DARKE

SEPTIMUS HEAP ✦ WIZARD APPRENTICE

ANGIE SAGE

BLOOMSBURY

LONDON OXFORD NEW YORK NEW DELHI SYDNEY

For my brother, Jason,
with love

Bloomsbury Publishing, London, Oxford, New York, New Delhi and Sydney

First published in Great Britain in 2011 by Bloomsbury Publishing Plc
50 Bedford Square, London, WC1B 3DP

Bloomsbury is a registered trademark of Bloomsbury Publishing Plc

First published in the United States
by HarperCollins Children's Books, a division of HarperCollins Publishers
10 East 53rd Street, New York, NY 10022

This edition published in July 2012

A CIP catalogue record for this book is available from the British Library

ISBN 978 1 4088 0627 2

Typeset by Hewer Text UK Ltd, Edinburgh
Printed and bound by CPI Group (UK) Ltd, Croydon, CR0 4YY

7 9 10 8 6

www.septimusheap.co.uk

A note from the author

DARKE was where I got to discover those lurking, scary places below the Castle that I always knew were there but had not wanted to visit. But now it was time. If Septimus had to do his Darke Week, then I would have to do my Darke year. So we did it together. The only difference was, Septimus had his Darke Disguise and I just had my laptop. This, by the way, is my favourite Beetle book. And, actually, my favourite Simon book too. It's the book where people begin to grow into who they truly are — and that is what the Septimus Heap series is all about.

Angie Sage

POSSESSED COTTAGE

BLEAK CREEK

THE BOTTOMLESS WHIRLPOOL

THE GHOST SHIP "VENGEANCE"

THE DARKE HALLS

UNDERGROUND

TO THE WONDROUS WITCHES

THE DRAGON HOUSE

INFIRMARY

THE RIVER

NORTH GATE

THE HEAPS' ROOM

RAMBLINGS

BOATYARD TUNNEL

JANNIT MAARTEN'S BOATYARD

FOREST

THE MOAT

THE OUTSIDE PATH

HOLE·IN·THE·WALL TAVERN

UNDERFLOW EXIT

RAVEN'S ROCK

MANUSCRIPTORIUM

WIZARD TOWER

ENTRANCE TO DUNGEON No.1

EAST GATE LOOKOUT TOWER FOUNDATIONS

OLD DOCKS

THE BEAKS

SNAKE SLIPWAY

WIZARD WAY

MAKERS MILE

RAMBLINGS

THE PALACE

TRADERS' MARKET

PALACE LANDING STAGE

SITE OF DROWNING

PALACE SUMMER HOUSE

NEW QUAY

TRADERS' DOCK

SOUTH GATE

FERRY

THE CASTLE

SALLY MULLIN'S TEA & ALE HOUSE

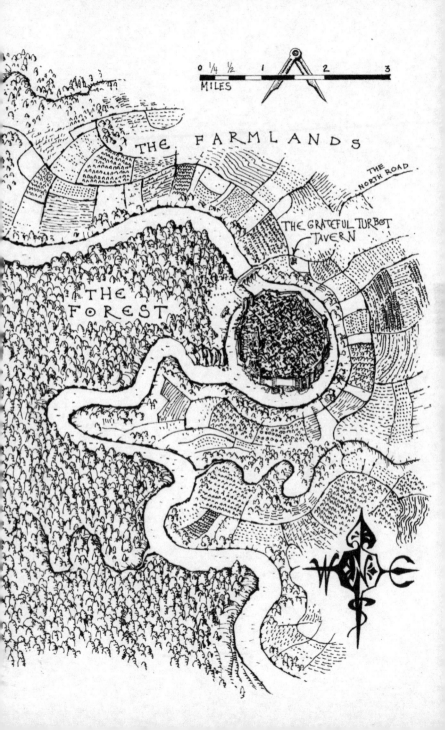

✣ PROLOGUE ✣
BANISHED

It is a Darke and stormy night.

Black clouds hang low over the Castle, shrouding the golden pyramid at the top of the Wizard Tower in a dim mist. In the houses far below, people stir uneasily in their sleep as the rumble of thunder enters their dreams and sends nightmares tumbling from the sky.

Like a giant lightning conductor, the Wizard Tower rears high above the Castle rooftops, Magykal purple and indigo lights playing around its iridescent silver sheen. Inside the Tower the duty Storm Wizard prowls the dimly lit Great Hall, checking the StormScreen and keeping an eye on the UnStable window, which has a tendency to panic in a storm. The duty Storm Wizard is a little on edge. Magyk is not usually affected by a storm, but all Wizards know about the Great Lightning Strike of Long Ago, which briefly drained the Wizard Tower of its Magyk and left the rooms of the ExtraOrdinary Wizard badly scorched. No one wants that to happen again – particularly the duty Storm Wizard.

At the top of the Wizard Tower in her as yet unscorched four-poster bed, Marcia Overstrand groans as a familiar nightmare flickers through her sleep. A loud *craaaack* of lightning splits open the cloud above the Tower and zips harmlessly to earth down the duty Storm Wizard's hastily conjured Conductor. Marcia sits bolt upright, dark curly hair awry, trapped in her nightmare. Suddenly her green eyes open wide with surprise as a purple ghost shoots through the wall and skids to a halt beside the bed.

"Alther!" gasps Marcia. "What are you *doing*?"

The tall ghost with long white hair tied back in a ponytail is wearing bloodstained ExtraOrdinary Wizard robes. He looks flustered.

"I really hate it when that happens," he gasps. "Got Passed Through. By lightning."

"I'm very sorry, Alther," Marcia replies grumpily, "but I don't see why you had to come and wake me up just to tell me that. *You* may not need to sleep any more, but *I* certainly do. Anyway, it serves you right for being out in a storm. Can't think why you want to do that – argh!"

Another *craaaack* of lightning illuminates the purple glass of Marcia's bedroom window and makes Alther appear almost transparent.

"I wasn't out there for the fun of it, Marcia, believe me," says Alther, equally grumpily. "I was coming to see you. As *you* requested."

"As I requested?" says Marcia blearily. She is still half in her nightmare about Dungeon Number One – a nightmare that always comes when a storm is playing around the top of the Wizard Tower.

"You requested – *ordered* would be a better way of putting it – that I track down Tertius Fume and tell you when I had found him," says Alther.

Marcia is suddenly wide awake. "Ah," she says.

"Ah, indeed, Marcia."

"So you have *found* him?"

The ghost looks pleased with himself. "Yup," he says.

"Where?"

"Where do you think?"

Marcia throws back the bedcovers, slips out of bed and pulls on her thick woollen gown – it is cold at the top of the Wizard Tower when the wind blows. "Oh, for goodness' sake, Alther," she snaps as she pushes her feet into the purple rabbit slippers that Septimus gave her for her birthday. "I wouldn't ask if I knew, would I?"

"He's in Dungeon Number One," Alther says quietly.

Marcia sits down on the bed rather suddenly. "Oh," she says, her nightmare replaying itself at double speed. "Bother."

Ten minutes later, two purple-clothed figures can be seen scurrying along Wizard Way. They are both trying to keep out of the needle-sharp rain that sweeps up the Way, Passing Through the leading figure and soaking the one close behind. Suddenly the first figure dives down a small alleyway, closely followed by the second. The alleyway is dark and smelly but at least it is sheltered from the near-horizontal rain.

"Are you sure it's down here?" asks Marcia, glancing behind. She doesn't like alleyways.

Alther slows his pace and drops back to walk beside Marcia. "You forget," he says with a smile, "that not so very long ago, I came down here quite often."

Marcia shudders. She knows that it was Alther's faithful visits that kept her alive in Dungeon Number One.

Alther has stopped beside a blackened, brick-built cone that looks like one of the many disused Lock-Ups that can still be seen scattered around the Castle. Somewhat unwillingly,

Marcia joins the ghost; her mouth is dry and she feels sick. This is where her nightmare always begins.

Lost in her thoughts, Marcia waits for Alther to unlock the small iron door, which is pockmarked with rust. The ghost gives her a quizzical look. "No can do, Marcia," he says.

"Huh?"

"Wish I could," says Alther wistfully, "but, unfortunately, you are going to have to open the door."

Marcia comes to her senses. "Sorry, Alther." She takes out the Universal Castle Key from her ExtraOrdinary Wizard belt. Only three of these keys were ever made, and Marcia has two of them: one of her own in her capacity as ExtraOrdinary Wizard, and one that she is keeping safe for Jenna Heap until the day she becomes Queen. The third is lost.

Making an effort to steady her hand, Marcia pushes the iron key into the lock and turns it. The door swings open with a creak that at once takes her back to a terrifying snowy night when a phalanx of guards threw her through the door and sent her tumbling into the darkness.

A foul smell of rotting meat and burned pumpkin tumbles out into the alleyway, and a trio of curious local cats screech and head for home. Marcia wishes she could do the same. Nervously she fingers the lapis lazuli amulet – the symbol and source of her power as ExtraOrdinary Wizard – that she wears around her neck and, to her relief, it is still there – unlike the last time she passed through the door.

Marcia's courage returns. "Right, Alther," she says. "Let's get him."

Alther grins, relieved to see Marcia back on form. "Follow me," he says.

Dungeon Number One is a deep, dark chimney with a long ladder attached to the inside of the top half. The bottom half is ladder-free, lined with a thick layer of bones and slime. Alther's purple floating form drifts down the ladder but Marcia steps carefully – very carefully – down each rung, chanting an UnHarm Spell under her breath, with a Begird and Preserve in readiness for both her and Alther – for even ghosts are not immune to the Darke Vortices that swirl around the base of Dungeon Number One.

Slowly, slowly, the figures descend into the thick gloom and stench of the dungeon. They are going much farther down than Marcia expected. Alther had assured her that their quarry was "only lurking around the top, Marcia. Nothing to worry about".

But Marcia *is* worried. She begins to fear a trap. "Where *is* he?" she hisses.

A deep, hollow laugh answers her question, and Marcia very nearly lets go of the ladder.

"There he is!" says Alther. "Look, down there." He points into the narrow depths and, far below, Marcia sees the goat-like face of Tertius Fume leering up at them, an eerie green glowing in the darkness. "You can see him, you can do the Banish from here," says Alther, lapsing into tutor mode with his ex-pupil. "The chimney will concentrate it."

"I know," says Marcia tetchily. "Please be quiet, Alther." She begins to chant the words that all ghosts dread – the words that will Banish them to the Darke Halls for ever.

"I, Marcia Overstrand ..."

The greenish figure of Tertius Fume begins to rise up the chimney towards them. "I am warning you, Marcia

Overstrand – stop that Banish now." His harsh voice echoes around them.

Tertius Fume gives Marcia the creeps, but she is not deflected. She carries on with the chant, which must last for precisely one minute and be completed without hesitation, repetition or deviation. Marcia knows that the slightest falter means she must begin again.

Tertius Fume knows this too. He continues his approach, walking up the side of the wall like a spider, hurling insults, counter chants and bizarre fragments of songs at Marcia to try to put her off.

But Marcia will not be deflected. Doggedly she continues, blanking out the ghost. But as she embarks upon the closing lines of the Banish – "your time above this earth is done, you'll see no more the sky, the sun" – out of the corner of her eye, Marcia sees the ghost of Tertius Fume drawing ever closer. A stab of worry shoots through her – *what is he doing?* Marcia reaches the very last line. The ghost is inches away from her and Alther. He looks up, excited – almost exultant.

Marcia ends the chant with the dreaded words, "By the power of Magyk, to the Darke Halls, I you . . ."

As Marcia reaches the very last word, Tertius Fume stretches his hand up to Alther and Merges with his big toe. Alther recoils from the touch but is too late.

"Banish!"

Suddenly Marcia is alone in the chimney of Dungeon Number One. Her nightmare has come true. "Alther!" she screams. "Alther, where are you?"

There is no reply. Alther is Banished.

❋ 1 ❋
THE VISIT

Lucy Gringe found the last space on the dawn Port barge. She squeezed in between a young man clutching an aggressive chicken and a thin, weary-looking woman wrapped in a woollen cloak. The woman – who had uncomfortably piercing blue eyes – quickly glanced at Lucy, then looked away. Lucy dumped her bag down by her feet to claim her space; there was no way she was going to be standing up for the entire journey to the Castle. The blue-eyed woman would have to get used to being squashed. Lucy swivelled around and looked back up at the quay. She saw the damp, lonely-looking figure of Simon Heap standing on the edge, and she gave him a brief smile.

It was a bleak, cold morning, with a threat of snow in the sky. Simon shivered and attempted a smile in return. He raised his voice against the bangs and thuds that accompanied the barge's sail being readied. "Take care, Lu!"

"And you!" Lucy replied, elbowing the chicken out of the way. "I'll be back the day after Longest Night. Promise!"

Simon nodded. "You got my letters?" he called out.

"'Course I have," returned Lucy. "*How* much?" This was addressed to the barge boy who was collecting the fares.

"Six pence, darlin'."

"*Don't* call me darlin'!" Lucy flared. She fished around in her purse and dumped a large collection of brass coins into the boy's outstretched hand. "Could buy my own boat for that," she said.

The boy shrugged. He handed her a ticket and moved along to a travel-stained woman next to her, who was, Lucy thought, a stranger who had just arrived at the Port. The woman gave the barge boy a large silver coin – a half crown – and waited patiently while the boy made a fuss with the change. When she politely thanked him, Lucy noticed that she had a strange accent, which reminded her of someone, although she couldn't think who. Lucy was too cold to think right then – and too anxious. She hadn't been back home for a long time, and now that she was sitting in the boat bound for the Castle, the thought scared her a little. She wasn't sure what kind of reception she would get. And she didn't like leaving Simon, either.

The Port barge was beginning to move. Two dockhands were pushing the long, narrow boat away from the shore, and the barge boy was raising the worn red sail. Lucy gave Simon a forlorn wave, and the barge drew away from the quay and moved towards the fast incoming tide running up the middle of the river. Every now and then Lucy glanced back to see Simon's solitary figure still standing on the quay, his long, fair hair blowing in the breeze, his pale wool cloak fluttering behind him like moth wings.

Simon watched the Port barge until it disappeared into the low mist that hung over the river towards the Marram Marshes. As the last vestige of the barge vanished, he stamped his feet to get some warmth into them, then headed off into the warren of streets that would take him back to his room in the attic of the Customs House.

At the top of the Customs House stairs Simon pushed open the battered door to his room and stepped across the threshold. A deep chill hit him so hard that it took his breath away. At once he knew that something was wrong – his attic room was cold, but it was never *this* cold. This was a Darke cold. Behind him the door slammed shut and, as if from the end of a long, deep tunnel, Simon heard the bolt shoot across the door, making him a prisoner in his own room. Heart pounding, Simon forced himself to look up. He was determined not to use any of his old Darke skills but some, once learned, kicked in automatically – and one of these was the ability to See in the Darke. And so, unlike most people who, if they have the misfortune to look at a Thing, see only shifting shadows and glimpses of decay, Simon saw the Thing in all its glorious detail, sitting on his narrow bed, Watching him with its hooded eyes. It made him feel sick.

"Welcome." The Thing's deep, menacing voice filled the room and sent a stream of goose bumps down Simon's spine.

"G-Ger ..." stuttered Simon.

Satisfied, the Thing noted the terrified expression in Simon's dark green eyes. It crossed its long, spindly legs and began to chew one of its peeling fingers while regarding Simon with a baleful stare.

Not so very ago, the Thing's stare would have meant nothing to Simon; one of his pastimes during his residency at the Observatory in the Badlands had been staring down the Things that he occasionally Summoned. But now Simon could hardly bear to look in the direction of the decaying bundle of rags and bones that sat on his bed, let alone meet its gaze.

The Thing duly noted Simon's reluctance and spat a blackened nail on to the floor. A brief thought of what Lucy would say if she found *that* on the floor ran through Simon's mind, and the thought of Lucy made him just about brave enough to speak.

"Wher-what do you want?" he whispered.

"You," came the hollow voice of the Thing.

"M-*me*?"

The Thing regarded Simon with disdain. "Y-you," it sneered.

"Why?"

"I have come to Fetch you. As per your contract."

"Contract . . . what *contract*?"

"The one you made with our late Master. You are still Bound."

"*What?* But . . . but he's dead. DomDaniel is dead."

"The Possessor of the Two-Faced Ring is not dead," intoned the Thing.

Simon, assuming – as the Thing intended – that the Possessor of the Two-Faced Ring could only be DomDaniel, was horrified. "DomDaniel's *not* dead?"

The Thing did not answer Simon's question; it merely repeated its instruction. "The Possessor of the Two-Faced Ring requires your presence. You will attend immediately."

Simon was too shocked to move. All his attempts to put the Darke behind him and make a new life with Lucy suddenly seemed futile. He put his head in his hands, wondering how he could have been so foolish as to think that he could escape the Darke. A creak in a floorboard made him look up. Simon saw the Thing advancing towards him, its bony hands outstretched.

Simon leaped to his feet. He didn't care what happened but he was not going back to the Darke. He raced to the door and pulled at the bolt but it would not shift. The Thing was close behind him now, so close that Simon could smell the decay and taste the bitterness of it on his tongue. He glanced at the window. It was a long way down.

His mind racing, Simon backed away towards the window. Maybe if he jumped he would land on the balcony two floors down. Maybe he could grab the drainpipe. Or haul himself up on to the roof.

The Thing regarded him with displeasure. "Apprentice, you will come with me. Or do I have to Fetch you?" Its voice filled the low-ceilinged room with threat.

Simon decided to go for the drainpipe. He threw open the window, half clambered out and seized the thick black pipe that ran down the rear wall of the Customs House. A howl of anger came after him and, as Simon tried to swing his feet off the window ledge, he felt an irresistible force dragging him back into the room – the Thing had put a Fetch on him.

Even though Simon knew that there was no resisting a Fetch, he clung desperately on to the pipe while his feet were being pulled so hard that he felt like the rope in a tug-of-war. Suddenly the rusty metal lurking below the drainpipe's thick black paint came away in his hands, and Simon shot back into the room, pipe and all. He slammed into the bony – yet disgustingly soft – body of the Thing and fell to the floor. Unable to move, Simon lay looking up.

The Thing smirked down at him. "You will follow me," it intoned.

Like a broken puppet, Simon was dragged to his feet. He staggered out of his room and lurched like an automaton down the long, narrow stairs. In front of him glided the Thing. As they emerged on to the quayside, the Thing became no more than an indistinct shadow, so that when Maureen from the Harbour and Dock Pie Shop glanced up from opening the shutters, all she saw was Simon walking stiffly across the quay, heading towards the shadows of Fore Street. Maureen wiped her hand across her eyes. Some dust must have got in them, she thought – everything around Simon looked strangely fuzzy. Maureen waved cheerily but Simon did not respond. She smiled and fastened open the last shutter. He was an odd one, that Simon. Always had his head in some Magyk book or chanting a spell.

"Pies ready in ten minutes. I'll save you a veg and bacon one!" she called out, but Simon had vanished into the side streets, and Maureen could once more see clearly across the empty quayside.

When a person is Fetched, there is no stopping, no rest, no respite, until the person has reached the place to which he is Fetched. For a whole day and half a night Simon waded through marshes, scrambled through hedges and stumbled along stony paths. Rain soaked him, winds buffeted him, snow flurries froze him, but he could stop for nothing. Relentlessly on he went until finally, in the cold, grey light of the next day's dawn, he swam an ice-cold river, hauled himself out, staggered across the early morning dew and climbed up a crumbling wall of ivy. At the very top he was dragged through an attic window and frogmarched to a windowless room. When the door was barred behind him and he was left alone, sprawled on the bare floor, Simon no longer knew or cared where – or who – he was.

❋ 2 ❋
VISITORS

Night and a cold drizzle were falling fast when the Port barge drew up at the New Quay, a recently built stone jetty just below Sally Mullin's Tea and Ale House. Accompanied by assorted children, chickens and bundles, the frazzled passengers rose stiffly from their seats and stumbled down the gangway. Many of them made their way unsteadily along the well-trodden path to the Tea and Ale House to warm themselves by the stove and fill up with Sally's winter specials: mulled Springo Ale and warm spiced barley cake. Others, longing to get home to a warm fireside, set off on the long trudge up the hill, past the Castle amenity rubbish dump, to the South Gate, which would remain open until midnight.

Lucy Gringe did not relish the thought of the walk up the hill one little bit, especially when she knew that the Port barge was probably passing by where she was headed. She glanced at the woman sitting beside her. Lucy had spent the first half of the journey trying to avoid her oddly unsettling gaze but, after her neighbour had ventured a tentative question about directions to the Palace – which was where Lucy's first errand was taking her – they had spent the second half of the journey in animated conversation. The woman now rose wearily to follow the other passengers.

"Wait a minute!" said Lucy to her. "I've got an idea . . . *'Scuse me?*" she shouted at the barge boy.

The barge boy swung around. "Yeah, darlin'?"

With some effort, Lucy ignored the *darlin.* "Where are you docking tonight?" she asked.

"With this north wind blowin' up, it'll be Jannit Maarten's," he replied. "Why?"

"Well, I just wondered . . ." Lucy gave the barge boy her best smile. "I just *wondered* if you could *possibly* let us off at a landing stage on your way there. It's *so* cold tonight. And dark too." Lucy shivered expressively and looked mournfully up at the barge boy with her big brown eyes. He was lost.

"'Course we could, darlin'. I'll tell Skip. Where d'you want to get off?"

"The Palace Landing Stage, please."

The barge boy blinked in surprise. "The Palace? You sure, darlin'?"

Lucy fought down an urge to yell "Don't call me darlin', creep boy!" "Yes, please," she said. "If it's not too much trouble."

"Nothin's too much trouble for *you*, darlin'," said creep boy, "though I wouldn't have put you down for the Palace meself."

"Oh?" Lucy was not sure how to take this.

"Yeah. You know that landing stage is haunted, don't you?"

Lucy shrugged. "Doesn't worry me," she said. "I never see ghosts."

The Port barge cast off from the New Quay. It made a U-turn in the wide part of the river, rocking scarily as it cut across the current and the chop of the waves whisked up by the wind. But as soon as the barge faced downstream all became quiet once more and, about ten minutes later, it was gliding to a halt beside the Palace Landing Stage.

"Here y'are, darlin'," said the barge boy, throwing a rope around one of the mooring posts. "Have fun." He winked at Lucy.

"Thank you," said Lucy rather primly. She got up and held out her hand to her neighbour. "We're here," she said. The woman gave Lucy a grateful smile. She got stiffly to her feet and followed Lucy off the barge.

The Port barge drew away from the landing stage. "See ya!" yelled the barge boy.

"Not if I see you first," Lucy muttered. She turned to her companion, who was gazing at the Palace in amazement. It was indeed a beautiful sight – a long, low building of ancient mellow stone with tall, elegant windows looking out over the well-tended lawns that swept down to the river. From every window, a welcoming candle flickered, making the whole building glimmer magically in the deepening twilight.

"She lives *here*?" the woman murmured in a sing-song accent.

Lucy nodded shortly. Anxious to get going, she started purposefully up the wide path that led to the Palace. But her companion was not following. The woman was still on the landing stage, talking to what appeared to be an empty space. Lucy sighed – why did she always pick the weird ones? Reluctant to interrupt the woman's one-sided conversation – which seemed to be a serious one, for she was now nodding sadly – Lucy carried on, heading towards the lights of the Palace.

Lucy did not feel good. She was tired and cold and, above all, she was beginning to be anxious about the kind of welcome she would receive at the Palace. She put her hand in her pocket and found Simon's letters. She drew them out and squinted at the names written in Simon's large, loopy handwriting: *Sarah Heap. Jenna Heap. Septimus Heap.* She placed the one addressed to Septimus back in her pocket and kept hold of the ones addressed to Jenna and Sarah. Lucy sighed. All she wanted to do was to run back to Simon and know that it was "all right, Lucy-Lu". But Simon had asked her to deliver the letters to his mother and sister, and – whatever Sarah Heap thought of her – deliver them she would.

Lucy's companion was now hurrying after her.

"Lucy, I am sorry," she said. "I have just heard such a sad story from a ghost. It is sad, so very sad. The love of her life – and of her death – has been Banished. By *mistake*. How can any Wizard make such a mistake? Oh, it is a terrible thing." The woman shook her head. "Truly terrible."

"I suppose that must be Alice Nettles," said Lucy. "Simon said he'd heard that something horrible had happened to Alther."

"Yes. Alice and Alther. So very sad . . ."

Lucy did not have much time for ghosts. The way she saw it, ghosts were dead – it was being with the person you wanted to be with while you were *alive* that mattered. Which was, she thought, why she was back at the Castle right now, shivering in the bitter north wind that was blowing in off the river, tired and wishing she was wrapped up warmly in bed.

"Shall we get going?" said Lucy. "I don't know about you, but I'm frozen."

The woman nodded. Tall and thin, her thick woollen cloak wrapped around her against the wind, she stepped carefully, her bright eyes scanning the scene in front of her because, unlike Lucy, she did not see a wide, empty path. For her, the path and the lawns bounding it were full of ghosts: hurrying Palace servants, young princesses playing tag, little page boys, ancient queens wandering through vanished shrubberies, and elderly Palace gardeners wheeling their ghostly wheelbarrows. She went carefully, because the trouble with being a Spirit-Seer was that ghosts did not get out of your way; they saw you as just another ghost – until you Passed Through them. And then, of course, they were horribly offended.

Unaware of any ghosts at all, Lucy strode up the path at a fast pace, and the ghosts, some of whom were well acquainted with Lucy and her big boots, got smartly out of her way. Lucy soon reached the top path that encircled the Palace and she turned around to check on her companion, who was lagging behind. The oddest sight met her eyes – the woman was dancing up the path on tiptoe, zigzagging to and fro, as if she was taking part in one of the old-fashioned Castle dances – on her own. Lucy shook her head. This did not bode well.

Eventually the woman – flustered and out of breath – joined her, and Lucy set off without a word. She had decided to take the path that led around the Palace and to head for the main front door rather than risk no one hearing her knock on the multitude of kitchen and side doors.

The Palace was a long building, and it was a good ten minutes before Lucy and the woman were at last crossing the flat wooden bridge over the decorative Palace moat. As they approached, a small boy pulled open the night door – a little door set into the main double doors.

"Welcome to the Palace," piped Barney Pot, resplendent in a grey Palace tunic and red leggings. "Who do you wish to see?"

Lucy did not have a chance to reply.

"Barney!" came a lilting voice from inside. "*There* you are. You must go to bed; you have school tomorrow."

Lucy's companion went pale.

Barney looked back inside. "But I *like* doing the door," he protested. "Please, just five more minutes."

"No, Barney. *Bed.*"

"*Snorri?*" The faltering word came from the woman.

A tall girl with pale blue eyes and long, white-blond hair stuck her head out of the night door and peered into the dark. She blinked, stared straight past Lucy and gasped. "Mamma!"

"Snorri ... oh, *Snorri!*" cried Alfrún Snorrelssen.

Snorri Snorrelssen threw herself into the arms of her mother. Lucy smiled wistfully. Maybe, she thought, it was a good omen. Maybe later that night, when she knocked on the door of the North Gate gatehouse, her mother would be just as pleased to see *her*. Maybe.

❊ 3 ❊

BIRTHDAY EVE

But Lucy did not go to the North Gate gatehouse that night – Sarah Heap would not allow it.

"Lucy, you are soaking wet and exhausted," Sarah said. "I am *not* having you wander through the streets at night in that state; you'll catch your death of cold. You need a long sleep in a nice warm bed – and besides, I want to hear all about Simon. Now let's find you some supper ..."

Lucy gave in gratefully. The relief she felt at Sarah's welcome made her feel suddenly tearful. She happily allowed herself to be led along the Long Walk with Snorri and Alfrún and sat down beside the fire in Sarah Heap's little sitting room at the back of the Palace.

That evening, as flurries of snow blew in from the Port, Sarah Heap's sitting room was the warmest room in the Palace. Piled on the table were the remains of Sarah's famous sausage and bean hotpot supper, and now everyone had gathered around the blazing fire, drinking herbal tea. Squashed in with Lucy and Sarah were Jenna, Septimus and Nicko Heap, along with Snorri and Alfrún Snorrelssen. Snorri and Alfrún sat close together, quietly talking, while Alfrún kept hold tightly of

Snorri's hand. Nicko sat a little apart from Snorri, talking with Jenna. Septimus, Sarah noticed, was not talking to anyone but was gazing into the fire.

There was also a menagerie of animals: a large black panther by the name of Ullr, which sat by Alfrún's feet; Maxie, an ancient, smelly wolfhound who lay steaming gently in front of the fire; and Ethel, a stubbly, featherless duck wearing a new knitted waistcoat. Ethel sat resplendent on Sarah's lap, nibbling delicately on a piece of sausage. The duck, Jenna noted disapprovingly, was getting fat. She suspected that Sarah had knitted the new waistcoat because the old one had got too small. But Sarah loved Ethel so much that Jenna merely admired the red stripes and the green buttons along the back and said nothing about Ethel's expanding girth.

Sarah Heap was happy. In her hand she clasped a precious letter from Simon – a letter that she had read and reread and now knew by heart. Sarah had her old Simon back again – the *good* Simon, the Simon she knew he had always been. And now here she was, planning the party for Jenna's and Septimus's fourteenth birthdays. Fourteen was a big milestone, particularly for Jenna as Princess of the Castle, and this year Sarah had at last got her wish: the celebrations for both Jenna's and Septimus's birthdays were to be held at the Palace rather than at the Wizard Tower.

Sarah glanced up at the old clock on the chimneypiece and suppressed a feeling of irritation that Silas was not back yet. Recently Silas had been what he called "busy", but Sarah did not believe it – she knew Silas well enough to know that he was up to something. She sighed. She wished he were there to share the moment of everyone being together.

Pushing her thoughts about Silas to one side, Sarah smiled at Lucy, her daughter-in-law-to-be. Having Lucy there made her feel as if Simon was with them too, for there were moments when Lucy echoed Simon's eager, intense way of talking. One day, thought Sarah, maybe she would have *all* her children *and* Silas with her – though how they would all fit into the sitting room she was not sure. But if she ever got the chance she'd give it her best try.

Septimus too was glancing at the clock, and at 8:15 PM precisely he excused himself from the gathering. Sarah watched her youngest son, grown tall and gangly in recent months, get up from his perch on the arm of her battered sofa and pick his way through people and piles of books towards the door. She saw with pride his purple Senior Apprentice ribbons shimmer on the hem of the sleeves of his green tunic, but what pleased her most was his quiet, easy confidence. She wished he'd comb his hair more often but Septimus was turning into a good-looking young man. She blew her son a kiss. He smiled – slightly strained, Sarah thought – and stepped out of the cosy sitting room into the chill of the Long Walk, the wide passageway that ran along the length of the Palace.

Jenna Heap slipped out after him.

"Sep, wait a mo," she called after Septimus, who was striding off in a hurry.

Septimus slowed down unwillingly. "I've got to be back at nine o'clock," he said.

"You've got tons of time, then," said Jenna, catching up and walking along beside him, matching his long strides with smaller, faster ones.

"Sep," she said, "you know how I told you last week it was really creepy up by the attic stairs? Well, it still is. In fact, it's worse. Even Ullr won't go there. Look, I've got the scratches to prove it." Jenna rolled up her gold-hemmed sleeve to show Septimus a flurry of cat scratches on her wrist. "I carried him to the bottom of the stairs and he totally panicked."

Septimus seemed unimpressed. "Ullr's a Spirit-Seer cat. He's bound to get spooked sometimes with all the ghosts around here."

Jenna was not to be put off. "But it doesn't feel like ghosts, Sep. Anyway, most of the Palace ghosts Appear to me. I see *tons* of them." As if to prove her point, Jenna nodded graciously – a real Princess nod, thought Septimus – at what appeared to him to be thin air. "There. I've just seen the three cooks who got poisoned by the jealous housekeeper."

"That was nice for you," said Septimus, speeding up so that Jenna had to trot to keep up with him. They travelled quickly along the Long Walk, moving from the dancing flames of each rushlight into shadows and back into the light of the next.

"So I'd *see* if it was ghosts," Jenna persisted. "And it's *not*. In fact, all the ghosts are keeping away from that part of the corridor. Which just goes to show."

"To show what?" Septimus said irritably.

"That there's something *bad* up there. And I can't ask Marcia to check it out because Mum would throw a fit, but you're almost as good as Marcia now, aren't you? So *please*, Sep. Please just come and see."

"Can't Dad do it?"

"Dad keeps saying he'll have a look but he doesn't get round to it. He's always off somewhere. You know what he's like."

They had reached the large entrance hall, the light from a forest of candles illuminating its elegant flight of stairs and the thick old doors. Barney Pot had at last gone to bed and the entrance hall was empty. Septimus stopped and turned to Jenna. "Look, Jen, I've *got* to go. There's loads I have to do."

"You don't believe me, do you?" Jenna sounded exasperated.

"Of course I do."

"Huh! Not enough to come and check out what's going on up there."

But Septimus wore the closed expression that Jenna had seen so much of over the previous few months. She hated it. It was as if, when she looked into Septimus's bright green eyes, there was something shielding him from her.

"Bye, Jen," he said. "Must go. Tomorrow's a big day."

Jenna made a big effort to shake off her disappointment. She didn't want Septimus to leave with bad feelings between them.

"I know," she agreed. "Happy birthday, Sep."

Jenna thought Septimus looked slightly surprised.

"Oh . . . yes. Thanks."

"It'll be such fun tomorrow," she said, linking her arm through his reluctant one and walking him towards the Palace doors. "It's great us having birthdays on the same day, don't you think? It's like we're twins. And on the Longest Night too, it's so special with all the Castle lit up. Like it's especially for us."

"Yeah." Septimus looked distracted, and Jenna could tell all he wanted to do was to get out of the door as fast as he could. "I really *must* go, Jen. I'll see you tomorrow evening."

"I'll walk you to the gates."

"Oh." Septimus did not sound very enthusiastic.

They made their way down the drive, Septimus hurrying, Jenna trotting along beside.

"Sep . . ." said Jenna, breathless.

"Yeah?" Septimus sounded wary.

"Dad says you're at the same stage in your Apprenticeship as he was when he gave up."

"Mmm. S'pose I am."

"And one of the reasons he gave up, he said, was because he was going to have to do a load of Darke stuff and he didn't want to bring it home."

Septimus slowed down. "There were lots of reasons Dad gave up, Jen. Like he'd heard about the Queste too soon, and Mum was finding it tough on her own and he was going to have to work nights. All kinds of stuff."

"It was the Darke, Sep. That's what he told me."

"Huh. He says that *now*."

"He's worried about you. And so am I."

"Well, you shouldn't be," Septimus said irritably.

"But, *Sep* –"

Septimus had had enough. Impatiently he shook Jenna's arm off.

"Jen, please – *leave me alone*. I have stuff to do and I'm going now. I'll see you tomorrow." With that Septimus strode off, and this time Jenna let him go.

Jenna walked slowly back across the grass, her feet crunching through a dusting of frost, and fought off tears – *Septimus hadn't even wished her "happy birthday"*. As she wandered miserably into the Palace, Jenna could not get him out of her mind. Recently she had begun to feel like an outsider in his life – an

annoying outsider from whom secrets had to be kept. In order
to understand more about what Septimus was doing, Jenna
had begun to ask Silas questions about his own Apprenticeship
to Alther long ago, and she did not always like what she heard.

Jenna did not feel like going back to the happy group clus-
tered around Sarah's sitting-room fire. She took a lighted candle
from one of the hall tables and made her way up the wide
flight of carved oak stairs that led from the Palace entrance
hall to the first floor. She walked slowly along the corridor,
her footsteps muffled on the threadbare carpet, nodding to
the assorted ghosts who always Appeared when they saw the
Princess. Ignoring the short, wide passageway that led to her
bedroom, Jenna decided to take one more look at the attic
stairs – Septimus had made her wonder if she was indeed
worrying about nothing.

A rushlight burned steadily at the foot of the stairs, for
which Jenna was grateful – because looking up the flight of
bare, worn wooden stairs that disappeared into the darkness
gave her the creeps. Telling herself that Septimus probably was
right and there was nothing at all to worry about, Jenna began
to climb the stairs. She told herself that if she got to the top
and everything was all right, she would forget all about it, but
when Jenna was one step below the top she stopped. In front
of her was a deep darkness that seemed to move and shift as she
looked at it. It felt as if it were *alive*. Jenna was confused – part
of her was terrified and yet another part of her suddenly felt
elated. She had the strangest feeling that if only she stepped
up into the darkness, she would see everything she had ever
wanted to see, even her real mother, Queen Cerys. And as she
thought about meeting her mother, the feeling of terror began

to fade and Jenna longed to step into the dark, into the best place to be in the whole world – the place she had always been searching for.

Suddenly Jenna felt a tap on her shoulder. She wheeled around and saw the ghost of the governess who Haunted the Palace looking for two lost princesses staring at her.

"Come away, Esmeralda, come away," wailed the ghost. "It is Darke in there. Come away . . ." Exhausted by having Caused a tap on Jenna's shoulder, the ghost of the governess faded away and was not seen for many years hence.

Jenna's desire to step into the darkness evaporated. She turned and ran, clattering down the stairs two at a time. She did not stop running until she reached the broad, bright corridor that led to her bedroom and saw the friendly figure of Sir Hereward, the ancient ghost who guarded the double doors to her bedroom.

Sir Hereward sprang to attention. "Good evening, Princess," he said. "Early to bed, I see. A big day tomorrow." The ghost smiled. "It's not every day a Princess turns fourteen."

"No," said Jenna despondently.

"Ah, the pressure of advancing years already, I see." Sir Hereward chuckled. "But let me tell you, fourteen is nothing to worry about, Princess. Look at me, I've had *hundreds* of birthdays – lost count of 'em in fact – and I'm fine."

Jenna could not help but smile. The ghost was anything but fine. Dusty and faded, his armour dented, he was missing an arm, quite a few teeth and – she had recently noticed when he had removed his helmet – his left ear and a fair chunk of the side of his head. Plus, of course, he was *dead*. But that didn't seem to worry Sir Hereward. Jenna sternly told herself to stop being so miserable and enjoy life. Septimus would get over whatever it was and things would be fine again. In fact, tomorrow she would go to the last day of the Traders' Market and get him something for his birthday that would make him laugh – something more fun than the *Compleat History of Magyk* that she had already bought him from Wyvald's Witchy Bookstore.

"There, that's better." Sir Hereward beamed. "Fourteen's an exciting day for a Princess, you'll see. Now, here's a good one. This will really cheer you up. How do you put a giraffe in a wardrobe?"

"I don't know, Sir Hereward. How *do* you put a giraffe in a wardrobe?"

"You open the wardrobe door, put it in and close the door. So how do you put an elephant in the wardrobe?"

"I don't know. How *do* you put an elephant in a wardrobe?"

"You open the door, take out the giraffe and put the elephant in. Hur hur."

Jenna laughed. "That is *so* silly, Sir Hereward."

Sir Hereward giggled. "Isn't it? I mean, I'm sure you could fit them *both* in if you really tried."

"Yes . . . well, goodnight, Sir Hereward. I'll see you tomorrow."

The ancient ghost bowed, and Jenna pushed opened the grand double doors and went into her bedroom. As the doors closed, Sir Hereward resumed his post on guard, extra vigilant. Every Palace ghost knew that birthdays could be a dangerous time for a Princess. Sir Hereward was determined that nothing was going to happen to Jenna on *his* watch.

Once inside her room, Jenna could not settle – she felt a strange mixture of excitement and melancholy. Restless, she went to one of the tall windows and drew back the heavy red curtains to look out at the river. Watching the river at night was something she had loved to do ever since Silas had made her a little box bed in the cupboard in the Ramblings, where there was a tiny window that looked directly down on the water. In Jenna's opinion, the view from her grand windows at the Palace was greatly inferior to the one she had had in her cupboard – from her old perch at the Ramblings she had been able to see the tide's ebb and flow, which had always fascinated her. Very often there had been a few fishing boats tied up to one of the huge rings set into the walls far below, and she would watch the fishermen clean their catch and mend their nets. Here all she ever saw were distant boats passing back and forth and the moonlight reflected in the water.

That night, however, there was no moon. It was, Jenna knew, the last night of the old moon, and the moon did not rise until very nearly sunrise. Tomorrow night – her birthday night – would be the Dark of the Moon, when it would not rise at all. But even without the moon, the night sky was still beautiful. The clouds had blown away and the stars shone bright and clear.

Jenna drew the heavy curtains behind her so she was in the dark, cold space between them and the window. She stood still, waiting for her eyes to become accustomed to the dark. Her warm breath began to mist the window; she rubbed the glass clear and peered out at the river.

At first sight it appeared deserted, which was not a surprise to Jenna. Not many boats went out at night. And then she caught sight of a movement down by the landing stage. Squeakily she rubbed the window once more and squinted out. There was someone on the landing stage – it was *Septimus*. He looked as if he were in conversation with someone, although there was no one to be seen. Jenna knew at once that he was talking to the ghost of Alice Nettles – poor Alice Nettles, who had lost her Alther for a second time. Since her terrible loss, Alice had DisAppeared and had taken to wandering around the Castle looking for Alther. She was the source of the disembodied voice that would sometimes whisper in people's ears, "Where has he gone? Have you seen him, have you seen him?"

Jenna cupped her hands over her nose to protect the glass from her breath and stared into the night. She saw Septimus finish his conversation and walk briskly away, speeding along beside the river, heading towards the side gate that would take him out near Wizard Way.

Jenna longed to throw open the window and climb down the ivy – as she had done many times before – then run across the lawns, waylay Septimus and tell him what had just happened at the top of the attic stairs. The old Septimus would have come back with her, there and then. But not now, Jenna thought sadly. Now Septimus had more important things to do – secret things.

Suddenly aware of how cold she was, Jenna slipped out from behind the curtains and went over to the fire, where three huge logs were blazing in the ancient stone fireplace. And as she stood holding her hands out to warm in front of the crackling fire, Jenna wondered what Septimus was talking to Alice about. She knew that even if she asked him he wouldn't tell her.

It wasn't only Alice who had lost someone, Jenna thought sadly.

�֎ 4 �֎

APPRENTICES

The morning of his fourteenth birthday, Septimus was up before dawn. Quickly he cleaned and tidied the Pyramid Library – as he did every morning, even on his birthday. He found an unwrapped present from Marcia hidden under a pile of books to be filed. It was a small but very beautiful gold and silver Enlarging Glass. Attached to its ivory handle was a purple tag, which read: *To Septimus. Happy Magykal Fourteenth Birthday. With love from Marcia.* Septimus put the Glass in his pocket with a smile. It wasn't often that Marcia signed her name "with love".

Some minutes later the heavy purple door that guarded the entrance to the ExtraOrdinary Wizard's rooms swung open, and Septimus headed for the silver spiral stairs at the end of the landing, setting off on a visit he had made every day since he had returned from the Isles of Syren. Taking a chance that there were no Wizards about so early, he put the stairs into emergency mode and whizzed down to the seventh floor. Dizzy but exhilarated – there was nothing quite like an emergency run to wake one up – Septimus stepped off the stairs and walked a little unsteadily along a dimly lit corridor towards a door marked ICK BAY (the S having recently evaporated during an Ordinary Apprentice's spell that had gone wrong).

The ICK BAY door opened quietly and Septimus stepped into a dimly lit, circular room with ten beds arranged around the wall like the numbers on a clockface. Only two of the beds were occupied – one by a Wizard who had fallen down the Wizard Tower steps and broken her toe, the other by an elderly Wizard who had "felt a bit funny" the previous day. Two of the clockface spaces were taken by doors – one that Septimus had just come through and another, at the seven o'clock space, leading away from the sick bay. In the centre was a circular desk, in the middle of which sat the night-duty Wizard and the new sick-bay Apprentice, Rose. Rose, her long brown hair tucked behind her ears, was busy as ever, scribbling in her project book and devising new Charms.

Septimus approached. Rose and the Wizard gave him friendly smiles. They knew him well, for he visited every day – although usually not so early.

"No change," whispered Rose.

Septimus nodded. He had long given up expecting to hear anything different.

Rose got up from her chair. It was her job to escort visitors to the DisEnchanting Chamber. Septimus followed her over to the narrow door set in the wall at the seven o'clock space. Its surface had a shifting quality to it, typical of the effect that strong Wizard Tower Magyk produced. Rose placed her hand on the surface and quickly withdrew it, leaving a fleeting purple handprint behind. The door swung open, then she and Septimus stepped into an antechamber. The door closed behind them and Rose repeated the process with another door in front of them. It too swung open, and this time Septimus alone walked through. He entered a small pentagonal room suffused with a deep blue light.

"I'll leave you now," whispered Rose. "Call me if there's anything you need or . . . well, if there's any change."

Septimus nodded.

There was a heady smell of Magyk in the chamber, for within it a gentle DisEnchanting force was allowed to run free. The force circled counterclockwise, and Septimus could feel it warm upon his skin, tingling like drying salt water after a swim in the ocean. He stood still and breathed in deeply a few times to balance himself. For anyone with any Magyk in them, DisEnchantment is a peculiar thing to be close to, and the first few times he had entered the chamber Septimus had become extremely dizzy. Now that he was used to it he merely felt wobbly for a few moments. However, something that he had never quite got used to was the eerie sight of the DisEnchantment cocoon – a delicate hammock made from the softest unspun sheep's wool – which appeared to float in mid-air, although it was actually suspended by invisible Forrest Bands, invented by a long-gone ExtraOrdinary Wizard.

Feeling as if he were walking underwater, Septimus slowly approached the cocoon, pushing through eddies of DisEnchantment. Swathed in the wool lay a figure so insubstantial that sometimes Septimus was afraid she might disappear at any moment. But so far Syrah Syara, the occupant of the cocoon, had resisted disappearing – although it was a known risk of DisEnchantment, and the longer the process went on, the greater the risk became.

Septimus looked at Syrah's bluish face, which reflected the light of the chamber and seemed almost transparent. Her brown hair had been neatly plaited, giving her a prim, doll-like appearance – so different from the wild, windblown Syrah he had first met on the Isle of Syren.

"Hello, Syrah," he said quietly. "It's me, Septimus." Syrah did not react, but Septimus knew that that did not necessarily mean she could not hear him. Many people who had successfully emerged from DisEnchantment were able to recount conversations that had taken place in the chamber.

"I'm early today," Septimus continued. "The sun isn't even up yet. I want to tell you that I won't be able to come and see you for the next few days." He stopped to see if his words were having any effect. There was no reaction and Septimus felt a little upset – he had half hoped that a flicker of disappointment might cross Syrah's face.

"It's my Darke Week coming up," Septimus continued. "And ... um ... I want to tell you what I'm going to be doing. Because you've done it and you know how scary it feels before you go ... and I can't tell anyone else. I mean, I can't tell anyone who's not completed an Apprenticeship to an ExtraOrdinary Wizard. Which doesn't leave many people – well, only Marcia and you, in fact. Of course there would have been Alther before, well ... you know what happened. Oh, I know he was a ghost and there are lots of ExtraOrdinary Wizard and Apprentice ghosts around but Alther is – I mean *was* – different. He felt real, like he was still alive. Oh, Syrah, I miss Alther. I really do. And ... that's what I wanted to tell you – I'm going to get Alther back. I *am*. Marcia doesn't want me to, but it's *my* choice and she can't stop me. All Apprentices have the right to choose what they do in their Darke Week and I've chosen. I'm going down into the Darke Halls."

Septimus paused. He wondered whether he had told Syrah too much. If she really could hear him and understand every word he said, then all he had done was to leave her alone to worry about him. Septimus told himself not to be silly. Just because he had grown to care about what happened to Syrah, it didn't mean that she cared equally about him. In fact, he told himself, if she was aware of his visits she was more likely to feel relieved at the prospect of getting a rest from him. He grinned ruefully. Something Jenna had said to him more than once recently came back to him: "Not *everything* revolves around you, Sep."

Feeling a little awkward, he finished his visit. "So, er, good-bye then. I'll be fine and, um, I hope you will be too. I'll see you when I get back." Septimus would have liked to give Syrah a quick goodbye kiss but that was not possible. A person in the process of DisEnchantment must not be connected to anything that is earthbound. This was why the Forrest Bands holding Syrah suspended had been such a breakthrough – they Magykally broke the connection with earth and allowed the DisEnchantment to work. Most of the time.

Septimus left the DisEnchanting Chamber, made his way through the antechamber and stepped out into the sick bay. Rose gave him a friendly wave, which he returned briefly and, still feeling embarrassed, he left the sick bay and walked back down the corridor, telling himself, "Not *everything* revolves around you, you dillop."

However, that day in the Wizard Tower it seemed that, dillop or not, everything *did* revolve around him. A fourteenth birth-day for an Apprentice was a special one – being twice the

Magykal number seven – and naturally the entire population of the Wizard Tower wanted to wish Septimus a happy birthday, particularly as there was no birthday banquet to look forward to that evening. Sarah Heap's determination to have Septimus at the Palace that night had not gone down well at the Wizard Tower.

However, as Septimus went about his morning errands – delivering requested Charms to various Wizards, Finding a lost pair of glasses, helping out with a tricky spell on floor four – he detected a melancholy undertone to all the birthday wishes. The Wizard Tower was notorious for gossip, and it seemed that every Wizard knew that Septimus was about to embark upon his Darke Week – the one week that separates the Ordinary from the ExtraOrdinary Apprenticeship. This was despite the fact that the timing of the Darke Week was meant to be a secret.

And so, along with the many "happy birthday" greetings, there were also fervent wishes for "and many more of them, Apprentice". On his rounds Septimus was offered a varied assortment of gifts, all unwrapped – as was the tradition among Wizards in order to avoid the Placement of creatures, an ancient Darke trick that had once given Marcia some trouble. A pair of purple hand-knitted "lucky" socks, a bag of self-renewing banana chews and three Magykal hairbrushes were among those he accepted, but the vast majority were SafeCharms, all of which he politely refused.

As Septimus took the stairs down to the Wizard Tower Hall on his very last errand, he felt unsettled by the sadness beneath the birthday wishes. It was odd, he thought; it felt as if someone close to him had died or – it occurred to him as he stepped off the stairs – as if *he* were about to die. Septimus walked slowly across the soft, Magykal floor, reading the messages, which were wishing him not only A VERY HAPPY FOURTEENTH BIRTHDAY, APPRENTICE, but also BE SAFE, APPRENTICE. He sighed – even the floor was at it.

Septimus knocked on the door of the duty Wizard's room, which was tucked in beside the huge silver doors that led out from the Wizard Tower. Hildegarde Pigeon, a young woman in pristine Ordinary sub-Wizard robes, opened it. Septimus smiled; he liked Hildegarde.

"Happy birthday!" Hildegarde greeted him.

"Thanks."

"It's a big day, fourteen. And Princess Jenna's birthday too."

"Yes." Septimus felt a bit guilty. He'd forgotten to get her a present.

"We'll be seeing her later, apparently. About midday, Madam Overstrand said. She didn't seem very pleased, though."

"Marcia's not very pleased about anything at the moment," said Septimus, wondering why Jenna hadn't told him about her visit to the Wizard Tower.

Hildegarde sensed that all was not well. "So ... are *you* having a good day?"

"Well, yes, I suppose. I've just been up to the DisEnchanting Chamber. Bet you're glad you're not there any more."

Hildegarde smiled. "Too right," she said. "But it did the job. And it will for Syrah too, don't you worry."

"Hope so," said Septimus. "I've come for my boots."

"Oh, yes. Hang on a mo." Hildegard disappeared into the tiny room and emerged carrying a box with "Terry Tarsal, by appointment" written on it in gold letters. Terry had recently upgraded his image.

Septimus lifted the lid and peered inside. He looked relieved. "Oh good," he said. "He repaired my old ones. Marcia was threatening to get him to make me a new pair in green with *purple laces.*"

"Oh dear." Hildegarde smiled. "Not a good look."

"No. Definitely not."

"There's a letter for you too." Hildegarde handed over a creased and slightly damp envelope.

Septimus looked at it. He couldn't place the writing but it looked oddly familiar. And then he realised why – it was a mixture of his own handwriting and his father's.

"Um, Septimus," Hildegarde broke into his thoughts.

"Yep?"

"I know I shouldn't say this as it's confidential and all that but, well . . . I just wanted to say good luck. And I'll be think-ing of you."

"Oh. Well, thank you. Thank you, Hildegarde. That's really nice."

Hildegarde went a little pink and disappeared back into the duty Wizard's room.

Septimus tucked the shoebox under his arm and headed for the silver spiral stairs, letter in hand. Only when he was back in his room on the twenty-first floor of the Wizard Tower with the door firmly closed, did he tear open the envelope and read:

> *Dear Septimus,*
>
> *I hope you have a very happy fourteenth birthday.*
>
> *I expect you are surprised to get a letter from me, but I wish to apologise for what I did to you. I have no excuse except to say that I do not think I was in my*

right mind at the time. I believe that my contact with the Darke made me crazy. But I take responsibility for that. On the night of your Apprentice Feast, I deliberately sought out the Darke and that is completely my fault.

I hope that one day you will forgive me.

I realise that you are well into your Apprenticeship now and will have much knowledge. But even so, I hope you will not mind your oldest brother giving you some advice: Beware of the Darke.

With best wishes,
Simon (Heap)

Septimus sat down on his bed and let out a low whistle. He felt spooked. Even Simon seemed to know about his Darke Week.

❊ 5 ❊

RUNAWAYS

While Septimus sat rereading his letter, the messenger who had delivered it was suffering from an attack of cold feet. Even the two pairs of thick, stripy socks that Lucy Gringe habitually wore in the winter were no help that cold morning as she hung back in the shadows of the North Gate gatehouse, trying to pluck up the courage to announce herself to her mother.

Lucy had arrived at the Gatehouse early. She wanted to speak to her father first, before her mother ventured outside with his early morning cocoa. Despite her father's gruff exterior, Lucy knew that Gringe would be thrilled to see her. "Dad's an old softy, really," she had told Simon before she had left. "It's Mum who'll be difficult."

But Lucy's plan had gone awry. She had been thrown by the unexpected appearance of a makeshift lean-to shelter along the side of the gatehouse, beside the road leading to the bridge. A sign on the shelter announced it to be CAFÉ LA GRINGE, from which came the (unfortunately) unforgettable smell of her mother's stew. This was accompanied by the equally unmistakable sound of her mother cooking – clanging saucepan lids, muttered curses and ill-tempered thumps and thuds.

Lucy stood in the shadows wondering what to do. Eventually the rank smell of the stew drove her to a decision. She waited until her mother was looking into one of the deep stew pans and then, head held high, Lucy marched right past CAFÉ LA GRINGE. It worked. Mrs Gringe, who was wondering if anyone would notice the mouse that had fallen in overnight and suffocated, did not look up.

Gringe, a heavy-set man with close-shorn hair and wearing a greasy leather jerkin, was sitting in the gatehouse keeper's lodge. He was keeping out of the chilly wind that blew off the Moat and, more importantly, out of the way of the stew. It was a quiet day. Everyone in the Castle was either at the last day of the Traders' Market – which had stayed later than usual that year – or were busy getting ready for the festivities of the Longest Night, when candles would be lit in every window throughout the Castle. And so, apart from taking toll money from a few bleary Northern Traders first thing that morning, Gringe had had nothing better to do than polish the few coins he had collected – a job he had taken over from Mrs Gringe, now that she was, as he frequently complained, obsessed with stew.

When Gringe looked up at the newcomer, who he assumed was about to add to his meagre pile of coins, he did not at first recognise his daughter. The young woman with big brown eyes and a nervous smile looked far too grown up to be his little Lucy, who, in her absence, had become ever younger in Gringe's fond memory. Even when the young woman said, *"Dad!"* a little tearfully, Gringe stared at Lucy uncomprehending, until his cold, bored brain at last made the connection. And then he sprang to his feet, enveloped

Lucy in a huge hug, lifted her off her feet and yelled, "Lucy! Lucy, *Lucy*!"

A wave of relief swept over Lucy – *it was going to be all right.*

An hour later, sitting in the room above the gatehouse with her parents (while the bridge boy looked after the bridge and the stew looked after itself), Lucy had revised this opinion: *It was possibly going to be all right, if she was very careful and didn't upset her mother too much.*

Mrs Gringe was in full flood, recounting for the umpteenth time the long list of Lucy's transgressions. "Running off with that *awful* Heap boy, not a care about me or your father, gone these last two years with never a word ..."

"I did write to you," Lucy protested. "But you never replied."

"You think I got time to write letters?" asked Mrs Gringe, insulted.

"But, *Mum* –"

"I got a gatehouse to run. Stew to cook. On me *own*." Mrs Gringe looked pointedly at both Lucy and Gringe, who, to his discomfort, now seemed to be included in Lucy's wrong-doings. He stepped in hastily.

"Come, come, dear. Lucy's all grown up now. She got better things to do than live with her old mum and dad –"

"Old?" said his wife indignantly.

"Well, I didn't mean –"

"No wonder I look old. All that worry. Ever since she was fourteen she's bin running after that Heap boy. Sneaking out with him, even trying to *marry* him, for goodness' sake, and getting us into terrible trouble with them Custodians. And after all that we take her back out of the goodness of our hearts and what does she do? She runs off again! And never a word. Not a word ..." Mrs Gringe got out a stew-stained handkerchief and began noisily blowing her nose into it.

Lucy hadn't expected it to be this bad. She glanced at her father. *Say sorry,* he mouthed.

"Er ... Mum," Lucy ventured.

"What?" came her muffled voice.

"I ... I'm sorry."

Mrs Gringe looked up. "Are you?" She seemed surprised.

"Yes. I am."

"Oh." Mrs Gringe blew her nose loudly.

"Look, Mum, Dad. The thing is, me and Simon, we want to get married."

"I'd 'ave thought you'd already done *that*," her mother sniffed accusingly.

Lucy shook her head. "No. After I ran away to find Simon – and I *did* find him –" (Lucy refrained from adding "so there," as she would have done not so long ago) – "well, after I found him I realised that I wanted us to be married *properly*. I want a white wedding –"

"White wedding? Huh!" said Mrs Gringe.

"Yes, Mum, that's what I want. And I want you and Dad to be there. And Simon's Mum and Dad too. And I want you to be happy about it."

"Happy!" Mrs Gringe exclaimed bitterly.

"Mum ... *please*, listen. I've come back to ask if you and Dad will come to our wedding."

Her mother sat for a while digesting this as Lucy and Gringe looked on anxiously. "You really *are* inviting us to your wedding?" she asked.

"*Yes,* Mum." Lucy pulled a crumpled card edged with white ribbon from her pocket and handed it to Mrs Gringe, who squinted at it suspiciously. Suddenly she leaped to her feet and flung her arms around Lucy. "My baby," she cried. "You're getting *married*." She looked at Gringe. "I'll need a new hat," she said.

There was a sudden sound of thudding boots on the steps leading to the room and the bridge boy burst in. "What d'you charge an 'orse?" he demanded.

Gringe looked annoyed. "You know what to charge. I left you the list. Horse and rider: one silver penny. Now go an' get the money before they stop hangin' around waitin' for an idiot like you to ask stupid questions."

"But what if it's *just* an 'orse?" the bridge boy persisted.

"What, a runaway horse?"

The bridge boy nodded.

"Charge the horse whatever it's got in its wallet," said Gringe, raising his eyes to heaven. "Or you can hang on to the 'orse and charge the owner when 'e catches up with it. What do *you* think?"

"Dunno," said the bridge boy. "That's why I come and asked."

Gringe heaved a heavy sigh. "I better go an' sort this," he said, getting to his feet.

"I'll give you a hand, Dad," said Lucy, not wanting to be left alone with her mother.

Gringe smiled. "That's me girl," he said.

Gringe and Lucy found a large black horse tied up to a ring in the gatehouse wall. The horse looked at Lucy, and Lucy looked at the horse.

"Thunder!" Lucy gasped.

"Nah," said Gringe, looking up at the clouds. "Looks more like snow to me."

"No, Dad," said Lucy, stroking the horse's mane, "the horse – it's *Thunder*. Simon's horse."

"Ah. So *that's* how you got here."

"No, Dad. I didn't come on the horse. I got the Port barge."

"Well, that's good. I were a bit worried. He's got no saddle or anything. Not safe riding like that."

Lucy looked puzzled. She stroked Thunder's muzzle and the horse pushed his nose into her shoulder. "Hello, Thunder," she said. "What are *you* doing here?"

Thunder looked at her. There was an expression deep in the horse's eyes that Lucy wished she understood. Simon would know, she thought. He and Thunder always knew what each other were thinking. Simon and Thunder ... suddenly Lucy knew. "Simon! Something's happened to Simon. Thunder's come to tell me!"

Gringe looked concerned. Not more trouble, he thought. Mrs Gringe was right. Ever since Lucy had met the Heap boy something was always going wrong. He looked at his daughter's worried expression and, not for the first time, he wished she had met a nice, straightforward Castle boy all those years ago.

"Lucy, love," he said gently. "It might not even be Thunder. There're a lot of black horses about. And even if it is 'im, well, it don't mean anything bad. In fact, it's a stroke a luck. The horse got loose, it's come all the way through the Farmlands and no one's pinched it – which is a miracle – it's found its way into the Castle and *now* it's found you." Gringe wanted so much to make it all right for Lucy. He smiled encouragingly. "Look, love. We'll find 'im a saddle and all that kind of horse stuff and you can ride 'im back to the Port. Better than that smelly old barge any day."

Lucy smiled uncertainly. She wanted everything to be all right too.

Lucy led a reluctant Thunder around to the gatehouse stable. When she left, after giving him fresh hay and water and covering him with a warm horse blanket, Thunder tried to follow her out. Lucy quickly closed the bottom half of the stable door. Thunder stuck his great head out of the open top door and looked reproachfully at her.

"Oh, Thunder, tell me Simon's all right. *Please*," she whispered.

But Thunder was saying nothing.

A few minutes later Mrs Gringe came down to check on the stew. She was just in time to see Lucy, ribbons flying, racing off into the warren of houses that backed up to the Castle walls. Convinced that Lucy was running away again, Mrs Gringe stomped over to the nearest stew pot and poked angrily at it. She was, however, pleased to see that the mouse had incorporated nicely into the brown sludge.

Lucy was not running away. She was heading for the steps up to the path that ran along the top of the Castle walls and would take her to the East Gate Lookout Tower – the headquarters of the Message Rat Service, run by Stanley, his four ratlets (now fully grown) and their assorted friends and hangers-on.

As Lucy strode along the walls, she composed a variety of messages to Simon. By the time she breathlessly pushed open the little door of the East Gate Lookout Tower and stepped into the Message Rat Office, she had decided on something short and simple (and also cheap): *Thunder here. Are you all right? Send return message. Lu xxxxxx*

Half an hour later, Stanley had just caught the mid-morning Port barge. He was unsure whether to be flattered or annoyed that Lucy had insisted that she trusted no rat but him to take the message. After half an hour spent hiding out in a fish basket, trying to avoid the barge cat, Stanley decided he was most definitely annoyed. He was going all the way to the Port just to deliver a weather report. Added to that, he had just realised who the recipient of the message was – Simon Heap was one of the Heap Wizarding family. And Stanley was of the same mind as Mrs Gringe on this one: Heap Wizards were bad news.

❀ 6 ❀
CHOICE

While Gringe was searching for "horse stuff", Septimus was, as Marcia put it, in conference. He was in Marcia's sitting room, sitting on a small stool beside the fire, with his blue and gold leather-bound Apprentice Diary on his knees. It was open at the page that read "Darke Week".

Marcia had been dreading the Darke Week for some time. Even though she knew that the most powerful Magyk – which Septimus would be using in the next stage of his Apprenticeship – needed a personal connection with the Darke, it frightened her. Some ExtraOrdinary Wizards were perfectly at ease with the Darke. They enjoyed playing with the delicate balance between Darke and Magyk, adjusting it as a skilled mechanic would a finely tuned engine and, in the process, getting the last ounce of power from their Magyk. Marcia, however, preferred to use as small an amount of Darke Magyk as possible, relying more on her personal Magykal power – some purists might have called her an unbalanced practitioner of Magyk (although not to her face). It was, however, true that the most powerful Wizards were those in perfect balance – and this was what the Darke Week was all about. It was the time when the ExtraOrdinary Apprentice acquired personal experience of the Darke that would enable him or her to move towards a Magykal skill that was in harmony with everything – even the Darke.

Marcia had an added reason for being uneasy about Septimus's Darke Week. Recently she had noticed that the Wizard Tower was requiring more Magyk than usual to keep everything running in perfect order. There had been a series of minor breakdowns – the stairs had suddenly stopped one day for no reason, and the floor had begun to display the odd, jumbled message. The previous week the Wizards had had to Fumigate a severe outbreak of Darke spiders, and only the day before Marcia had needed to reset the Password on the doors twice. Each incident on its own would not have worried her – these things happened occasionally – but the cumulative effect had made Marcia jumpy. Which was why she now said to her Apprentice, "I know it's your choice, Septimus, but I would rather you didn't begin your Darke Week right *now*."

Marcia was perched precariously at one end of her sofa. This was because most of the sofa was already occupied by a willowy man with a pointy beard who was curled up like a cat, fast asleep. The man's long, elegant fingers rested delicately on the purple velvet of Marcia's sofa, the colour of which contrasted vividly with the yellow of his costume and his tall hat, which looked like a pile of ever-decreasing doughnuts crammed on to his head. This bizarre sleeping figure was Jim Knee – Septimus's jinnee – who had gone into hibernation. He had been asleep for some four weeks now, ever since the weather had turned wintry. His breathing was slow and regular, except for a loud snore that escaped now and then.

Marcia did not welcome having to share her sofa, but she preferred it to the alternative of Jim Knee being awake. Ignoring a sudden *snurrrufff* from the jinnee, she opened the *Apprentice Almanac* – a large, ancient book bound in what had once been bright green leather – which she was balancing on her knee. Slowly she turned the parchment pages until she found what she was looking for. She peered through her new tiny gold spectacles at the closely written text.

"Luckily you became Apprentice at a time that gives you the widest choice of when to do this. You actually have up to seven weeks after the Mid-Winter Feast in which to undertake your Darke Week. Is that not right, Marcellus?" Marcia looked over her spectacles at a man sitting opposite Septimus in an upright chair, daring him to disagree.

It was only the second time that Marcia had invited Marcellus Pye to her rooms in the Wizard Tower, and she had done so out of a wish to honour an old tradition. In days past, the Castle Alchemist – which Marcellus had once been – was consulted in the timing of the ExtraOrdinary Apprentice's Darke Week. The moment when an Apprentice went alone into the realm of the Darke was an important one, and Alchemists were known to have a much closer connection with all things Darke – not to mention something of an obsession with propitious timing.

The consulting of the Castle Alchemist had, naturally, lapsed with the demise of Alchemie in the Castle. But now, for the first time in many hundreds of years, there was, with Marcellus Pye, a true Alchemist available once again. After much thought, Marcia had decided to include Marcellus in the discussion. She was now regretting her decision – something told her he was going to be awkward.

Marcellus Pye glinted spectacularly in the firelight. He was dressed in a long, black, fur-lined velvet coat, which sported an extravagant array of shiny gold fastenings. The most unusual thing about him, however, was his shoes. Long and pointy, in soft red leather, they tapered to three-foot-long thin strips of leather that ended in black ribbons, which were tied just below his knees so that he did not (very often) trip over them. The onlooker, if they managed to stop looking at his shoes for a moment, would also see that below his dark hair brushed low over his forehead — which gave him an old-fashioned appearance — he too wore a small pair of gold spectacles. He also had a book on his knees, although it was smaller than Marcia's tome. His book, written by himself, was called *I, Marcellus*. Marcellus Pye was carefully consulting the last section, titled "The Almanac", before he answered Marcia's question.

"That may be true according to the Apprentice calendar," he said. "But —"

"But *what*?" Marcia interrupted irritably.

"*Snur . . . snurrrufff!*"

"Goodness me, what is that noise?"

"It's Jim Knee, Mr Pye. I told you before — he *snores*. I do wish you would listen."

"Jim Knee?"

"I *told* you — Septimus's jinnee. Ignore him. I do."

"Ah, yes. Well, well. As I was saying before I was interrupted, according to my own Almanac, which gives considerably more accurate detail, and which my Apprentice helped to —"

"*Ex*-Apprentice," said Marcia tetchily.

"I have never revoked his Indentures, Marcia," Marcellus countered, equally tetchily. "I regard him as my Apprentice."

The subject of their discussion squirmed uncomfortably.

"Those Indentures were meaningless," snapped Marcia, refusing to let the subject drop. "Septimus was not free to become your Apprentice – he was already Apprenticed to *me*."

"I think you will find he was Apprenticed to *me* before he was Apprenticed to you. About *five hundred years* before, in fact," Marcellus said with a slight smile that Marcia found intensely annoying.

"As far as Septimus was concerned," countered Marcia, "*your* Apprenticeship came later. And *Septimus* is the one who matters. In fact, he is the very reason we are both here right now – because we are concerned for his safety, are we not, Mr Pye?"

"*That* goes without saying," Marcellus Pye said stiffly.

"And so let me repeat what I said earlier, just in case that too has slipped your mind. Septimus has a window of seven weeks in which to commence his Darke Week. I am worried that if he goes tonight, at the Dark of the Moon, as you have suggested –"

"And as *he* wishes," interrupted Marcellus.

"He wishes it because you have suggested it, Mr Pye – don't think I don't know that. If Septimus embarks on his Darke Week tonight, he will be in greater danger than on any other night. Far better that he waits until the full moon in two weeks' time, when it will be less risky for him and also for the ..." Marcia trailed off. She was anxious that if Septimus entered the Darke at such a potent time it would unbalance the Magyk in the Tower even further, but she had no wish to tell Marcellus Pye her concerns – it was none of his business.

"Less risky for him and also for the *what*?" Marcellus asked suspiciously. He knew Marcia was keeping something from him.

"Nothing *you* need to worry about, Marcellus," Marcia replied.

Marcellus was annoyed. He snapped his book closed and got to his feet. He made a slight, old-fashioned bow. "ExtraOrdinary Wizard. As you requested, I have given my opinion. I regret that it was not to your liking, but I repeat: *the Dark of the Moon is the most effective time for Septimus to embark upon his* Darke Week. It is the most effective time for him to go and, as I understand it, *effective* is what Septimus wishes it to be. He is fourteen now – today, I believe." Marcellus smiled at Septimus. "Fourteen is considered old enough to make important decisions, Marcia. I think you should respect that. I have nothing further to add and I bid you good day." Marcellus bowed once again – deeper this time – and headed for the large purple door.

Septimus leaped to his feet. "I'll get the stairs for you," he said. Marcellus had had trouble with the stairs when he came up and had arrived in Marcia's room somewhat dizzy and dishevelled.

As Septimus escorted Marcellus Pye along the landing, his old tutor looked behind him to check that Marcia had not sent some kind of eavesdropping creature to follow him. He saw nothing and said in a low voice, "Septimus, I hope you realise that I would never have advised you to go into the Darke at this time if I did not have something for you that I truly believe will completely protect you." Marcellus fixed his deep brown eyes on his Apprentice – or not, depending on who you sided with. "I care about you, just as much as Madam Marcia Overstrand does."

Septimus turned a little pink. He nodded.

Marcellus Pye continued, "I did not mention this to Marcia because I believe that even now there are things that should be kept secret from the Wizarding community. They are *such* gossips. But for you, as my Alchemie Apprentice, it is different. Come and see me this afternoon; there is something I wish to give you."

Septimus nodded. "Thank you, Marcellus. I'll see you later."

Septimus helped Marcellus on to the stairs and set them moving downwards on delicate mode – normally used for elderly Wizards and visiting parents. He watched the apparently young Marcellus Pye disappear from view. He smiled – it was in the little details that Marcellus gave his true age away.

Septimus returned to his place by the fire. He and Marcia sat in silence for a while until Marcia broke it by saying, "I don't want to lose my Apprentice. More than that, Septimus, I don't want to lose *you*."

"You won't. I promise," Septimus replied.

"Don't make promises that you can't be sure to keep," Marcia told him.

A silence hung in the air.

"*Sner . . . urrrufff!*"

"Oh, for goodness' sake," Marcia muttered, casting an irritated glance at the jinnee. "Septimus, I didn't want to mention this in front of Mr Pye, but I am concerned about the recent glitches we've had here in the Tower. Going into the Darke is a two-way thing. It can open up channels for the Darke to come this way too."

"I know," said Septimus. "I've been practising Barriers all last week."

"Yes, indeed you have. But it's still risky – and particularly so at the Dark of the Moon. I am asking you to reconsider your decision and go at the full moon instead."

"But Marcellus says that this timing is my best chance to get Alther back," said Septimus. "Probably my *only* chance."

"Marcellus! What does he know?" snapped Marcia. And then, knowing she was not playing fair, said, "*Alther* would agree with me."

"How can you know what Alther would think?" retorted Septimus. "You don't even know if he *can* think any more."

"Oh, Septimus, *don't*," Marcia protested. "You don't know how often I wish I had stopped the Banish in time. Not a day passes when that awful moment doesn't come back to me. And then telling Alice . . ." She shook her head, unable to go on.

They were silent for a while and then Septimus said, "Marcia?"

"Yes?"

"You know how you are always saying that we must be honest with each other?"

"Yeees?"

"*Sner . . . snurrrufff . . .*"

"There's something I want to ask you and I want you to be honest with me."

"Of *course* I will be, Septimus." Marcia sounded offended.

"If you were me and you had this one chance to bring Alther back – even with all the risks – would you take it?"

"But I don't *have* that chance. I have already been into the Darke and therefore I am Known. There is no way I could get into the Darke Halls now."

Septimus got to his feet and stood by the fire. He felt he needed the advantage of some extra height. "You haven't answered my question," he said, looking down at Marcia.

"No, I suppose I haven't," Marcia replied meekly.

"So, if you were me and had this one chance to bring Alther back, *would you take it?*"

A silence ensued into which even Jim Knee's snores dared not intrude. At last Marcia answered.

"Yes," she said quietly. "Yes, I think I would."

"Thank you," said Septimus. "Then I shall go tonight. At midnight."

"Very well," said Marcia with a sigh. "I'll start getting things ready." She got to her feet, picked up the *Apprentice Almanac* and walked out to her study. She was back a few minutes later carrying a large iron key on a loop of black cord. "You'd better take it now, before I change my mind," she told Septimus. "It's the key to Dungeon Number One."

Septimus buttoned the key into his secure pocket. It felt heavy and awkward – a weight he would rather not carry. He'd be glad when he no longer needed it, he thought.

Hoping to make Marcia feel better, Septimus said, "I'll be OK. I shall have something to protect me."

Marcia looked very annoyed. "If that Marcellus Pye has promised you some kind of Alchemie KeepSafe knick-knack – he has, hasn't he – don't you dare believe it's going to make a scrap of difference. *It won't.* All it will do is lull you into a false sense of security. Alchemie stuff is nothing but smoke and mirrors, Septimus. All talk and no action. None of their stuff ever did work. It was complete *rubbish.*"

"But Marcia, I'm sure Marcellus –"

"Marcellus! Forget about Marcellus. Septimus, you must rely *only* on yourself and your own Magykal powers." Marcia looked at her timepiece and sighed. "Midday already. As if it isn't enough that I have to put up with a meddling Alchemist – any minute now there will be a meddling *Princess* at my door declaiming from that wretched book with its tiddly-squiddly type, which is the bane of every ExtraOrdinary Wizard's life. I really could be doing without fourteenth birthdays right now." With that, Marcia stormed off to her study.

Septimus sat for some time, looking into the fire and relishing the quiet – apart from an occasional *snurrrufff*. He thought about what Marcia had said. Deep down he felt she was wrong about Marcellus – not all Alchemie was rubbish, he'd seen that for himself. But he knew Marcia would never agree. The build-up to the Darke Week was horrible, Septimus thought. Somehow it drove a wedge between you and everyone you cared about. He really wanted Marcia's approval for what he was going to do, but it was he who was going into the Darke, not Marcia. He must do it his way – not hers.

Snurrruuuuufff.

Septimus got to his feet. It was time to go and see Marcellus.

THE BRINGER OF THE BOOK

The meddling Princess, like Septimus, had had an unusually formal birthday morning. At nine o'clock precisely, a tall woman dressed in Palace robes so ancient that they actually had long gold ribbons dangling from their sleeves banged on the Palace doors.

The duty Door Wizard was having his breakfast, so it was Sarah Heap who eventually opened them. "Yes?" she asked irritably.

"I am the Bringer of the Book," the woman announced imperiously. Without waiting to be asked, she swept inside, bringing with her a pungent smell of mothballs and the faint whiff of fish.

"Presents go on the table," said Sarah, indicating a large table already piled with assorted colourful packages. "We are not opening them until this evening."

The Bringer of the Book made not the slightest move in the direction of the table. She towered over Sarah, her height increased by great swathes of white hair piled precariously on the top of her head and secured with a wild assortment of combs. She looked at Sarah in disbelief. "But I am the *Bringer of the Book,*" she said.

"I know. You already said. That's very nice; Jenna enjoys reading. Just put it on the table. Now excuse me, I really must get on. You know the way out." Sarah indicated the doors, which were still thrown wide open.

"The way out?" The woman sounded incredulous. "I am not going *out*. I have come to see the Princess. Now, my good woman, I will trouble you to announce my presence."

Sarah spluttered indignantly, but Jenna's timely arrival stopped any further escalation of hostilities.

"Mum!" she said, rushing in from the Long Walk. "Have you seen my – oh!" Jenna stopped and stared at the tall, imperious woman in the ancient Palace uniform. The old red and grey robes with their gold ribbons gave her the weirdest feeling, transporting her back to the frightening few days she had spent at the Palace in the ghastly Queen Etheldredda's Time. "Who . . . who are you?" she stammered.

The Bringer of the Book swept down into a deep curtsy, her long, fragile ribbons falling gracefully to the dusty floor.

"Your Grace," she murmured. "May I offer you my humble congratulations upon your Day of Recognition. I am the Bringer of the Book. I come to you as I came to your mother, and as my mother came to her mother before her, and as her mother came to her mother before her. I come to you to bring you *the Book*."

Sarah felt the need to translate. "She's brought you a book, Jenna. That's nice, isn't it? I've told her to put it on the table as we're not opening the presents until this evening."

The Bringer of the Book rounded on Sarah. "Mistress, I would ask you to hold your tongue. You may return to your duties – whatever they may be."

"Now look here —" Sarah began. She was stopped by Jenna, who was beginning to understand that something important was going on.

"Mum," said Jenna. "It's OK. I think it's — *you know* — Princess stuff." She turned to the woman and spoke in her best Princess voice. "Thank you, Bringer of the Book," she said. "May I introduce to you my mother, Madam Sarah Heap?"

The Bringer of the Book gave Sarah a small, perfunctory curtsy. "I apologise, Mistress Heap. I assumed from your dress that you were a menial."

"There's a lot of work to do around here and someone has to do it," snapped Sarah. "You can talk to Jenna in my sitting room if you want to go somewhere warm. I've just lit the fire." With that she walked off, head held high, stray wisps of straw-coloured hair bouncing crossly as she strode into the Long Walk in search of Silas Heap.

The Bringer of the Book looked disapprovingly at the retreating Sarah. She did not lose the expression when she turned to Jenna. "A sitting room will *not* be suitable for this important occasion," she said. "It is traditional for the Presentation to take place in the Throne Room. Perhaps you will be so kind as to lead the way."

The last time Jenna had been in the Throne Room was five hundred years ago, in Queen Etheldredda's Time. It did not hold good memories. Before then — or, strictly speaking time-wise, after — she had been in the Throne Room only once, and luckily she did not remember it. That was fourteen years ago to the very day, the day that her real mother, Queen Cerys, was shot dead. The idea of going into the Throne Room dismayed her, especially on this day of all days.

"The Throne Room is locked," Jenna said coolly. "I do not use it."

For the first time the Bringer of the Book regarded Jenna with something like approval. "Of course you do not use it, Princess. That is exactly how it should be. You have had no need for it until today. But today, the occasion of your fourteenth birthday, is the day of your first official engagement. Traditionally this takes place in the Throne Room – as you know." The Bringer of the Book smiled at Jenna as though they were in on the same joke – a joke that no one else was clever enough to understand. Jenna had known girls like that at school and she hadn't liked them. She felt the same way about the Bringer of the Book.

Jenna was about to retort that she didn't care what the occasion was, she wasn't going to unlock the Throne Room for anyone and anyway, she didn't have the key, when Silas appeared. Jenna felt in need of his support.

"Dad," she said, forgetting her Princess manners in her distress at being asked to unlock the Throne Room. "Dad, we *don't* have the key to the Throne Room, *do* we?"

Silas surprised her. From his pocket he took a heavy, red-jewelled key and presented it to her with a small bow.

"Don't be silly, Dad." Jenna laughed, deliberately not taking the key. "You don't have to bow."

Silas looked serious. "Maybe I should now that you're fourteen," he said.

"Dad?" Jenna began to feel concerned. What was happening? It sounded as though something was about to change, and she didn't want it to.

Silas looked uncomfortable. "Marcia told me last week about, er ... *her*." He waved his hand at the increasingly affronted Bringer of the Book. "She gave me the key. She said that from your fourteenth birthday forward it is possible at any time that The Time May Be Right."

"Right for *what*?" Jenna demanded crossly. She hated it when people arranged things without telling her and then expected her to go along with it. It took her right back to her tenth birthday, when she was suddenly taken away from her family. And, as ever, Marcia was involved.

Silas was conciliatory. "You know for what, love," he said. "For you to be crowned Queen. You are old enough now. It doesn't mean you are going to be, just that it is possible. And that is why this lady –"

The Bringer of the Book glared at Silas.

Silas coughed. "Ahem, I mean this very, er ... *important*, very *official* lady has come today. She is the hereditary Bringer of the Book. And traditionally you receive it in the Throne Room." Silas caught Jenna's gaze. She looked upset. "It's uh ... symbolic, you see. Of, um, of what you will be one day."

"So why didn't you tell me?" demanded Jenna. "Or Mum?"

Silas looked upset. "I didn't want to spoil your birthday for you or Mum. I know how you feel about the Throne Room. I'm sorry, I suppose I should have said."

Jenna sighed. "Oh, it's all right, Dad. I'll do it – as long as you come and *sort the key out*. OK?" She gave Silas a meaningful glare.

"Ah. OK. Right. I'll come with you."

The Bringer of the Book objected. "This is a private ceremony. It is not suitable for a member of the public to attend," she said.

"He's not a member of the public," snapped Jenna. "He's my dad."

"He is *not* your father."

Jenna exploded. "No, he's *not*. Of course he isn't. It's my birthday and you wouldn't expect my *father* to be here, would you?" Jenna took Silas's arm. "This is my *dad*. He's here. And he's coming with me." With that, Jenna and Silas slowly and sedately climbed the sweeping stairs up to the first floor. The Bringer of the Book had no alternative but to follow.

They arrived outside the huge double doors that led into the Throne Room, which occupied the very centre of the Palace. The doors were covered in ancient gold leaf, worn so thin that the squares of gold showed the red beneath. Jenna thought they looked beautiful – but she had no intention of opening them. "OK, Dad?" she said.

Silas nodded. He put the key in the lock, and Jenna thought she saw a small flash of Magyk – at least, she hoped she did. Silas turned the key. It went halfway around and stuck.

"It's Jammed," he said. "You try it, Jenna."

To Jenna's relief, the key was indeed stuck fast. "It is," she agreed. "It's Jammed."

The Bringer of the Book wore a distinctly suspicious expression.

"Would you like to try?" Jenna asked, offering her the key.

The Bringer of the Book snatched the key, pushed it into the lock and gave it a fearsome twist. Jenna could see she meant business and hoped that Silas's spell held out. It did. Reluctantly, after a lot of vigorous twisting and poking at the lock, the Bringer of the Book returned the key.

"Very well," she sighed. "The ReTiring Room will do just as well."

Jenna refrained from asking why she hadn't said that in the first place. She reckoned she knew the answer already. The Bringer of the Book wanted to bask in the reflected glory of the Throne Room. Jenna had met many people like her in Queen Etheldredda's Palace, which was where she had begun to learn how to deal with them.

The ReTiring Room was intended as a personal space for the Queen to put on her ceremonial robes and to retreat to from the Throne Room if she needed. It was dusty and dark, but Jenna liked it and often used it as a quiet place to work. With the Bringer of the Book trailing behind her, Jenna led the way into the ReTiring Room. Silas excused himself and left; this time Jenna did not object.

The ReTiring Room was long and narrow, with one tall window at the end that looked out over Wizard Way. A shabby curtain on the right side of the room covered a door that led to the Throne Room, which was impassable due to a large plank Jenna had hammered across it. The room was extremely chilly, but a fire was laid ready in the small grate. Jenna took the tinderbox from the chimneypiece and struck a yellow flame into the dry moss at the base of the fire. She used the flame to light the candles as well, and soon the room glowed with a yellow light and looked much warmer than it actually was.

The Bringer of the Book fussily settled herself at a small desk below the window. From an array of mismatched but comfortable chairs Jenna took the chair she liked to curl up and read in – a battered red and gold one with a pile of cushions and a wonky leg – and pushed it towards the fire.

It was a long and tedious three hours but at the end of it, as she stood at the Palace door, watching the Bringer of the Book sail off down the Palace Drive, her ribbons fluttering in the cold wind that was blowing in off the river, Jenna held in her hand a small red book entitled *The Queen Rules*.

Jenna went straight back up to the ReTiring Room. She closed the door with a feeling of relief to have the place to herself once more, then pulled her chair even closer to the fire and looked at the little red leather book. It was so delicate. The pale red leather was soft to the touch, well worn and rubbed – she realised with a shiver of goose bumps – by the fingers of her mother, her grandmother and her many great-grandmothers before her. The pages, edged with gold leaf, were made of delicate paper so transparent that they were printed only on one side. The spelling was bizarre and the type was tiny and full of swirls and curlicues, which was why it had taken so long for the Bringer of the Book to read – and explain – the entire contents to Jenna. But now that she was at last alone with her book, Jenna turned to the page that she wanted to reread the most:

Protocol: Wizard Tower
(N.B. Substitute P-I-W for Queen if appropriate)

After her three-hour tutorial, Jenna now knew that "P-I-W" meant Princess-in-Waiting. There were two sections that particularly interested Jenna.

SECTION I: THE RIGHT TO KNOW
The P-I-W has a Right To Know all facts pertain-
ing to the security and wellbeing of the Castle and the
Palace. The ExtraOrdinary Wizard (or, in absentia, the
ExtraOrdinary Apprentice) is required to answer all the
P-I-W's questions truthfully, fully and without delay.

Jenna smiled. She liked the sound of that, but she was willing
to bet Marcia didn't. She read the second section even more
carefully.

SECTION II: PALACE SECURITY
It is for the P-I-W to deem if a matter relates to Palace
Security. If she deems it to be so, she may Call upon the
ExtraOrdinary Wizard or the ExtraOrdinary Apprentice
to assist at Any Time. This Call will be given priority over
all other matters at the Wizard Tower. So Be It.

Huh, thought Jenna. Sep had obviously not read *this*.

She reread the second passage, smiling at the hand-drawn,
heavy red lines below the words "P-I-W", "Any Time" and
"all". It seemed that she was not the only Princess-in-Waiting
to have this kind of trouble. She particularly liked what was
written at the foot of the page in a different but equally determined hand: "Wizards are replaceable. The Queen is not."

Jenna uncurled herself from her chair like a cat. She got
up, dampened the fire and closed the door on the ReTiring
Room, leaving it to settle into its stillness once more. She
would go straight to the Wizard Tower and do a bit of deem-
ing. Right now.

On her way out, Jenna bumped into Sarah, who, with the help of Billy Pot and the cook, had begun to put up bunting in the entrance hall.

"Has Dolly gone?" asked Sarah.

"Who?"

"Dolly Bingle. She works in the fish shop down by the New Quay. I *knew* I'd seen her before. Funny how different she looks with a bit of gold flummery and her hair out of a fish net."

"The Bringer of the Book was *Dolly Bingle*?" Jenna was stunned.

"Yes, it was. And Dolly knows perfectly well who I am. I shall expect some cheap haddock when I next go there," said Sarah with a wicked grin.

✳ 8 ✳

CHEMISTRY

On the way down the Palace drive Jenna remembered her walk with Septimus the previous evening. The memory still upset her but now, with *The Queen Rules* safely in her pocket, it annoyed her too. Septimus had treated her as though she was no more than an irritating child. And here she was chasing after him again, about to give him the opportunity to behave in exactly the same way. Why did she need his opinion on what was going on in the Palace attic? He wasn't the only one who knew stuff – there was someone much nearer who would actually be glad to help.

A few minutes later Jenna was standing outside Larry's Dead Languages Translation Service. She took a deep breath and readied herself to step inside. Jenna didn't like Larry and Larry clearly didn't like her. However, she did not take this personally because, so far as she could tell, Larry didn't like *anyone*. Which made it very odd, she thought, that Beetle had not only taken a job as Larry's transcription scribe but, now that his mother had moved down to the Port, was living there too.

Bracing herself for the caustic remarks that always accompanied her entrance, Jenna put her shoulder to the shop door and shoved (the door was notoriously stiff – Larry liked people to really want to get into his shop). The door flew open with unusual ease, Jenna hurtled across the shop and crashed into a pile of manuscripts on which a tall, expensive-looking vase was precariously balanced.

Accompanied by the sound of Larry's throaty chuckle coming from the upstairs gallery, Beetle performed an impressive flying catch and saved the vase just before it crashed to the floor.

He helped Jenna to her feet. "Hey, are you all right?" he asked.

Winded, Jenna nodded.

Beetle took Jenna's arm and led her through the shop to the library at the back, saying loudly, "I have your translations ready, Princess Jenna. Perhaps you'd like to take a look?"

As they disappeared out of Larry's earshot, Beetle said, "I'm really, really sorry about the door. I didn't have time to warn you. Larry oiled it yesterday afternoon and set up the vase on top of the manuscripts. Since then he's sat upstairs in the gallery waiting for people to do exactly what you did just now. He's charged three people for breaking the vase – *and* they've paid."

"Three?"

"Yep. He sticks it back together after each time."

Bemused, Jenna shook her head. "Beetle, I really don't know why you want to work here – let alone *live* here. Especially as Marcia offered you a place at the Wizard Tower."

Beetle shrugged. "I love the old manuscripts and their weird languages. And I'm learning all kinds of stuff; you'd be amazed at what people bring in. Besides, I'm not Magykal. The Wizard Tower would drive me nuts."

Jenna nodded. The Wizard Tower would drive her nuts too. But so would working for Larry.

As if he'd read her mind, Beetle said, "You know, after working for Jillie Djinn, Larry's not so bad. And I like living on Wizard Way. It's fun. Fancy a FizzFroot?"

Jenna smiled. "You got one in chocolate?"

Beetle looked crestfallen. "Sorry, no. They only come in fruit flavours."

Jenna took her much-loved Chocolate Charm from her pocket. "We could try them with this," she said.

"OK," said Beetle a little doubtfully. "Larry!" he called out. "I'm going for my break."

Jenna heard a gruff, "Ten minutes and *no more*," from the gallery and followed Beetle to a small, incredibly filthy kitchen right at the back of the shop.

"Happy Birthday," said Beetle. He looked embarrassed. "I . . . I've got something for you but it's not wrapped up yet. I wasn't expecting to see you until this evening."

Jenna looked embarrassed too. "Oh. Gosh. That's not why I came. I wasn't expecting anything."

"Oh. And, um, sorry about the mess," Beetle said, suddenly seeing the kitchen through Jenna's eyes. "Larry gets really angry if I clear it up. He says mould is good for you."

"Slime too?" asked Jenna, looking at a bag of carrots that were pooling across the floor.

Beetle felt mortified. "Let's go to Wizard Sandwiches," he said. "I'm owed some time."

Some ten minutes later – after Jenna had witnessed a new and impressive Beetle telling Larry he was taking his lunch hour *now* and it was actually going to be one whole hour – they were sitting at a small window table in Wizard Sandwiches' newly opened upstairs café. They made a striking couple. Beetle wore his blue and gold admiral's jacket and his thick black hair was, for once, behaving just the way he wanted it to. Jenna's gold circlet shone softly in the light of the small candle that stood in a pool of wax on their table. She sat with her red, fur-lined cloak still pulled around her, slowly warming up after the chill of the outside, while she gazed around the exuberantly painted room with its steamed-up windows. Jenna noticed with relief that no one was staring at her (the members of the Wizard Sandwiches Cooperative did not believe in hierarchical systems and acted accordingly). She felt like an everyday person – a grown-up everyday person *going out to lunch*. Even better than that, she had her happy and excited birthday feeling back.

"What would you like?" asked Beetle. He offered Jenna the menu, which was covered with Wizard Sandwiches in-jokes and colourful drawings of sandwiches but offered no clue as to what the sandwiches might contain.

Jenna picked a tall, triangular stack of small sandwiches called "Edifice". Beetle chose a large cube-shaped sandwich called "Chemistry". He took the menu and went up to the counter to order (Wizard Sandwiches did not believe in the servitude of waiting staff. This also kept the wage bills down). Beetle returned carrying two WizzFizz specials, which were as near to a FizzFroot as it was possible to get. He set a pink and green drink in front of Jenna with a flourish.

"Minty strawberry," he said. "It's new."

"Thank you," Jenna said, feeling suddenly shy. Being out with Beetle like this felt different from being with Beetle in the everyday way she had become used to. It seemed that Beetle felt the same, as for some minutes they both looked intently out of the window, although there was little to see apart from a wintry Wizard Way and a couple of people scurrying along with boxes of candles in preparation for the Longest Night illuminations.

Eventually Jenna spoke. "Actually, I wanted to ask you something," she said.

"Did you?" Beetle felt pleased.

"Yes. I asked Sep last night and he won't do *anything*."

Beetle felt rather less pleased. Jenna did not notice. She carried on, "Sep's weird at the moment, don't you think? I've asked him a few times now and he's always made excuses."

Beetle now felt distinctly *un*-pleased. He was tired of being second best to Septimus. It was, in fact, one of the reasons why he had refused Marcia's offer of a place at the Wizard Tower.

"Edifice! Chemistry!" A shout came from the counter.

Beetle got up to collect the sandwiches, leaving Jenna with a vague feeling that she had said something wrong. He returned with a teetering stack of triangles and a huge cube.

"Wow," said Jenna. "Thank you." She tentatively took the top triangle off the pile and bit into it. It was a delicious mixture of chopped smoked fish and cucumber with Wizard Sandwiches' famous sandwich sauce.

Beetle regarded his large cube with dismay. It was one solid lump of bread made from half a loaf. In it were drilled nine holes filled with different coloured jams and sauces, and from the centre hole a wisp of smoke was rising. Beetle knew at once he had made a mistake; he just *knew* that when he tried to eat it, the coloured gloop would run down his face and drip on the table and he would look like a kid. Why hadn't he chosen something simple?

Beetle began sawing at his cube. The multicoloured gloop ran across his plate and swirled into a thick rainbow puddle. Beetle began to turn pink. His sandwich was an utter disaster.

"So ... um, what is it you wanted Sep to do?" he asked, trying to deflect attention from the accident on his plate.

"There's something going on in the Palace. In the attic," said Jenna. "No one's allowed up there since that stuff with Dad and the Sealed Room – even I don't go there – but sometimes when I'm in my room I hear footsteps above my head."

"Probably rats," said Beetle, staring at "Chemistry" in dismay. "There're some big ones down by the river."

"It's *human*," whispered Jenna.

"But some ghosts make footstep noises," said Beetle. "It's one of the easiest things a ghost can Cause. And you have a *load* of ghosts at the Palace."

Jenna shook her head. That was what Silas and Sarah had said too.

"But Beetle, someone is using those stairs – the dust is worn away from the middle of the treads. I thought it was Mum, as she does wander around a bit at night when she can't sleep, but when I asked her about it she said she hadn't been up there for ages. So yesterday I decided to go up and have a look."

Beetle looked up from the mangled mess on his plate. "What did you see?"

Jenna told Beetle what had happened the previous evening. By the time she had finished, Beetle wore a look of consternation.

"That's not good. Sounds like you might have an Infestation," he said.

"What, like cockroaches or something?" Jenna was puzzled.

"No. I didn't mean *that* kind of infestation. It's what we used to call it in the Manuscriptorium. I suppose Wizards might have a different name for it."

"For what?"

Beetle also lowered his voice – it wasn't good to talk about the Darke in a public place. "For when something Darke moves into someone's house. In fact, it sounds like something might be setting up a –"he glanced around to check that no one was listening – "a Darke Domaine."

Jenna shivered. She didn't like the sound of that at all. "What's a Darke Domaine?" she whispered.

"It's like a kind of foggy pool of Darke. It can get really powerful if it's not got rid of. It grows by drawing strength from people, and it lures them in with promises of all the things they long for."

"You mean there might *really* be something nasty in the attic?" Jenna looked scared. She hadn't quite believed it until now.

From what Jenna had just told him, Beetle thought it was highly likely. "Well, yes. You know, I think you should really get Marcia to have a look."

"But if I ask Marcia to come today, Mum will have a fit." Jenna thought for a moment. "Beetle, I'd really appreciate your advice first. If you say it's a –" she too glanced around – "*you-know-what*, then I'll go straight to Marcia. I promise."

Beetle could not refuse. "OK," he said.

"Oh, *thank you*." Jenna smiled.

Beetle took out his treasured timepiece. "Suppose I come round, let's see ... about half-past three. Gives me time to pick up a SafeCharm from the Charm desk at the Wizard Tower. It will still be daylight then. You don't want to go near that kind of stuff after dark."

It was then that Jenna remembered that the last time Beetle helped her, he had lost his job. "But what about Larry? What about your job?"

Beetle grinned. "Don't worry, I'll fix it with Larry. He owes me buckets of time. And Larry's OK as long as you tell him what you're doing. He's nothing like Jillie Djinn, so don't you worry about *that*. Half-past three at the Palace Gate?"

"Oh, thank you, Beetle. *Thank you*." Jenna regarded the gooey mess on Beetle's plate, which was beginning to fizz alarmingly. She pushed her stack of sandwiches to the middle of the table. "Let's share," she said. "I can't possibly eat them all."

9

CHARMING

Beetle and Jenna emerged from the warmth of Wizard Sandwiches into the grey chill of Wizard Way. A few stray snowflakes drifted down and Jenna pulled her red fur-lined cloak tightly around her. Beetle buttoned up his admiral's jacket and wound his long woolly scarf around his neck.

"Hey, Beetle!" came a shout.

A tall, impossibly thin young man was walking towards them from the upper reaches of Wizard Way. He waved and picked up speed.

"Good morning … Princess Jenna," the young man said, out of breath. He bowed his head and Jenna felt embarrassed.

"Wotcha, Foxy," said Beetle.

"Wotcha, Beet," replied Foxy, stamping his feet and rubbing his hands together. His long, pointy nose glowed like a bright red triangle set in his thin, pale face, and his teeth chattered. He looked cold in his grey scribe's tunic. "Ser-sausage sandwich?" he asked.

Beetle shook his head. "Not today, Foxy. Gotta go and get a SafeCharm from the Wizard Tower."

Foxy grinned, his slightly pointy teeth shining in the warm light from Wizard Sandwiches' windows. "Hey, don't go to the competition. You're talking to the Chief Charm Scribe here."

"Since when?"

"Since this morning at eight fifty-two *precisely*," Foxy replied with a grin, mimicking his boss, Miss Jillie Djinn, Chief Hermetic Scribe, to perfection.

"Wow. Hey, congratulations," said Beetle.

"And it would be an honour, Mr Beetle, if you would consent to be my first commission."

"Okey-dokey." Beetle grinned.

"We'll just run through the formalities, shall we?"

Beetle looked uneasy. "Actually, Foxy, I don't really want to go into the Manuscriptorium."

"No need. I have, as of this moment, in my capacity as Chief Charm Scribe, instigated the Manuscriptorium's pioneering mobile Charm service." Foxy took what Beetle recognised as a standard-issue scribe notebook from his book pocket and unclipped the pencil from its holder.

"OK," said Foxy, pencil poised. "Just a few questions, Mr Beetle, and then I guarantee we will have the perfect SafeCharm for you. Unlike the WT Charm Desk One-Charm-Fits-All policy, we tailor our Charms to your *personal* requirements. Inside or out?"

"Um . . . inside," answered Beetle, somewhat taken aback by Foxy's sales patter.

"Up or down?"

"What do you mean?"

"I dunno. Sounds good, though, don't you think?"

"*Foxy.*" Beetle laughed. "For a weird moment I thought you actually knew what you were doing."

"I *do* know what I'm doing," protested Foxy. "Just trying to make it more exciting, that's all. *Inside* is all I need to know."

"What about the strength?" asked Beetle.

"Bother," said Foxy. "Forgot that. Small, medium or large . . . no, I don't mean that."

"Minor, major or maximum," Beetle supplied.

"Yeah, that's it. So waddyou want?"

Beetle glanced at Jenna. "Maximum," said Jenna. "Just in case."

"Okey-dokey. I'll see what we got. Delivery to place of work in one hour OK?"

"Thanks. Just ask for me. Say it's business."

"Will do, Beet. Sausage sandwich tomorrow then?"

"Yep. See you, Foxo."

With that, Foxy – looking not unlike a large heron picking its way through the shallows – headed for the multicoloured door of Wizard Sandwiches.

Ten minutes later Jenna was wandering through the Northern Traders' Market. She was looking for a fun birthday present for Septimus, but she was also avoiding going home until her appointment with Beetle. Jenna knew that if she went back to the Palace, Sarah would find her and she would end up in yet another discussion about the letters from Simon. Unlike Sarah Heap, Jenna had read her letter from Simon only once and had left it screwed up on her bedroom floor. When Sarah had asked her what he'd said, Jenna had been curt. "Sorry," she'd replied.

Every year the Castle inhabitants flocked to the Traders' Market to stock up on winter provisions of woollen cloth, candles, lanterns, salted fish, dried meats and fruits, fur and sheepskins before the Big Freeze blew in and cut off the Castle for six weeks or so. People also ate the hot pies, roasted nuts and crumbly cakes and drank gallons of the huge varieties of spiced mulled drinks for sale. And when they were weary of shopping, they would sit and watch jugglers, fire dancers and acrobats tumbling in the roped-off space in front of the Traders' Office.

Despite the apparent chaos, the market was meticulously organised. Rigorous standards were applied to all traders, pitches were allocated under a strict licensing system and the marketplace was divided into sectors according to the kinds of goods sold. Generally the Northern Traders' Market was an orderly affair, but the final day was a frenetic time and the market was packed. Crowds of people moved from stall to stall, grabbing bargains, buying things they didn't really need "just in case", taking a last chance to buy Mid-Winter feast presents. The tall, pale-eyed Northern Traders cried out their wares at the tops of their voices, trying to sell all the odds and ends that no one had wanted – up until now. The urgency in their lilt-ing sing-song voices carried over the hubbub and reminded people that the Mid-Winter Feast was only a few days away, and then the Big Freeze was coming.

Every year of her life – bar one, the year she had turned ten – Jenna had visited the craft section, known as Makers' Mile. Makers' Mile was a relatively new section of the market; it extended out of the official market place, straggled along the road and ran around the outside of the large, brick-paved circle at the end of Ceremonial Way. As Jenna had grown older she would wander along the Mile, silently planning her perfect present list for her birthday. She had rarely received anything on the list, but it didn't take away the fun of dreaming. This year Jenna had found nothing remotely funny to give to Septimus in the main market and decided to head out along Makers' Mile for a last visit. As she elbowed her way towards it through the fur and prepared skins area and caught the overpowering smell of Foryx fur, Jenna noted wryly that the normal Castle respect for the Princess did not apply in the market.

At last she emerged into the infinitely more sweet-smelling Makers' Mile. With her old feeling of birthday anticipation, Jenna began to wander along, browsing the stalls. By the time she had walked around the circle twice, Jenna had still not found anything funny to give Septimus, but she suspected the reason had more to do with how she was feeling about Septimus than any of the goods that were on offer. She decided to head for her favourite stall – silver jewellery and lucky charms – which she had spotted near the Makers' Mile Tally Hut.

The stall belonged to Sophie Barley, a talented young Port jeweller. (Unlike the rest of the market, Makers' Mile had stalls available to those who were not Northern Traders. They were mainly taken by those who lived in the Port, as Castle people preferred to buy from the market rather than sell.) Jenna was surprised to find that instead of the friendly Sophie, the stall was manned by three odd-looking women dressed in varying shades of black. Behind the stall, in an old armchair, was slumped an elderly woman with her face plastered in thick white make-up and her eyes closed. The old woman was watched over by a slight figure swathed in a muddy black cloak with a voluminous hood.

"Ooh, it's the *Princess*!" Jenna heard an excited whisper escape from beneath the hood.

"Leave this to me, dingbat," came the response from the fiercest-looking woman in the stall, who was clearly the boss and who – Jenna saw as she briefly glanced up – had a very nasty stare.

The boss eyeballed Jenna. "*How* may I help you?" she asked. The two other stallholders – a lanky woman with her hair piled on top of her head like a spike and a short, dumpy one with food stains down her front – nudged each other and giggled behind the boss's back.

The last thing Jenna wanted was help. Sophie always let her browse and try on anything she liked. And Sophie certainly didn't snatch the first thing she picked up and say, "That will be half a crown. We don't give change. Wrap it up, Daphne," which is what the boss-with-the-stare did with the delicate heart-shaped pendant with tiny wings that Jenna had lifted from its velvet pad.

"But I don't want to buy it," Jenna protested.

"So what'd you pick it up for?"

"I just wanted to look at it."

"You can look at it on the table. We charge extra for *picking up*."

Jenna stared at the woman. She was sure she'd seen her somewhere before – and her sidekicks too.

"Where's Sophie?" she asked.

"Who?"

"Sophie. Sophie Barley. It's *her* stall. Where is she?"

The boss-with-the-stare bared a row of blackened teeth. "She couldn't make it. She's a bit ... *tied up* at the moment." Her two sidekicks giggled nastily.

Jenna began to move away. The jewellery didn't seem nearly as nice without Sophie.

"*Wait a minute!*" a high voice shouted urgently. Jenna stopped and turned. "We've got some lovely Charms. And we don't charge for picking up Charms, *do we?*"

"Shut up, Dorinda!" The boss-with-the-stare wheeled around and glared at the hooded figure standing beside the old woman. "*I'm* doing this." The boss turned back to face Jenna and her mouth twitched into a kind of U-shape which, Jenna realised, was meant to be a smile. "We do indeed have a delightful new range of Charms, Princess. Very pretty. Quite *charming*, in fact." A strange spluttering ensued, which Jenna thought was probably meant to be laughter, although quite possibly the woman was choking on something. It was hard to tell.

The boss indicated two little wooden boxes at the front of the stall. Intrigued, Jenna looked at them – they were so very different from the rest of Sophie's jewellery. Nestled on white down inside each box was a tiny jewel-like bird. The birds had a beautiful greenish-blue sheen and shimmered like the kingfishers Jenna had once loved to watch from her window in the Ramblings. Despite herself, Jenna was fascinated. She gazed at the birds, amazed at their minute feathers, which were so detailed that she could almost believe the birds were real. Tentatively she reached out a finger and stroked the plumage of one of the birds – and snatched her hand away as if it had been bitten. *The bird was real.* It was soft and warm and lay breathing terrified, fast breaths.

The old woman in the armchair snapped her eyes open like a doll that has just been sat up. "Pick up the birdie, dearie," she said in a wheedling whine.

Jenna stepped back from the stall and shook her head.

The boss-with-the-stare swung around and glared at the old woman. "I said *leave it to me*, didn't I?" she snapped. "Idiot!"

"*Oooh!*" A gasp of thrilled horror came from the hooded figure.

The old woman was not as decrepit as Jenna had taken her to be. She rose menacingly from her armchair and pointed a long, dirty fingernail at the boss-with-the-stare. "Never, *ever*, talk to me like that again," she hissed.

The boss-with-the-stare went as white as the old woman's plastered face. "Sorry, Wi—" She stopped herself hurriedly. "Sorry," she mumbled.

Suddenly Jenna realised who the stallholders were. "Hey!" she exclaimed. "You're –"

The boss-with-the-stare leaned forward and glared at Jenna. "Yeah – *what*?" she challenged.

Jenna decided against saying she thought the women were witches from the Port Witch Coven. "Not very nice," she said, a little lamely. Then she made a hasty exit, leaving all five witches – for she was right – cackling uproariously.

The Port Witch Coven watched Jenna disappear into the crowd.

"I knew it wouldn't work," Daphne – the dumpy one with the food stains – said morosely. "Princesses are hard to catch. The Wendrons tried and they couldn't get her."

"Pah!" snorted the boss-with-the-stare, whose name was Linda. "The Wendrons are fools. They've got a few lessons to learn. And *I'm* looking forward to teaching them." She laughed unpleasantly.

A plaintive wail came from inside the hooded figure sitting beside the old woman – who was, of course, the Witch Mother of the Port Witch Coven. "But she didn't take the bird, she didn't take the bird!"

"And you can shut up too, Dorinda," snarled Linda. "Anyway, it doesn't matter – she touched the bird, didn't she?"

Linda leaned over the two little birds. She took a deep breath in, then breathed out, sending what looked like a long stream of grey smoke curling around them. The blanket of breath settled over the tiny boxes and the witches gathered around to watch. A few moments later fluttering could be seen, and two minute, iridescent birds flew up from their boxes. Fast as a cat, Linda snatched the birds out of the air and held them up triumphantly, one in each hand.

The other witches looked on, impressed.

From somewhere inside her tattered black robes, Linda drew out a small silver cage on a chain, as delicate and beautiful as any of the jewellery in the stall. She unscrewed the bottom of the cage, opened her right hand and slammed the cage down over the bird. Then she poked the panicking bird into the cage with a prodding finger – it was a tight fit even though the bird was tiny. Quickly Linda tipped the cage upside down and screwed the floor back on, then she swung the cage over her neck so that it hung dangling by its chain like an exotic pendant. Inside the cage the bird blinked in shock.

"Hostage," Linda informed the other witches. They nodded, impressed, and – as they always were with Linda – slightly scared.

Linda held her left fist up to the cage and slowly unfurled her fingers. Inside her fist sat the other bird, trembling. It gave a despairing tweet at the sight of the caged bird and fell silent. Linda raised the bird up to her eyes and began to mutter in a low, threatening monotone. The bird stood on her palm, transfixed. Linda finished whatever ghastly thing she was saying and the bird flew up and hovered, looking down at the silver cage dangling from Linda's grubby neck. Linda pointed a long-nailed finger at the fluttering scrap of blue and the bird vanished. UnSeen, it flew off on an erratic course, which followed Jenna's path as she headed for the Palace.

"Lovebirds!" Linda commented scathingly. "*Love*. What rubbish." She laughed. "But useful rubbish. I *still* have that bird in the palm of my hand." She held out her empty hand and snapped her fingers shut. "*And* the Princess."

Jenna and her invisible bird reached the Palace Gate at the same time as Beetle. Beetle looked flustered.

"Thought I was going to be late," he puffed. "Foxy . . . Chief Charm Scribe, *my foot*."

"You mean he isn't?" Jenna was surprised.

"Well, he is – if Jillie Djinn would only let him. Foxy said when he got back she'd taken all the Charms into the Hermetic Chamber for what she called *stocktaking* and wouldn't let him have them."

Jenna raised her eyes to heaven. "That *woman*. You're well out of that place, Beetle." She looked concerned. "But that means you haven't got a SafeCharm."

Beetle grinned. "That's OK. I probably won't need one. Anyway, I've got this. Foxy found it in the Pending Cupboard." He took a small, slightly curved, flat piece of wood from the inside top pocket of his admiral's jacket and showed it to Jenna. "Foxy reckons it'll be more use than a SafeCharm. He said a sea captain came in a couple of days ago and swapped it for a love Charm. It's a heartbeat thingy. You put it next to your heart like so . . ." Beetle put the Charm back into his top left pocket. "Foxy says that if you get really scared it knows and brings you back to the last place you were safe. Shall we get going?"

Beetle and Jenna walked up the Palace drive under a dark cloud that had blown in from the Port. Jenna did not want to meet Sarah right then, so she took the path around the back of the Palace. By the time they reached the small door into the turret at the far end, a cold wind was blustering up from the river and fat drops of sleety rain were beginning to fall. Jenna pushed open the door and they stepped inside. The door slammed in a sudden gust, the noise echoing down the Long Walk.

It was unusually dark inside the Palace. When Nicko had at long last returned safely home, Jenna had celebrated having both Septimus and Nicko in the Castle once more by asking Maizie Smalls, who lit the torches in Wizard Way, to live at the Palace. In return for two rooms looking out on the river and supper every night, Maizie had agreed to light a candle in every room in the Palace and to light the Long Walk with rushlights. But Maizie did not start "operation light up", as she called it, until a half-hour before sunset. And there was, despite the gloom, still more than an hour to go before then.

Jenna always found the Long Walk – with its odd assortment of objects lining the walls – creepy, and that afternoon, in the failing light, she found it particularly so. So when Beetle took his old Ice Tunnel lamp (one of his mementos from his time at the Manuscriptorium) and flicked on its eerie blue light just as they passed a trio of grinning shrunken heads, Jenna shrieked out loud, then clapped her hand to her mouth.

"Sorry," she said, a little embarrassed. "Got a bit spooked."

"Whoooo," said Beetle in a mock-ghostly voice, holding the light beneath his chin and grinning.

"Oh *don't,* Beetle – that's even more horrible!"

Beetle swung the light away from his face and shone it down the wide, amazingly long corridor. Strong as its beam was, it did not reach the end. "Actually, I feel a bit spooked too," he said in a half-whisper. He glanced behind him. "I keep thinking something is kind of fluttering behind us ... but I can't see anything."

Jenna looked around too. She had felt the same thing though she hadn't wanted to say anything. The word *fluttering* reminded her of the two little birds lying trembling in their boxes. Loudly – to reassure herself more than anything – she said, "No, there's nothing there."

The UnSeen little bird rested a few minutes on one of the shrunken heads, its tiny wings tired with having to keep airborne for so long, and then continued following Jenna.

They walked on quickly past the door to Sarah Heap's sitting room and a door with PALACE PAMPHLETS INC. scrawled on it in chalk, which was Silas's office. Jenna was pleased to see both rooms were empty. They soon arrived at some narrow backstairs and climbed up to the first floor of the Palace. Here were mainly suites of private rooms at the rear of the building looking out over the river, and more public rooms – including the locked Throne Room – at the front. The wide upstairs corridor had a hushed, subdued quality to it. Thick, dusty curtains hung down in front of many of the draughty windows and doors and down the centre ran what was known as the longest carpet in the world, which had actually been made there, in the corridor, by an itinerant group of carpet weavers.

They walked silently through the muffled gloom. Jenna

was not expecting to see anyone but as they went past Maizie Small's room, the door opened and Maizie rushed out.

"Oh!" said Maizie, surprised. "Oh, hello, Princess Jenna. And Beetle. I didn't expect to bump into you." Maizie cast a disapproving glance at Beetle. "Not *upstairs.*"

Beetle went pink but he hoped it was too dark for anyone to notice.

"You're early, Maizie," Jenna said, rather irritated.

"It's the Longest Night tonight, Princess Jenna. I have to get every torch lit by nightfall, and I always help out with some of the displays on the Way. It's a crazy rush." Maizie took a small timepiece out of her pocket and consulted it hurriedly. "Now then, I've lit all new candles upstairs, and Mr Pot's coming in to do the downstairs. You're all sorted." A loud spattering of sleet on one of the roof lanterns made everyone look up. "Shocking day to be out," said Maizie. "I must be off."

Beetle and Jenna walked on in an awkward silence past the wide corridor that led to the large double doors – and the ghost of Sir Hereward – guarding Jenna's bedroom. The faint figure of Sir Hereward raised his one ghostly arm in salute as they hurried by, and not long after they arrived at the foot of the attic stairs.

"Oh!" exclaimed Jenna. The entrance to the stairs was covered by an old red velvet curtain, which had been skewered to the wall by an assortment of large rusty nails. Jenna recognised Silas Heap's handiwork immediately. "Dad must have just done this," she whispered. "So he *did* listen to what I said ..."

Beetle regarded the old curtain. "It's a bit makeshift," he said.

"That's Dad for you."

"I suppose he's put some kind of SafetyGate on there," said

Beetle. "And he's nailed that up to hide it. SafetyGates do look a bit weird sometimes. Shall I have a look?"

Jenna nodded. "Yes please, Beetle."

Beetle took out his pocket knife. He unfolded the tool for pulling-long-rusty-nails-out-of-plaster and set to work doing exactly that. Immediately a great lump of plaster came off the wall and the curtain fell on his head – *crump*.

"Oof!" gasped Beetle as the curtain enveloped him in a cloud of dust and dead spiders. "Oof – eurgh. Gerroff! *Gerroff me!*"

The curtain did not do as requested and Beetle, convinced that he had been attacked by something nasty from the attic, began stabbing at it with his pulling-long-rusty-nails-out-of-plaster tool. "Argh . . . *help!*"

"Beetle, Beetle!" yelled Jenna, trying to pull the curtain off. "Beetle, stand *still*. Stop fighting!"

Finally her voice got through. "Huh?" said the curtain.

"Beetle, please, just stay still a moment. And stop trying to kill the curtain."

The curtain settled down and Jenna heaved it off its prey in a cloud of dust.

"Atchooo!" Beetle sneezed.

Jenna regarded the pile of shredded curtain on the floor. "Beetle: one. Curtain: nil." She laughed.

"Yeah," said Beetle, not quite so amused. He dusted off his admiral's jacket and then tentatively waved his arm through the gap that the curtain had covered.

"There's no SafetyGate there," he said. "Or if there was, it's come away with the curtain. I s'pose it could have been Bonded to it. Come to think of it, it did tingle a bit when it landed on me. That's what made me think I was . . . well, being attacked. It wasn't panic, you know. It felt really weird."

"So . . . if Dad *did* put some kind of barrier up and now it's gone, maybe we should go and tell him?" said Jenna.

"I could have a look first," said Beetle, badly needing to do something constructive after the curtain fight.

"Well . . ."

Unwilling to let his chance to impress Jenna slip away, Beetle headed up the stairs quickly, before she had time to say no.

Jenna's voice came after him. "Beetle, maybe you shouldn't . . ."

Beetle stopped and turned. "It's fine," he said.

"It doesn't *look* fine," said Jenna. She could see the familiar shifting darkness hovering at the top of the stairs.

"I'll just have a quick look so that we can tell Marcia exactly what's going on," said Beetle.

Jenna followed Beetle up the stairs. He stopped and barred her way. "No, Jenna," he said rather formally. "Let me do this. You did ask me, after all."

Jenna looked past Beetle up to the top of the stairs. "But, Beetle, that weird misty stuff is still there. I'd forgot how scary it is. I think we should get Dad, or maybe even Marcia. I really do."

Beetle did not want to give way. "It's all right," he insisted. "I said I'd have a look and I will. OK?"

There was something in the way Beetle stood that made him seem so solid, so commanding, that made Jenna step back.

"OK," she said reluctantly. "But please . . . be careful."

"Of course I will." Beetle pulled out a long chain from his admiral's coat pocket, unclipped his timepiece and placed it in Jenna's hand. "I'm only going to be a few seconds; I'll just have a quick look and see what's going on. If I'm not back in . . . oh, three minutes . . . you can go and get Silas, OK?"

Jenna nodded uncertainly.

Beetle set off up the long, straight flight of stairs, aware that Jenna was watching his every move. As he drew closer to the top, a feeling of fear came over him and he stopped. In front of him, no more than three steps away, was a wall of a shifting, dancing, swirling blackness, which clearly was not just late winter afternoon darkness mixed with some old spell vapours that, deep down, Beetle had hoped it would be.

"Can you see anything?" Jenna's voice drifted up to him. It already sounded far away.

"No . . . not really."

"Maybe you should come down."

Beetle thought that too. But when he looked back and saw Jenna far below, gazing up at him expectantly, he knew he had to go on. And so, determined not to act scared in front of Jenna *again*, Beetle forced himself to take the last few steps to the top of the stairs.

At the foot of the stairs Jenna saw a few tendrils of darkness move out and curl around Beetle's feet. At the top of the stairs Beetle was overwhelmed by a sudden desire to step into the darkness. He was convinced that his father was waiting for him there. He knew he would find him if only he would step into the swirling grey mist. And so he did. He took a step forward – and disappeared.

Jenna watched Beetle go. She looked down at his timepiece and began to count the minutes. Above her a small, invisible bird noiselessly fluttered, counting long bird minutes, waiting and watching for the moment it could bring the Princess home to its imprisoned mate.

❊ 11 ❊
A DARK DOMAINE

Beetle stepped into the gloom and a wave of happiness came over him. Suddenly he knew that his father was not dead from a spider bite – as his mother and a well-worn, faded letter of condolence from the Port authorities had always told him. His father was *alive*. Not only alive but here in this very place, waiting to see him – his *son*.

Feeling as though he was walking in lead boots beneath a dark and swirling sea, Beetle moved dreamily deeper into the gloom. Everything felt muffled and his breath came slowly. Indistinct shadows of Things – although Beetle did not see them as such – moved and swayed on the edge of his vision, plucking at his clothes, pushing him forward. Feeling that this was the biggest moment in his life, Beetle walked slowly, almost reverentially, knowing that all he had to do was to push open the right door and he would find the person that he had always longed to meet.

Beetle progressed along the seemingly endless corridor, passing rooms piled high with old mattresses, bedsteads and broken furniture – but not one containing Mr Beetle. As Beetle neared the end, he heard the sound of a sneeze. His heart leaped. This was it. The sneeze belonged to his father – he *knew* it. What had his mother so often told him? *If only your father had not been allergic to just about everything, he would never have swelled up like a balloon when that spider bit him and he would still be alive today.* And here, at the end of the corridor, was his father – sneezing just like his mother said he always did. Nervously Beetle approached the room where the sneeze had come from. The door was half open and through it he could see a figure lying on a narrow bed, the blankets pulled up around his ears. As Beetle tiptoed in, the figure shook with another violent sneeze. Beetle stopped. The words he had longed to say, but he had never had anyone to say them to, sat on the tip of his tongue. He took a deep breath and let them go.

"Hello, Dad. It's me, B –"

"Whaa?" The figure in the bed sat up.

"You!" gasped Beetle, shocked. "*You*. But you're not my . . ."

Merrin Meredith, hair sticking up on end, nose red raw, looked even more shocked. He sneezed violently and blew his nose on the bedsheet.

Beetle came to his senses and realised that he was not *ever* going to see his father. A great feeling of loss swept over him, which was quickly replaced by fear. His mind cleared and he suddenly knew what he had done – he had walked into a Darke Domaine. Beetle forced himself to stay calm. He looked at Merrin, who was a pathetic sight, hunched up in bed. His long, greasy hair straggled over a fresh crop of spots, his thin, bony fingers played nervously with the blanket, while his swollen and discoloured left thumb sported the heavy Two-Faced Ring that Beetle remembered him wearing in what he now thought of as the old days in the Manuscriptorium.

It's only Merrin Meredith, Beetle told himself. *He's a complete prat. He couldn't do a decent* Darke Domaine *in a million years.*

But Beetle could not quite convince himself of this. The scary thing was, as soon as he had walked into Merrin's room, he had come to his senses. And if Merrin really was Engendering a Darke Domaine, then that was exactly what Beetle would have expected to happen. Merrin would be at the very centre of the Domaine – in its eye – where all is calm and free of Darke disturbances. One way to test it was to step outside the room, but Beetle was loath to risk it. He knew that in a Darke Domaine your sense of time and space could change. In what might seem like a few steps you could actually be walking miles – sometimes hundreds of miles. And it had indeed felt like a long, long walk down the corridor. Supposing he was no longer in the Palace attic? He could be anywhere – in the Badlands, in Bleak Creek, in Dungeon Number One – *anywhere.*

Beetle decided that his only chance was to convince Merrin that his Darke Domaine had failed and get Merrin to walk out with him. That way he'd have a safe passage back. It would be tricky, but it might just work. Taking care not to lie – because lies can fuel anything Darke – Beetle took a deep breath and launched into the attack.

"Merrin Meredith, what are you doing in the Palace?" he demanded.

"*Atchoo!* I could say the same to you. Someone *else* fired you, have they? Got nothing better to do than go snooping in people's bedrooms?"

"You'd know all about snooping," Beetle retorted. "And as for being fired – I hear Jillie Djinn's at last seen sense and fired *you.* What took her so long I don't know."

"Stupid cow," sniffed Merrin.

Beetle did not disagree.

"Anyway, she didn't fire me – not for long, anyway. Jillie haddock-face Djinn does what *I* say now, because I've got *this*." Merrin jabbed his left thumb in the air, taunting Beetle with the Two-Faced Ring – a thick gold ring with two evil-looking faces carved from dark green jade.

Beetle looked at the ring disdainfully. "Gothyk Grotto junk," he said scornfully.

"That shows how much *you* know, beetlebrain," Merrin retorted. "This is the *real thing*. Those stupid scribes don't dare mess with me any more. I call the shots at that dump." Merrin was enjoying boasting to Beetle. Surreptitiously, he slipped his hand under his pillow to check – for the twentieth time that day – that *The Darke Index* was still there. It was. The small but deadly book that Merrin had acquired during his time working for Simon Heap at the Observatory – and which had led him to the Two-Faced Ring – felt crumpled and slightly damp to the touch, but it gave Merrin a sudden burst of confidence. "Soon I'll be calling the shots in the whole Castle. That stupid Septimus Heap and his pathetic dragon had better watch out, 'cause anything he can do I can do ten times better!" Merrin waved his arms expansively. "There's no way he could even begin to do *this*."

"Do what?" said Beetle. "Hide up in the Palace attic and *sniff*?"

Beetle thought he noticed a flicker of uncertainty pass over Merrin's face.

"Nah. You know what I mean. *This*. And I can get anyone to come here I want. Yesterday I got the prissy Princess to put her little foot in, and this morning I got the old Heap Wizard to put his stupid head in. They both got scared and ran away but it didn't matter. We got what we needed."

"We?" asked Beetle.

"Yeah. I've got back-up. You want to watch out, *office boy*, because today I got *you* good and proper." Merrin laughed. "You thought you were coming to see your stupid *dad*!"

Beetle had forgotten how obnoxious Merrin was. He fought down the urge to punch him. It wasn't – as Jenna would no doubt have told him – worth it.

"I am here," Beetle said, "because Princess Jenna asked me to investigate some noises in the attic. I told her it was probably rats and it turns out I was right. It's one big *stupid* rat."

"Don't call me stupid," Merrin flared. "I'll show you who's the stupid one here. *You.* You walked right in."

"Into what – your smelly bedroom?" Beetle said scornfully.

Merrin began to look less confident. "Didn't you notice anything?" he asked.

"A load of old junk and empty rooms," Beetle replied dismissively, careful to still speak the truth.

"That all?"

Beetle sensed he was winning. He avoided a direct answer and snapped, "Merrin, what *are* you talking about?"

Merrin's confidence suddenly left him. His shoulders sagged. "Nothing ever goes right," he moaned. He looked up at Beetle as if expecting sympathy. "It's 'cause I'm not well," he said. "I could do it if I didn't have this horrible cold."

"Do what?"

"None of your business," said Merrin gloomily.

Beetle reckoned it was time to make a move. He turned to leave, hoping that he'd done enough to convince Merrin that his Darke Domaine had failed. "Right. I'll be off then," he said. "I'll tell the Heaps where to find you." He began to walk slowly to the door.

"No! Hey, wait!" Merrin called out.

Beetle stopped. He felt immensely relieved but did not want to show it. "Why?" he demanded.

"Please, Beetle, *please* don't tell them. I've got nowhere else to go. I feel *awful* and no one even *cares*." Merrin inspected the sheet for a space where he hadn't blown his nose and blew noisily into it.

"And whose fault is that?"

"Oh, I expect it's *my* fault," said Merrin. "It always *is* my fault. It's just not *fair*." He twisted the Two-Faced Ring anxiously.

A sudden spatter of sleet drummed on the window. Merrin looked up pathetically. "Beetle. It . . . it's cold outside. It's wet and it's nearly dark. I've nowhere to go. *Please* don't tell."

Beetle hurried on with his plan. "Look, Merrin, Sarah Heap is really nice. She won't throw you out, not in the state you're in." Beetle reckoned he was telling the truth here. "She'll take care of you until you're better."

"Will she?"

"Of course she will. Sarah Heap will take care of anything. Even *you*."

Merrin had run out of dry sheet. He blew his nose on his blanket.

Beetle pressed on. "So why don't you come downstairs with me to where it's nice and warm?"

"All right then," said Merrin. He coughed and fell back against his stained pillow. "Oh . . . I think I'm too weak to get up."

"Don't be ridiculous. You've only got a cold," said Beetle scathingly.

"I've got . . . *flu*. Probably pneu . . . pneumonia in fact."

Beetle wondered if Merrin might, for once, be telling the truth. He did actually look ill. His eyes were bright and feverish and he seemed to be having trouble breathing.

"I'll come with you . . . I'll give myself up, I will," wheezed Merrin. "But you'll have to help me. Please."

Reluctantly Beetle went over to the bed. It smelled of dirty, damp clothes, sweat and sickness.

"Thank you, Beetle," Merrin murmured, gazing oddly over his shoulder into the distance. The hairs on the back of Beetle's neck began to prickle uncomfortably and the temperature in the chilly little room dropped a few degrees lower. Merrin held out his snotty hand and as Beetle leaned forward, steeling himself to take it, Merrin sat bolt upright and grabbed hold of Beetle's arm. Tight as a vice Merrin's bony fingers encircled his forearm. The ring on Merrin's thumb pressed into his flesh and began to burn into it. Beetle gasped.

"Never, *ever* call me stupid," Merrin hissed, looking intently over Beetle's shoulder. "*I* am not stupid – *you* are."

Beetle felt chilled. He knew that something very nasty was standing behind him and he dared not turn around. Beetle did not reply. His throat had suddenly gone dry.

Behind Beetle was a mass of Things, which had sensed Merrin losing his grip on the Darke Domaine. Merrin had acquired them in the Badlands some eighteen months previously, when he had taken possession of the Two-Faced Ring. Once the ring reached its full power, Merrin had Summoned the Things to the Palace because he had what he called "plans".

Merrin's confidence had returned. "You are in my Darke Domaine and you know it," he crowed. "And I *know* you know it."

Beetle swayed. Merrin's ring was sending stabs of pain shooting up his arm and into his head. He felt sick and very, very dizzy. He tried to pull away but Merrin held him fast. With his free hand Merrin pulled a small, dog-eared book from under the bedcovers and waved it triumphantly at Beetle. "See this? I've read *all* of this and I can do stuff you can't even dream of," he hissed into Beetle's ear. "You wait, *office boy*. I am going to show them all in this smelly little Castle and that stuck-up Manuscriptorium that they should have been nice to me. They're going to regret it big time. This is *my* Palace now, not the stupid Princess's. Soon the Castle will be mine and I am going to have everything I want. Everything!" Merrin was spitting with excitement. Beetle longed to wipe the spittle off his cheek but he could not move. Merrin had a pincer grip. "And that stupid Septimus Heap, he'll be sorry he stole my name. I'll get him, you'll see. *I'm* going to be the only Septimus Heap around here. It will be *my* Wizard Tower, *my* Manuscriptorium and I'll have a ten-times better dragon than that moth-eaten Spit Fyre he prances around on. You'll see!"

"In your dreams," Beetle retorted, sounding more confident than he felt. Merrin's rant spooked him. There was such a crazy kind of power behind it that Beetle almost believed him.

Merrin did not bother to reply. With one hand keeping an iron grasp on Beetle and the other clutching his open book, Merrin began to chant the words on the page in a low, monotonous voice. A Darke mist began to envelop Beetle. As Merrin came towards the end of the chant, the terrible words reached down to Beetle as if he were at the bottom of a deep, dark pit. His heart raced and he could hardly breathe from the fear that came over him. His vision closed in so that all he could see was a tunnel with Merrin at the end of it, waving his book and opening his huge red mouth to say …

But Beetle never heard what Merrin said. With his last conscious effort he reached out and snatched the book from Merrin's grasp.

"BeGone!" yelled Merrin. And then, "Oi! Give it back!"

But Beetle didn't give it back. Beetle was gone.

12
BOOMERANG

Beetle was somewhere dark and uncomfortable – very uncomfortable. He was crushed into a tiny space, his knees folded up to his chest and his arms twisted up around his head. He tried to move, but he was wedged so tightly that he felt as though he were in a clamp. He fought down panic. What had Merrin done to him?

Beetle's discomfort was quickly turning into something much more nasty. Pins and needles were running down his legs and already he couldn't feel his feet. His hands buzzed and tingled. His left hand was closed tightly around the book he had snatched from Merrin and was wedged in the same corner that his head was stuck in. His elbows and knees were jammed up against something hard and they hurt – *really* hurt. But the worst thing was the overwhelming feeling, growing stronger every passing moment, that if he didn't stretch out *right now* he would go crazy.

Beetle took a few deep breaths and tried to quell his panic. He opened his eyes wide and stared into the dark, but although some light did seem to be filtering through from somewhere, he could not make sense of anything. The small amount of light helped Beetle get some control over his panic and he discovered that he could wiggle – just a little – the fingers of his right hand. Painfully he stretched them out and tapped, then scratched, the confining walls, trying to discover what they were made of. A splinter under his fingernail gave him the answer – wood. A great stab of fear shot through him – *he was in his own coffin*. Beetle heard a wild, despairing cry like that of an animal caught in a trap and a chill ran down his spine. It took him a few seconds to realise that the cry came from him.

Beneath the sound of his heart thudding in his ears, Beetle was becoming aware of noises filtering through from some-where outside the coffin. It was an indistinct, muffled murmur-ing. In his dark prison, Beetle's imagination flipped into over-drive. He'd read that Things murmured. Particularly when they were hungry – or was it angry? Beetle tried to remember. Did Things get hungry? Did they even eat? If they did, would they eat *him*? Maybe they were just angry. But angry wasn't good either. In fact, it was probably worse. But what did it matter? Right now he'd give anything to get out of the coffin, to be able to stretch out his arms and legs and to uncurl his spine. In fact, he'd happily face a thousand Things in exchange for just being able to stretch out to his full height once more.

Beetle groaned out loud. The murmuring grew louder and drowned out the thumping of his heart, and then one of the sides of the coffin began to shake. Beetle closed his eyes. He knew that, any minute now, a Thing would wrench off the side of his coffin and that would be it. If he was lucky he'd get a few seconds to uncurl himself, to straighten his twisted arms and legs – but only if he was lucky. And after that? After that it would be the end of O. Beetle Beetle. Beetle thought of his mother and suppressed a sob. *Mum, oh Mum*. She would never

Luckily, due to her cost-cutting measures, the lights were very dim and she could not clearly see what was happening in the shadows beside the cupboard.

Jillie Djinn sneezed again. "It seems you cannot keep control of even a simple Charm, Mr Fox," she snapped. "If there is another incident – *atchoo atchoo* – like this – *atchoooo* – I shall be forced to reconsider your recent appointment."

"I . . . I . . ." Foxy stammered.

Jillie Djinn blew her nose loudly and with great attention to detail. It was not a pretty sight. "Why, pray, was the Charm not given to me for stocktaking?" she demanded.

Romilly could see that Foxy was struggling with an answer. "It's only just come back, Miss Djinn," she said.

"Miss Badger, I asked the Charm Scribe, not you," said Jillie Djinn. "And it is from the Charm Scribe that I require an answer."

"It's only just come back, Miss Djinn," Foxy repeated.

Jillie Djinn was not pleased. "*Atchoo!* Well, now that it is back, I require it for stocktaking. *Immediately*, Mr Fox."

In a panic, Foxy hissed at Beetle. "Give it here, Beet. Quick. Before she comes over to get it."

At last Beetle understood what had happened. He put his still trembling hand into the top left pocket of his admiral's jacket, pulled out the tiny curved piece of polished wood and handed it to Foxy. "Thanks, Foxo," he muttered.

The desks in the Manuscriptorium stood tall and dark under their dim lights, like winter trees at sunset. Quickly Foxy loped through them to the far side of the Manuscriptorium and gave his Chief Scribe the tiny Boomerang. Jillie Djinn took it and looked at Foxy suspiciously.

"What are all the scribes doing away from their desks?" she asked.

"Um. Well, we had a bit of trouble," said Foxy. "But it's all right now."

"What kind of – *atchoo* – trouble?"

"Hmm . . ." Thinking on his feet was not Foxy's strong point.

"Well, Mr Fox, if you can't explain I shall have to go and see for myself. Oh, for goodness' sake, get out of my way, will you?" Foxy was hovering in front of Jillie Djinn as though guarding an invisible goal, but unfortunately his talents did not lie in the goalkeeping arena either. The Chief Hermetic Scribe elbowed him out of the way and headed off through the closely packed lines of desks.

The scribes, who had gathered protectively around Beetle, watched the ball of navy blue silk trundle towards them. They bunched themselves into a tight-knit group and prepared for her attack.

"*What* is going on?" Jillie Djinn demanded. "*Why* are you not working?"

"There's been an accident." Romilly's voice came from the back of the group.

"An *accident*?"

"Something fell out of the cupboard unexpectedly," said Romilly.

"Accidents usually *are* unexpected," Jillie Djinn observed tartly. "Enter full details along with the *exact* time of the incident in the accident log immediately – *atchoo atchoo* – and bring it to me to sign."

"Yes, Miss Djinn. I'll just go to the physik room for a plaster first. I won't be long."

"Very well, Miss Badger." Jillie Djinn sniffed irritably. She knew something was not quite right. She tried to peer over the heads of the scribes but to her annoyance she found that the tallest scribes – corralled by the quick-thinking Barnaby Ewe, whose head always banged the doorframe – were clustering around her.

"Excuse me, Miss Djinn," said one of them, a gangly young man with wispy brown hair. "While Miss Badger is in the physik room I wonder if you could check my calculations? I'm not sure if I've correctly worked out the average number of seconds that people have been late for their first appointments over the last seven weeks. I think I may have got a decimal point in the wrong place."

Jillie Djinn sighed. "Mr Partridge, will you never understand the decimal point?"

"I'm sure I very nearly *do* understand, Miss Djinn. If you could only run over it once more for me, I know all will be clear."

Partridge knew that Jillie Djinn never could resist explaining the decimal point. And so, while Partridge stifled numerous yawns and Jillie Djinn began a tortuous explanation, accompanied by much nose blowing, Romilly Badger smuggled Beetle into the physik room.

The physik room was small and dingy, with a tiny slit of a window that looked out on to the Manuscriptorium backyard. Squashed into the room were a lumpy bed, two chairs and a table with a large red box on it. Romilly sat Beetle down on the edge of the bed and draped a blanket over his shoulders – Beetle was shivering with shock. Foxy came in, quietly closed the door behind him and stayed leaning against it.

"You look terrible," he told Beetle.

Beetle managed a smile. "Thanks, Foxo."

"Sorry, Beet. I thought it'd bring you back to the last place *you* had been safe – didn't think it would come back to the last place *it* had been. Stupid thing."

"Don't apologise, Foxo. That cupboard's a hundred times better than where I probably *was* headed. Just wish I'd worked it out earlier, that's all. I wouldn't have made such a racket." Beetle grinned sheepishly. He couldn't quite remember what he'd said. He had a feeling he'd yelled out "Mum" – or even worse, "Mummy" – but he hoped that maybe it had only been inside his head.

"Nah, you were OK," said Foxy with a smile. He turned to Romilly. "Are you all right?" he asked. "Where did you cut yourself?"

"I'm fine, Foxy," said Romilly patiently. "I didn't cut myself. The plaster was an excuse to get Beetle out of the way."

"Oh, I *see*. That's really clever."

Beetle and Foxy watched Romilly open the red box, take out a large plaster and wrap it around her thumb.

Foxy looked puzzled. "But I thought . . ."

"Corroboration," said Romilly mysteriously. "OK, Beetle. I'll go and check if the coast is clear, then we can get you out without you-know-who seeing anything."

Foxy held the door open for Romilly, then he quietly closed it and resumed his position leaning against it. "She's clever," he said admiringly.

Beetle nodded. He still felt very odd, although he suspected that it was as much being back in his old place of work – a place that he had once loved – as anything Merrin had done.

"We still miss you," said Foxy suddenly.

"Yeah. Me too . . ." mumbled Beetle.

"It's horrible here now," said Foxy. "It's not been the same since you went. Actually, I'm thinking of leaving. And so are Partridge and Romilly."

"Leaving?" Beetle was shocked.

"Yeah." Foxy grinned. "D'you think Larry might want three more assistants?"

"I wish," said Beetle.

Neither said anything for a moment, and then Foxy spoke. "So, ah, what were you doing, Beet – I mean, why did you need a SafeCharm? And why did it bring you back? Things must have been really scary."

"They were. You know that Merrin Meredith kid who's been hanging around here?"

"Him!" spat Foxy.

"Well, he did a BeGone."

"On *you?*"

"Yeah."

"No wonder you look so rough," said Foxy.

"Yeah. But that's not the worst of it. He's holed up in the Palace attic –"

"You're kidding!"

"– and I think he's started a Darke Domaine."

Foxy stared at Beetle in disbelief. "No! *No.* How?"

"You know that ring he wears – that nasty Two-Faced thing? Well, I always thought it was a fake from Gothyk Grotto, but now I'm not so sure. I think it might be the real thing."

Foxy sat down on the chair beside Beetle. He looked worried. "It could be. It kind of makes sense if it is," he said in a low voice. "He's got some hold over Miss Djinn. She lets him do exactly what he likes – I think she's scared of him. The weird thing is, I know for a fact she's fired him at least three times, but he comes back just like nothing happened – and she *never remembers*. And recently she's started going really strange when he's here, kind of vacant, like she's not there any more. It's scary."

"I'll bet," said Beetle.

"Yeah." Foxy looked down at his feet, and Beetle knew he was about to say something that he'd had to really think about. There was a silence while Beetle waited and Foxy got his words together. "The thing is, Beet," said Foxy eventually, "this has happened here before. Remember all the stuff with my dad?"

Beetle nodded. Foxy's father had been the Chief Hermetic Scribe before Jillie Djinn. He had left in disgrace after becoming involved in a plot with Simon Heap – in his Darke days – to kill Marcia Overstrand.

"I know no one will ever believe it," said Foxy, "but my dad never wanted to do all that bones stuff for Simon Heap. He had no idea what it was for – he really didn't. But he said the Darke just pulled him in. And once you're in, it ties you up in knots and you can't escape – however much you try."

Beetle nodded.

"I went to see my dad last week," Foxy said tentatively.

Beetle was amazed. "You went to *see* him? But I thought Marcia banished him to the Far Countries."

Foxy looked awkward. "Yes, she did. But he got *so* home-sick. He came back secretly. He's changed his name and he lives down in the Port now. It's not in a very nice part of the Port, but he doesn't mind. You won't tell anyone, will you?"

"Of course I won't."

"Thanks. I don't go and see him much, just in case anyone notices, but recently I've been really worried about stuff here and I wanted to talk to him about it. He says it sounds bad. That Meredith kid – he's got Jillie Djinn right *there*." Foxy pressed his thumb into his opposite palm. "Under his thumb. Just like Simon Heap had my dad."

"He's been trouble right from the start," agreed Beetle. "I remember the first day he turned up, he was wearing that ring."

Foxy glanced at the door. "You know, I don't think it's fake either," he muttered.

"But how did he get it, Foxy? The real one belonged to DomDaniel."

"Well, *he's* dead."

"But you know the ring will only come off the Other way? He *can't* have chopped DomDaniel's thumb off."

"Nothing would surprise me about that little tick," said Foxy.

"I reckon I should go to Gothyk Grotto and see if they do copies," said Beetle. "If they don't I'll go and ask Marcia what she thinks."

"Well, don't be surprised if a couple of Wizards randomly turn up at the Grot and ask you why you want one," warned Foxy. "I asked for a copy of a Darke Charm once – just to play a joke on old Partridge – and they got quite funny about it."

A quiet *ratta-tippy-tap* sounded on the door. Beetle jumped.

"'S OK," said Foxy. "Scribe code. All clear. Time to go."

A minute later Beetle had been bundled out of the Manuscriptorium and was standing on Wizard Way. It was surprisingly busy. The Traders' Market had closed at sunset and people were now flocking to Wizard Way to watch the lighting of the candle displays for the Longest Night. Beetle leaned against the Manuscriptorium torch post, trying to take in the events of the previous hour or so. He saw Maizie Smalls advancing purposefully towards him. The throng parted to let her through, their upturned faces illuminated as they watched her lean her ladder against the post and nimbly climb up, her flaming TorchLighter at the ready.

The little band of children who had followed Maizie all along the Way gathered around the blackened silver base of the torch post and cheered as the Manuscriptorium torch flared up into the deepening twilight. It was a happy moment, but Beetle was not there to enjoy it. The sight of Maizie had jogged his memory and taken away the last of the fuzziness in his head.

"Jenna!" he gasped.

He set off at a run down the Way, dodging between the oncoming pedestrians, heading for the Palace.

✳ 13 ✳

GOTHYK GROTTO

Halfway down Wizard Way, Beetle saw Jenna racing up the other side. With her long hair streaming out behind her, the light from the torchlights glinting off her gold circlet and her red cloak flying, she sent oncoming pedestrians jumping out of her way and left them staring after her. Above her a small, invisible lovebird desperately tried to follow the glinting circlet through the crowds as it zigzagged towards the Wizard Tower.

Beetle walked quickly across the wide thoroughfare of the Way. He still found it hard to shake off one of the rules of the Manuscriptorium that all scribes signed up for: *no running, shouting, swearing, singing or dancing in Wizard Way*. It was a rule that, during his time at the Manuscriptorium, was taken very seriously, and up until now Beetle had not broken it. But as Jenna disappeared fast towards the Great Arch that led into the Wizard Tower courtyard, he broke two of its tenets at once. He set off at a run and yelled, "Jenna! *Jenna!*" And then, as people stopped and stared at him, he felt that maybe he was being disrespectful, so he yelled, "Hey, *Princess Jenna.* Stop!"

Jenna did stop, not for Beetle but to push through the crowd that had gathered around Maizie Smalls, who had crossed the Way to light the very last torch. As Jenna tried to dodge around

Beetle – just another body in her way – he put his arm out to stop her.

Jenna looked up, eyes blazing in anger. "Get out of my way – *oh, Beetle, it's you, it's you!*" She threw her arms around him.

"Ooh," said someone in the crowd. "Ooh, *look*! It's the Princess and that boy who was the –"

"Let's get out of here," said Beetle, reluctantly disengaging himself. He took hold of Jenna's arm and walked her briskly away.

"Beetle – what *happened*? You didn't come back! I was *so* scared. How did you get *here*? Hey, *where are we going*?" Jenna demanded in rapid fire while Beetle steered her across the Way and into the shadows of The Skinny Bones' Bob – an extremely narrow opening that led off Wizard Way and would take them into Ramblings Alley.

"We are going to Gothyk Grotto," said Beetle.

"Why?" Like a stubborn pony, Jenna stopped in her tracks and shook her head. Beetle halted – when a pony stops in The Skinny Bones' Bob, everyone stops. Jenna regarded Beetle with one of her finest Princess stares. "Beetle," she informed him, "I am not going another step until you tell me *what is going on*."

"I'll tell you on the way, OK?" he said.

"What, to Gothyk Grotto – that *dump* where all the weirdos hang out?"

"Yes. *Please,* Jenna, can we get going? It smells horrible here."

Jenna gave up. "OK. But this had better be good."

Jenna was entirely accurate in her description of Gothyk Grotto. It was a run-down, dark and dingy shop at the end of Little Creep Cut, somewhere in the middle of the scruffiest part of the Ramblings. As Beetle pushed open the door, the sound of a theatrical monster-style roar blared out above their heads and made Jenna – and the Unseen bird – jump. The bird recovered itself and flew in just as the door banged closed.

Beetle and Jenna stood for a moment, trying to make sense of the place. At first it seemed to be in total darkness, but soon they noticed a few flickering candles, which were moving slowly, randomly appearing and disappearing. The unearthly sound of a nose flute drifted out from some distant place, and the stuffy air was filled with the smell of particularly pungent incense, which set Jenna off sneezing. As their eyes became accustomed to the dark, Jenna and Beetle could see dim shapes of figures holding the candles as they wandered between towering stacks and teetering shelves.

Suddenly a flame flared in the gloom and they saw a tall boy lighting two candles nearby. The boy walked over and handed the candles to Jenna and Beetle with the words, "Welcome to Gothyk Grotto."

"Wolf Boy!" gasped Jenna. "What are *you* doing here?"

"Huh?" said what sounded like Wolf Boy's voice.

Jenna raised her candle and looked at the boy. It wasn't Wolf Boy, but there was something about him that reminded her of him. The boy was about the same height and build as Wolf Boy, but his hair was short and spiky and even in the dark, Jenna could see it was black, unlike Wolf Boy's light brown.

"Sorry," said Jenna. "I thought you were someone else."

"Yeah. Well, sorry I'm not Wolf Boy, whoever he is. Cool name."

"It's odd, you sound just like him. Don't you think, Beetle?"

"Just like," agreed Beetle.

"Beetle's a cool name too. Yeah. Hey. Wow. Man, you're the *Princess*. Wow. What're *you* doing here?"

"We've come to see if you sell copies of the Two-Faced Ring," said Jenna.

"You *what*?"

"We want to know," said Beetle very clearly and slowly, "if you sell – or have ever sold – copies of the Darke Two-Faced Ring?"

"Huh?"

"The Darke Two-Faced Ring," Beetle repeated.

"Jeez," said the boy.

"So . . . do you sell them? Have you *ever* sold them?"

"You really want to know?" The boy seemed flummoxed.

"Yes, please," said Beetle, trying to be patient. "Have you? Ever sold them? To *anyone*?"

"You'd better come this way," said the boy. "Follow me, please."

With a distinct feeling that they had done something wrong, Beetle and Jenna set off after him. Following the boy was no easy task. He wore a long black robe, which swept the ground and blended into the dakness, and he obviously knew his way around well enough not to need a candle as he weaved quickly between the shelves and stacks, which were set out as a double labyrinth. Jenna went first, and the only way she kept up with the boy was by following the swish of his gown over the rough wooden floorboards. They wound their way through the seemingly endless canyons of merchandise (the labyrinth was planned to lead customers past everything twice), trying to keep up with the boy at the same time as not tripping over assorted plaster bones, cheap black cloaks and tunics, false Gragull teeth (a Gragull being a mythical bloodsucking human), bottles of fake blood, buckets of heavy jewellery embellished with skulls, Charms, bits of dead hamster (the latest craze), stacks of books of popular spells, piles of board games, glow-in-the-dark paint, jelly insects in jars, spider's webs, wolverine eyes and a thousand other examples of what was known in the Castle as "Gothyk Grot".

At last they emerged from the labyrinth into the back of the shop – a dusty space piled high with unopened boxes and lit by a few tall, black candles. The eerie sound of the nose flute was louder here and came from behind a small door (painted black, naturally) that was set deep into an ornate gothic arch. The boy beckoned them to follow him and headed for the door. Jenna hurried after him, tripped over a pile of cardboard skulls, and steadied herself against the arch. It wobbled alarmingly.

The boy knocked on the door. The sound of the nose flute ceased – much to their relief – and a voice called out, "Yes?"

"It's me, Matt. I've got a nine-nine-nine here. It's the Princess and the ex-Manuscriptorium Clerk."

"Very funny, Marcus. Get me a cup of tea, will you?"

"No, really, I *have*. And it's the Princess, Mr Igor. Honest."

The voice on the other side of the door sounded irritated. "Marcus, I've told you about telling stories before. Now go and get me my cup of tea. OK?"

The boy turned around to Jenna and Beetle and shrugged. "Sorry," he said. "He gets funny at twilight. I'll go and get him a cup of tea. He'll see you after that."

"But we don't *need* to see him," said Beetle, exasperated. "We only want to know if you have ever had any fake Two-Faced Rings."

"Exactly. So you have to see him. It's the rules. Sorry." The boy grinned apologetically and disappeared back into the labyrinth.

"This is stupid," said Jenna, "I'm not waiting here all night." She rapped loudly on the little black door and then, without waiting for a reply, she went in. Beetle followed.

A man with a long, extremely white face ending in a wispy, pointy beard was sitting at a small desk playing a solitary card game. He did not look up but murmured, "That was quick, Marcus. Just put it down here, will you?" When no cup of tea appeared in his line of sight the man looked up. His jaw dropped. "Good ghouls!" he gasped. He leaped to his feet, scattering the cards, and bowed awkwardly. "Princess Jenna! It *is* you. I am so sorry. I had no idea . . ." He looked around. "Where's Marcus gone? Why didn't he say you were here?"

"Well, *Matt* said I was here," said Jenna, confused.

"Matt, Marcus, same thing," said the man obscurely. "Oh, please, please sit down, Princess. And you, scribe Beetle." He waved his hand to stop Beetle from explaining. "No, don't say anything. I know what happened. But once a scribe always a scribe, eh? Now to what do I owe the pleasure of this visit? What can I do for you, eh?"

Jenna got to the point. "We need to know if you have ever sold copies of the Two-Faced Ring."

Igor went a shade whiter. "So it *is* a nine-nine-nine. Oh dear, how very embarrassing. I do apologise. But it's part of the terms of our licence, eh?" Igor reached below the desk and pressed a large red button. Then he looked up and smiled awkwardly. "Purely a formality of course," he said. "Do please sit down." He indicated two unsteady wooden chairs that were pushed up against the wall. Igor watched them gingerly sit down, not taking his eyes off them for a moment. "Well, your Grace —"

"Please, just call me Jenna," Jenna interrupted.

"It seems a little familiar. *Princess* Jenna if I may. Eh?" Jenna nodded.

"Well, Princess Jenna, if it had been anyone else asking this I would have to keep you in custody here until the arrival of the duty Wizard. But as it's you, eh, I wouldn't dream of keeping you against your wishes. Naturally." Igor looked highly embarrassed.

"What do you mean?" asked Jenna.

"Well, it's like this, eh? We have what we call a Notification List of certain Darke objects, potions, Charms, Spells, etcetera. Top of the list is the Two-Faced Ring. It is, as Marcus said, code nine-nine-nine. If anyone asks for something on the list, we have to notify the Wizard Tower."

"But why?" asked Jenna.

Igor shrugged. "I don't know, eh. The Wizard Tower doesn't actually tell us anything. But I would guess that knowing that these things exist, and then wanting copies of them, shows a knowledge of Darke things that is suspicious, eh? Maybe even dangerous. Excepting yourself, Princess, of course," he added hurriedly. "Of course you have a right to be interested in *everything*. Totally understandable – *totally*."

"So is that a *yes* or a *no*?" asked Jenna.

"A yes or no what?" Igor looked puzzled.

"Have you ever sold copies of the Two-Faced Ring?"

Igor looked shocked. "Good ghoul, *no*. Of course we haven't. What do you take us for?"

"I'm sorry," said Jenna. "I . . . we didn't mean anything bad. We just needed to know."

Igor lowered his voice. "Do not seek to know. Keep this ring from your thoughts. Take care, Princess Jenna. Do not meddle with this. Do not name it again." He gazed at a point a few feet above Jenna's head and a frown flitted across his brow. "Be careful, Princess," he muttered. "Walk with the Darke and you do not walk alone." He stood up and bowed solemnly. "Your travelling companions may not be what you would wish for. Marcus will see you out."

Still feeling as though they had done something wrong, Beetle and Jenna followed Marcus – or was it Matt? – back through the labyrinth in silence. As they passed a large jar of Gragull teeth, Jenna stopped and took a set.

"How much are these?" she asked.

"Free to you," grinned Matt – or was it Marcus?

"Oh, thank you," said Jenna with a smile.

The boy led them out of the maze and opened the door for them.

"Excuse me," said Jenna, intrigued, "but is your name Marcus or Matt?"

The boy grinned. "Matt."

"So why did Igor call you Marcus?"

"Marcus is my brother. We're identical. Igor thinks we play tricks on him and pretend we're each other, but we don't – that is just *so* lame. But Igor thinks he's being clever and when we tell him who we are, he always calls us by the other name." Matt shrugged. "It's like that in here. Weird."

"Weird," agreed Jenna.

$\star$ $\star$ $\star$

Accompanied by the roar of the door monster, Jenna and Beetle stepped out into the wind funnelling down Little Creep Cut. Beetle turned to her, his hair blowing into his eyes, the sharp drops of sleety rain making him blink. "So Foxy *was* right," he said. "Merrin's got the real thing. This is serious – we need to tell Marcia right away."

Jenna wound her cloak around her, pulling the fur edging tight under her chin to keep out the rain. "I know," she said miserably. "Mum is going to be *so* upset. She's been looking forward to tonight for *ages*. It's the first time she's had me and Sep together for our birthdays – *ever*."

Beetle and Jenna walked in silence back along Little Creep Cut, heading towards a large signpost that read TO THE WIZARD TOWER. Above them flew the little UnSeen lovebird, buffeted by the wind, stung by the rain, but now with a ray of hope that it might soon see its own true love once again.

"Beetle," said Jenna.

"Mmm?"

"I never mentioned this to anyone before because I thought they'd think I was weird or something, but I think Merrin's been living in the Palace for ages."

"*What?*" Beetle looked astonished.

"Well . . . every now and then I've thought I've seen him kind of disappearing around the corner, although I was never totally sure. I even mentioned it to Mum once, but she thought it was just a ghost. But you remember what Barney Pot told Aunt Zelda – that Merrin had ambushed him in the Long Walk? I know no one else believed him, but Barney doesn't tell fibs. And if that *is* true, then Merrin's been hanging around for at least eighteen months. Which is really creepy." Jenna shivered.

"That's horrible," said Beetle. "The thought of him just lurking up there. Watching you. Wandering around at night –"

"Oh, stop it, Beetle!" Jenna protested. "I don't even want to *think* about it."

They had reached the TO THE WIZARD TOWER signpost, which was illuminated by a small torch burning brightly in a holder on the top. The sign pointed down a well-lit lane known locally as Wiz Way. They turned down it and walked briskly between the neat houses, all with their Longest Night candles burning in their windows. As they progressed, Beetle noticed Jenna was becoming increasingly uneasy.

"Is this the right way?" she asked Beetle after a while.

"Of course it is." Beetle cast Jenna a wondering glance. He knew that she knew the lanes around the Ramblings backwards.

"But . . . it doesn't feel like it."

"Well, it *is*. You *know* it is. It's Wiz Way." Beetle was flummoxed.

Jenna had stopped and was looking around, as though seeing the alleyway for the first time. Above her the UnSeen lovebird fluttered hopefully. It was nearly home.

"What's wrong?" asked Beetle. He glanced up. It felt as if something was hovering above Jenna's head, just outside his field of vision.

Jenna rounded on him angrily. "Nothing's wrong. Stop nagging me, Beetle. I'm just not going your stupid way, that's all!" And with that she turned and ran back along Wiz Way, then suddenly scooted to the left and disappeared into a tiny, dark alleyway – the notorious Dagger Dan's Dive.

14

DAGGER DAN'S DIVE

Beetle tore after Jenna but, unlike her, he was not a natural runner. He soon lost sight of her flying red cloak as she drew ahead of him, leaping over puddles and skidding around blind corners, slipping through the twists and turns of the narrow, dark alleyway as though she had run down it a hundred times before. Doggedly Beetle followed the increasingly faint echoes of her footsteps, and soon he could hear nothing but the sound of his own boots thudding on the stones. Of Jenna there was no trace at all.

Of all the alleyways that led off Wiz Way, Dagger Dan's Dive was the worst. The twisting, narrow passage was named after a notorious mugger and cut-throat who had used it as a foolproof escape. Even if closely pursued, Dagger Dan would always get away – and mystify his pursuers – by jumping into the open drain at the alley's dead end, then creeping through the water and filth to his small boat tied up on the river by the drain's mouth.

Beetle could not understand why Jenna had chosen to run down Dagger Dan's Dive, of all places. Like him, she had grown up in the Ramblings. She had been to a Ramblings school, and she too would have passed her Ramblings Proficiency Test by memorising the Ramblings map and undertaking three timed journeys on her own. This was the test that all children had to pass before they were allowed to become Ramblers and wander freely (or Ramble) on their own. But even for a Rambler there were forbidden alleys – and Dagger Dan's Dive was at the top of the list.

The Dive, as it was known locally, was inhabited by the more shadowy denizens of the Castle – the kind of people who one never saw out in daylight hours and hoped not to see out at night. With its decrepit overhanging buildings exuding the sickly sweet smell of rot (and worse) and the inhabitants' habit of jostling strangers or staring from their windows at every echo of footsteps – usually armed and ready to throw a bucket of slop if they didn't like the look of those making them – Dagger Dan's Dive was a place no one chose to go, especially at night.

But as Jenna ran, she was oblivious to everything she knew about the Dive. Escorted by the UnSeen bird, she raced along, jumping over potholes, skidding around stinking piles of rubbish, ignoring catcalls and curses shouted from windows far above and even a well-aimed rotten tomato that hit the back of her cloak. Towards the end of the Dive, Jenna began to slow down, and she finally came to a halt under the dull light of a rusty lantern. She stopped to catch her breath and looked about, suddenly confused by where she found herself. Above her head the lantern squeaked as it swung mournfully above a dilapidated door studded with nails. Behind her was a boarded-up window with faded lettering above it proclaiming:

FORTUNES TOLD, FORTUNES SOLD.
ENTER HERE IF YOU BE BOLD.
POSITIVELY NO CREDIT.

A gust of wind rattled the lantern alarmingly. Jenna shivered. Where was she – and *what* was she was doing here? The long-ago chanted list of forbidden alleyways came back to her and she realised with a sinking feeling that, not only had she run down Dagger Dan's Dive, but she was now standing outside the notorious Doom Dump, which some years ago had been the centre of great excitement when it had been Fumigated and Locked by a posse of Wizards led by the ExtraOrdinary Wizard herself.

Every Ramblings child knew that Doom Dump was near the end of Dan's Dive and Jenna, well aware that the Dive was a dead end, knew she must turn around and go back the way she had come. The thought frightened her, and she felt unwilling to move. The lantern squeaked and a spatter of rain soaked into her cloak. Jenna shook her head to get rid of an odd buzzing, muzzy feeling.

Just as Jenna was getting the courage to go back up the Dive she heard the sound of pounding footsteps coming towards her. She froze. The footsteps drew closer, and she shrank back into the shadows of Doom Dump, pressing against the wall in the hope that whoever it was coming down the alley would not see her.

To her huge relief it was Beetle who came skidding around the corner.

"Jenna!" puffed Beetle, equally relieved to see Jenna waiting for him. "What are you doing? Why'd you come down *here*?"

"I . . . I don't know." It was true; Jenna didn't know why. She felt as if she had just woken up from a bizarre dream.

"Let's get out of here," said Beetle, glancing around uneasily. "We'll have to go back the way we came. It's a dead end just around the corner and you don't want to end up *there*."

"I know," said Jenna, "I *know*."

Beetle set off quickly and Jenna went to follow – *but she could not move*. She swung around to check that her cloak was not caught in something but it hung freely. She tugged at her long robe, which, to her dismay, was spattered with mud, but that was not stuck either. Trying not to panic, she lifted first one foot and then the other, and neither of them were stuck – but when she once again tried to follow Beetle, she could not move.

Jenna lost the fight against panic. "Beetle!" she yelled. *"Beeee . . . tle!"* To her horror, no sound came from her mouth. Above her the lantern fizzled out and Jenna was plunged into darkness.

Beetle had not got far when he realised that Jenna was not following him. He felt exasperated – what was she playing at? Annoyed now, he went back to get her, but as he once more rounded the corner he saw that the lantern above the studded door had gone out and Jenna was not there.

Beetle stopped outside the door. "Jenna?" he said in a half-whisper. *"Jenna?"*

There was no reply. A cold spatter of rain fell; Beetle shivered in his admiral's jacket and wound his woolly scarf another turn around his neck. He wished he were somewhere else. And he wished he understood what Jenna was up to – sometimes he just could not work her out. Assuming that Jenna had plans that she was not telling him about and had tried to get rid of him once again, Beetle grumpily set off towards the Dive's notorious dead end. Whatever Jenna might have planned, he was not going to leave her on her own at the end of Dagger Dan's Dive.

The dead end was deserted. Beetle's irritation began to be replaced with concern. He peered down into the open drain, beside which someone had thoughtfully placed a rotten plank with the words "Watch Out!" scrawled on it. Beetle took out his blue light and flicked it open, then he gingerly kneeled down and peered into the drain. A bad smell hit him.

"Jenna ... Jenna?" he called nervously, his voice sounding hollow in the darkness below.

There was no reply, for which Beetle was grateful, until a horrible image flashed in his mind – Jenna lying unconscious far below. He leaned forward and held out his light. Deep down he saw the dark, sluggish waters of the drain half covering – *oh no* – a dark lump of something.

"Jenna!" Beetle called down, his voice echoing hollowly inside the drain.

Behind him came a cough. "Hey. Lost something?" asked a familiar voice.

"Wolf Boy!" Then Beetle looked up. "Oh, sorry. It's *you*."

"Yeah, I guess you're right. It *is* me," said the boy. "So who are you?"

"Beetle. You remember, at Goth – oh, I see. You must be Marcus."

Marcus grinned. "You've been to the Grot, yeah? Matt still there?"

"Oh . . . yes. Yes, he is." Beetle's voice echoed into the drain.

"Good," said Marcus. "I'm late for my shift. Wouldn't come this way if I wasn't in a hurry – it's a short cut over the wall." He looked closely at Beetle. "So why'd *you* come here, then?"

Beetle pointed his blue light into the drain. "I think Jenna's fallen in. Look."

"Hey, cool light," said Marcus. He peered into the drain, and Beetle played his light on the form lying far below in the water. "Nah, that's not anyone," said Marcus. "It's just some old clothes and stuff."

Beetle wasn't so sure.

"You can go down and check if you like," said Marcus. "See if it is – who did you say?"

"Jenna. Princess Jenna."

Marcus whistled in amazement. "*Princess Jenna?* Hey, what's *she* doing down here?" He peered in once more. "Well, if you think it really *is* Princess Jenna, you'd better take a look. There are some rungs going down the side – see?"

The last thing Beetle wanted to do was climb down into the stinking drain, but he knew he had no choice.

"I'll keep watch for you," said Marcus as Beetle carefully removed the two planks and swung himself over the edge. "I won't let anyone do a Ransom on you."

Beetle's head was just visible above the manhole. "Do a *what*?" he asked.

"A Ransom. You know, when they push you in the drain and won't let you get out until you give 'em all your stuff."

"All your stuff?" Beetle was distracted, looking into the drain.

"Yeah." Marcus grinned. "Not much fun running up the Dive with no clothes on, I can tell you. Be careful, the rungs are rusty."

"Ah. OK." Very carefully Beetle began to climb down into the drain. The rungs were indeed rusty. They felt loose against the brickwork and as Beetle cautiously placed his boot into the slime at the bottom of the drain, the last one came away in his hand. He dropped it into the mud with a dull *thub* and shone his light along the drain.

Beetle's blue light didn't show much; it was made for the clean whiteness of ice, not the brown muckiness of sludge. But it did show enough for him to see that the lump that he had feared was an unconscious Jenna was indeed a pile of old clothes. Just to make sure, Beetle waded through the muck, trying to ignore the wetness seeping into his boots, and tentatively poked at the lump with his foot. It moved. Beetle yelled. A huge rat ran out and scuttled off into the dark.

"You all right?" Marcus's face appeared in the manhole opening.

"Yeah." Beetle felt a little foolish. "A rat. Big one."

"There's a lot around here," said Marcus. "And they're not Message Rats, that's for sure. It's a whole different species, I reckon. Bite you as soon as look at you. You were lucky."

"Ah . . ."

"I take it that's not the Princess?" Marcus asked.

"No."

"You don't want to stay down too long. It's been raining for days now. There might be a rush."

"A what?" Beetle couldn't hear Marcus clearly as a low thunder like the rush of blood in his head was filling his ears.

"A *rush*. Oh sheesh – hey, *look out!*"

Beetle didn't hear a word Marcus said, but he did hear what was coming along the drain. He leaped up, grasping for the rung, only to find that it was gone. It was, he remembered, lying in the mud where he had thrown it. The roar in his ears grew louder, and the next thing Beetle knew, a hand was reaching down and Marcus was yelling, "Grab hold. Quick!"

A few seconds later Beetle and Marcus were lying on the wet cobblestones at the end of Dan's Dive, staring down at the wall of water rushing along the drain below.

"Thanks," gasped Beetle.

"No worries," puffed Marcus. "Good thing Princess Jenna *wasn't* down there."

Beetle sat up. He ran his hands through his hair as he always did when he was worried – and immediately wished he hadn't. Where *was* Jenna?

✷ 15 ✷

DOOM DUMP

Jenna was in Doom Dump.

As she wordlessly yelled for Beetle and the lantern fizzled out, Jenna had heard the studded door creak open behind her. Terrified, she had tried to run, but her feet had stayed planted firmly outside the door. And when an arm had stretched out and a hand grabbed the back of her cloak and began to pull her inside, Jenna's feet had taken her across the threshold of Doom Dump and waited patiently while a girl, wearing witch robes that would not have looked out of place in Gothyk Grotto, Locked and Barred the door.

"Marissa!" gasped Jenna, but once again she made no sound.

"Goldfish." Marissa smirked. Mockingly she opened and closed her mouth like a fish.

Keeping her hand firmly on Jenna's cloak, Marissa shoved Jenna along the corridor of a typical long, narrow Castle house. It was totally dark, but Marissa knew her way. She threw open the first door leading off the corridor and pushed Jenna into a tunnel-like room, lit at the far end by a pair of rushlights and a tiny fire sputtering in a huge fireplace. The rushlights illuminated what at first appeared to be a comforting scene – a table around which a group of woman were seated for a meal. But

Jenna felt anything but comforted. Sitting at the table was the Port Witch Coven.

All eyes were upon Jenna as Marissa delivered the unwilling addition to the party. As they reached the table – which had two empty chairs – Marissa tightened her grip on Jenna, afraid that her prize might elude her at the last minute. This was her first test set by the Coven and she knew she'd done well. Both the Silent and the FootLock Spells had worked, but Marissa knew from past experience how elusive Princesses could be and she wasn't taking any chances.

Marissa pushed Jenna down into one of the vacant seats and took her place beside her. Jenna did not react. She stared at the table in front of her, at first because she was determined not to catch a witch's gaze and then because of a horrified fascination with what the witches were actually eating. It was, she thought, worse than Aunt Zelda's offerings – and that was saying something. At least Aunt Zelda made an effort to cook whatever weird ingredients she used until they were reasonably unrecognisable, but the bowls of squirming salted earwigs and a large dish of skinned mice covered with a lumpy, pale sauce made no effort at disguise. Jenna felt sick. She switched her gaze to the tablecloth, which was covered in Darke symbols and old gravy.

Linda – the boss-with-the-stare from the jewellery stall – pushed her chair back with a teeth-on-edge scrape and got to her feet. Slowly and menacingly she made her way around the table towards Jenna. Linda loomed close and Jenna could smell the musty damp of the witch's robes mixed with a stale, heavy smell of dead roses. Suddenly, as if to land a slap, Linda's arm shot out and, despite herself, Jenna flinched. But Linda's open palm travelled to a spot just above Jenna's head and snatched something out of the air.

Linda drew down her closed fist and held it in front of Jenna. She muttered a few words to reverse the UnSeen and snapped open her fingers. Lying in the witch's palm was the tiny shimmering bird that Jenna had – so long ago, it seemed – refused to pick up from the stall.

"There, little birdie," Linda crooned. "You have done well. You have Brought the Princess. You may have your reward." From inside her robes, she pulled out the tiny cage that hung around her neck, took it off and swung the cage and its prisoner in front of the terrified bird lying in her hand. "Here is your little friend. Take a look."

Both birds looked at each other. Neither made a move or a sound.

Taking everyone by surprise, Linda suddenly threw the bird in her hand into the air. At the same time, she hurled the tiny cage to the floor. She raised her foot to stamp on the cage, but the Witch Mother shouted out, "Linda! Stop that *right now!*"

Linda's foot stopped in mid-air.

"You made a bargain, you keep it," said the Witch Mother.

"It's only a poxy *bird*," said Linda, her foot hovering above the cage.

The Witch Mother hauled herself to her feet. "You renege on a Darke bargain at your peril. Remember that. Sometimes, Linda, I think you forget the Rules. It is not good for a witch to forget the Rules. Is it, Linda?" She leaned across the table, eyeballing the witch. *"Is . . . it?"* the Witch Mother repeated menacingly.

Linda slowly lowered her foot away from the tiny cage. "No, Witch Mother," she said sulkily.

Daphne, the dumpy witch who looked, Jenna thought, as if she had been sewn into a sack that someone had left some rotten rubbish in, got up quietly. She tiptoed up behind Linda and picked up the cage.

"You're horrible," Daphne bravely told Linda. "Just because you stamp on my giant woodworm all the time doesn't mean you can go stamping on *everything*." Daphne's fat, mouse-stained fingers fumbled with the cage door and managed to open it. The trapped bird fell out on to the table next to a neat pile of mouse bones – which the Witch Mother was using to pick her teeth – and lay there, stunned.

Jenna watched with horror, all the while desperately trying to make a plan but unable to think of anything. She saw the hovering bird – the one that had brought her to Doom Dump – fly down to its companion and nudge it gently. The stunned bird fluttered its wings, shook its feathers and, a few moments later, both birds flew unsteadily off into a dark corner of the room. Jenna found herself envying them.

The Witch Mother turned her attention to Jenna. "Well, well," she said with a ghastly grimace. "We have our Princess." She looked Jenna up and down as though she were buying a horse and trying to get it cheap. "It will do, I suppose."

"I *still* don't see why we need one," came a querulous voice from the shadows. It belonged to a young witch with a large towel wrapped around her head.

"Dorinda, I have already told you why," said the Witch Mother. "I'd have thought with those ears your memory might have improved."

Dorinda gave a loud wail. "It's not my fault. I didn't *want* elephant ears. And I don't see why we want a Princess either. She'll just spoil things. I *know* she will."

"Shut up, Dorinda," snapped Linda. "Or else."

Dorinda shrank back into the shadows – it was Linda who had Bestowed the elephant ears upon her.

"As I told you before, Dorinda – the possession of a Princess gives a coven the right to rule all other covens," said the Witch Mother. She turned to Marissa and patted her arm. "You made the right choice to come to us, dearie." Marissa looked smug.

As if they had already lost interest in their new acquisition, the witches switched their attention from Jenna to the remains of their meal and carried on talking and arguing as though she was not there.

Jenna watched them suck the rest of the mouse bones clean and then pick out the biggest earwigs and pop them into their mouths. The only thing that gave her any satisfaction was the expression on Marissa's face as she tried to force down an earwig. Marissa's old coven, the Wendron Witches, ate normal, forest-gathered food. Jenna had once had dinner there and had actually enjoyed it. That was, she remembered, the night they had tried to kidnap her.

Once supper was over, the Witch Mother called out in a rasping voice, "Nursie! Nursie! Clear the plates. *Nursie!*"

A rotund figure, whom Jenna recognised but could not place, bustled into the room carrying a bucket over the crook of her arm like a handbag. She stacked up the plates, scraping the revolting leftovers into the bucket, and staggered out, balancing the plates precariously. A few minutes later she returned with the same bucket, but this time it contained a concoction of foul-smelling Witches' Brew, which she ladled into cups for the witches. Nursie glanced at Jenna briefly, showing no interest in her, but as she left the room once again, Jenna remembered where she had seen her before. Nursie was the landlady of The Doll House – a guesthouse next door to the coven's residence in the Port, where Jenna had once had the misfortune to spend a night.

The witches slurped their Witches' Brew and continued to ignore Jenna. The Witch Mother tipped her head back and noisily drained her cup, then she patted her stomach and regarded Jenna with a satisfied sigh. Mouse and maggot casserole followed by a slug of Witches' Brew always improved her temper – the coven's new acquisition wasn't so bad, all things considered.

"Welcome, Princess," the Witch Mother said, pulling at a piece of mouse ear stuck in a gap between her teeth. "You are one of us now."

"I am not," retorted Jenna silently, causing the rest of the coven to fall about laughing.

"As near as makes no difference, dearie," said the Witch Mother, who, after many years of goldfish spells, was a whizz at lip-reading. "By midnight tonight you will be one of us, like it or not."

Jenna shook her head violently.

The Witch Mother rubbed her hands together and perused Jenna once more. "Yes. You'll do nicely." She gave Jenna her best smile – formed by parting her lips and showing two rows of blackened teeth. "*Very* nicely."

Jenna was not sure how to take this. She wasn't sure that being considered good witch material was exactly a compliment.

Linda looked irritated. "You're such a toady, Witch Mother. She'll be a rubbish witch. We wouldn't even look at her if she wasn't a Princess."

The Witch Mother glared at Linda and turned to Marissa, who was rapidly becoming her new favourite. "Now, this is a special job for you, Marissa dearie. Take the Princess to the room we've prepared and make her put on her witch robe. Take all that she has away from her. You can have her nice circlet if you want, it will suit you."

"No!" Jenna gave a silent yell and her hand flew up to her head. "You are not having it. You are *not*."

"Oh, I so *love* goldfish spells," spluttered the witch with her hair matted into a tall spike on top of her head.

"Quiet, Veronica," said the Witch Mother sternly. "Now, Marissa, take the Princess away."

Marissa looked very pleased with herself. She grasped Jenna's arm and pulled her to her feet, then she propelled her towards a heavy curtain hanging at the far end of the room. Jenna tried to resist but her feet betrayed her and took her seemingly willingly along with Marissa. As they reached the curtain the Witch Mother called out, "Bring me her nice red furry cloak when you're done, Marissa. It gets so cold here. Shakes my old bones, it does."

Linda glared at the departing Marissa; her long-nurtured position as Witch-Mother-in-waiting was looking precarious. She got to her feet. The Witch Mother looked up suspiciously.

"Linda, where are you going?" she asked.

Linda passed a hand wearily across her forehead. "It's been a long day, Witch Mother. I think I'll take a little nap. I do so want to be at my best for tonight's . . . *proceedings*."

"Very well. Don't be late. We start at midnight *on the dot.*"

Gimlet-eyed, the Witch Mother watched Linda leave. She listened to the witch's footsteps clumping loudly up the stairs; she heard the creaking of the bedroom floorboards above and the squeak of Linda's bedsprings.

However, although Linda's footsteps had gone upstairs to bed, Linda had not. The Witch Mother had never mastered the art of Throwing footsteps and consequently did not believe it was possible. But it was. When Linda left the room, her footsteps had stomped up the stairs and into her bedroom, then they had jumped up and down on her bed and squeaked the bedsprings. Linda herself, however, had somewhere else to go.

Unaware of Linda's deception, the Witch Mother surveyed the remaining three witches with an air of satisfaction. "We are on the up," she said. "Not only are we now six in our coven, we will soon be seven – and our seventh member will be a *Princess.*"

From somewhere at the back of the house came the sound of a scream.

"Goodness me, what *is* Marissa doing to our dear Princess?" the Witch Mother said with an indulgent smile. But the Witch Mother was – as Linda often commented – getting forgetful. And what she had forgot was that Jenna was still Silent.

It was Marissa's scream.

❊ 16 ❊
CALL-OUT

Beetle arrived at the Wizard Tower breathless and flustered. Hildegarde opened the door to him. She looked surprised.

"What are *you* doing here?" she said. "You and Princess Jenna have just been the subject of a nine-nine-nine from Gothyk Grotto. You should be there waiting for the Emergency Wizard."

Beetle fought to get his breath back. "I . . . she . . . they . . . let us go. Must see Marcia . . . now . . . urgent."

Hildegarde knew Beetle well enough to send an express messenger straight up to Marcia's rooms. While the messenger set the stairs on emergency and disappeared in a whirl of blue, Beetle paced the Great Hall impatiently, not daring to hope that it would have any result. He was as amazed as Hildegarde when, no more than a few minutes later, a flash of purple appeared at the top of the spiral stairs and whizzed its way down. In a moment Marcia was hurrying across to the agitated Beetle.

Marcia listened to Beetle's story of Merrin in the Palace attic, the Two-Faced Ring, the Darke Domaine and finally, Jenna's disappearance, with increasing concern.

"I knew it," she muttered. "I *knew* it."

Marcia heard Beetle out and then sprang into action. She sent Hildegarde up to the Search and Rescue Centre on the nineteenth floor of the Wizard Tower to begin a Search for Jenna at once.

"And now," said Marcia, "we must do a Call-Out to the Palace. There is no time to lose."

It was a relatively easy matter to Call-Out all the Wizard Tower Wizards. The Tower had an extremely ancient Magykal intercom system that no one understood any more, but which still worked – although Marcia did not dare use it too often. A fine spiderlike web of Magykal threads connected all the private rooms and public spaces in the Tower. The control point was a tiny circle of lapis lazuli set high up in the wall beside the Wizard Tower doors. Beetle watched Marcia ball her right hand into a fist and then throw it open, letting go of a well-aimed stream of Magykal purple that hit the centre of the circle, whereupon a wafer of paper-thin lapis detached itself and floated down into Marcia's outstretched hands. Marcia pressed the flimsy circle of blue into her left palm. Then she held her hand up to her mouth and addressed her palm in an oddly flat monotone.

"Calling all Wizards, Calling all Wizards. This is a non-optional Call-Out. Please make your way immediately, I repeat, *immediately*, to the Great Hall."

Marcia's monotone sounded in every room in the Wizard Tower, as loud and undistorted as though she were there in person – much to the dismay of one elderly Wizard taking a bath.

The effect was immediate. The silver spiral stairs slowed to steady mode – a setting that allowed easy access for all – and a few seconds later, Beetle saw the blue cloaks of the first Wizards descending.

Wizards and Apprentices gathered in the Hall – the Wizards grumbling that the ExtraOrdinary Wizard had chosen to do a Call-Out practice just as they were about to have tea, the Apprentices chattering with excitement. Beetle kept an eye on the stairs for Septimus, but although plenty of green robes were mixed in with the blue, his was not among them.

The last Wizard stepped off the stairs and Marcia addressed the crowd. "This is not a Call-Out practice," she said. "This is the real thing."

A surprised murmur greeted her announcement.

"All Wizards are required to form a Cordon around the Palace within the next half-hour. I intend to put the Palace into Quarantine as soon as possible."

A collective gasp of shock echoed through the Great Hall, and the lights inside the Tower – which, if there was nothing else to do, reflected the Wizards' collective feelings – turned a slightly surprised pink.

Marcia continued. "To that effect I am asking you to exit the Tower with Mr Beetle. En route to the Palace you will provide back-up to Mr Beetle while he Calls Out the Manuscriptorium Scribes."

It was Beetle's turn to look shocked.

Marcia continued. "You will then proceed to the Palace Gate and assemble there silently please. I must impress the need for *absolute silence* upon you all. It is imperative that our target in the Palace does not realise what is happening. Understood?"

A murmur of assent ran through the Hall.

"Raise your arm, Beetle, so that they all know who you are."

Beetle obeyed, thinking that it was pretty easy to see who he was, as he was the only one wearing an admiral's jacket. But right then – after learning that Merrin had been living in the Palace for nearly two years and Silas Heap had not noticed – Marcia had a poor opinion of the observational powers of the average Ordinary Wizard. She was taking no chances.

"Beetle, I now declare you to be my Call-Out Emissary," Marcia said rather formally. From her ExtraOrdinary Wizard belt she took a tiny scroll tied in a wisp of purple ribbon and gave it to Beetle.

The scroll lay in Beetle's palm, surprisingly heavy for its size.

"Gosh . . ." he said.

"The scroll is a twice-tap," Marcia informed him. "Make sure you hold it at arm's length when it is Enlarging, as they can get a bit hot. Once it's full size, all you have to do is read out what it says. Emissary scrolls are reasonably intelligent, so this one should respond to most things Miss Djinn throws at you. I have given you the adversarial model." Marcia sighed. "I suspect you will need it."

Beetle suspected he would too.

"Also, Beetle, although the Chief Hermetic Scribe is *obliged* to let all Indentured Scribes go on a Call-Out, she herself does not have to attend. And frankly I would prefer it if she didn't. Understood?"

Beetle nodded. He totally understood.

Marcia raised her voice and addressed the assembled Wizards and Apprentices. "Now, please leave the Tower with Mr Beetle in an orderly fashion."

"But Septimus hasn't come down yet," said Beetle.

"No, indeed Septimus hasn't." Marcia sounded cross. "At

the very moment when I should be relying on my Senior Apprentice, he has chosen to absent himself and go listening to some ridiculous *twaddle* peddled by Marcellus Pye. I shall be sending a Wizard to get him." And, thought Marcia, to tell him that he will most certainly *not* be beginning his Darke Week that night.

Now Beetle understood why he was Emissary – once again, he was Septimus's replacement. It took the shine off it a little. But only a little.

And so, while Marcia embarked on the more time-consuming Castle Call-Out, Beetle led the Wizards and Apprentices out of the Wizard Tower. Like a gooseherd with a gaggle of disorderly geese, he took them down the wide, white marble steps, across the cobbles of the courtyard, shining and slippery with watery sleet, and through the lapis lazuli-lined Great Arch into Wizard Way.

Beetle's entourage created quite a stir among the Longest Night promenaders. Even the brightest window display could not compete with the impressive sight of a Wizard Tower Call-Out. The gold braid on his admiral's jacket glinting in the torchlight, Beetle walked proudly along Wizard Way at the head of a sea of blue flecked with green, and the crowds parted respectfully to let them through. It was a wonderful moment but all he could think about was – *where was Jenna?*

On the nineteenth floor of the Wizard Tower, Hildegarde was sitting at the huge Searching Glass, scanning the Castle. The three portly and somewhat self-important Search and Rescue Wizards were annoyed at not being asked to conduct the Search themselves, especially as Hildegarde was only a mere sub-Wizard, but as she had been sent by the ExtraOrdinary Wizard, there was nothing they could do but proffer patronizing advice and hover irritatingly close by.

Hildegarde studiously paid them no attention. She focused all her energy on the Searching Glass, bringing her slowly growing Magykal powers to guide it. But all the Glass did was insist on focusing on Doom Dump, which was where Hildegarde knew that Beetle had last seen Jenna. She wasn't very good at this, she thought gloomily. Jenna was sure to be far away by now.

❄ 17 ❄

WITCH PRINCESS

While Hildegarde was peering through the Searching Glass at the decrepit roof of Doom Dump, deep inside the house itself Linda was skulking in the shadows outside the scullery where Marissa had taken Jenna.

Linda needed a few minutes to get her spell ready for the upstart Marissa – a spell that would make Dorinda's elephant ears look like a party trick. And as she went over the spell in her mind for the last time, strengthening it, making it just that *little* bit nastier (more warts), Linda heard the same scream from the scullery that the Witch Mother had heard. Preoccupied with her spell, Linda was not thinking straight. She too assumed the scream came from Jenna, so she waited a few seconds more so that Marissa could finish whatever she was doing. But as the sound of choking came through the door, Linda began to get worried. It wouldn't do to have their Princess throttled just yet – not until they had thoroughly defeated the Wendron Witches. She threw open the scullery door and stopped in amazement. Linda was impressed. She couldn't have done better herself.

Jenna had Marissa in a headlock – and it was a good one too, Linda noticed. In her younger days Linda had been a big fan of headlocks, although now she let her spells do the work for her.

Marissa's face was an interesting shade of purple. "Lemme go!" she was gasping. *"Lemme . . . aaah . . . go!"*

Jenna looked up and saw Linda. Marissa was in no position to look up, but she knew from the pointy boots with the dragon spikes up the back who it was.

"Get her . . . off me," Marissa gasped in a hoarse whisper.

You touch her and you'll regret it, Jenna mouthed Silently at Linda.

Linda looked amused. She liked fights, and one between a witch and a Princess was pretty much top of her fight wish list. Unfortunately however, there was business to attend to and she needed to get on with it before the Witch Mother came tottering along to see what was happening.

"Well *done,*" Linda told Jenna. "Very impressive. You carry on like this and I might just change my mind about Princesses. Possibly. Now just keep holding her right there. *Perfect.*"

Jenna saw that Linda was eyeing Marissa like a snake working out where to strike. Something was about to happen and she could see it wasn't going to be good – particularly for Marissa.

Linda raised her hands up to her face and then pointed both index fingers at Marissa's head, squinting down them like a marksman. It reminded Jenna horribly of how the Hunter had once lined her up in the sights of his pistol.

"Keep her still," Linda instructed Jenna. "Hold her *right there.*"

Marissa whimpered.

Jenna did not like the turn events had taken. Suddenly she was Linda's accomplice. She knew that Linda was about to do something very bad to Marissa and she did not want to be part of it, but she dared not let go. If she did, Marissa would immediately turn on her – as would Linda. She was stuck.

Slowly Linda lowered her pointing fingers and, as she did so, two thin beams of brilliant blue light streamed from her eyes and rested on Marissa's face. Then the witch began to chant:

> *"Heart and brain*
> *Flame and pain*
> *Blood and bone*
> *Rattle and moan*
> *Lung and liver*
> *Shriek and shiver . . ."*

Marissa let out a terrified wail. She knew that this was the beginning of the dreaded Exit spell, the spell that takes away human form and replaces it with another – for ever. It was, like most of Linda's nastiest spells, Permanent.

"No!" yelled Marissa. "Please, *noooooooooo!*"

Linda's yellow incisors slipped over her bottom lip as they always did when she was concentrating. The Exit was long and complicated. It required a great concentration of energy, but it was already off to a good start. Linda was very pleased with the way the Princess was helping; it was so much easier with an assistant. Excited, Linda now moved into the main body of the spell, where all Human parts of Marissa were one by one reassigned to Toad. Her voice descended to a low monotone so that the words became blurred into one long, sing-song chant.

From Marissa's terror, Jenna was beginning to realise that if she kept Marissa in her headlock she would be party to something truly awful. She had to do something – but what?

Linda's menacing chant continued, the witch's voice rising ever higher. The gloom in the scullery deepened and the thin beams of light from Linda's blue-black eyes cut through the dark like needles, joining the witch with her victim.

"Princess Jenna. Please. Let me go," Marissa whispered desperately. "I'll do anything, anything you want. I *promise*."

Jenna didn't believe Marissa's promises. She had to get what she wanted while she still had the witch in her grasp – but how could she? She was Silenced. Very slightly she loosened the headlock. Marissa looked up, tears welling in her eyes.

"Princess Jenna. I'm sorry. I'm *really* sorry. Please help me. Please, oh *please*."

Jenna pointed to her mouth and Marissa understood. She muttered a few words and whispered, "OK. It's gone."

Linda's voice suddenly regained its normal pitch, the chant slowed down and once more the words became gruesomely clear:

> *"Pinprick bones and*
> *Poison glands,*
> *Warty skin*
> *And creeping hands . . ."*

Marissa screamed. She knew the end was coming very, very soon. "*Please* let me go," she gasped.

Jenna tested her voice. "Fix the feet thing," she hissed.

Marissa gabbled something under her breath and hissed, "It's gone, it's gone. Now, please, please, *please*."

Jenna cautiously tried a small step back, taking Marissa with her – *she was free*. She released the headlock.

Chaos ensued.

Marissa sprang up and Jenna raced off past Linda, heading for the door. Mouth open, Linda stopped mid-chant. Marissa hurled herself at Linda, biting, kicking and screaming, Linda fell backwards under the onslaught and hit her head with a *craaack* on the stone-flagged floor.

Jenna had just got out of the door and was running down the corridor when, through the gloom, she saw the large bulk of the Witch Mother teetering on her tall, spiked shoes, blocking the far end of it.

"Marissa, is that you?" the Witch Mother's suspicious voice called out of the dark. "What's going on down there?"

Trapped, Jenna hurtled back to the scullery, slammed the door and leaned against it, holding it shut. Marissa was sitting on Linda and, as far as Jenna could make out, trying to strangle her. At Jenna's return she looked up in surprise.

"She's coming," gasped Jenna.

Marissa stared at her, uncomprehending. "Who's coming?"

"*Her*. The Witch Mother."

Marissa went pale. She had assumed that when Linda had tried to Exit her, she had been acting on the Witch Mother's instructions. She leaped up from Linda – who gave a small moan, but did not move – and pointed at the door that Jenna was leaning against. Jenna squared up for a fight, but a fight was the last thing on Marissa's mind. "Lock, Stop and Bar!" she shouted. A small but definite *click* came from the door.

"It won't last long," said Marissa, "not against *her*. We've got to get out of here." She headed for the only window in the dingy scullery, which was set high above a table heaped with a pile of black cloth. Marissa leaped up on to the table and pushed the window open. "It's the only way out. There's a bit of a drop but it's a soft landing. Here, put this on." Marissa picked up the pile of black cloth and threw it at Jenna, who ducked. It landed on the floor beside her.

Marissa looked annoyed. "Do you want to get out or not?" she demanded.

"Of course I do."

"Well, those are your witch robes. You've got to put them on."

"Why?"

Marissa sighed impatiently. "Because you won't get out if you don't. The window's Barred to all Cowan."

"*Cowan?*"

"Yeah. Cowan. Non-witches. Like *you*, dumbo."

The door handle rattled. "Marissa?" came the Witch Mother's voice. "What's going on in there?"

"Nothing, Witch Mother. It's fine. Nearly done," Marissa called out. "*Put them on – quick,*" she hissed to Jenna. "There's enough witch stuff in them to fool a stupid window. *Hurry!*"

Jenna picked up the robes as though she were picking up a shovel of cat poo.

The door handle rattled again, louder. "Marissa, why is the door Locked?" The Witch Mother sounded suspicious.

"She got out, Witch Mother. But it's OK. I've got her. Nearly done!" Marissa trilled out cheerfully. To Jenna she whispered, "*Are you going to put them on or not? Because I'm going right now.*"

"All right, *all right*," whispered Jenna. They were only clothes, she reasoned. Wearing witches' robes didn't actually mean anything. She threw the musty black cloak over her head, pulled it down over her own red robe and quickly did up the buttons.

"Suits you," said Marissa with a grin. "Come on," she beckoned Jenna up on to the table, and Jenna scrambled up. Marissa opened the window and the cold, sleety night air blew in. "Put your arm out," she said.

Jenna went to put her arm out but her hand came up against something solid, which felt like congealed slime. "Yuck!" she gasped, and snatched it back.

The Witch Mother had surprisingly good hearing. *"Marissa?"* came her voice suspiciously through the door. "Is there someone else in there with you?"

"Just the Princess, Witch Mother," Marissa called out and then whispered to Jenna, *"Rats – the robes aren't enough."*

Jenna looked down at her black witch cloak, which enveloped her like the night and made her feel very peculiar. It seemed quite enough to her. "What do you mean?" she asked.

"If you want to get out, I'm going to have to do something else."

Jenna didn't like the sound of that. "Like what exactly?"

The door handle rattled once again. "Marissa, I can hear voices," the Witch Mother shouted. "What are you doing?"

"Nothing, Witch Mother! She's got her robes on. We'll be out soon," Marissa called. And then to Jenna, *"Like I'm going to have to make you a witch."*

"No *way!*"

"Marissa!" The door handle rattled angrily. "I heard the Princess. She's not Silent any more. What's going on in there?"

"Nothing. Honestly. It was *me*, Witch Mother."

"Don't lie to me, Marissa. *Let me in!*" The Witch Mother rattled the door handle so violently that it fell off, bounced its way across the floor and hit Linda on the head.

"Aargh . . ." Linda groaned.

"What was *that*? If you don't let me in *right now*, I shall Smash the door and then there'll be *trouble*," the Witch Mother yelled.

Marissa looked panic-stricken. "I'm going," she told Jenna. "You can stay here and good luck to you. Don't say I didn't try. See ya!" And with that she pulled herself up to the window. She was halfway through when a loud *craaaaaack* came from the door and a long split ran through the wood from top to bottom.

"Marissa. Wait!" yelled Jenna. "Do the something else — *whatever* it is."

Marissa's head appeared at the window. "OK. This is a bit yucky," she said, "but it's got to be done." She poked her head back through the window and kissed Jenna. Jenna leaped back in surprise. "Told you it was yucky." Marissa grinned. "But you're a witch now. You don't belong to the Coven yet, you'd have to kiss them *all* for that."

"No *thanks*." Jenna grimaced.

The sound of splintering wood heralded the metal tip of the Witch Mother's boot appearing through the door.

"Time to go, Witch," said Marissa.

Jenna scrambled through the window and leaped into the dark. She landed on an old compost heap.

"Run!" hissed Marissa.

With brambles tearing at them, Jenna and Marissa raced through the overgrown garden, scrambled over the wall and dropped down into the back alley. Behind them the Witch Mother – her large bulk stuck in the tiny window – screamed in fury and Sent curses after them. The curses skittered around the garden, bounced off the walls and ReBounded on the Witch Mother.

The two witches tore up the dark back alley, heading towards the welcoming lights of Gothyk Grotto. As Jenna slammed the door shut behind her to the accompaniment of the door monster, she grinned. Suddenly Gothyk Grotto looked so *normal*.

Marcus approached, unfazed by the sight of two witches in the shop. It was not unusual for people to dress up on the Longest Night festivities – he had just sold all their remaining skeleton suits to the staff of Wizard Sandwiches.

"Need any help?" he asked.

Jenna threw back her voluminous witch's hood.

Marcus gasped. "Princess Jenna, you're *safe*. Your friend, wotsisname . . . Earwig – he was looking for you."

The mention of earwigs made Jenna feel sick. "Beetle! Is he here?"

"Nah. He'll be pleased you're safe; he was going nuts. But there's someone here from the Wizard Tower for you." Marcus winked at Jenna. "Good luck."

The door monster roared again and Hildegarde rushed in. She skidded to a halt and stared at Jenna and Marissa.

"It *is* you!" she gasped. The Searching Glass had told her that the fleeing witch was Jenna, but she had not believed it. Catching her breath, Hildegarde said, "Princess Jenna, you do know those robes are the real thing, don't you?"

"Of course I do," said Jenna stonily.

Hildegarde looked disapprovingly at Jenna and the company she was keeping.

"Madam Marcia has asked me to take you straight to the Palace at once. She will be meeting you there. Witches' robes are not appropriate attire and I suggest you take them off right away."

Hildegarde's attitude annoyed Jenna. "No," she said. "These robes are mine and I'm wearing them."

Marissa grinned. She could get to like Jenna.

❈ 18 ❈

THE EMISSARY

The tide of Ordinary Wizards flowed to a halt outside a small, dimly lit shopfront about a hundred yards down Wizard Way, on the right-hand side. A sign above the shop announced it to be NUMBER THIRTEEN, MAGYKAL MANUSCRIPTORIUM AND SPELL CHECKERS INCORPORATED.

Beetle stepped out of the protective pool of Wizards and looked up at his old, once loved, workplace. The windows were misted with the breath of twenty-one scribes toiling away inside, and through the strip of cloudy glass above the teetering piles of books and manuscripts he could see a yellow glow of light. But it was a gloomy window for the Longest Night – no wasteful candle displays were allowed under Jillie Djinn's regime.

Beetle felt sorry for the scribes working while Wizard Way was abuzz, but he was pleased they were still there. He had been worried that they might have left early that night, as they always had done in his time as Front Office Clerk and General Dogsbody. But Jillie Djinn's grip on the Manuscriptorium had tightened since Beetle left. She did not believe in leaving early – especially to have fun.

Two Wizards, sisters Pascalle and Thomasinn Thyme, stepped forward. "We are happy to be your escort, Mr Beetle, if you need one."

Beetle thought he could do with all the help he could get. "Thank you," he said. He took a deep breath and pushed open the door. There was a loud *ping* and the door counter clicked over to the next number. The Front Office was a shambles and it made Beetle feel sad. The large desk, which he had kept so neat and organised, was a disgusting mess of papers and half-eaten sweets, the floor was unswept and sticky underfoot and there was a distinct smell of something small and furry having died under one of the many untended stacks of papers.

Beetle's gaze travelled around the dingy room, taking in the flimsy half-wood, half-glass panel that separated the Front Office from the Manuscriptorium itself, the ancient greyish paint peeling off the walls and the festoons of cobwebs looping down from the ceiling. He wondered if perhaps he hadn't noticed how run down it all was when he had worked there. But one thing he knew he would have noticed was the state of the small, reinforced door behind the desk that led to the Wild Book and Charm Store – it was nailed shut, with two thick planks across it. Beetle wondered how anyone managed to get in to clean. He presumed they didn't. The state of the Wild Book and Charm Store did not bear thinking about.

Suddenly the half-glass door that led into the Manuscriptorium flew open and the Chief Hermetic Scribe bustled out. She carried a large handkerchief on which, Beetle noticed, in addition to the letters CHS, her collection of qualifications were carefully embroidered around the edge in different colours. So that's what Jillie Djinn did in her long evenings alone in her rooms at the top of the Manuscriptorium, thought Beetle.

Jillie Djinn blinked in surprise at the sight of Beetle flanked by two Wizards.

"Yes?" she snapped.

Beetle had been clutching the Emissary scroll tightly, waiting for this very moment. Quickly he twice-tapped the scroll and held it at arm's length. With a faint buzz a flicker of purple ran around the edges of the scroll, a waft of heat hit him, and suddenly he was holding the full-size version. It felt surprisingly thin and delicate (because in Magyk matter can neither be created nor destroyed), but Beetle thought that only added to its air of mystery and importance. He caught Jillie Djinn's gaze and saw she was, for a moment, impressed – then her default expression of mild irritation quickly reasserted itself.

Beetle was determined to be scrupulously polite. "Good evening, Chief Hermetic Scribe," he said. "I am here as Emissary of the ExtraOrdinary Wizard."

"So I see," Jillie Djinn replied coolly. "And what does she want *now*?"

Getting into his official role with some relish, Beetle began to read from the words busily arranging themselves on the scroll.

"Please be informed that a Castle Call-Out is in progress. The presence of all Indentured Scribes is Called for with immediate effect," he proclaimed.

Jillie Djinn went straight to major annoyance.

"You can tell the ExtraOrdinary Wizard that important work is in progress here," she snapped. "Manuscriptorium scribes will not drop everything and rush off on the whim of the ExtraOrdinary Wizard." From one of her many pockets she took out a small timepiece and squinted at it. "They will be available when the Manuscriptorium closes in two hours, forty-two minutes and thirty-five seconds precisely."

Marcia Overstrand's Emissary was having none of it. He tried – not entirely successfully – to suppress a smile as the exact words he needed scrolled up before him. Savouring the moment, Beetle slowly read them out.

"Please be advised that Call-Out Conditions state that Manuscriptorium scribes will be available as and when required. Failure to provide them *on demand* will invalidate your Terms of Office."

Jillie Djinn sneezed into her overqualified handkerchief. "*Why* are they required?" she demanded in an indignant splutter.

The words on the Emissary scroll continued to roll up, all gaining Beetle's approval – he could not have put it better himself.

"Please be informed that I am not at liberty to divulge that information. Any questions or complaints relating to this matter may be addressed in writing to the Wizard Tower once the Call-Out is stood down. You will receive an answer within seven days. I now require you to make your scribes available *immediately*. So be it."

Jillie Djinn spun on her heel and flounced off into the Manuscriptorium, slamming the flimsy door behind her. Beetle glanced at his two escorts, who looked taken aback.

"We'd heard she was difficult," whispered Pascalle.

"But we didn't know she was *that* bad," finished Thomasinn.

"She's got worse," said Beetle. "Much worse."

From behind the partition Beetle heard a sudden burst of excited chatter, followed by the thudding of twenty-one pairs of boots as the scribes jumped down from their desks.

Above the hubbub came Jillie Djinn's squawk, "No, Mr Fox, this is *not* time off. You will all stay two hours, thirty-nine minutes and seven seconds later tomorrow."

The door to the front office burst open and Foxy emerged at the head of the scribes. At the sight of Beetle he looked startled.

"Hey, Beet. I'd make yourself scarce. We're on a Call-Out practice and you-know-who is in a foul temper."

"I know." Beetle grinned, waving his scroll at Foxy. "I've just told her."

Foxy gave a low whistle. He grinned too. "Wish I'd thought of that. So we've got the Longest Night off after all. Thanks, Beet!"

"No, Foxy. This is for real. You *are* on a Call-Out."

"And you're running it? I'm impressed."

"I'm just the messenger, Foxo." With a flourish, Beetle twice-tapped the end of the scroll and popped the Reduced – and now very cold – version safely into his pocket. He raised his voice. "Outside please, everyone, and join the Ordinaries. We are to make our way to the Palace Gate, where we will assemble and await further instructions. Once outside, please be quiet – this is a silent Call-Out. Fast as you can, please – ouch! Partridge, mind where you're putting your fat feet, will you?"

"Nice to see you too, Beetle." Partridge grinned as he and Romilly Badger squeezed by in the crush of eager scribes. The excitement of the Call-Out was infectious, and no one seemed to mind that they would have to work late the next day. Beetle counted the scribes out until it was just himself and Foxy left in the Front Office.

"D'you want Miss Djinn too?" asked Foxy warily. "I can go and get her if you do."

"Thanks, Foxo, but Marcia said she'd rather not."

"Yeah. Quite understand," said Foxy. "Look, I gotta go and Lock the Charm cupboard. Part of the job. Not that I got any Charms to Lock up, but it doesn't look good if I don't."

Beetle glanced outside. The crowd of Wizards, Apprentices and scribes were waiting, looking expectantly at him. "Be quick," he said.

Foxy nodded and scooted off. A minute later, Foxy was back, beckoning frantically to Beetle.

"Beetle – he's here. *Again*."

"Who's here?"

"Who do you think? Daniel Dingbat Hunter."

"Merrin?"

"Yeah. Whateverhecallshimself. *Him*."

Beetle asked his two Wizard escorts to take the waiting Wizards and scribes down to the Palace. "I'll catch up with you as soon as I can," he promised. "OK," he said to Foxy. "Quick. Show me."

Very quietly Foxy pushed open the door into the Manuscriptorium and pointed inside. Beetle peered in. All he could see were the ranks of tall, empty desks, each under its own pool of dim yellow light. Of Merrin there was no sign – or, indeed, of Jillie Djinn.

"I can't see him," Beetle whispered.

Foxy looked over Beetle's shoulder. "Bother. I did see him. I *know* I did. He's probably in the Hermetic Chamber."

Beetle was indignant. "He shouldn't go in *there*."

"Try telling Miss Djinn that – he goes wherever he wants,"

said Foxy gloomily as he quietly closed the door. "He's up to something, Beet."

Beetle nodded. That was most certainly true.

"Little toad," said Foxy.

The little toad was indeed up to something. He was, as Foxy had suspected, in the Hermetic Chamber.

Merrin was waiting – and he didn't like it. To pass the time he was eating a long liquorice bootlace pulled from the secret siege drawer of the large round table in the middle of the Hermetic Chamber. The drawer was now crammed with a stash of sticky liquorice, while its rightful contents languished in the rubbish bin in the yard.

Merrin was pleased with his afternoon's work. He was getting good at this Darke stuff, he thought. He'd used a Darke Screen and had walked out of the Palace right under Sarah Heap's nose, which had been fun, especially when he had deliberately trodden on her foot. And now, because Jillie Djinn had been snappy with him, he'd fixed that too. She wouldn't ever do that again, thought Merrin, as he smirked into the ancient Glass propped up against the wall.

Merrin peered into the darkness of the Glass and behind him he saw the reflection of the Chief Hermetic Scribe, sitting hunched over the table. He tried out a few more expressions in the Glass, tapped his feet impatiently and wandered over to the Abacus, where he began clicking the beads endlessly back and forth in such an irritating way that anyone else but the cowed Jillie Djinn would have yelled at him to *stop it right now*!

Merrin sighed loudly. He was bored and there were not

even any scribes to annoy. He toyed with the idea of going down to the basement and smashing a few things, but the Conservation Scribe scared him. He wished the Things would *hurry up*. What was taking them so long? All they had to do was bring the stupid Darke Domaine with them — what was so difficult about that? He kicked the wall impatiently. *Stupid Things.*

Leaving Jillie Djinn staring into space, Merrin wandered out along the seven-cornered passageway and surveyed the dark and empty Manuscriptorium. It was oddly spooky without the scribes. He wouldn't be spending any time in this dump, he thought, but it would suit the Things nicely. It would keep them out of his way too, and he could hang out wherever he wanted. And do whatever he liked. So there.

❇ 19 ❇

THE SAFECHAMBER

As Beetle resumed his place at head of the Call-Out, the person who should have been leading it was immured in the cellar of a house on Snake Slipway. Not far above him, a loud knocking on the front door by a breathless Wizard went unheard.

Septimus was listening to Marcellus Pye discussing the dangers of, and defences against, the Darke. Time was ticking on. Very slowly. So far there had been at least an hour's worth of dangers, if not more.

Alchemist and Apprentice were sitting inside a tunnel-like, windowless chamber. The atmosphere was oppressive; the air was fuggy with candle-wax fumes, and a faint taint of lingering Darke made Septimus edgy. Unlike Marcellus Pye, who sat opposite him in a comfortable tall-backed chair, Septimus was perched uncomfortably on a bumpy stone bench. Between them was a small table, thick with candle grease, on which yet another burning candle added its contribution.

Marcellus, however, looked at ease. He was in his secret SafeChamber with his Apprentice, instructing him in the defence of the Darke, and that — as far as he was concerned — was how things should be. A SafeChamber was something every self-respecting alchemist always possessed, but never admitted to. In what Marcellus now called "his first life" as an alchemist, five hundred years in the past, he had installed his SafeChamber between two adjoining rooms in the cellar of his house. It occupied the space so cleverly that none of the subsequent inhabitants had ever noticed the few feet lost from each room.

Marcellus had constructed the chamber himself – he had had no other choice. In the days of the Castle alchemists, one of the drawbacks of the profession had been that it was impossible to get a builder. Once a builder knew that a job was for an alchemist, he would suddenly become very busy, or fall off a ladder and "break a leg", or have to go away to a distant relative's sickbed. Whatever the excuse, he would certainly never be seen again. The reason for this was that the perils of working for an alchemist had become legend among Castle builders, passed down from Master to Apprentice: "Never work for an alchemist, lad," (or lass, but usually lad). "As soon as the job's done, you'll surely be found floating face down in the Moat to keep the secrets of what you've just built. However much gold they offer you, it just isn't worth it. Believe me." Although this wasn't true for all alchemists, it has to be said that there was some basis for this belief.

Marcellus Pye possessed many talents but building was not one of them. The outside of the chamber was passable because Marcellus had covered his rough brickwork by putting up great sheets of wooden panelling in both the affected rooms. However, the inside of the chamber was a mess. Marcellus had not realised how hard it was to build walls that went up straight – and stayed that way – so the walls grew closer and closer together, almost meeting at the top. Once he had installed the false wall behind which he kept his most arcane treasures, the SafeChamber was no more than a claustrophobic corridor.

Septimus was almost lulled into a trance by the flickering of a multitude of candles perched in the various nooks and crannies provided by Marcellus Pye's unusual approach to bricklaying. The chamber was streaked black with the soot from their flames, and thick rivulets of wax ran down the walls, glistening in the yellow light. The only thing that kept Septimus from drifting off was the way the bricks in the wall pressed their sharp corners into him as though they were jabbing at him with angry fingers. Every now and then he would wriggle uncomfortably and lean against another, slightly different, pointy bit.

"Stop fidgeting and pay attention, Apprentice," said Marcellus Pye sternly from his comfortable chair. "Your life may – indeed, it most probably *will* – depend upon it."

Septimus suppressed a sigh.

At last Marcellus got down to the reason that Septimus had come to see him. "You will, I presume, be attempting to retrieve Alther Mella's ghost from the Darke Halls tonight?"

"Yes. Yes . . . I'm going to the Darke Halls. At midnight." As he said the words Septimus felt a thrill of excitement mixed with fear. Suddenly it all began to feel very real.

"And you will seek to enter the Darke Halls through the Dungeon Number One Portal?"

"Yes, I will. Isn't that the only place where you can get in?" Septimus asked.

Marcellus Pye looked quizzical. "Not at all," he said. "But it *is* the only place you can get to in time for midnight tonight. There are other Portals, some of them extremely effective for matters like this, where you might find your timing is less important. However, none are in the Castle."

Leaving Septimus to wonder why Marcia hadn't told him about these other, possibly more effective Portals, Marcellus took the candle from the table and got up from his chair with a small groan. Looking like the old man he really was, the alchemist shuffled along the length of the chamber to the false wall at the end, which was, Septimus noticed, panelled like the room outside. Marcellus pressed his hand on to one of the panels, slid it to one side and reached into the space behind. Septimus heard the clink of glass on glass, the rattle of small dried things in a metal box, the thud of a book, then a relieved, "Got it!"

As Marcellus shuffled back, Septimus very nearly leaped to his feet and ran for it. The light from his candle threw dramatic shadows on to the alchemist's face, and as he advanced towards Septimus, hand outstretched, Marcellus looked exactly as he had when Septimus had first seen him – a five-hundred-year-old man grabbing at him, pulling him through a glass into a secret world below the Castle. It was not a good moment. It unsettled Septimus more than anything else had in the tense build-up to his Darke Week.

Unaware of the effect he had had, Marcellus Pye resumed his place next to Septimus. He looked pleased. "Apprentice, I have in my hand something that will give you safe passage through the Portal and into the Darke."

He unclasped his fist to reveal a small, dented tinderbox. Septimus felt horribly disappointed. What was Marcellus thinking? He owned his own tinderbox and it was a lot better looking than that one. And it probably worked better too

– Septimus prided himself on being able to get a fire going in fifteen seconds. He and Beetle had had a fire-start competition not long ago and he had won best of five.

Marcellus handed him the tinderbox. "Open it," he said.

Septimus did as he was asked. Inside were the usual components of a tinderbox – a small, pronged wheel, a flint, some thin strips of cloth infused with the Castle's well-known, highly flammable wax and some dried moss.

Septimus had had enough. Marcia's parting shot came back to him: "Alchemie stuff is nothing but smoke and mirrors, Septimus. All talk and no do. None of their stuff ever did work. It was complete *rubbish*."

Septimus got to his feet. Marcia was right – as usual. He *had* to get out of the oppressive little chamber dripping with candle wax, fusty with Darke secrets. He longed to be part of the everyday Castle world once more. He wanted to run through the streets, breathe the cold fresh air, see the myriad of Castle lights twinkling in the windows, watch people as they promenaded back and forth admiring – or not – their neighbours' lights. But more than anything, he wanted to be with people who weren't fussy five-hundred-year-old alchemists who thought you were still their Apprentice.

Marcellus had other ideas. "Sit down, Apprentice," he said sternly. "This is important."

Septimus remained standing. "No, it's not. It's an old tinderbox. That's all. You can't fool me."

Marcellus Pye smiled. "It seems I already have, Apprentice. For this is not what it appears to be."

Septimus sighed. Nothing ever was where Marcellus was concerned.

"Patience, Apprentice, patience. I know this chamber is cramped, I know it is stuffy and foul, but what I am going to show you can only be revealed here. It will not survive outside the Darke for long." Marcellus looked up at Septimus, his expression serious. "Septimus, I cannot – I *will* not – let you venture defenceless into the Darke. Sit down. Please."

With another sigh, Septimus reluctantly sat down.

"You see," said Marcellus, picking up the tinderbox, "like all Darke Disguises, this is not what it appears to be. As you too must be when you go into the Darke."

"I *know*. Masks, MindScreens, Bluffs – I've done all that stuff with Marcia."

"Well, of course you have." Marcellus sounded conciliatory. "That is no more than I would expect. But there are some things to which even the ExtraOrdinary Wizard does not have access. That's what we alchemists are – or *were* – for. We kept in touch with the Darke. We went where Wizards did not dare."

This was no more than Septimus had suspected, given Marcia's warnings about alchemists, but this was the first time he had heard Marcellus admit to it.

Marcellus continued. "As an Alchemie Apprentice it is only right that you too should know how to work with the Darke. It is all very well the Wizards sticking their heads in the sand like one of those birds . . . oh, what are they called?"

Septimus was not sure. "Chickens?" he suggested.

Marcellus chuckled. "Chickens will do nicely. Like chickens, they peck at what is in front of them but they do not understand what it truly is. Sometimes they call it something else, like Other, or Reverse, but that does not change anything. Darke remains Darke, whatever you call it. So now, Apprentice, you must decide whether to take your first step into the Darke the Alchemie way – and see what is really inside the tinderbox – or the Wizard way, and see no more than an old flint and some dried-up moss. Which is it to be?"

Septimus thought of Marcia and he knew what she would say. He thought of Beetle and he really wasn't sure what he would say. And then he thought of Alther. Suddenly Septimus had the oddest feeling that Alther was sitting right next to him. He turned and thought he saw a momentary flash of purple, a suggestion of a white beard. Then it was gone, leaving Septimus with the certain knowledge that he would never see Alther again unless he said, "The Alchemie way."

Marcellus smiled with relief. He had been extremely worried at the thought of Septimus venturing into the Darke in the customary *just think good thoughts and it will be all right* Wizard style. The old Alchemist was also just a little triumphant. He had, for the moment, won his Apprentice back.

"Very wise," Marcellus said. "Now you stop being a chicken and embark on your first conscious step into the Darke. Septimus, you understand that this is only to be taken if you truly wish to do it. Do you?"

Septimus nodded.

"Then say it."

"Say what?"

"That you want to do this. Say 'I do'."

Septimus hesitated. Marcellus waited.

There was a long pause. Septimus had the heady sensation of being about to step over a threshold that even Marcia had not crossed.

"I do," he said.

As though someone had thrown a switch, all the candles in the chamber went out. The temperature plummeted.

Septimus gasped.

"We must not be afraid of the Darke." Marcellus's voice came through the fumes of extinguished candles. Septimus heard the Alchemist click his fingers. At once the candles burst back into flame, but the chamber remained cold – so cold that Septimus could see clouds of breath misting the air.

Marcellus now had Septimus's full attention. "Apprentice, your first step is to choose a name to use when you are dealing with the Darke. Wizards – if they venture this far – usually reverse their whole name, but they do not realise how dangerous this is. You will never be free of the Darke if you do this, you can always be Found. We Alchemists know better. We take the last three letters from our name and reverse them. I suggest you do that."

"S – U – M," Septimus said.

Marcellus smiled. "*Sum*: I am. Very good. If you have to use your name, this is what you say. It is close enough to pass for the truth, but not true enough for you to be Found. Now we get to the reason we are here: Apprentice, do you wish to take on the Darke Disguise?"

Septimus nodded.

"Say it," prompted Marcellus. "I cannot take you through these steps on a mere nod of the head. I must be clear that you wish to proceed."

"I do," said Septimus, his voice trembling a little.

"Very well. Apprentice, place the tinderbox over your heart, like so . . ."

Septimus held the tinderbox over his heart. It sent a stab of cold right through him like a dagger of ice.

Marcellus continued his instructions. "Keep your hand stone still – no more fidgeting. Good. Now repeat these words after me."

And so the old Alchemist began, using Reverse words that Septimus had never heard before, words that he suspected Marcia too had never heard. They chilled him more than the icy press of the tinderbox, more than the freezing air inside the chamber. By the time Septimus had spoken the last words – "I dnammoc siht ot eb: draug sum" – his teeth were chattering with cold.

"Open the box," said Marcellus.

At first Septimus thought the tinderbox was empty. All he could see was the dull grey metal of the insides, and yet when he looked closely he was not sure that it *was* metal that he was seeing. It looked misty, as though something was there and yet not there. Tentatively, as though something might bite, he put his finger into the box. His finger told him that there was indeed something in the tinderbox – something soft and delicate.

"You have found it." Marcellus looked pleased. "Or rather, it has found you. That is good. Now take it out and put it on."

Feeling as though he was playing a "let's pretend" game with Barney Pot, Septimus pinched his thumb and forefinger together and got hold of something elusive, barely there. It felt like pulling spider's webs from a jar – spider's webs that the spider in the jar did not want him to have. Septimus pulled hard, and as he raised his hand high he saw that he was drawing a long stream of gossamer-thin fabric from the tinderbox.

Marcellus Pye's dark eyes shone with excitement in the candlelight. "You've done it . . ." he whispered, sounding very relieved. "You've found the Darke Disguise."

The Darke Disguise reminded Septimus of one of Sarah Heap's floaty scarves, although Sarah favoured brighter colours. This was an indeterminate colour that Sarah would have condemned as dull; it was also much larger than any scarf that Sarah possessed. Septimus kept on pulling it from the tinderbox, and the Darke Disguise kept on coming, falling in fine, weightless folds across his lap, tumbling down to the floor. Septimus began to wonder how long it actually was.

Marcellus answered his unspoken question. "Its length will be right for whatever you need. Now, Apprentice, a word of advice. I suggest you pull a thread from it now – it is easily done – and keep it with you. It will be as strong as a rope and, in my experience, it can be useful to have something a little Darke that comes easily to hand when one is venturing into these realms."

Not for the first time, Septimus wondered what secrets Marcellus had in his past. But what he said made sense. He pulled a thread from the loose weave and began to wind it into a neat coil.

Marcellus looked on approvingly. "Confidently done. Remember, the Darke power of this exposed thread will begin to evaporate after about twenty-four hours. Do not keep it in your Apprentice belt; you do not want to upset any Charms or Spells. A pocket will do."

Septimus nodded – he'd worked *that* out for himself.

"Now I suggest you return the Darke Disguise to the tinderbox," said Marcellus. "Any time spent out, even in here, dilutes its power a fraction."

As instructed by Marcellus, Septimus spoke the words "I

knaht uoy, esaelp eriter," and the Darke Disguise evaporated into the tinderbox like a wisp of smoke.

Marcellus regarded his Apprentice with satisfaction. "Very good indeed. It obeys you well. Just before you enter the Darke Portal, open the box and instruct it so – 'ehtolc Sum.' Now that it Knows you it will stick to you like a second skin. Take care not to wear it away from the Darke, as it will soon dissolve into nothing, which is why I have to show it to you in this chamber. Use it well."

Septimus nodded. "I will," he said.

"And one last thing."

"Yes?"

"The Darke Disguise may corrupt Magyk. Do *not* take this box into the Wizard Tower."

Septimus was dismayed. "But ... what about my Dragon Ring?"

"You are wearing the ring. It is part of you, and the Darke Disguise will protect all parts of you." Marcellus smiled. "Do not worry, it will shine as brightly as ever for you, Apprentice, although others will not see it."

Septimus looked at his ring, which was glowing in the gloom of the SafeChamber. He was relieved. He would feel lost without it.

Marcellus issued his last instruction. "When you return with Alther – as I know you will – you must bring the Disguise straight back here to store it. Understand?"

"I understand," said Septimus. "Thank you. Thank you very much, Marcellus." Carefully he put the tinderbox in the deepest, most secret pocket of his Apprentice tunic. "I'll see you later. At the party," he said.

"Party?" asked Marcellus.

"You know – my birthday party. With Jenna. At the Palace."

"Ah, yes. Of course, Apprentice. I forget."

Septimus rose to go. This time Marcellus Pye did not stop him.

❄ 20 ❄
CORDON

Night had fallen while Septimus had been marooned in the SafeChamber. He stepped out into the cold, crisp air and headed up Snake Slipway, pulling his cloak tight and walking fast to try and rid himself of the chill that seemed to have settled into his bones. At the end of the slipway he took the Rat Run, a well-trodden alley that led straight to the middle of Wizard Way.

The Longest Night was one of Septimus's favourite times. As a boy soldier in the Young Army, Septimus had looked forward to it; even though he had had no idea at the time that the day was also his birthday, it had felt special. He had loved seeing all the candles placed in every window in the Castle. The practice had been frowned on by the Supreme Custodian and his cronies, but it was too ancient a custom to dislodge and it had become a small symbol of resistance. That particular meaning had been lost on the young Septimus – all he knew was that seeing the lights made him feel happy.

But now the Longest Night had a much greater significance for him: it was a symbol of hope and renewal – the anniversary of his rescue from the Young Army by Marcia. Despite the task ahead of him that night, Septimus strode along the Rat Run with the familiar feeling of excitement and happiness running through him. A few cold specks of sleet settled briefly on his upturned face as he smiled at the ancient houses, all with a single, brave candle burning in each window. He breathed in the fresh air, ridding himself of the cloying fumes of the old Alchemist's house, and pushed away his feelings of guilt about Marcia and what he knew she would see as disloyalty with Marcellus.

Septimus was determined to do what *he* felt was right. It was his fourteenth birthday – a day recognised throughout the Castle as the beginning of independence. He was no longer a child. He was his own person and he made his own decisions.

A few streets away, the Drapers Yard Clock began to chime. Septimus counted six and picked up speed. He was late. He'd promised to be with his mother by six.

As Septimus hurried into Wizard Way he found that things were not quite as he had expected. The Way was crowded – as it usually was on the Longest Night – but instead of people wandering along, chatting and pointing out some of the more interesting windows (for the last few years there had been a serious outbreak of competitive tableaux in many of the shop fronts) everyone was standing quite still, gazing towards the Palace. That was in itself strange enough, but what really worried Septimus was the anxious silence.

"I'm surprised you're not down there too, Apprentice," a voice somewhere near his elbow said. At the word "Apprentice" several heads turned towards Septimus.

He looked around to find Maizie Smalls, who lived up – or was it down? – to her name, standing beside him. She looked worried. "You know, at the Cordon. Around the Palace," she elaborated.

"Cordon? Around the *Palace*?"

"Yes. I do hope my cat's all right. Binkie hates changes to his routine. He's an old cat now, you see, and – *oh* . . ."

But Septimus had gone. He was off, heading for the Palace. He made his way through the crowd faster than he'd expected. As soon as anyone saw that it was the ExtraOrdinary Apprentice pushing past or treading on their toes, they stepped back respectfully – apart from Gringe, who stopped him and growled, "Better get a move on, lad. Bit late, aren't you?" But he let him go when Lucy protested, "Leave it, Dad. Can't you see he's in a hurry?"

Septimus looked gratefully at Lucy and pushed on, catching as he went a glance of Nicko talking to Lucy's brother, Rupert. But there was no time to lose saying hello to Nicko; Septimus was desperate to get to the Palace.

By the time he had reached the Palace Gate, Septimus knew that Gringe was right; he was indeed late – too late. Stretching across the Palace lawns, a few yards inside the Gate, was the Cordon: a long line of Wizards, Apprentices and scribes, encircling the Palace, each holding a piece of purple cord that linked them to the next person. From the stillness and the concentration of those forming it, Septimus knew the Cordon was complete. Septimus had never seen a Cordon for real, although the Wizard Tower occasionally held practices in the courtyard and some Apprentices had once – to Gringe's disgust – placed a Cordon around the North Gate gatehouse as a joke. Septimus knew that, ideally, all in the Cordon would have been holding hands, like children in the popular Castle game "Here We Go Around the Wizard Tower", but in order to encircle the longest building in the Castle, each person forming the Cordon needed to use a piece of Magykal Conducting Cord, a length of which all Wizards, Apprentices and indentured scribes always carried with them.

Septimus stood at the front of the subdued crowd watching the Cordon, trying to work out what was going on. Being on the outside of something Magykal was an unfamiliar feeling for Septimus – and he didn't like it at all. But he soon began to realise that he had had a narrow escape. If he had been a few minutes earlier, Marcia would have expected him to take part, and with the Darke Disguise deep in his secret pocket, he would not have dared. The relief of not having to explain that to Marcia almost made up for missing out on a historic piece of Magyk – *almost*.

Septimus could not resist a closer look. He slipped through the Palace Gate and walked slowly across the grass. As he drew nearer he saw four figures inside the Cordon making their way rapidly towards the Palace doors. One was, of course, Marcia. The second, Septimus realised with a stab of something that could have been jealousy, was *Beetle*. Beetle was taking the place that should have been his. And there were two others following behind. One he was pretty sure was Hildegarde and the other was a witch. *What was going on?*

Septimus had stopped at what he thought would be a safe distance from the Cordon. He realised he must have muttered something, because the sick-bay Apprentice, Rose, who was part of the Cordon, turned around. She smiled at Septimus and mouthed, "Shh. It's silent."

"Why?" Septimus mouthed. Rose shrugged and made an *I have no idea* face.

Septimus felt beside himself with frustration. A thousand questions ran through his mind. What had happened – had

Silas done something stupid? Where was Jenna? Where were his parents? Were they safe? And then an awful thought occurred to him: Was this something to do with the whatever-it-was in the attic that Jenna had asked him to look at the previous evening? *Was this all his fault?*

Septimus set off along the outside of the Cordon. The air was cold, and a sparse fall of sleety snow was drifting down, landing on the winter cloaks of the Wizards and scribes, settling briefly on woolly hats and bare heads alike before melting away. Already the hands holding on to the cords (gloves were not permitted, as they broke the Connection) looked red and cold, and some of the younger Apprentices, who in their excitement had rushed out without their cloaks, were shivering.

Keeping watch on the Palace as he went, Septimus tried to think what it was that Jenna had said the night before. *There's something bad up there* – that was all he could remember her saying. But he knew that he hadn't given her a chance to tell him anything else. He scanned the Palace for clues to what was happening. It looked the same as ever, solid and peaceful in the winter's night – but then something caught his eye. A candle in an upstairs window went out. Septimus stopped behind a line of elderly Wizards wearing an assortment of colourful scarves and woolly hats and stared up at the Palace windows. Another candle died, and then another. One by one, like dominoes slowly falling, *click … click … click*, the candles were being snuffed out. Septimus knew that Jenna had been right – something bad *was* up there.

"You wouldn't help Jenna because you were so uptight about keeping your stupid head clear for your Darke Week, and *now* look what's happened," he told himself angrily. "And you went off to some Darke Alchemie chamber when you know Marcia didn't want you to, and so now you've missed taking part in the most amazing Magyk you are ever likely to see. That, dillop brain, is what getting close to the Darke does. It makes you think only of yourself. It takes you away from people you care about. And now you don't have anyone to talk to and it *serves you right*."

Septimus veered away from the Cordon and its Magykal camaraderie and headed off into the night. He had reached the riverbank and was jogging towards the Palace Landing Stage when the ghost of Alice Nettles suddenly Appeared to him. Since Alther's Banishment, Alice didn't Appear any more, but she made an exception for Septimus. Alice was the only ghost Septimus knew who always seemed to react to the weather and tonight, even though he knew she could not feel the cold, she looked frozen.

"Hello, Alice," he said.

"Hello, Septimus," said Alice in a faraway voice. She turned to Septimus and, for the first time ever, the ghost of Alice Nettles reached out to a human being. She put her hands on Septimus's shoulders and said, "Bring my Alther back, Apprentice. Bring him back."

"I'll do my best, Alice," Septimus replied, thinking how cold Alice's touch was.

"You will go tonight?" she asked.

The key to Dungeon Number One – and the beginning of his Darke Week – hung heavy in his pocket. But the Cordon had thrown all of Septimus's plans into confusion. He had absolutely no idea what was going on or what Marcia would be doing at midnight. He hesitated.

Alice looked anxiously at Septimus. "You do not answer, Apprentice."

Septimus saw the stricken look in Alice's eyes and he made a decision. He may have let Jenna down but he was not going to do the same with Alice. He would enter Dungeon Number One whether Marcia was there or not. "Yes, Alice. I will go and get Alther."

A slow smile dawned on Alice's face. "Thank you," she said. "Thank you from the bottom of my heart."

Septimus left Alice wandering along the Landing Stage, gazing dreamily at the river. He walked slowly along the riverbank, plunged into gloom. Never – not even in the Young Army – had Septimus felt so alone. He realised how he had become used to being in the very centre of things, to being an integral and important part of the Magykal life of the Castle. Now that he suddenly found himself on the outside of the Magykal circle – literally – he felt bereft.

Septimus trudged through the long grass right at the edge of the riverbank, while the dark, cold waters of the river ran silently by. Tiny snowflakes drifted down and settled on his thick woollen cloak, and the grass felt crisp with frost beneath his feet. As he walked, Septimus felt the presence of the Palace looming up on his left side. Like the scene of a horrible accident, his eyes felt drawn to it. And every time he glanced up with a feeling of dread, he saw yet another window go dark, and he could not help but imagine that Jenna was still in there, trapped somewhere.

He ploughed on along the riverbank, convinced he could have stopped whatever was happening to the Palace if only he had helped Jenna when she had asked him. But it was all too late. Jenna wasn't here to ask him now. He was on his own – and he had only himself to blame.

Septimus reached the gate that led through the tall hedge into the Dragon Field. He pushed it open. There was only one creature left for him to talk to – his dragon, Spit Fyre.

21

QUARANTINE

Inside the Palace, unaware of the events silently unfolding around her, Sarah Heap was perched precariously at the top of a step-ladder in the Palace entrance hall. By the light of a beautiful chandelier (it had taken Billy Pot ten whole minutes to light all of its candles) Sarah was busy nailing up a banner that read HAPPY 14TH BIRTHDAY JENNA AND SEPTIMUS above the arch-way that led into the Long Walk. She was not pleased to hear the sound of approaching footsteps outside.

"Botheration," Sarah muttered under her breath. She knew that one set of footsteps belonged to Marcia Overstrand – somehow Marcia always managed to walk everywhere as though she owned the place. Sarah struggled irritably with the unwieldy banner above her head. Trust Marcia to turn up early, she thought. Well, she would have to make herself useful until the party started. Goodness knows there was plenty to do. *Oops.* She could hold the stepladder steady for a start.

The sound of the footsteps changed from cinder scrunches on the path to purposeful *tippy-taps* of purple python on wood as they crossed the bridge over the ornamental moat. They were followed by equally purposeful – but less proprietary – thuds of the footsteps of Marcia's companions.

The Palace doors were pushed open and the *tippy-taps* strode across the stone floor of the entrance hall. They halted below Sarah's ladder.

"Sarah Heap," Marcia announced.

Why, Sarah wondered crossly, did Marcia have to sound so officious? She turned around, hammer raised, the last two nails held between her lips.

"Mrgh?" said Sarah, finally deigning to look down at her visitors. "Ah, hrr Brrr n Hrrrr," she said, actually pleased to see two of Marcia's companions, Beetle and Hildegarde, although less pleased to see the young witch they had with them. She took the nails out of her mouth. "You're early," she said. "But I could do with some help. There's always more to do than you think to get a party ready."

"Mum," said the young witch.

Sarah nearly dropped her hammer. "Goodness, Jenna. It's *you*. I didn't know this was going to be a fancy dress party."

"Mum, it's *not*, but –" Jenna began, wanting to explain before Marcia jumped in with both feet.

Sarah looked disapproving. "Well, I don't know why you are walking around in that *witch stuff*," she said. "You really shouldn't. It's not nice."

"Sorry. It's been a bit of a rush. But –"

"You're telling me. We're not nearly ready for the party, and now –"

"Mum, listen –"

"The party's cancelled," said Marcia.

Sarah dropped the hammer, narrowly missing Marcia's right foot. *"What?"* she said angrily.

"Cancelled. You and everyone inside the Palace have five minutes to leave."

Sarah was down the ladder in a flash. "Marcia Overstrand, how *dare* you?"

"Mum," said Jenna. "Please listen, it's important, something has —"

"Thank you, Jenna, I'll handle this," said Marcia. "Sarah, it is my job to ensure the safety of the Palace. There's a Cordon encircling the building and I am now putting it in Quarantine."

Sarah looked exasperated. "Look here, Marcia, there is no need to go to such extremes. I don't know what Septimus or Jenna have been telling you about the party, but you really mustn't take any notice. Their father and I will be here and we have no intention of letting things get out of hand."

"It seems they already *have* got out of hand, Sarah," said Marcia. She put her hand up to stop Sarah's protests. "Sarah, listen to me, I am *not* talking about the party. And may I say, the fact that you and Silas have been here appears to have been no safeguard against anything *whatsoever*. Indeed, I am surprised – and not a little disappointed – that Silas has allowed this to happen."

"It's only a little birthday party, Marcia," Sarah said snappily. "Of *course* we've allowed it to happen."

"Sarah, for goodness' sake, *listen* to what I am saying. I am *not* talking about the birthday party," Marcia replied, equally snappily. "And you can stop waving that hammer around too."

Sarah looked at the hammer in her hand as though she was surprised to find it there. She shrugged and placed it on the stepladder.

"Thank you," said Marcia.

"So what are you talking about?" Sarah demanded.

"I am talking about your *lodger* in the attic."

"What lodger? We don't have lodgers," Sarah said indignantly. "Things may be a bit tough sometimes but we haven't had to rent the Palace out as a guesthouse quite yet. And even if we did, I hardly think we need your permission, thank you very much." Sarah folded up the stepladder with an angry *bang* and began to heave it into the Long Walk. Beetle stepped forward and took it from her.

"Thank you, Beetle," said Sarah, "that's very sweet of you. Excuse me, Marcia, I have things to do." With that she began gathering up the remains of streamers that were scattered across the floor.

"Mum," said Jenna, handing her some fallen streamers. "Mum, please. There's something horrible here. We have to –"

But Sarah was not in a mood to listen. "And you can take that witch cloak off right now, Jenna. It smells awful – just like the real thing."

Marcia raised her voice. "This is my final warning. I am about to Quarantine this building." She got out her timepiece and laid it on her palm. "You have five minutes from *now* to vacate the premises."

This was too much for Sarah. She stood up and, hands on hips, hair angrily awry, she raised her voice even louder. "Now look here, Marcia Overstrand, I have had *quite* enough of you barging in on my daughter's birthday – and my son's too, as it happens – and tearing everything apart. I will thank you to *go away* and *leave us in peace*."

Hildegarde had been watching Marcia's handling of the proceedings with dismay. Before her promotion to the Wizard Tower, Hildegarde had been on door duty at the Palace. She knew Sarah Heap well and she liked her a lot. Hildegarde stepped forward and laid her hand on Sarah's arm.

"Sarah, I'm very sorry, but this is extremely serious," she said. "There really *is* someone in your attic and he has, so it seems, set up a Darke Domaine in there. Madam Marcia has placed a protective Cordon around the Palace to prevent the Domaine escaping and now, for the safety of all of us in the Castle, she needs to place the Palace in Quarantine. I'm so sorry this had to happen today of all days, but we dare not leave it a moment longer. You do understand, don't you?"

Sarah stared at Hildegarde in disbelief. She wiped a hand across her forehead and sank into a battered old armchair. A faint groan came from the chair, and Sarah sprang to her feet. "Oh, sorry, Godric," she said, apologising to the very faded ghost who had fallen asleep in the chair some years ago. The ghost slept on.

"Is this true?" Sarah asked Marcia.

"That's what I've been trying to tell you, if only you'd listen."

"You haven't been trying to *tell* me anything," Sarah pointed out. "You have been issuing instructions. As usual." She looked around, worried. "Where's Silas?"

Her question was answered by the sound of running foot-steps above. Silas Heap, blue Ordinary Wizard robes flying as, two at a time, he raced down the sweeping stairs that led down to the entrance hall, was yelling, "Everyone – get out, *get out!*"

Silas skidded to a halt at the foot of the stairs and, for the first time in his life, he looked pleased to see Marcia. "Marcia," he puffed. "Oh, thank goodness you're here. My SafetyGate has been broken. It's got out of the attic. It's upstairs now and it's filling the place up – *fast*. We've got to get a Quarantine put on. Marcia, you need to do a Call-Out, get a Cordon around if we've got time —"

"All done," Marcia told Silas briskly. "The Cordon of Wizards is in position."

Silas was stunned into silence.

Marcia got down to business. "Is there anyone else in the Palace?"

Sarah shook her head. "Snorri and her mother have gone off on their boat. The Pots have gone to see the lights. Maizie's out lighting up, Cook's gone home with a cold, and no one's arrived for the party yet."

"Good," said Marcia. She glanced up to the top of the wide flight of stairs, which led to a gallery from which the upstairs corridor ran the length of the Palace. Along the gallery, the rushlights were burning as usual, but the dimming of the light where the corridor stretched away both to the left and right told Marcia that the more distant lights were being extinguished. The Darke Domaine was getting closer.

"Everyone will exit the premises," she said. *"Now!"*

"Ethel!" gasped Sarah. She raced off and disappeared into the Long Walk.

"Ethel? Who on earth is Ethel?" Marcia glanced up to the gallery. The flame on the farthest rushlight began to dim.

"Ethel's a duck," said Silas.

"A *duck*?"

But Silas was gone, racing off in pursuit of Sarah — and Maxie, who he just remembered he had left sitting by the fire that morning.

Up on the gallery the first rushlight had gone out and the flame on a second, nearer rushlight was faltering. Marcia looked at Jenna, Beetle and Hildegarde. "It's moving fast. If I don't do the Quarantine now, this is going to get out. And frankly, I am not sure that our Cordon will hold it. We are very widely spaced. And I certainly won't have time to Raise a Safety Curtain."

"You *can't* leave Mum and Dad," gasped Jenna.

"I have no choice. They're putting the whole Castle at risk – for a *duck*."

"*You can't do that!* I'm going to go and get them." With that Jenna raced off. Hildegarde darted after her and grabbed her witch's cloak.

Jenna spun around angrily. "Let go!"

The cloak felt horrible to the touch, but Hildegarde doggedly hung on. "No, Princess Jenna, you mustn't go. It's too risky. *I'll* go. They'll be in Sarah's sitting room, yes?"

Jenna nodded. "Yes, but –"

"I'll get them out of the window." Hildegarde glanced at Marcia, calculating how long it would take to get to Sarah's sitting room. "Give me ... count me to a hundred and then do it. OK?"

Marcia looked up at the landing. A wall of darkness now blocked any view of the corridors. She shook her head. "Seventy-five."

Hildegarde gulped. "OK. Seventy-five." And she was gone.

"One," began Marcia. "Two, three, four ..." She signed to Beetle and Jenna to leave. Jenna shook her head.

Beetle took Jenna's arm. "You must leave," he said. "Your parents would not want you to stay. Hildegarde will get them out."

"*No*. I can't go without Mum and Dad."

"Jenna, you have to. You are the Princess. You must be safe."

"I'm sick of being *safe*," she hissed.

But Beetle backed out of the Palace doors, taking Jenna with him. Once outside he took a small, fat tube from his pocket. "I've got the Flare," he called to Marcia.

Marcia gave him a thumbs-up. "Thirty-five, thirty-six ..."

"What Flare?" asked Jenna.

"To Activate the Cordon. Just in case."

"In case what?"

"Well, in case the Quarantine doesn't work. In case something escapes."

"Like Mum and Dad, you mean?" Jenna said, wrenching her arm from Beetle's grasp.

"*No*. In case something Darke escapes."

But Jenna was not there to hear. Witch cloak flying, she was racing off along the small path that ran around to the back of the Palace. Beetle sighed. He wished Jenna would take off the witch cloak. She didn't seem like Jenna any more.

Feeling wretched, Beetle waited between the two burning torches on either side of the bridge. Through the open Palace doors he saw the pile of abandoned birthday presents, the discarded streamers, the HAPPY BIRTHDAY banner, all looking oddly out of place now as Marcia – purple-robed and intense – paced back and forth, continuing her count. Beetle saw the last rushlight at the top of the stairs flicker and go out and the wall of Darkenesse – not night-time darkness but something thicker, more solid – begin to move down towards the pacing figure below.

Beetle watched Marcia like a hawk, terrified of missing her signal. The ExtraOrdinary Wizard was backing towards the door now. She was still counting, going on for as long as she dared in order to give Hildegarde the best possible chance.

"One hundred and four, one hundred and five . . ."

With every step backwards that Marcia took, the Darkenesse advanced. It reminded Beetle of a giant cider press he had once visited where you could stand inside and watch the pressing plate move down towards you. It had terrified Beetle at the time – and now it terrified him all over again.

The descending roof of Darkenesse reached the chandelier, and suddenly all the candles sputtered out. Beetle saw Marcia raise her right hand. He pushed the Ignite pin into the side of the Flare, held the Flare at arm's length and was blown off his feet by the sudden blast of light that shot into the sky. A gasp of "oohs" came from the crowd beyond, but from the Cordon came the quieter sound of a sustained humming, as though the Palace were surrounded by a gigantic swarm of bees. The Cordon was now Active. Marcia leaped outside, slammed the thick wooden doors shut, laid a hand on each door and began the Quarantine.

The Magyk was so strong that even Beetle – who was not a very Magykal person – could see the purple shimmering haze of Magyk playing around the doors and, as the sound of the humming from the huge circle of Wizards, Apprentices and scribes filled the air, the Magyk spread out from the doors, creeping across the darkened windows of the Palace, Quarantining everything that lay within in a thin veil of purple.

Beetle hoped that what lay within did not include Hildegarde, Sarah and Silas. Or Jenna.

22

ETHEL

"Sarah, forget that contrary duck and get out!" Silas was yelling.

Silas and Hildegarde were anxiously hopping up and down on the path outside Sarah's open sitting-room window. Maxie was whining fretfully. Inside, Sarah was frantically searching for Ethel.

"I can't just *abandon* her," Sarah shouted back, hurling a pile of washing off the sofa and throwing the cushions on to the floor. "She's hiding because she's *frightened*."

"Sarah, *get out!*"

To Hildegarde's dismay, Silas clambered back in through the open window. Maxie went to follow; Hildegarde pulled the protesting wolfhound away.

"Mr Heap, Mr Heap!" she called in through the window. "Come back, *please*! No, Maxie. *Down.*"

Inside the room Silas was propelling a reluctant Sarah towards the open window. "Sarah," he told her, "duck or no duck, it is time to go. Come *on.*"

Sarah gave one last try. "Ethel, dear," she called out, "Ethel, where are you? Come to Mummy!"

An exasperated Silas manoeuvred Sarah out of the window. "Ethel is a *duck*, Sarah, and you are *not* her mummy. You have eight children to be mummy to, and they all need you more than that duck does. Now get *out*!"

A moment later, much to Hildegarde's relief, both Silas and Sarah were standing beside her. Suddenly the candle flickering in the room next door to Sarah's went out. Quickly Hildegarde reached up to close the window.

"Quack!" A flurry of movement came from underneath a pile of old curtains propped up beside the door and a yellow beak poked out.

"Ethel!"

Neither Silas, who was distracted by the sudden appearance of Jenna rounding the corner at the far end of the Palace, nor Hildegarde, who was pulling down the window, were quick enough to stop Sarah leaping back inside. Hildegarde was, however, quick enough to stop Silas clambering in after Sarah.

"No, Mr Heap. Stay here," she said firmly, hanging on to Silas's sleeve just to make sure. "Mistress Heap, please come back, *oh no* –"

As Sarah scooped Ethel out from the pile of curtains, the door to her sitting room crashed open. A wave of Darkenesse flooded inside, and Sarah screamed a terrified, piercing scream that Jenna would never forget. Sarah clutched her duck to her, mouth wide open in a shriek, and was lost to human sight. As the Darkenesse swirled towards the open window, Hildegarde had no choice but to slam the window shut and put a rapid Anti-Darke on it just to make sure nothing escaped.

"Sarah!" Silas yelled, banging on the window. *"Saraaaaaah!"*

Jenna arrived, breathless. "Mum!" she gasped. "Where's Mum?"

Unable to speak, Silas pointed into the room.

"Get her out, Dad, *get her out!*" yelled Jenna.

Silas shook his head. "It's too late. Too late . . ." As he spoke the candle on the little table beside the window guttered and went out. Sarah's sitting room was Darke.

There was a stunned silence on the path outside the window. With reluctance, Hildegarde broke it. "I think," she said softly, "I think we should go now. There's nothing we can do."

"I'm not leaving Mum," said Jenna stubbornly.

"Princess Jenna, I am so sorry, but there is nothing we can do for her now," Hildegarde said gently. "Marcia has instructed that we go outside the Cordon."

"I don't care what Marcia has instructed," snapped Jenna. *"I'm not leaving Mum."*

Silas put his arm around Jenna. "What Hildegarde says is true, Jenny," he said, using his old baby name for her, something Jenna had not heard for years. "Your mum would not want us to stay here. She would want us – and you in particular – to be safe. Come on."

Jenna shook her head, not trusting herself to speak. But she stopped resisting and allowed Silas to lead her away.

The subdued party walked slowly across the grass, which was becoming dusted with white as the sleet began to turn to snow in the cold of the encroaching night. They headed towards the silent circle of Wizards, scribes and Apprentices holding their purple Cords. Suddenly the sky lit up with a *whoosh*. Jenna jumped.

"It's all right," said Hildegarde. "It's only the signal to the Cordon to Activate." At that a strange humming sound, like a mass of bees on a warm summer's day, drifted towards them. It was oddly unsettling – bees did not belong to a dark winter's night with snowflakes falling.

Jenna looked back at the Palace – *her* Palace, as she now thought of it. Every night, since Alther had been Banished, she would walk down the river and talk to the forlorn ghost of Alice Nettles. She and Alice would look up at the Palace and Alice would say how beautiful it looked now that every window had a light in it, and Jenna would agree. But now, like Alther, the lights were gone – every one of her candles snuffed out. It reminded Jenna of how the Palace had been when she had first moved in with Silas and Sarah, but there was one important difference: there had always been one window with a light in it – Sarah's sitting room, where they had sat every evening. Now there was nothing.

All eyes were upon them as Hildegarde, Silas, Jenna and Maxie walked slowly towards the Cordon. Hildegarde chose a spot between two scribes, Partridge and Romilly Badger, who were holding either end of the Cord in front of the entrance to Sarah Heap's herb garden. Somehow Partridge had managed to share his Cord with Romilly, rather than have a Wizard spacer between them, as was recommended practice. On either side of Romilly and Partridge, the circle of Wizards, scribes and Apprentices, linked with various lengths of purple cord, stretched out into the night. All were making the long, low drone that prepared the Cord for Marcia to raise the Safety Curtain.

Romilly and Partridge nodded at Jenna but neither smiled – they had both seen what had happened. Resolutely they continued their low drone.

Silas stepped forward.

"Don't touch!" yelled Hildegarde, somewhat frazzled and – after his leap into the sitting room – not entirely trusting Silas to be sensible.

Silas looked annoyed. "I wasn't *going* to," he said indignantly. "We can't touch the Cord," he whispered to Jenna. "It will break the Magyk."

"So how are we supposed to get out?" Jenna asked irritably.

"It's all right, Princess Jenna," Hildegarde said soothingly. "We can get out, but there's a particular way of doing it. We need some of this . . ." Hildegarde reached into her sub-Wizard belt for her own piece of Conducting Cord. She drew it out and held up a very short length of purple cord. "Oh," she said. "I don't think that's long enough."

"Standard sub-Wizard length," said Silas. "Enough for one person only." He took a much longer length from his Ordinary Wizard belt. "Use mine. I may as well do *something* useful. Now, this is what we do; we all stand really close together and – *Maxie, come back!*"

Jenna raced after Maxie and dragged him back; the wolf-hound regarded her with big, brown, accusing eyes. She held Maxie close and Silas proceeded to encircle them all with his purple Conducting Cord. A few minutes later, a walking parcel of three people and a wolfhound shuffled towards the Cord held by Partridge and Romilly. Any other time Jenna would have giggled her way along, but now it was all she could do to blink back tears – every step took her away from Sarah, marooned in the Darke. She glanced back at the Palace and saw that a Magykal shimmer of purple had crept over it like a veil, Quarantining everything within. She wondered if Sarah knew what had happened. She wondered if Sarah now knew anything at all . . .

Silas meanwhile was carefully tying both ends of his Conducting Cord to the main Cordon Cord, without actually touching it himself. Partridge and Romilly obligingly lifted their Cord like a skipping rope and the parcel of people and wolfhound shuffled underneath the Cord and out the other side.

"Well, that's it," sighed Silas. "We're out."

"*Mum's* not," said Jenna as they set off slowly through the kitchen garden, along Sarah's neat paths that wound through the herb beds.

"I know," Silas said quietly. "But she won't be there for ever, Jenna."

"How do you know that?" asked Jenna.

"Because I am not going to let that happen," said Silas. "We are going to help Marcia sort this out."

"Marcia is the one who made all this happen," Jenna said, crossly. "If she hadn't tried to boss Mum around and if she had bothered to explain things, then Mum would have had time to get out."

"And if your mother hadn't gone running off after a duck she would have had time to get out too," Silas pointed out. "But that is beside the point," he added quickly, noticing Jenna's stormy expression. "We must get to the Wizard Tower. Marcia will need all the help she can get."

They walked out of the door in the kitchen-garden wall and stepped into the small alleyway that ran along the back, going towards Wizard Way to the left and to the river to the right. Silas led the way with Maxie; Jenna and Hildegarde followed in silence. At the end of the alleyway Jenna stopped.

"I'm not going to the Wizard Tower," she said angrily. "I'm

sick of Wizards. And I'm sick of Wizards messing everything up – especially on my birthday."

Silas looked at her sadly. He didn't know what to say. Jenna seemed so irritable nowadays, and whatever he said was never quite right – and, he thought, it didn't help that she was dressed in that awful witch costume, either. He rummaged in his pocket, brought out a large brass key and handed it to her.

"What's that for?" asked Jenna.

"Home," said Silas. "Our place in the Ramblings. I've been doing it up. Making it just how your mum always wanted it to be. It . . . it was going to be a surprise for her next birthday. She's always wanted to go home. But now . . . well, now *you* at least can go home."

Jenna looked at the key lying heavy and cold in her palm. "That's not home, Dad. Home is where Mum is. Home is *there*." She pointed back at the Palace, the top row of Darke attic windows just visible over the alley wall.

Silas sighed. "I know. But we'll need somewhere to sleep for now. I'll meet you there later – Big Red Door, There and Back Again Row. You know the way."

Jenna nodded. She watched Silas walk briskly off, heading towards Wizard Way.

"Shall I come with you?" asked Hildegarde, who had kept a discreet distance behind Jenna and Silas. And then, receiving no answer, asked, "Jenna – Princess Jenna, are you all right?"

"No. And *no*," Jenna said sharply, cutting Hildegarde short before her sympathy got too much for her. She turned and ran back up the alley.

Hildegarde decided not to follow. Princess Jenna needed some time on her own.

Jenna followed the alley back up past the kitchen-garden wall, around the dogleg turn that skirted the edge of the Dragon Field, and headed towards the river. The freezing night air bit into her as she ran, and she pulled her witch's hood up over her head to keep warm. The dark, dull shine of the river came into view and, breathless now, she slowed to a walking pace. The alley came to an end at a small, neglected jetty, which Jenna wandered on to. At the very end of the jetty she sat down on the damp and mossy wooden boards, wrapped her cloak around her and gazed at the sluggish black waters flowing silently beneath her feet. And there she sat, thinking of Sarah imprisoned in the Palace, wondering what was happening to her. She remembered childhood stories, Darke tales told around the fire late at night when she was meant to be asleep, tales told by visiting Wizards to the Heaps' crowded room in the Ramblings, of people emerging after years inside a Darke Domaine, their eyes wild and empty, their minds gone, their voices babbling gibberish. She remembered the whispered discussions on what could have reduced people to such a state, all kinds of ghastly details that came into people's heads late at night. And she could not help but think that all these terrible things could now, *at that very moment*, be happening to *her mum*.

Jenna sat, silent tears dripping down her neck, gazing out at the river. Flakes of snow began to settle on her witch's cloak, and the cold coming from the water set her shivering, but she did not notice. All she wanted was to find Septimus and tell him what had happened.

But where was he?

✵ 23 ✵

SAFETY CURTAIN

Marcia and Beetle crossed the Cordon using the same method that
Silas had, although with greater efficiency. Once they were on
the other side, Marcia stood back and looked at the Palace.
She saw the purple Magykal shimmer covering it and the two
torches on the outside of the main doors, which were still lit.
Her Quarantine had worked. There was, however, no sign of
Hildegarde, Sarah or Silas. Marcia felt worried. She scanned
the inscrutable windows of the Palace and concentrated hard.
Her heart sank. There was no escaping it – she Felt the presence of two humans inside the building. It did not bode well
for Sarah and Silas – or was it Hildegarde and Silas – or Sarah
and . . . Marcia briskly told herself to stop worrying. She would
find out soon enough.

Marcia now began the next stage of isolating the Palace from
the rest of the Castle. This was the stand down, from which the
raising of the Safety Curtain would follow. She picked the two
nearest members of the Cordon: Bertie Bott, Ordinary Wizard
and dealer in used (or pre-loved, as Bertie liked to say) Wizard
cloaks, and Rose, the sick-bay Apprentice. To each one she
said the pre-arranged stand-down password. Immediately they
stopped their low hum. Rose sent the password around to her

right, and Bertie sent it to his left. Like a retreating wave, the low drone faded and was replaced by the whispering of the password. Soon silence had fallen. It spread to the crowds who had gathered at the end of Wizard Way, waiting expectantly for the next stage. Word was that the Raising of a Safety Curtain was worth watching.

At first it did not seem particularly promising. Each person in the Cordon was now busy knotting his or her Cord to their neighbour's. They laid their joined Cord on the ground, making sure it had no twists or kinks in it, and walked carefully away so as not disturb the delicate Magyk – for Magyk involving so many participants was a fragile thing. Within minutes of Marcia giving the password, a huge circle of Cord lay on the ground like a purple snake encircling the Palace. Beetle, who was feeling rather melancholy after Jenna's outburst, thought the fragile Cord looked sad as it lay abandoned in the trampled grass.

Meanwhile, the Wizard Way audience had drifted in through the Palace Gate in order to get a closer look. People waited patiently, with only the occasional smothered cough giving their presence away. They watched as the ExtraOrdinary Wizard kneeled down and placed her hands a few inches above the Cord. Nudges and excited glances were exchanged – now at last something was happening.

Totally unaware of her audience, Marcia was concentrating hard. She felt a faint current of Magyk running unimpeded through the Cord, which told her that everyone had let go. Now for the difficult part, she thought. Still kneeling, Marcia kept her hands low and close to the Cord. What she had to do now required a huge amount of energy. She took a long, deep breath in. Beetle, who was watching Marcia intently, had never seen anyone breathe in for so long. He half expected Marcia to blow up like a balloon and float away. Indeed her cloak seemed to him to be moving outwards as if it really was filling with air.

Beetle was actually stepping back in case Marcia did indeed go *pop*, when she at last stopped breathing in. Now she began to breathe out, her lips pursed as though she were blowing on hot soup. From her mouth came a shimmering stream of purple, which was drawn to the Cord like iron filings to a magnet. The stream of purple kept on coming; it settled on the section of Cord in front of Marcia and grew steadily brighter. When it was so bright that Beetle had to look away, Marcia at last stopped breathing out.

Now came the part that demanded real skill. Marcia placed her hands in the brilliant light and very slowly she began to raise her hands. Behind her the crowd gave a subdued murmur of appreciation as the blinding purple light began to move upwards, following her hands while still remaining anchored to the Cord. Slowly, carefully, biting her lip in concentration, Marcia drew up the light, taking care not to pull it too fast, which could create weak spots or even holes in what was now a shimmering purple curtain. Beetle saw Marcia's muscles trembling with the effort, as though she were lifting a tremendously heavy weight. The curtain of light followed Marcia as, arms painfully outstretched, she got up from her knees and staggered awkwardly to her feet. Beetle resisted his instinct to help her up, knowing well enough not to break Marcia's immense concentration, which reduced her brilliant green eyes to pinpoints of light in her pale skin.

Suddenly, what everyone in the audience had been waiting

for happened. With a shout of something long and complicated – that later no one could remember – Marcia threw her arms into the air. There was a loud *whoosh*, and a curtain of blindingly bright purple light shot as high as the very tips of Marcia's fingers, then raced off along the Cord with the zipping fizz of fire along a fuse.

A loud and appreciative "ooh" rose from the crowd, which seemed to startle Marcia. She swung around and glared at the assembled throng.

"Shh!" she hissed.

Abashed, the crowd fell silent. Some began to sidle away, but the more knowledgeable stayed, knowing that the best was yet to come.

Marcia had set the curtain of light racing off in one direction only – to her right. The reason for this was that she wanted to be present at the place where the light joined up. The join in a Safety Curtain was a delicate thing, and although some Wizards, for dramatic effect, would have sent the light racing off in both directions and hope that it successfully melded somewhere on the other side of the Palace, Marcia was more careful. She also disapproved of drama; she thought it devalued Magyk and encouraged people to see it as an entertainment – hence her irritation with the crowd.

Now the wait began for the return of the purple fire. It took a while. The nearly seven-foot-high purple curtain had to travel all around the Palace and, at the back of the building, where there had been too many people on the Cordon, down through the garden too – fairly close, in fact, to the hedge that divided the Dragon Field from the Palace garden.

★   ★   ★

Spit Fyre slept through the oncoming rush, but his Imprintor and Pilot, Septimus Heap, was wide awake. He had been expecting a Safety Curtain, as he knew Marcia did not do things by halves. At the sight of the swathe of Magykal purple moving behind the top of the Dragon Field hedge, Septimus looked gloomily at the oncoming purple wall, admiring its evenness and brilliance. Marcia had clearly performed a textbook piece of Magyk – and *he* had not been part of it. Septimus watched the Safety Curtain travel on its way, and then he went back to the Dragon House, unwilling to face Marcia just then. He knew what she would say. It would be exactly what he would say to an Apprentice of his own if he or she ever missed something like this. And he didn't want to hear it.

At last the crowd saw the purple curtain reappear on the other side of the Palace. Conscious of the disapproving presence of the ExtraOrdinary Wizard, they greeted it with a restrained murmur of excitement and watched with bated breath as one end of the shimmering curtain travelled towards the other.

Later some said that the Closing of the Safety Curtain was an anticlimax, but others said it was the most amazing thing they had ever seen. It depended – like many things in life – on what you expected to see. All saw the meeting of the two sheets of light and the violent flash that accompanied it, but those who truly looked saw, for a few amazing seconds, the history of the Castle played out before them. The Safety Curtain was ancient Magyk (which always involved some form of breath control) and had been used by Castle Dwellers in a more primitive form even before the advent of the very first ExtraOrdinary Wizard. Before the Castle Walls had been built, a Safety Curtain had often been put around the Castle at the dark of the moon in an effort to keep out marauders from the Forest. It hadn't worked too well at first but every time it was used it grew stronger. And like the ancient pictures on the walls inside the Wizard Tower, deep inside it were echoes and snatches of wild moments in its long existence. As the Curtains met and melded together, it was possible to briefly see wonderful things within the shifting lights: fierce horsemen galloping through, screaming witches riding upon giant wolverines, giant tree fiends hurling Gargle Toad bombs; all played their brief part in breaching — and thus strengthening — the Safety Curtain. And then they were gone. The Magykal Curtain settled into a completely fused circle. The moving quality of the purple light changed to a steady glow and all was still.

Those who had glimpsed these visions stood stunned for a few seconds, then broke into excited chatter. Marcia rounded on the crowd.

"Quiet!" she shouted.

The chatter died away instantly.

"This is serious Magyk. I have put this Safety Curtain in place to *protect* you, not to give you ten minutes of free entertainment."

"We're paying for it now!" shouted one brave soul from the safety of the crowd.

Marcia glared in the direction of the heckler and her voice took on an edge of steel. "You must understand that I have placed the Safety Curtain there to protect us *all* against a Darke Domaine that has engulfed the Palace." She paused to let this information sink in and saw, with some satisfaction, the crowd's mood become suitably serious and worried.

"I ask you to respect it. This is for your safety. For the safety of the Castle."

The crowd was silent. A small girl at the front – whose hero was Marcia and who longed one day to be a Wizard – said in a very small voice, "Madam Marcia . . ."

Despite somewhat creaky knees, Marcia squatted down. "Yes?"

"What if the Darke 'maine gets out?"

"It won't," Marcia said confidently. "You mustn't worry, you will be perfectly safe. The Palace is Quarantined. The Safety Curtain is there just in case." She stood up and addressed the crowd. "I can do nothing more until sunrise. Tomorrow, at first light, I shall Fumigate the Palace and all will be well. I bid you goodnight."

There were a few murmurings of "thank you" and "g'night ExtraOrdinary" as people wandered off to find their way home – somehow the lights in Wizard Way no longer seemed interesting. Marcia watched the crowd disperse with some relief. It worried her to have too many people near something as powerful as a Safety Curtain. The various Wizards, scribes and Apprentices also began to wander off to their homes.

"Mr Bott!" Marcia called out as the rotund purveyor of cloaks scuttled off for his dinner.

"Drat," Bertie muttered under his breath. But he dared not ignore the boss, as Marcia was known in the Wizard Tower. "Yes, Madam Marcia?" he said with a slight bow.

"No need for that, Mr Bott," snapped Marcia, who hated any sign of what she called bowing and scraping. "You will take the first watch at the fusion point. It is, as I am sure you know, always a possible weak spot. I will send a relief at midnight."

"Midnight?" gasped Bertie, his stomach already rumbling at the thought of the sausages, mash and gravy that his wife always prepared on the Longest Night and that was surely waiting for him at home.

Unlike Bertie Bott, Rose seemed loath to leave. She was gazing up at the Safety Curtain in wonder. "I'll take the watch, Madam Marcia," she offered.

"Thank you, Rose," said Marcia. "But I have already asked Mr Bott."

Bertie ran a limp hand across his forehead. "Actually, Madam Marcia, I do believe I am feeling a little faint," he said.

"Really?" said Marcia. "Well, if Rose takes your turn without any supper, she *will* faint. Whereas you, Mr Bott, have plenty of . . . *reserves*."

Rose took courage from Marcia's half-smile as she regarded the discomforted Bertie Bott. "I would love to take the watch, Madam Marcia," she persisted. "Truly, I would. The Safety Curtain is amazing. I have never seen anything like it."

Marcia gave in. She liked Rose and did not want to dent her enthusiasm. And after the conspicuous absence of her own Apprentice, Marcia appreciated some enthusiasm. "Very well, Rose. But go back to the Wizard Tower and have something to eat first. Take at least an hour. Then you may return and take Mr Bott's watch. Now, Mr Bott, what do you say to Rose?"

"Thank you, Rose," said Bertie Bott meekly.

Bertie watched Rose and Marcia walk off into Wizard Way and sighed. He stamped his feet in the chill air and drew his cloak around him as another flurry of snow came in from the river. It was going to be a very long hour.

✳ 24 ✳

PALACE THINGS

While Merrin wandered around the Manuscriptorium, intimidating Jillie Djinn and writing rude words on the scribes' desks, the events he had set in motion were beginning to unfold.

At the top of the Palace, a Thing UnLocked the door of a tiny, windowless room at the end of Merrin's corridor.

"It . . . is . . . time," it said.

Muddy, dishevelled and aching all over from being Fetched, Simon Heap slowly got to his feet.

"Follow," came the Thing's hollow voice.

Simon did not move.

"Follow."

"No," croaked Simon, his throat painfully dry from lack of water.

The Thing leaned nonchalantly against the doorframe and looked at Simon with what might have been a mixture of amusement and boredom. "If you do not follow, the door will be Locked," it intoned. "It will be Locked for a year. After a year has passed, the only person able to UnLock it will be your mother."

"My *mother?*"

"She will be pleased to see you again, no doubt." The Thing made a noise like a strangled chicken, which Simon knew was, in Thing terms, a laugh. "Even though you will be no more than a pile of slimy rags in her attic."

"*In her attic?* Is that where I am?" asked Simon, who had no memory of the Fetch.

"You are in the Palace." The Thing moved back through the doorway. "If you do not follow *now*, I shall shut the door. Then I shall Lock it." The door began to close. Simon imagined Sarah Heap pushing it open some time in the future — maybe years later.

"Wait!" He ran out of the room.

Simon followed the Thing as it moved in its peculiar crab-like shuffle along the attic corridor and descended *cler-clump cler-clump* the same narrow stairs that Jenna and Beetle had climbed that afternoon. Simon dreaded what he was going to find. Were his parents prisoners of the Thing too — or worse? And what about Jenna? He knew that if any of them saw him with the Thing, they would assume this was *his* doing. They would blame him for everything. Simon felt a wave of his old self-pity come over him but he pushed it away. He only had himself to blame, he told himself sternly.

The Thing shambled surprisingly swiftly along the wide upstairs corridor and Simon followed in its wake, feeling as though he were wading through treacle. He took this as a good sign; he had been told that this was what walking through the Darke felt like but he had never noticed before.

An oppressive silence pervaded the Palace. Even the night-time ghosts who regularly haunted the Palace were quiet and stilled, except for one — a governess — who was in a complete panic. Her intermittent screams cut through the air and sent shivers down Simon's spine. Many of the ghosts had been making their regular evening promenade along the corridor, hoping for a glimpse of the Princess, when the Darke had unexpectedly descended. They were now stuck, unable to move through the thickness of the Darke, and Simon could not help but Pass Through them. Every time he felt the soft waft of chill, slightly stale, air he felt sick. But one ghost that Simon did not Pass Through was Sir Hereward – Sir Hereward Passed Through *him*.

During the onset of the Darke Domaine, Sir Hereward had remained faithfully at his post outside Jenna's bedroom, his sword at the ready. What it was at the ready for, Sir Hereward was not sure, but the ghost was not going to be caught napping by a little bit of Darke. But as the Darke deepened and infiltrated every last nook, every last cranny, even Sir Hereward got twitchy. Twice the ghost had felt *something* go into Jenna's room – he had heard the telltale groan of the door and the squeak of the curtain rings as the curtain was pushed aside – but twice his sword had run through nothing but air. Sir Hereward longed for some light to see by and a good clean fight with something real. So when Simon's human footsteps crept by, creaking the ancient floorboards, disturbing the air in a way that ghosts and Things do not, Sir Hereward ran up the passageway that led to Jenna's room and ambushed Simon with a bloodcurdling yell of, *"Have at you, Sirrah!"*

"Argh!" yelled Simon, totally spooked. The Thing looked back briefly and continued its crab walk towards the gallery at the top of the main stairs. Simon resolutely followed the Thing, but Sir Hereward was not going to let his enemy escape so easily. He chased after him, aiming sword swipes at him as he went. Simon felt as if he were being attacked by a demented windmill. Again and again, Sir Hereward's sword came swishing down on him. Even though Sir Hereward's sword had no substance, it was a highly unpleasant sensation having a ghostly sword slashing through him. Indeed such was the anger of the ghost wielding it, that the sword actually Caused a sound – a sharp *whoosh* – as it sliced through the air. Simon knew that if Sir Hereward's sword had been real, he would no longer be in one piece, or quite possibly even two or three. It was not a comforting thought.

"*You*, sir, I know who you are!" *Whoosh whoosh*.

Sir Hereward's surprisingly powerful boom of a voice filled the thick silence – and stunned the governess into welcome silence.

"I see your Heap hair –" *whoosh* – "and your scar. The Princess has told me all about you –" *whoosh whoosh*. "You, Sirrah, are the black sheep Heap" – *whoosh*. "You are the wicked brother who kidnapped your own defenceless sister!" *Whoosh whoosh whoosh* Sir Hereward raged.

Doggedly Simon kept going, following the Thing while he tried to work out what on earth he was going to do. But it is hard to think when a one-armed ghost is unleashing a string of abuse and a torrent of well-aimed sword swipes.

Sir Hereward did not let up. "Do not –" *whoosh* – "think you can escape justice, you cur! I will have revenge!" *Whoosh whoosh*. "How could you treat a young Princess in such a –" *whoosh* – "dastardly fashion?"

Simon thought it best to ignore the ghost and keep going, but this only seemed to anger Sir Hereward more. "Sirrah!

You run like the coward you surely are —" *whoosh*. "Stand and fight like a man!" *Whoosh whoosh whoosh!*

Suddenly Simon had had enough. He stopped and turned to face his tormentor. "I *am* a man," he said, "which is more than I can say for *you*."

Sir Hereward lowered his sword and looked at Simon with disgust. "A cheap jibe, Sir, but no more than I would expect. Stand and fight your ground."

Simon felt very weary. He spread out his hands to show he had no weapon. "Look, Sir Whatever-your-name-is, I do not want a fight. Not right now. There's quite enough going on here without that, don't you think?"

"Hah!" scoffed Sir Hereward.

"And I am truly sorry about Jenna — *Princess* Jenna. I did a terrible thing and I would do anything to undo it, but I cannot. I have written to ask her to forgive me and I hope one day she will. I can do no more than that."

"Silence!" the Thing commanded.

Sir Hereward peered into the Darke and saw the faint shadow of the Thing. But the Thing did not see — or hear — the ghost. Sir Hereward had chosen only to Appear to Simon; he was far too experienced to risk Appearing to anything Darke.

"You scum, Heap," said Sir Hereward, waving his sword around once more. "You have brought Darke Things into the Palace."

Simon felt exasperated. Why did people — and even ghosts — always think the worst of him? "Look, you silly old fool," he snapped, "will you just get this into your head? I *hate* this Darke stuff."

The Thing — a paranoid entity at the best of times — took this badly. "Silence!" it shrieked.

Sir Hereward took it no better. "How dare you insult me, you blackguard!"

Simon was reckless now. He turned on Sir Hereward. "I'll insult you if I choose, you stupid – *aaaaaaaaaargh*!" The Thing's hands were suddenly gripping Simon's neck, pushing his windpipe back towards his spine.

"You mock me at your peril," hissed the Thing.

"*Garrrr* . . ." Simon was choking. The smell of decay filled his nostrils and the Thing's long, filthy fingernails cut into his skin.

Shocked, Sir Hereward lowered his sword.

"When I tell you to be silent, you *will* be silent," Sir Hereward heard the bullying Thing hiss to his victim. "If you will not be silent when I command it, I shall ensure that you will be silent *for ever*. Understand?"

Simon just about managed to nod his head.

The Thing let go. Simon reeled back and fell, retching, on to the carpet.

"Oh *dear*," muttered Sir Hereward.

The Thing stood over Simon. "Get up. Follow," it ordered.

Sir Hereward watched Simon drag himself to his feet and, clasping his bruised neck, stagger after the Thing like a naughty puppy. The ghost began to think that perhaps things were not quite what he had taken them for – and, quite possibly, that Simon Heap was not what he had taken him for either. Determined to find out what was going on, Sir Hereward set off after Simon.

Taking advantage of the fact that the Thing could not hear him, the ghost said, "Look here, Heap, I want some answers."

Simon looked at the ghost in despair. Why wouldn't he *go away*? Didn't he see he had enough trouble right then?

"Now, this is just between you and me, Heap." He caught Simon's anxious glance at the Thing. "Don't worry, I do not Appear to Things. It can't hear me."

Simon looked at the ghost and saw a brief, conspiratorial smile. A small ray of hope flitted across his mind.

"Heap, I want to get some facts straight. I do not want any lies. Just nod or shake your head. Got that?"

Easier said than done, thought Simon. He felt as if his head might fall off. Cautiously, he nodded.

The motley procession of the stooping, ragged Thing, followed by the battered young man in his muddy, torn robes and the one-armed ghost moved slowly along the corridor. The ghost began his questions.

"Did you come to the Palace of your own free will?"

Simon shook his head – very carefully.

"Do you know why you are here?"

A slow shake.

"Do you know where the Princess is?"

Yet another slow shake.

"We must find her. And to find her we must rid the Palace of this . . . this *infestation*." Sir Hereward sounded disgusted. "Do you agree, Heap?"

With some relief, Simon nodded. It was less painful than shaking his head.

"And are you willing to help me get rid of these . . . Things?"

Simon nodded too vehemently and a groan escaped him. The Thing swung around, the procession stopped and Simon's heart raced. He put his hands up to his bruised throat as though trying to ease his neck. The Thing glared at Simon, then turned and continued its crab shuffle into the galleried landing.

"We need a plan of action," said Sir Hereward, getting into campaign mode. "First we need to –"

Simon did not hear any of Sir Hereward's plans. The Thing, tired of Simon lagging behind, was waiting for him. As Simon drew level, it grabbed hold of his torn robes, dragged him along the gallery and pushed him down the stairs. Simon half ran, half fell down to the entrance hall below, where a crowd of twenty-four Things waited for him.

Sir Hereward ventured cautiously down the stairs. From his vantage point, he saw Simon's painful progress across the hall, pinched and punched as he was pushed and prodded towards the Palace doors. The ghost reached the foot of the stairs and, with some trepidation, he stepped into the crowd of Things. It was not a good experience. No ghost likes to be Passed Through, but to be Passed Through by something Darke is a truly awful experience. It had never happened to Sir Hereward before, but as he followed Simon across the hall, it happened to him at least ten times. Resolutely the ghost kept going. His job was to protect the Princess, and to do that he reckoned he needed to keep close to Simon. Sir Hereward knew that if anyone had the strength to get rid of the Things, to get the Palace back for the Princess, it would be a Living young man, not an ancient one-armed ghost. And besides, he didn't like bullies. He'd had Simon Heap down as one, but now the boot was on the other foot. Or feet. If Things had feet.

Simon had reached the Palace doors. A thin film of Magykal purple flickered across them, to which every Thing gave a respectful distance.

"Open the doors," instructed the Thing.

"Don't you dare!" said Sir Hereward, who had suddenly grasped what was happening. "We don't want *them* all over the Castle."

Simon ignored Sir Hereward – he had enough to think about. He stared blankly at the Thing but his thoughts were racing. He now understood why he had been Fetched – it was to break a Quarantine. A truly Darke entity can never get through a Quarantine, which is a powerful form of Anti-Darke. It needed a human being with Darke knowledge – knowledge that the Things knew Simon had. It was well known that Things would seek humans out to do this for them, for no human can be completely Darke – all have some small remnant of good feeling left lurking somewhere. Even DomDaniel had had a tiny bit: the old necromancer had once taken in a stray cat and given it a saucer of milk – a Thing would have skinned and eaten it.

The crowd of Things was growing impatient. *"Open . . . open . . . open!"* They whispered in unison.

Simon decided that, whatever the consequences for himself, he would not open the doors. If someone – he was sure it was Marcia – had put a Quarantine on the Palace it was for a good reason, most probably to keep the Darke Domaine isolated to one place and to protect the Castle. He himself would have done the same, and reinforced it with a Cordon too. No doubt Marcia had done something even better – and he wasn't about to mess it up.

"No," Simon croaked. "I won't. I won't open the doors."

"Well said!" harrumphed Sir Hereward.

"Open . . . the . . . doors," repeated the Thing, who had half strangled him.

"No," said Simon.

"Then perhaps your *mother* will persuade you." The Thing clasped its ragged, peeling hands together and, one by one, Simon heard its knuckles crack. He watched it push its way through the crowd of Things and, taking four other Things with it, lope off down the Long Walk in the direction of Sarah's sitting room.

Surely, thought Simon, his mother wasn't still in the Palace – was she?

❄ 25 ❄

SIMON AND SARAH

Sarah Heap looked much smaller than Simon remembered. In fact, when the Things that had gone to fetch her came back into the entrance hall, Simon could see no sign of Sarah. For a brief moment of hope he thought his mother was not there after all. But as they drew near, Simon saw Sarah's faded yellow curls just visible inside the press of Things that surrounded her.

Murmuring in the excited way that Things have when they know something unpleasant is going to happen to someone, they pushed and poked the terrified Sarah Heap towards Simon. Sarah stared at Simon in horror, and on her face Simon read what he had been so afraid he would see – his mother thought that this was *his* doing.

"Mum, Mum, *please*, I didn't do this. *I didn't!*" said Simon, instantly back to being a little boy wrongly accused of something.

Sarah clearly did not believe him. "Oh, *Simon*," she sighed.

But the next few seconds made Sarah change her mind.

"You will open the door now," the strangler-Thing intoned.

"N-no," stuttered Simon.

"You *will*," the Thing informed him. It shoved a smaller Thing standing beside Sarah out of the way, then it raised its bony hands and placed them around Sarah's neck, which looked, Simon thought, so very thin and fragile.

"Simon," whispered Sarah. "What do they want?"

"They want to get out, Mum. But they can't. They want me to do it for them."

"Out into the Castle?" Sarah looked horrified. "All of them? Out there? With all those poor people?"

"Yes, Mum."

Sarah looked outraged. "No son of mine will do *that*, Simon."

"But, Mum, if I don't . . ."

"Don't!" said Sarah fiercely. She closed her eyes.

The Thing tightened its fingers around Sarah's neck. Sarah began to choke.

"No!" yelled Simon. He sprung forward to wrench the Thing from his mother but the four other Things pounced on him and held him fast. "Stop it, stop it, *please!*" Simon yelled.

"When you open the door, I shall stop," replied the Thing, pressing into her throat with its thumbs.

Sarah's hands clawed uselessly at the Thing and gasping sounds came from her throat as she struggled for air.

Simon was in despair. "*No . . .* please *stop.*"

The Thing's blank eyes stared back at Simon. "Open . . . the . . . door," it commanded.

Desperately Simon glanced around, looking for Sir Hereward for help. But the ghost had been pushed backwards by the throng of Things that had gathered for a better view, and all Simon could see was the tip of his sword waving uselessly in the air. He was on his own.

Sarah drew in a loud, rasping gasp and went limp.

Simon could stand it no more – *he was killing his own mother*. All he had to do was to open one stupid door and she would live. If he didn't, she would die. That one certainty overwhelmed him. Nothing else mattered. Everything else was in the future, but his mother was dying *right now*, before his eyes. Simon made a decision: everyone would have to take their chance; at least they would have a chance – unlike Sarah, who had none unless he gave in. He stepped up to the Palace doors and placed his hands on the thin film of Magyk that covered the ancient wood. And then, hating every moment of what he was doing, Simon Heap spoke the Reverse for the Quarantine.

The Thing dropped Sarah like a hot potato – humans were not pleasant objects for Things to touch. "Open it," it hissed at Simon.

Simon turned the huge brass door handle and pulled open the heavy double doors. The Things poured out of the Palace like a stream of dirty oil, but Simon paid them no attention – he was kneeling on the worn limestone flags, holding Sarah. She took in a long, wheezing breath, so long that Simon wondered if she would ever stop. Slowly the mottled blue of her face suffused with pink and Sarah's eyes flickered open. She looked up at her oldest son in confusion.

"Simon?" she croaked in a painfully hoarse whisper. She looked at him as if seeing him for the first time. *"Simon?"*

Gently Simon helped her sit up. A sudden gust of snow blew in through the open doors. Sarah was staring at him, remembering now. "Simon, you *haven't*?" she whispered. Simon glanced up at Sir Hereward, not daring to reply.

The ghost looked down at Simon sadly. There was nothing to say. He would have done the same for his own mother, he thought.

"Simon," said Sarah. "You *didn't* let them out. Did you? Oh no ..."

Sarah sank back to the floor and Simon gently let her go. He sat beside her, head in his hands. He'd done wrong. He knew he had. But he'd had a choice only between two wrongs. And what choice was that?

✳ 26 ✳
ABSENCES

"Beetle," said Marcia as they halted outside Larry's Dead Languages and Beetle fumbled for his key. "What are your plans for tonight?"

Beetle thought glumly what his plans had been: Jenna's fourteenth-birthday party at the Palace. He'd been looking forward to it for months. He knew that the cancellation of a party paled in significance against what had happened at the Palace that night, but if you'd asked Beetle which he regretted most right then, he would have admitted it was the party.

"None," he replied.

"In the continued *absence* of my Apprentice –" there was an edge in Marcia's voice – "I would greatly appreciate an assistant – a knowledgeable assistant. An assistant who does not run off and spend his valuable time with a *disreputable old Alchemist.*" Marcia almost spat the last few words. She recovered her poise and continued. "So, Beetle, what do you say to spending the night at the Wizard Tower and helping us with our preparations for the Fumigation tomorrow?"

Once again Beetle had the uncomfortable feeling of being second choice to an unavailable Septimus. But the offer was not one he wanted to refuse. The alternative was creeping up to his tiny room at the back of Larry's Dead Languages while trying not to wake the irascible Larry – something he had not yet managed to do. Larry was a light sleeper and always woke with a string of Latin curses, which, with his recently acquired knowledge, Beetle now understood perfectly.

And so he replied, "Yes, I'd like that very much."

"Good." Marcia looked pleased.

As Beetle and Marcia walked up Wizard Way, the Safety Curtain lighting up the night behind them, both were occupied with thoughts of who might be marooned in the Palace inside the Darke Domaine. Beetle's thoughts led to his terrifying afternoon – and it was only then he remembered the book he had snatched from Merrin's grasp.

He fished it out of his pocket and handed it to Marcia. "I forgot. Merrin had this. I snatched it just as he was doing the BeGone. I'm sure you've got a copy but I thought you'd be interested."

Marcia stopped in her tracks, which happened to be under a torch post. She stared at the unprepossessing, sticky little book in her hands and let out a long, low whistle. Beetle was a little shocked – he didn't know Marcia *whistled*.

"Beetle, I most certainly do not have a copy – there is only *one* of these," said Marcia, turning over the dog-eared book in amazement. "I have wanted to get my hands on this for *years*. It is the index – the key to the secrets – of a very important book." She looked at Beetle, her eyes shining with excitement. "Beetle, I cannot tell you what a relief this is. I have to confess that what I saw at the Palace tonight frightened me and frankly, I wasn't at all sure we could get rid of it. I was afraid we might never be able to use the Palace again – that it would be Quarantined for ever." Marcia shook her head in dismay.

Quickly Marcia flicked through *The Darke Index*. "Amazing ... just wonderful. This is the real thing. Beetle — you have saved the day!"

Beetle grinned. "Gosh," he said. "I didn't realise it was *that* important."

Marcia turned to him. "It is *pivotal*. You see, now — for the first time for hundreds of years — we can use the Paired Codes. They are our protection against the Darke, but we have been unable to read them ever since this disappeared along with *The Undoing of the Darkenesse*. I found *that* mouldering in the Marram Marshes, but it's no good for the really important stuff without this." She waved *The Darke Index* triumphantly. "Now we shall be able to get rid of that nasty little concoction of Merrin Meredith's down at the Palace with *no trouble at all!*" Marcia looked at Beetle with a broad smile. "I do hope it will be all right if I borrow this tonight?"

Beetle was quite taken aback. "Oh ... yes. Of course," he said. "In fact, I'd like you to keep it. Something like that should only belong to the ExtraOrdinary Wizard."

"Very true," said Marcia approvingly. "But thank you all the same, Beetle." She put *The Darke Index* into her most secure pocket. "So now," she said, "we shall pay a visit to the Manuscriptorium. There is something there I need to collect."

Bother, thought Beetle.

The door to the Manuscriptorium was locked but Marcia had a key. This was a source of great indignation to Jillie Djinn but there was nothing she could do about it. ExtraOrdinary Wizards always had a key to the Manuscriptorium for use in emergencies — which Marcia considered this to be. She turned the key in the unwilling lock and the door swung open without the usual *ping*. The counter was disconnected every evening before the scribes left the building.

Reluctantly Beetle followed Marcia into the scruffy front office. He had been there too many times that day for his liking.

"It's not *my* favourite place, either," Marcia said in a half-whisper. "But I need to collect the Manuscriptorium half of the Paired Code. Of course we have the Wizard Tower half of the Pair, but unfortunately the Manuscriptorium half is somewhere here in a place known only to the Chief Hermetic Scribe." Marcia sighed. "I just wish it wasn't *this* Chief Hermetic Scribe, that's all." She looked at Beetle hopefully. "I don't suppose you happen to know where it might be?" she asked.

Beetle shook his head. "I've no idea what a Paired Code even looks like," he said.

"The Manuscriptorium one is a small silver disc with lines radiating out. I think there's a hole in the middle where the ancient Hermetic Scribes used to put a thread and wear it around their neck. They used the Paired Codes a lot in those days," Marcia said wistfully. "The Manuscriptorium half is much smaller than the Wizard Tower half, which we have up in the Pyramid Library. Neither of them look like much on their own, but when you put them together it's quite something, apparently. As we will soon find out." Marcia looked delighted. The thought of once more being able to perform such ancient Magyk thrilled her.

They went through to the Manuscriptorium, which was deserted. It was wreathed in shadows, illuminated only by the light that shone up from the basement where the Conservation, Preservation and Protection Scribe, Ephaniah Grebe, lived and worked. Of Jillie Djinn there was no sign.

"Miss Djinn will be in her rooms," Beetle whispered to Marcia. "She never stays down here after the scribes have gone home. She goes upstairs and eats biscuits. And counts things."

Beetle led Marcia through the lines of desks to the back of the Manuscriptorium to a short flight of worn stairs with a battered blue door at the top. Marcia *tippy-tapped* up the stairs and tugged irritably at the silver bell pull beside the door. The faraway tinkle of a bell rang forlornly somewhere at the top of the building. They waited for the sound of Jillie Djinn's footsteps descending, but none came. Impatiently Marcia rang the bell again. There was no response.

"It really is too bad," muttered Marcia. "The Chief Hermetic Scribe should always be available in emergencies." She stomped back down the steps. "We'll just have to search this wretched place until we find her. She's got to be here somewhere."

Suddenly something caught Marcia's attention. She pointed to the narrow stone arch at the side of the Manuscriptorium that led to the Hermetic Chamber. "I thought I saw someone go in. Out of the corner of my eye. But she must have seen us – what *is* she playing at?" Marcia hurried over, her python shoes tapping on the old oak floorboards.

Beetle hung back as Marcia stepped through the arch into the pitch-black passageway that led to the Chamber, but she beckoned him to come with her. He followed her in.

The Hermetic Chamber, the inner sanctum of the Manuscriptorium, was reached by a seven-cornered passage, which was specially designed to catch any stray Magyk that might try to escape from the Chamber or, indeed, enter and disturb the delicate balance within. It was also completely light-tight and soundproof – and somewhat unnerving.

As Beetle followed the rustle of Marcia's cloak brushing along the stone floor of the passageway, he had the uncomfortable feeling from the way she had slowed down that she was a little spooked. As he went deeper into the passage and lost any glimmer of light, Beetle began to feel pretty spooked himself, but as they turned the seventh and last corner, the light from the Hermetic Chamber flooded the final few feet of the passageway and Beetle relaxed. Half obscured by Marcia's flowing cloak, he saw with some relief – for he'd had the distinct impression that Marcia had been expecting something altogether different – the Chief Hermetic Scribe, Jillie Djinn, sitting at the familiar round table.

The white walls of the Hermetic Chamber made it feel dazzling after the darkness of the passageway. Beetle glanced around – everything looked just as he remembered it. The ancient dark Glass was propped up against the roughly plastered walls, as was the old-fashioned abacus. The large, round table was in the middle and underneath it, Jillie Djinn's tiny feet in their sensible – and sadly scuffed – black lace-ups were resting on the main Ice Tunnel hatch, which, Beetle noticed with relief, was closed and clearly had been for a long time, judging by the dust covering it.

Jillie Djinn seemed smaller than Beetle remembered. The harsh light in the Chamber showed up the shabbiness of her dark blue silk robes – a shabbiness that he had not seen before. Jillie Djinn had always been rather fond of new silk robes and was very particular about keeping them clean, but now they were creased and had what looked suspiciously like gravy stains down the front. Beetle was shocked. But what he found most concerning was that Jillie Djinn was not actually doing anything. There were no books of calculating tables open in front of her, no fat ledgers filled with endless columns of her tiny figures, ready for an unfortunate scribe to transcribe in triplicate the next day. She sat hunched over the bare table, staring into space and hardly seemed to register the intrusion of her visitors. It was as if she wasn't there.

A flash of concern crossed Marcia's face but she got straight down to business. "Miss Djinn," she said briskly. "I have come to collect the Manuscriptorium half of the Paired Code."

Jillie Djinn sniffed and, to Beetle's shock, wiped her nose on her sleeve. But she did not reply.

"Miss Djinn," said Marcia, "this is a serious matter. You must make available to the ExtraOrdinary Wizard the Manuscriptorium half of the Paired Code upon request at any time of day or night. I realise this has not been requested for many hundreds of years, but I am requesting it *now*."

Jillie Djinn did not react. It was as if she did not understand a word that was said.

Marcia looked concerned. "Miss Djinn," she said quietly. "May I remind you that Paired Code Protocol forms part of the induction Oath of a Chief Hermetic Scribe."

Jillie Djinn shifted uncomfortably and sniffed again. She looked pathetic, thought Beetle. Once so upright and proper, she was now weighed down by her cares. He had never liked the Chief Hermetic Scribe, but now his dislike was mixed with sadness for her. And disquiet – something was very wrong. Beetle glanced at Marcia. She was regarding the Chief Hermetic Scribe with a new light in her eye – like a cat getting ready to pounce. And then, suddenly, she did. Marcia leaped forward and clapped both hands on Jillie Djinn's shoulders. "Depart!" she commanded. A flash of purple lit up the white chamber and Jillie Djinn gave a sharp scream. A loud hiss came from beneath Marcia's hands, and Beetle was aware of something small and dark – he couldn't see exactly what – leaping to the ground and scuttling out.

"A Maund," muttered Marcia. "Someone's put a Maund on her. Vicious beasts and *so* heavy. *What* is going on here?" She glanced around the Hermetic Chamber anxiously. So did Beetle. It appeared to be empty, but he was no longer so sure.

"Miss Djinn," said Marcia quickly. "This is of the utmost urgency. You must *immediately* give me the Paired Code."

Jillie Djinn, relieved of her burden, was no longer hunched. But she still looked haunted. She glanced around the chamber, then quickly ran her hand across the table in a zigzag movement. There was a quiet whirring noise and a tiny drawer opened in front of her. Looking about her uneasily, Jillie Djinn took out a small, polished silver box and placed it on the desk.

"Thank you, Miss Djinn," said Marcia. "I would like to check that the Code is indeed in the box."

Jillie Djinn was gazing out somewhere in the distance over Marcia's shoulder. She nodded absently, then an expression of fright flashed across her features.

Marcia was busy opening the box. Inside she saw a small silver disc with a raised central boss, which was exactly like the textbook drawing that she was familiar with. Marcia put her spectacles on and took a closer look. A mass of fine lines radiated from the tiny hole at the centre of the disc and scattered along these was an array of Magykal symbols, some of which she had not seen since her advanced codacology week in her final Apprentice year. Marcia was satisfied – it was indeed the Manuscriptorium half of the Paired Code.

There was sudden disturbance in the air. Marcia spun around. She lunged forward, and Beetle saw the little silver disc fly into the air and disappear – then something gave him a sharp punch in the stomach.

"*Oof!*" He doubled over, gasping for breath.

"Beetle, block the passageway!" Marcia shouted.

Still winded, Beetle threw himself in front of the entrance to the seven-cornered passage. Something bony with sharp elbows hurtled into him and Beetle staggered back. He braced himself, arms across both sides of the narrow passageway so that whatever it was could not pass. As an invisible hand gripped his arm and tried to wrench it away from the wall, Beetle felt something burning dig deep into his flesh.

"Aargh!" he gasped.

"Don't move, Beetle," said Marcia, advancing towards him. "Just . . . stay . . . there."

Beetle's arm felt as though the pointed end of a red-hot stick was being thrust into it, and the look on Marcia's face as she came forward was terrifying. But he did not move. Marcia stopped a little way in front of him, her green eyes flashing furiously. She stretched out her arms and grasped something, as though she were picking up a two-handled pot.

"Reveal!" she said triumphantly. A cloud of purple filled the exit to the Hermetic Chamber and showed a dark shape within it. As the cloud cleared, the gangly form of Merrin Meredith was Revealed, both ears held firmly in Marcia's iron grip.

Merrin swallowed hard and winced. The Paired Code had sharp edges.

"He's *swallowed* it!" Marcia cried incredulously.

BOTT'S BRIDGE

Rose was late. Things were somewhat chaotic at the Wizard Tower and she had had to fill in at the sick bay until the duty Wizard had eventually turned up from the Call-Out. But now, excited by the prospect of being part of the amazing piece of Magyk that was the Safety Curtain, Rose raced down Wizard Way, trying not to be any later for Bertie Bott than she possibly could.

In front of the dazzling Safety Curtain, Bertie Bott stood resolutely guarding the fusion point, unaware that only a few feet behind him, on the other side of the shimmering purple wall, twenty-five Things were patrolling to and fro, silently looking for the join.

Bertie's stomach was grumbling. He was having cruel visions of supper: sausages and mashed potatoes dripping with gravy, treacle tart and custard and possibly even a small square of chocolate fudge, if he could manage it. Bertie sighed inwardly. He was sure he could. As Bertie wondered whether he would prefer peas or a double helping of mash with his sausages, his stomach emitted the loudest rumble yet. A mere arm's length behind him, the strangler Thing stopped and listened hard.

Bertie was getting extremely cold. Even his finest pre-loved, fur-lined cloak was not keeping out the chill of the Longest

Night. Bertie took it off to shake the fur out and thicken it up for a while – a trick he knew from the cloak business – but as he shook it, the edge of the cloak touched the Safety Curtain. Bertie never knew what hit him.

Lightning fast, the Thing punched a hole through the fusion point, grabbed Bertie's cloak with one hand and pulled hard. Bertie toppled backwards into the Safety Curtain. In a moment the strangler Thing had its hands around Bertie's throat and was pulling him in so that he lay across the Safety Curtain like a small, humpbacked bridge – later immortalised in Apprentice textbooks as Bott's Bridge.

On either side of Bertie the Magykal purple light still shone like a luminous wall, but now there was a dark gap, like a broken tooth in a smile. As Bertie Bott lay face up on the snow-dusted grass, a Darke tide of Things began to flow across him. (Many years later, when the Safety Curtain was Raised by one who wished he had not missed his only chance to see it done, this scene was the first to be replayed.)

Rose arrived at the two torches that flanked the Palace Gate. She stopped for a moment to catch her breath and then pushed open the gate, on which a large notice had been stuck that tersely read: PARTY CANCELLED. Gudrun the Great – the faded old ghost on guard at the Palace Gate – smiled at Rose, but Rose, almost blinded by the startling brilliance of the Safety Curtain, did not see her.

"Take care, Apprentice," whispered Gudrun. "Take care." But all Rose heard was the whispering of the wind blowing in off the river.

As Rose approached the Safety Curtain she began to feel uneasy. Rose was a sensitive Apprentice who was aware – some said far too aware – of the Darke. And Rose had a talent that she did not yet know she possessed but was soon to discover: she could See Things. Looking out for Bertie Bott, Rose walked slowly across the grass, heading to where she knew the join in the Safety Curtain was – directly in front of the Palace Gate. The twinge of anxiety that had been niggling at her grew greater. *Where was Bertie Bott?* She could not see him anywhere. It wasn't as if he was hard to spot. There was plenty of Bertie to see. She wondered if, because she was late, he had already gone home for his supper, but Rose was sure that not even a ravenous Bertie Bott would dare desert such an important post.

Reluctant to get any closer, Rose slowed to a halt. She had the oddest sensation that the harder she looked for Bertie, the less she could see. She shivered and pulled her green Apprentice cloak around her, not to keep warm – she was still warm from her run – but to protect herself. Against what, she was not sure.

"Bertie?" she called in a half-whisper. *"Bertie?"*

There was no reply.

Rose decided to use an old Wizard trick. She stood still and turned her head slowly from side to side, letting her eyes "see what they will see". And they did. Suddenly Rose saw the gap in the Safety Curtain, and pouring through the gap were Things. Monstrous, shadowy Things loping towards her like all her nightmares rolled into one.

Rose ran. She ran so fast that she was halfway up Wizard Way before the true meaning of what she had seen struck her. And then she kept on running, as fast as she could, back to the Wizard Tower to tell Marcia.

But Marcia was not there.

Marcia was still at the Manuscriptorium.

✳ 28 ✳

HERMETICALLY SEALED

As Rose raced past the dark windows of the Manuscriptorium, Marcia was inside struggling to place a Locking Band around Merrin's wrists.

Merrin was fighting her all the way, and Marcia was shocked at how powerful he had become. She was using the strongest Restrain she could without putting him at risk, and still he was not totally subdued. Merrin's dark eyes blazed with anger and his feet twitched as he tried to kick out. The gold on his Two-Faced Ring flashed as he pulled and twisted his wrists, stretching the Locking Band almost to the breaking point. After a torrent of verbal abuse, Marcia had also placed a Silent on Merrin, but that did not stop his mouth moving. Marcia was – to her regret right then – a good lip-reader.

A loud knocking came suddenly on the outside door. Marcia looked annoyed. "Beetle, see who it is and tell them to go away."

Beetle went into the front office. He opened the door to find Marcellus Pye on the other side. "Ah, Scribe Beetle." Marcellus sounded relieved. "I am glad it is you."

Beetle had long ago given up trying to explain to Marcellus Pye that he was no longer – and indeed never had been – a scribe at the Manuscriptorium.

"Excuse me, Mr Pye," he said, closing the door, "we're a bit busy at the moment."

Marcellus stuck his foot in the door. "I have just been to the Palace for the party, only to find there is a Safety Curtain up." He sounded worried. "My Apprentice, Septimus Heap, was going there and I am concerned for his safety. I thought I'd call in on my way to the Wizard Tower. Is he here, by any chance?"

"No, he's not. I haven't seen him and no, before you ask, I *don't* know where he is." Beetle sounded annoyed. He was tired of everyone asking him about Septimus. "Excuse me, Mr Pye, but do you mind leaving now? We have things to do. Would you move your foot *please*?"

But Marcellus did not move – his attention was suddenly taken by something down at the Palace end of Wizard Way. Beetle took the opportunity to close the door. He had to lean against it hard to shut it, and as he turned the key he saw that Marcellus was executing an odd kind of dance.

Beetle decided to ignore him.

Marcellus began banging on the door.

Marcia came into the front office, grasping Merrin by his Locking Band. Jillie Djinn trailed behind like a ghost. "Beetle, what's going on?" Marcia demanded.

"It's Marcellus," said Beetle. "He won't go. He's looking for Septimus."

A look of concern flashed across Marcia's face. "But I thought Septimus was with *him*."

"Apparently not," said Beetle, a trifle sulkily.

"What's that in the door?" asked Marcia. A long, thin piece of red leather was poking between the door and the doorjamb.

"Bother," said Beetle. "It's his shoe." He unlocked the door and it flew open to reveal Marcellus Pye, equally irritable, on the other side, nursing the squashed tip of his precious red shoe – a birthday present from Septimus a few years back.

"It's ruined," said Marcellus. "Look." He pointed to the torn ribbons that were tied just below his knee.

"You shouldn't wear such ridiculous shoes," snapped Marcia.

"Well, you'd know all about *that*, Marcia," Marcellus retorted.

While Marcia and Marcellus were bickering, something had caught Beetle's attention – the two torches burning on either side of the Palace Gate had just gone out. Beetle had a bad feeling – why had both torches gone out at the same time? He soon had his answer.

"No . . . no, it *can't* be!" he gasped.

"What?" asked Marcia, stopping midway through a shoe-based insult.

Beetle pointed down Wizard Way. Like water through a sluice gate, the thick fog of the Darke Domaine was pouring out through the Palace Gate and swirling into the lower reaches of Wizard Way. "The Safety Curtain! It's been breached!"

"What?"

Merrin smirked.

"Marcellus," said Marcia. "Make yourself useful for once. Hold on to this . . . this *creature* for me. I must see what's happening." She handed Merrin over to Marcellus and hurried out into Wizard Way. She was just in time to see the first torch at the Palace end of the Way extinguished by what looked like a bank of black fog.

Marcia ran back into the front office, slammed the door and leaned against it. She looked as white as a sheet of best

Manuscriptorium paper. "You're right. It's breached." And then, to Beetle's shock, Marcia swore.

Merrin broke through his Silent with a snigger.

Marcia glared at him. "You won't be laughing soon, Merrin Meredith," she snapped. "Not when we are getting that Paired Code out of you."

Merrin went pale. He hadn't thought about that.

"Get him out of here, Marcellus," said Marcia. "Beetle, you take Miss Djinn. We must get back to the Wizard Tower *now*."

Beetle was reluctant. "But we can't abandon the Man-uscriptorium," he said.

"The Manuscriptorium must take its chance."

Beetle was horrified. "No. *No*. If the Darke Domaine gets in everything will be destroyed. All the arcane Magyk in the Hermetic Chamber *and* in the old Chamber of Alchemie . . . it will all be gone. Nothing will remain. *Nothing*."

"Beetle, I'm sorry, there is nothing we can do."

"Yes, there is," Beetle retorted. "The Hermetic Chamber can be Hermetically Sealed. That's why it's built like it is. And the ExtraOrdinary Wizard can Seal it. That is true, isn't it?"

Marcia answered with great reluctance. "Yes, it is true. But to Seal Miss Djinn in there would be nothing short of murder. She wouldn't know what was happening to her. She'd have no chance."

"But I might," said Beetle quietly.

"You?"

"Yes. Seal *me* in the Hermetic Chamber. *I'd* guard it."

Marcia was grave. "Beetle, there's only enough air for about twenty-four hours – after that you'll have to do a Suspension. You do know that not all those Sealed in the Chamber have survived, don't you?"

"I'll take a chance. Fifty–fifty isn't bad."

Marcia shook her head. So often Beetle knew far more than she expected. "Three lived, three died," she muttered. "Not great odds."

"Could be worse. Please, Marcia. I don't want to lose the Manuscriptorium. I'd do anything to stop that. *Anything*."

Marcia knew that Beetle was not going to change his mind. "Very well, Beetle. I'll do as you ask. I'll Activate the Hermetic Seal."

Leaving Marcellus Pye with a firm grasp on Merrin and Jillie Djinn staring into space, Marcia and Beetle made their way to the entrance of the seven-cornered passage. They stopped outside.

"You'll find the secret siege drawer in the table by tapping the tiny black circle in the centre seven times. The drawer contains emergency supplies and the Suspension Charm with instructions," Marcia told him.

"I know," said Beetle.

"You're a brave young man, Beetle. Good luck."

"Thanks."

Marcia wondered if she'd ever see Beetle again. "Right then. You'd better go in. As soon as you get into the Chamber, sit in the Chief Hermetic Scribe's seat. It's in the very centre and you'll be all right there. The Sealing Magyk will be very intense and that isn't always pleasant."

"Oh. Right."

Marcia gave Beetle a strained smile. "I'll count to twenty-one and then I'll Activate the Seal. Understood?"

"Yep. I'll count too. One . . . two . . ."

Beetle was gone. He ran through the narrow stone archway into the darkness of the seven-cornered passageway, and before he had finished counting to ten he was in the brightness of the circular Hermetic Chamber. Feeling as though he shouldn't, Beetle sat down in the Chief Hermetic Scribe's seat at the table and, still counting, he watched the archway that he had just run through. The next few seconds were the longest of his life.

The Activating of the Seal began. A hissing sound filled the Chamber, immediately followed by a rush of cold air as the Seal was driven along the seven-cornered passage. Beetle watched in awe as a shining wall of purple Magyk came around the last corner and stopped at the arch that led into the Chamber. The brilliant Magykal light pulsed over the archway and the circular white walls of the Hermetic Chamber intensified it, sending currents of Magyk swirling while Beetle sat in the calm at the very centre of it, hardly daring to breathe. After a few minutes he could see that the purple light was beginning to fade, wisps of Magyk were drifting off. They hung in the air, and the bittersweet taste of Magyk caught in Beetle's throat and made him cough.

As the last vestiges of Magyk disappeared, Beetle understood what it meant to be Sealed in the Chamber. Where the arch had been there was now solid wall, indistinguishable from any other part of the walls that surrounded him. He was entombed. Above his head rose the dome of white stone that formed the ceiling of the Hermetic Chamber and below his feet was the Sealed hatch to the Ice Tunnels.

Remembering what Marcia had told him, Beetle tapped the tiny black circle in the centre of the table seven times. A small drawer below the table sprung open. He reached in for the Suspension Charm – and drew out a handful of liquorice bootlaces.

✳ 29 ✳
RETREAT

The Darke Fog was rolling on. It had reached the door to Larry's Dead Languages. It seeped in around the edges, finding out the cracks, pouring through the knotholes, needling through the woodworm burrows. It gathered around the piles of translated papers, swirled into the much-repaired vase and snuffed out the candles in the window display that had been lovingly created by Beetle. It rolled on through the shop, up into the gallery, along the landing and up the rickety winding stairs. In his little room deep in the back of his house, Larry awoke. He sat up in bed and pulled the bedclothes around his chin. He stared into the darkness, listening hard. Something was wrong. Larry swung his sticklike legs out of bed and, as his bare feet flinched at the cold touch of the floorboards, he saw black smoke pouring underneath the door. Aghast, he leaped up – *the house was on fire!*

The smoke advanced towards him; it began to curl around his frozen toes and slowly, as if in a dream, Larry sat down again. A great feeling of contentment overwhelmed him. He was back in his old school, getting the Latin prize for the seventh time, and he had just seen his father in the audience, in the front row, smiling at him. Smiling at *him*. Larry. Clever Larry . . .

As the Darke Fog layered around him, Larry sank back on to the bed. His breathing slowed and, like a tortoise in the depths of winter, he slipped into a dark and dreamless state somewhere between life and death.

Marcia ushered Jillie Djinn and Marcellus, who had custody of Merrin, out into Wizard Way. She quickly locked the Manuscriptorium door behind her. Marcia could hardly bear to think about what she had left behind, but what was facing her was even worse. Advancing up Wizard Way like a pulsating black toad was a Darke shifting blackness.

Marcia was horrified to see that the rolling Fog was accompanied by a line of Things – the outriders of the Darke Domaine. Like the sweep of a terrifying search party, they spread out across Wizard Way, with the Fog tumbling behind. She stared in shock, unable to tear herself away from the disaster unfolding before her.

Marcellus tried to draw Marcia back. "Marcia, you must get to the Wizard Tower at once," he said.

Merrin's eyes flashed angrily at Marcellus. With the Darke Domaine advancing ever nearer he felt he was growing stronger. The Two-Faced Ring was growing hot on his thumb and the vicious green faces were beginning to glow. The top face winked up at Merrin, and suddenly he knew he could beat Marcia. He could beat them all. *He* was in charge now. He was the *best*.

First Merrin broke the Silent with the worst insult in the Castle, then he broke the Restrain. With a violent twist, he tore himself from Marcellus's grasp and delivered a vicious kick to the Alchemist's shins. As Marcellus hopped up and down, gasping in pain, Merrin raised his arms in the air and, in a taunting gesture, he pulled his wrists apart, snapping the Locking Band as if it were no more than tissue paper. Relishing his moment of triumph, Merrin darted forward and waved his left thumb in Marcia's face, laughing as she instinctively drew back. The ring's evil-looking faces glowered at her, their jade complexions gleaming.

Marcia knew that there was only one possible reason for Merrin's sudden surge of power – the oncoming Darke Domaine had indeed been Engendered by him. Up to that moment she had found it hard to believe that Merrin was capable of such a thing but now, as he pranced away, defiantly punching the air with his fist, with his Two-Faced Ring glittering, Marcia realised just how much control Merrin now had. It was a terrifying thought.

"You *idiot*!" she yelled at him. "You have no idea what you are messing with, do you?"

"Neither do you, Wizard-face." Merrin laughed. "Run away to your twinkly little Tower and take old haddock-brain with you. I don't need her any more. See ya! Ha, ha, ha!" Merrin could hardly contain himself. He had never had such an attentive – such an astonished – audience. It was wonderful. It was what he had always wanted.

"*That's* what I think of your stupid Magyk!" he yelled at Marcia, flicking his fingers at her. Gesticulating and laughing, Merrin danced backwards, his pale face lit by the still-burning torches and the ghostly candle displays shining on to the empty streets. "Come and get me if you dare!" he yelled.

Marcia did dare. It was undignified but she didn't care. Inside Merrin's nasty little stomach the precious half of the

Paired Codes was churning, and she was not having her last chance to defeat him escape her. She tore down Wizard Way in pursuit. Merrin laughed and ran, his scribe's cloak streaming behind him, his outstretched arms flapping like a demented bird flying towards his flock.

Marcellus raced after Marcia. It was a long time since he had run anywhere and his shoes were not ideal for the job – particularly after their encounter with the Manuscriptorium door. But Marcia's pointy purple pythons were even less suited to running and he soon caught up with her.

"Marcia . . ." he puffed. *"Stop."*

Marcia shook Marcellus's hand off her arm. "Let *go*," she hissed.

Marcellus stood firm. "No. Marcia, don't you see? The closer you get to *that* –" he waved his free hand at the advancing Darke Domaine and its outriders – "the more power it gives him and the more it takes from you. Come away before something awful happens."

"Something awful *has* happened," snapped Marcia, setting off in pursuit once more.

Marcellus kept up with difficulty. "It could be worse . . . you still have the Wizard Tower . . . don't risk it all on a nasty little scribe."

Marcia stopped. "You don't understand – he's got the Paired Code!"

Marcellus looked shocked, but he quickly recovered himself. "You must leave the Code to its fate. You must go back to the Wizard Tower." His voice shook with urgency. *"You must not lose that too."*

"I shall lose neither." Marcia flared angrily. "Just watch me."

Marcellus and Marcia were now more than halfway down Wizard Way. Only a hundred yards or so in front of them, the wall of Darke Fog rolled slowly towards them. At the base of the Fog a line of Things stretched out, shifting and blending in with the Darke, loping slowly forward, pulling the Darke Domaine with them.

Merrin was heading erratically for the Fog. Spinning around to check that Marcia and Marcellus were still watching him, flashing rude signs, screaming obscenities, he drew ever closer to his Darke Domaine.

Marcia focused hard on Merrin, gauging the distance. Muttering the words for a Fast Freeze, she raised her arm and a streak of ice-blue light left her hand and arced into the air. It landed with a brilliant white flash in the middle of Merrin's back. He staggered forward and gave a loud cry.

"Good shot," muttered Marcellus.

Marcia grimaced. She had never before performed Magyk behind someone's back. It was considered the lowest form of Magyk, but now was not the time for such refinements. She had held back from Freezing Merrin, assuming she would get him to the Wizard Tower and deal with things there. Freezing someone was dangerous and not to be undertaken lightly. But now, with the lives of everyone in the Castle at stake, Merrin's safety was no longer a consideration.

Slowly Merrin turned around. Outlined in a blue-white crackle of the Freeze trying to take, he shivered and shook as though caught in an icy blast – but he did not Freeze. He stared at Marcia for some seconds, as though his brain had slowed and he was trying to work out what had happened. Marcia returned the stare, waiting impatiently for the Magyk to take effect. In the frost of the spell, Merrin shone out against the Darke Fog, but slowly he began to shine a little less. Horrified, Marcia saw the icy brilliance fade and Merrin shake himself, throwing off the Freeze like a dog throwing off water.

Marcia's Magyk had failed. It was then that she really understood what she was up against.

Marcellus stepped up beside her. "You *must* go now," he said quietly.

"Yes. I know," Marcia said, but she did not move.

Merrin was ecstatic – *he had defeated the ExtraOrdinary Wizard*. High on success, he turned to the line of Things and yelled, "Get her!"

Marcellus saw three Things step forward as one. He saw them take another step and that was all he waited to see. He grabbed Marcia's hand and ran, dragging her up Wizard Way, not daring to look behind. Breathless, they reached the Manuscriptorium, where Jillie Djinn was patiently, vacantly, waiting.

Marcia recovered her senses. She wheeled around to see how far away the Things were and saw to her great relief that they had barely moved. An encroaching Darke Domaine takes a lot of energy, and the Things were slow and ponderous. Knowing that it could do no more than cause a brief delay, Marcia threw an emergency Barrier across Wizard Way, then with the Chief Hermetic Scribe sleepwalking between them, she and Marcellus set off towards the Wizard Tower.

At the Great Arch an extremely anxious Hildegarde was hovering, waiting for Marcia's return.

"Madam Marcia! Oh, thank *goodness* you are here!"

Marcia wasted no time. "Is Septimus back?" she asked.

"No." Hildegarde sounded worried. "We thought he was with you."

"I feared as much." Marcia turned to Marcellus and laid her hand on his arm. "Marcellus. Please, will you find Septimus for me? And keep him safe?"

"Marcia, *that* is why I came to the Manuscriptorium. I *am* looking for him. I will not stop until I find him – I promise you."

Marcia gave Marcellus a strained smile. "Thank you. You know I trust you, don't you?"

"Well, I never thought I'd hear you say *that*," said Marcellus. "Things must be bad."

"They are," said Marcia. "Marcellus, if . . . if anything happens, I give you guardianship of my Apprentice. Farewell." With that she turned away abruptly and walked quickly into the dark blue shadows of the Great Arch, the *tippy-tappy* sound of her shoes echoing as she went.

Marcellus stood for a moment and watched something that he had only seen once before, in his first life as the Castle's greatest Alchemist. He saw the Barricade – a thick slab of ancient pitted metal – silently slice down through the centre of the Great Arch, closing the main entrance into the Wizard Tower courtyard. It was, Marcellus knew, the first of many shields that would be sliding into place, readying the Tower for its strongest and most ancient Magyk of defence.

Next came the beginnings of a four-sided Living SafetyShield (this was the strongest SafetyShield possible; it was known as Living because it required the energy of many living presences within it to keep it active. It could also, in extremis, act independently). Like the Barricade, a Living SafetyShield was extremely rare. Marcellus watched it rise slowly from the walls surrounding the Wizard Tower courtyard, a blue shimmering skin that cast its eerie light into Wizard Way.

Satisfied that the Tower would be protected – for a while, at least – Marcellus slipped away, leaving Wizard Way to its fate. With his cloak blending into the shadows, the old Alchemist disappeared into the very narrowest of gaps between two ancient houses. Marcellus walked quickly through what, in his Time, had been known as the Canyons – formed in the earliest days of the Castle when the houses that lay between Wizard Way and the Moat were built. To protect against the spread of fire, houses had been built in blocks of two or three, with a tiny gap left between the blocks – a gap so small that Bertie Bott would not have been able to squeeze in. But Marcellus Pye moved fast through the Canyons like a snake down a pipe, heading for what he guessed was his last chance to find Septimus before the Darkenesse fell.

❈ 30 ❈

IN THE DRAGON HOUSE

Jenna walked slowly back along the jetty to the overgrown path at the river's edge. She saw the purple glow of the Safety Curtain lighting up the sky and guessed it was some kind of Magyk isolating the Palace – and her mother inside it. She stuffed her hands deep into her pockets and the smooth brass of the key that Silas had given her met her hand. Jenna sighed. She did not want to spend the night alone in her old home. She wanted to be with Septimus, but if Septimus was not around, the next best thing was his dragon. She set off along the path beside the river, wading through the long, frosty grass until she reached a tall gate at the end. Nailed on to the gate was a rough, and somewhat charred, wooden sign. It read:

DRAGON FIELD
ENTER ENTIRELY AT OWN RISK
POSITIVELY *No* COMPENSATION PAYABLE
FOR ANY EVENTUALITY, FORESEEN OR OTHERWISE.
SINGED: BILLY POT (MR)
DRAGON KEEPER BY APPOINTMENT

Jenna could not help but smile. The sign actually *was* singed, so Billy's spelling was unusually accurate. She opened the gate and stepped inside. On the far side of the field she could see the long, low shape of the Dragon House silhouetted against the purple light. Carefully weaving her way around several suspiciously smelly heaps in the grass, she headed towards the Dragon House. Sometimes talking to a dragon was the only thing that made sense.

Now that Spit Fyre was no longer an unwelcome squatter in the Wizard Tower courtyard but master of his very own field, his Dragon House was left open all night. When Sarah Heap had queried this, Billy Pot had indignantly told her that, "Mr Spit Fyre is a gentleman, Mistress Heap, and gentlemen are not locked up at night." The more pressing reason, which Billy had omitted to mention, was that on his very first night in the Dragon House, Spit Fyre had eaten the doors.

And so, as Jenna carefully crossed the field, she saw the dark outline of Spit Fyre's blunt snout resting on the edge of the ramp that led up to the shed. Jenna drew her witch's cloak around her and pulled the hood down low on her face, enjoying the feeling it gave her of blending in with her surroundings. Silently she approached the Dragon House, planning to creep into the warm straw and curl up beside Spit Fyre's comforting bulk.

The Dragon House was a dark and smelly place. It was also noisy. Dragons as a rule do not sleep quietly and Spit Fyre was no exception. He snuffled, he grunted, he snorted, he sniffed. His fire stomach rumbled and his ordinary stomach gurgled. Every now and then an enormous snore would shake the roof of the Dragon House and send Billy Pot's rack of dragon-poo shovels rattling.

Deep inside the Dragon House, Septimus was leaning against the warmth of Spit Fyre's fire stomach. He had made a decision – it was time to go back to the Wizard Tower. Time to face Marcia and explain why he had missed the most important Magyk in the Castle in many years. Slowly he got to his feet and – *what was that?* A rustle in the straw like a rat ... but bigger than a rat ... much bigger ... moving stealthily ... purposefully ... with a subtle taint of Darke about it. *It was coming towards him.* Muscles tensed, Septimus did not move. Spit Fyre, he noticed, continued sleeping, which was odd. He peered into the dark, straining his eyes to see. *The rustling was getting nearer.*

There was a sudden stumble in the straw, but still Spit Fyre slept on. Why, thought Septimus, didn't Spit Fyre wake up? The dragon was very touchy about who came into his house. He hated strangers – only a few months ago Spit Fyre had very nearly eaten a sightseer who had run in for a dare.

It was then that Septimus saw the intruder move out of the shadows and he realised why Spit Fyre did not wake up. It was a witch; she must have put some kind of sleep spell on him. It was a Darke witch too; the front-buttoned cloak with the embroidered symbols all over it was just like the ones worn by the Port Witch Coven. Septimus crouched down and watched the fumbling figure approaching, feeling its way along the spines. From his pocket he took out his neat coil of Darke thread. He waited until the witch was so close that her next step would tread on him – then he pounced. He threw the thread, which had a surprising weight to it, around the witch's ankles and pulled. She toppled on to him with a piercing scream.

"Arrrgh! Ouch ouch *ouch!*"

"*Jen?*" gasped Septimus.

"*Sep?* My ankles. Oh, Sep, there's a *snake*. Get it off me — *getitoffme!* Oh, it hurts. *It's burning me!*"

"Oh, Jen. I'm sorry, oh, I'm sorry! I'll get it off you. Keep still. *Keep still!*"

Jenna stayed as still as she could bear and Septimus unwound the Darke thread as fast as he could. As soon as it was gone Jenna began rubbing her ankles furiously.

"Ouch ouch ouch . . . *Aargh!*"

Septimus leaped to his feet. "Back in a mo, Jen. Don't move."

"Fat chance," muttered Jenna. "I think my feet are going to fall off."

Septimus squeezed past Spit Fyre's leathery folded wings and disappeared behind the dragon's spiny head. He emerged a few moments later and quickly made his way back to Jenna.

"Ouch ouch ouch . . ." Jenna was muttering fiercely to herself. *"Ouch."* Bright red welts had sprung up wherever the Darke thread had touched her skin and she felt as though a red-hot wire were cutting into her.

Septimus kneeled down and rubbed a damp and somewhat sticky cloth carefully over the angry red lines. Immediately the vicious sting left them and Jenna gave a sigh of relief.

"Oh, Sep, that's amazing. It's stopped. Oh, it's *stopped*. What *is* it?"

"It's my handkerchief."

"I know *that*, silly. But what's the sticky stuff on it?"

Septimus avoided answering. "You need to leave it on for twenty-four hours. OK?"

"OK." Jenna nodded and poked tentatively at her ankles; she now felt no more than a warm buzz along the fading red lines. "It's brilliant stuff. What is it?"

"Well. Um . . ."

Jenna looked at Septimus suspiciously. "Sep, *tell* me. What *is* it?"

"Dragon dribble."

"Oh, yuck!"

"It's powerful stuff, Jen."

"I've got to have dried dragon dribble on me for *twenty-four hours*?"

Septimus shrugged. "If you don't want the Darke stuff back."

"Darke stuff?" Jenna looked at Septimus. Her voice dropped to a whisper. "Is that what it was? What are you doing messing with Darke stuff, Sep?"

"I could ask you the same thing," said Septimus.

"Huh?"

"Jen, you might think that's a nice fancy dress witch's cloak, but it's not. It's the real thing."

"I know," said Jenna quietly.

"You *know*?"

Jenna nodded.

"But I thought that no one could wear a Darke witch's cloak unless they're . . ." Septimus looked at Jenna. She returned his gaze steadily. "Jen – you're *not*?"

Jenna was defensive. "I'm only a novice,"

"*Only a novice?* Jen. I . . . I . . ." Septimus ran out of words.

"Sep, stuff's happened."

"You're telling me."

Jenna stifled a sob. "Oh, it's been so horrible. It's *Mum* . . ."

They sat in the straw at the back of the Dragon House and Jenna told Septimus about Merrin, about the Darke Domaine and about what had happened to Sarah. Now, at last, Septimus understood what had been going on since he had left Marcia that afternoon.

Jenna reached the end of her story and fell silent. Septimus said nothing; he felt as if his whole world was falling apart.

"It's all so rubbish, Jen," he muttered eventually.

"I *hate* birthdays," said Jenna. "Stuff happens on birthdays. Everything you love gets messed up. It's awful."

They were silent for a while, then Septimus said, "Jen. I'm really, *really* sorry."

Jenna looked at Septimus, his face lit by the soft yellow light shining up from his Dragon Ring. She didn't think she'd ever seen him look so unhappy, not even when he was a small, frightened boy soldier. "It's not *your* fault, Sep," she said gently.

"Yes, it is. It wouldn't have happened if I had helped you when you asked me – if I had listened properly to what you were saying. But I was so taken up with ... with all my stuff. And now look at the mess we're in."

Jenna put her arm around Septimus's shoulders. "It's OK, Sep. There are so many *ifs*. *If* I had taken more care of the Palace. *If* I'd searched it ages ago when I first thought I saw Merrin. *If* Dad had done something when I'd asked him. *If* I'd gone to Marcia earlier instead of asking Beetle. *If* Marcia had explained things properly to Mum. If if if. You were just one of a long trail of them."

"Thanks, Jen. I'm so glad you're here."

"Me too,"

They sat quietly together, lulled by the regular breathing of the sleeping Spit Fyre. They were beginning to drift off to sleep themselves when they heard something that made the hairs on the backs of their necks prickle. From outside the Dragon House came a scraping sound, as though someone was scratching fingernails on brick.

"What is it?" whispered Jenna.

Septimus felt Spit Fyre's muscles suddenly tense – the dragon was awake. "I'll go and see."

"Not on your own, you won't," said Jenna.

The scraping was making its way towards the front of the Dragon House. Spit Fyre gave a warning snort. The scraping sound stopped for a moment and then continued. Septimus felt Jenna grab his arm. "Use this," she mouthed, pointing to her witch's cloak.

Septimus nodded – it seemed that a witch's cloak had its uses after all. Hiding beneath the cloak to disguise their human presence, they crept forward, squeezing between Spit Fyre and the rough sides of the Dragon House. Suddenly Spit Fyre made an odd movement that almost flattened Jenna and Septimus against the wall. Keeping his head on the ground, the dragon raised himself on his rear haunches. His back spines stabbed at the rafters of the Dragon House, deepening the grooves they had already made. He snorted and his fire stomach gurgled.

Septimus glanced at Jenna; something was wrong. They inched around Spit Fyre's wings and stopped dead – black against the purple glow of the Safety Curtain were the unmistakable shapes of three Things.

One of the Things had hold of Spit Fyre's sensitive nose spine and was pushing the dragon's head down into the straw. Spit Fyre snorted once more, trying to draw in enough air to make Fyre – but because the Thing was holding his head down, his fire stomach could not work. A dragon can only make Fyre with his lungs full and his head held high.

On either side of Spit Fyre's head, the other two Things were closing in. A sudden glint of steel – purple in the glow of the *Safety Curtain* – flashed a warning. The Things had knives. Long, sharp, dragon-stabbing blades.

Jenna had seen the knives too. She made a sign that Septimus took to mean *you get one and I'll get the other one*. It was only after Jenna took off like a rocket and launched herself and her cloak on to the nearest Thing that Septimus realised Jenna had no weapon – except surprise. But he thought no further. While Jenna landed on the Thing, knocked it to the ground and smothered it in the swathes of her cloak, Septimus leaped over Spit Fyre's neck and hurled himself at the other Thing. The Thing knew nothing until it was felled by a burning hot wire around his neck and the rapid incantation of a Freeze.

Bemused, the third Thing – which still had hold of Spit Fyre's nose spine – stopped and stared. It was the very last Thing to have been Engendered by Merrin and was the runt of the litter, with few of the nastier Thing attributes. It survived by mimicking other Things and generally playing follow-the-leader, but it had a tendency to dither when left on its own – which is what it did now.

The next few seconds were a blur. Spit Fyre felt the Thing's grip loosen. With a fierce, fast movement he threw his head high. The nose-spine Thing went flying. Like a ragged bundle of wash hurled by an angry washerwoman, it travelled into the air, crashed through the branches of an overhanging fir tree and disappeared over the high hedge that divided the Dragon Field from the Palace grounds. As it flew through the air it hit the purple force field of the Safety Curtain – which still worked fine everywhere but at the fusion point – bounced off and was sent on an opposite trajectory towards the river. Some seconds later a faint but extremely satisfying splash was heard as it hit the river.

Jenna and Septimus grinned at each other cautiously. Three down – but how many to go?

The Thing felled by Septimus lay inert in the straw with a long strand of Darke Thread almost lost in the scraggly folds of its neck. Jenna still had her cloak wrapped around the other Thing's head, but it wasn't something she wanted to do for long.

"Sep, I'm stuck," she whispered. "If I get up then this Thing will too."

"Just leave your cloak over it, Jen. It's a Darke cloak and you shouldn't be messing with it. Leave it there and it will carry on smothering the Thing all on its own."

Jenna was not impressed. "I'm not leaving my cloak. No way."

Septimus glanced around nervously, wondering if there were any more Things. He didn't want a discussion with Jenna right then, but some things just had to be said.

"Jen," he whispered urgently. "You don't seem to realise. Your cloak is a Darke *witch cloak*. It's not good. You shouldn't be playing around with it."

"I am *not* playing around with anything."

"You are. Leave the cloak."

"No."

"Jen," Septimus protested. "This is the cloak talking, not you. *Leave it.*"

Jenna fixed Septimus with her Princess look. "Listen, Sep, this is *me* talking – not some lump of wool, OK? This cloak is my responsibility. When I want to get rid of it I will do it properly so that no one else can get hold of it. But right now I want to keep it. You forget that you've got all this weird Magyk stuff to protect you. You know what to do against the Darke. I don't. This cloak is all I have. It was given to me and *I am not leaving it on this disgusting* Thing."

Septimus knew when to give up. "OK, Jen. You take your cloak. I'll Freeze that one as well."

Expertly Septimus muttered a quick Freeze. "You can get your cloak back now, Jen," he said. "If you really want it."

"Yes, Sep. I *do* really want it." Jenna snatched her cloak off the Thing and to Septimus's amazement she put it on.

Septimus decided to leave his Darke thread buried deep into the raggedy skin folds of the other Thing's neck. There were some things he never wanted to do and diving into the folds of a Thing's neck was one of them. Close up, Things have a foul, dead-rat kind of smell and there is something truly revolting about direct contact with them. When a human touches them, strips of slimy skin peel off and stick to flesh like glue.

Spit Fyre had watched with interest as his Pilot and Navigator so very effectively immobilised his attackers. There is a widespread theory that dragons do not feel gratitude, but this is not true – they just don't show it in a way that people reconise. Spit Fyre lumbered obediently out of the Dragon House. He carefully avoided treading on any toes and refrained from snorting in Septimus's face – this was dragon gratitude at its fullest.

Septimus stood close to the comforting bulk of Spit Fyre and scanned the eerily purple Dragon Field.

"Do you think there are more Things?" Jenna whispered, looking uneasily behind her.

"I dunno, Jen," muttered Septimus. "They could be anywhere ... everywhere. Who can tell?"

"Not *everywhere*, Sep. There's one place they can't go." Jenna pointed skywards.

Septimus grinned. "Come on, Spit Fyre," he said. "Let's get out of here."

❄ 31 ❄
HORSE STUFF

The Gringe family was upstairs in the gatehouse. They had come home early from their traditional Longest Night wander down Wizard Way because Mrs Gringe had felt ignored by Rupert – who had been talking to Nicko for much of the time – and had demanded to go home. Consequently they had missed the Raising of the Safety Curtain, although it would have meant little to them as the Gringes treated Magyk with great suspicion.

Mrs Gringe was sitting in her chair, unravelling a knitted sock with quick, irritable movements, while Gringe was poking at the small log fire that they allowed themselves on the Longest Night. The chimney was cold and choked with soot, and the fire was refusing to draw and was filling the room with smoke.

Rupert Gringe, his filial duty of the Wizard Way promenade done for another year, stood hovering by the door, anxious to be away. He had a new girlfriend – the skipper of one of the Port barges – and he wanted to be there to meet her when the late-night barge arrived at the boatyard.

Beside Rupert stood Nicko Heap, equally anxious to be gone. Nicko had come along because Rupert had asked him.

"There's not so much shouting if someone else is there," Rupert had said. But that was not the only reason Nicko had come. The truth was, he was feeling unsettled. Snorri and her mother had taken their boat, the *Alfrún*, on a trip to the Port and "only a little way out to sea, Nicko. We'll be back in a few days", Snorri had promised. When he had asked her why, Snorri had been evasive. But Nicko knew why – they were testing the *Alfrún's* seaworthiness. He knew that Snorri's mother wanted Snorri and the *Alfrún* to come home with her, and something told Nicko that Snorri wanted that too. And when Nicko thought about it – which he tried not to – he felt a sense of freedom at the thought of Snorri going away. But it was tinged with sadness, and after Lucy's excited talk of weddings, Nicko longed to get back to the boatyard. At least you knew where you were with boats, he thought.

Lucy smiled at her brother trying to edge out of the door. She knew exactly how he felt. Tomorrow she would be away on the early morning Port barge and she couldn't wait.

"You definitely booked a horse space, Rupe?" she asked him, not for the first time.

Rupert looked exasperated. "Yes, Luce. I *told* you. The early morning barge has two horse berths and Thunder's got one. For sure. Maggie said."

"Maggie?" asked his mother, looking up from her sock unravelling, suddenly alert.

"The skipper, Mother," Rupert said quickly.

It was not lost on Mrs Gringe that Rupert had gone bright pink, his face clashing with his spiky, carrot-coloured hair. "Oh. She's a *skipper*, is she?" Mrs Gringe tugged at a knot, determined to unpick it. "Funny job for a girl, that."

Rupert was old enough now not rise to the bait. He ignored his mother's comments and continued his conversation with Lucy. "Come down to the boatyard early tomorrow morning, Luce. About six. We'll – I mean *I'll* help you load him before the passengers arrive."

Lucy smiled at her brother. "Thanks, Rupe. Sorry. I'm just a bit edgy."

"Aren't we all," said Rupert. He hugged his sister and Lucy returned his hug. She didn't see much of Rupert and she missed him.

After Rupert had left, Lucy felt the eyes of both her parents on her. It was not a comfortable feeling. "I'll go and check on Thunder," she said. "I thought I heard him whinny just then."

"Don't be long," said her mother. "Supper's nearly done. Shame your brother couldn't wait for supper," she sniffed. "It's stew."

"Thought it might be," muttered Lucy.

"What?"

"Nothing, Ma. Back in a tick."

Lucy clattered down the wooden stairs and pushed open the battered old door that led on to the run up to the draw-bridge. She took a few deep breaths of smoke-free, snowy air and walked briskly around to the old stable at the back of the gatehouse, where Thunder was residing. Lucy pushed open the door and the horse, lit by the lamp that she had left in the tiny high window, looked at her, the whites of his eyes glistening. He pawed the straw, shook his head with its dark, heavy mane and gave a restless whinny.

Lucy was not a great horse person, and Thunder was bit of a mystery to her. She was fond of the horse because Simon loved him so much, but she was also wary. It was his hooves that worried her – they were big and heavy and she was never quite sure what Thunder was going to do with them. She knew that even Simon took care not to stand behind the horse in case he kicked.

Lucy approached Thunder cautiously and very gently patted the horse's nose. "Silly old horse coming all this way to see me. Simon must be so upset that you've gone. Won't he be pleased to see you? Silly old horse …"

Lucy suddenly had a vivid picture in her mind of riding Thunder off the Port barge and Simon's look of amazement when he saw what she could do. She knew it was possible; she had seen the daredevil boys who rode their horses off the barge instead of leading them. It couldn't be that difficult, she thought. It was only up the gangplank, which was not exactly far to ride a horse. Then Simon could take over and they could ride back together. It would be such fun …

Lost in her daydream, Lucy decided to see how easy it was to actually get up on to Thunder. Not at all, was the answer. Lucy regarded the horse, which stood so much taller than her – his back was as high as her head. How *did* people get on to horses? Ah, thought Lucy, saddles. They had saddles. With things for your feet. But Lucy did not have a saddle. Gringe had not found one cheap enough, and Thunder had had to make do with a thick horse blanket – which Lucy rather liked, as it was covered in stars. It was also, in the cold, much more useful to him.

Lucy was not deterred; she was determined to get up on Thunder. She fetched the set of wooden steps that reached to the hay manger and set them beside the horse. Then she climbed the steps, wobbled precariously at the top and clambered on to the horse's broad back. Thunder's only reaction was to shift his weight a little. He was a steady horse and it seemed to Lucy as though he hardly noticed her. She was right. Thunder had barely registered her presence; the horse had someone else on his mind – Simon.

"Bother!" An exclamation came from somewhere near the floor.

Lucy recognised the voice. "Stanley!" she said, looking down from her great height. "Where are you?"

"Here." The voice sounded rather aggrieved. "I think I've trodden in something." A rather portly brown rat was peering at his foot. "It's not very nice if you don't wear shoes," he complained.

Lucy felt excited – a reply from Simon, and so soon. But Stanley was fully occupied inspecting his foot with an expression of disgust. Lucy knew that the sooner he got the horse poo off his foot, the sooner she would hear Simon's reply to her message.

"Here, have my hanky," she said. A small square of purple dotted with pink spots and edged in green lace floated down from Thunder. The rat caught the scrap of cloth, gave it a bemused look, and then scrubbed his foot with it.

"Thanks," he said. With a surprisingly agile leap, Stanley hopped up the steps and jumped on to Thunder, landing just in front of Lucy. He presented her with the handkerchief.

"Mmm, thank you, Stanley," said Lucy, taking it carefully between finger and thumb. "Now, please, *tell me the message*."

With one hand holding on to Thunder's coarse black mane for support, Stanley stood up and put on his official message-delivering voice.

"No message received. Recipient marked as gone away."

"Gone away? What do you mean, *gone away*?"

"Gone away. As in, not present to receive message."

"Well, he was probably out doing something. Didn't you wait? I paid extra for that, Stanley, you know I did." Lucy sounded cross.

Stanley was peeved. "I waited as agreed," he said. "And then, seeing as it was you, I went to the trouble of asking around, which was when I discovered that there was no point waiting any longer. I only just got the last barge home, *actually*."

"What do you mean, no point waiting any longer?" asked Lucy.

"Simon Heap is not expected to return, so his domestics told me."

"Domestics – *what domestics*? Simon doesn't have any cleaners," Lucy said snappily.

"Domestics as in the rats that live in his room."

"Simon doesn't have rats in his room," said Lucy, slightly affronted.

Stanley chuckled. "Of *course* he has rats. Everyone has rats. He has – or had – six families under his floor. But not any more. They left when something rather nasty turned up and took him away. It was sheer luck I bumped into them. They were looking for another place on the quayside but it's not easy; very desirable properties there are already stuffed to the brim with rats, you wouldn't believe how many –"

"Something nasty took him away?" Lucy was aghast. "Stanley, whatever do you mean?"

The rat shrugged. "I don't know. Look, I must go home and see what my brood are doing. I've been out all day. Goodness knows what state the place will be in." Stanley went to jump down but Lucy grabbed hold of his tail. Stanley looked shocked. "*Don't* do that. It's extremely bad manners."

"I don't care," Lucy told him. "You're not going until you've told me *exactly* what you heard about Simon."

Stanley was saved from answering by a sudden gust of wind, which blew the stable door wide open.

Thunder raised his head and sniffed the air. He pawed the ground restlessly and Lucy began to feel slightly unsafe – there was something Magykal about Thunder and he was a little scary. Thunder had been Simon's faithful horse through his master's Darkest moments and there was an indissoluble connection between them. And now Thunder Knew his master was near. And where his master was, Thunder must be.

And so Thunder went. He threw his head back, whinnied and was out of the stable door, his hooves slipping on the snowy cobbles as he cantered out into the night. Paying Lucy no more attention than if she had been a gnat on his back, the horse galloped off to the place where he Knew his master awaited him.

The clattering of Thunder's hooves was the only sound to disturb the warren of deserted streets that led from the North Gate gatehouse to Wizard Way – apart from some extremely piercing screams.

"Stop! *Stop*, you stupid horse!"

✳ 32 ✳

DAY OF RECOGNITION

After Spit Fyre had taken off from the Dragon Field, Septimus had flown him away from the Palace and out above the river. They had wheeled to the right just before the jagged crag of Raven's Rock and were now flying above the Moat. Septimus craned over Spit Fyre's wide, muscled neck and stared down at the Castle below on his right-hand side. He gasped. It looked as though someone had dropped a large pool of ink on to the Palace and Wizard Way. The dark irregular shape was, even as he watched, moving outwards as yet more candles and torches were extinguished.

Jenna was sitting in her usual Navigator space, in the dip between the dragon's shoulders, just behind Septimus.

"It's so dark down there!" she shouted above the noise of Spit Fyre's wings.

Septimus searched for a sign of Marcia's Safety Curtain. He thought that maybe, just possibly, he could see a faint purple glimmer deep within the blackness, but he could not be sure. The only thing he could be sure of was that the Safety Curtain had failed.

At least, Septimus noted with relief, Marcia knew what was happening. The spreading blackness had halted at the wall surrounding the Wizard Tower courtyard and from its boundaries he saw the Living SafeShield begin to grow upwards into the night sky, encasing the entire tower in a cone of brilliant indigo and purple lights, the colours of which showed, to Septimus's knowledgeable eye, that Marcia was in residence. It was a magnificent sight and made him feel proud to be part of the Wizard Tower – although once again unhappy to be outside the Magyk.

They flew slowly along the Moat, keeping the Castle Walls on their right. The Darke Domaine was spreading fast and he knew that nowhere in the Castle would be safe for long. The one beacon of light – the Wizard Tower and his *home* – was now closed to him and to Jenna. They had a simple choice: leave the Castle and flee to safety or find somewhere within the Castle where they could hide out and keep the Darke at bay.

Jenna tapped him on the shoulder. "Sep, what are you *doing?* We have to get to the Palace. We have to get Mum out of there!"

They had now reached the other end of the Moat. The One Way Bridge was to their left and in front of them; on the other side of the river, lights ablaze, was the ramshackle shape of the Grateful Turbot Tavern. Septimus contemplated landing there – the lights looked so welcoming – but he needed time to think. He wheeled Spit Fyre around in a tight turn and began to retrace their path.

Septimus flew Spit Fyre slowly so that he could see how far – and how fast – the Darke Domaine was spreading. They flew over the drawbridge, which was raised as it always was at night. The Darkenesse had not yet reached there, although the Gringes' rather mean single candle in the upstairs window of the gatehouse did not make it easy to tell. But there were other signs that all was still well; Septimus could still see the thin covering of snow on the road reflecting the light from candles in houses set back from the gatehouse. He also saw, as he dipped down for a closer look, a rectangle of lamplight thrown on to the road from an open door at the back of the gatehouse.

Septimus took Spit Fyre down low along the Moat. He was relieved to see that candles were still burning in the windows of the houses that backed on to the Castle walls, as were the lamps in Jannit Maarten's boatyard and on the newly arrived late-night Port barge, which was just docking. But farther down, the Manuscriptorium boathouse was Darke. Not merely unlit but so dark as to be almost invisible. If Septimus had not known it was there, he would have thought it was an empty space. And yet, strangely, the houses on either side of it were still lit.

What Septimus could not see was that the Darke Domaine had followed Merrin to the Manuscriptorium and had spread through the entire premises, which extended down to the Moat. Merrin intended to make the Manuscriptorium his temporary headquarters until he got into the Wizard Tower. But being in charge was not as much fun as he had expected now that Jillie Djinn was no longer there to intimidate. The empty old place felt rather creepy, especially with the Seal on the Hermetic Chamber glowing eerily through the Darke, behind which – unknown to Merrin – Beetle was frantically searching for the Suspension Charm, which was now languishing in the rubbish bin out in the yard along with the rest of the contents of the siege drawer.

With the Paired Code feeling like it was stuck in his throat, Merrin had gone upstairs to Jillie Djinn's rooms to wash it down with her stash of biscuits and plan his next move. His mouth full of stale biscuit, Merrin stared out of the window and caught a glimpse of Spit Fyre as he flew past. *What was he doing up there?* Merrin cursed. Stupid Things. They couldn't even do a simple job like getting rid of a pathetic dragon. Well, he'd show that dragon. He'd get it. Merrin smiled at his dark reflection in the grubby window. Oh, he'd get it all right – one way or another. It wouldn't stand a chance. Not against what he'd got planned. This was, Merrin told himself, going to be *fun*.

Spit Fyre flew slowly on, past tiny attic windows containing flickering candles until they came to Snake Slipway. Below them, to the left of the Slipway was Rupert Gringe's boat-house, still happily ablaze with a couple of buckets containing torches. The houses on either side of the slipway were also still untouched; many of them seemed to have caught Marcellus's habit of burning forests of candles, and the whole slipway shone brightly.

Septimus had made his decision – Alther must wait. He would use his Darke Disguise to rescue Sarah and then he would stay and fight the spreading Darkenesse. But he could not risk Jenna's safety. He wheeled Spit Fyre out across the Moat and over the Forest borders in order to give the dragon space to turn for a good run into Snake Slipway, where he planned to land.

"What are you doing?" yelled Jenna.

"Landing!" yelled Septimus.

"Here?"

"Not here. Snake Slipway!"

Jenna leaned forward and yelled in Septimus's ear, "No, Sep! We have to get Mum!"

Septimus turned to face Jenna. "Not you, Jen. Too dangerous. I'll go!"

"No way! I'm coming too!" Jenna shouted above the *whooshing* of the air as the dragon's wings swept down.

Spit Fyre was lining up for the tricky swoop down into Snake Slipway, but Septimus could not concentrate with Jenna yelling in his ear. He wheeled the dragon around once more.

"No, Jen!" Septimus yelled as Spit Fyre flew back across the Moat towards the Forest again. "I'm taking you somewhere safe first. We don't know what's in the Palace now!"

"Mum's in there, you – you *total dumbrain!"*

Septimus was shocked. Jenna never used language like that normally. He blamed the witch's cloak. He turned Spit Fyre around and lined him up once more for landing on Snake Slipway.

Spit Fyre began his second attempt to land.

"Septimus Heap, you are *not* dumping me!" Jenna yelled.

"But, Jen –"

"Spit Fyre!" yelled his Navigator. "Go up!"

Spit Fyre – who obeyed his Navigator's instructions in the absence of any from his Pilot – began to go up. But not for long.

"Down, Spit Fyre!" his Pilot countermanded. Spit Fyre went down. His Pilot was in charge.

"Up!" yelled Jenna.

Spit Fyre went up.

"Down!" Septimus yelled. His dragon obeyed. Septimus had one last go at persuading Jenna.

"Jen, please, listen to me! The Palace is *dangerous*! If something happens to you, that's it. No more Queens in the Castle. *Ever*. We can land here and I'll take you to Marcellus's house – he's got a SafeChamber – or we can even go to Aunt Zelda's. You choose. But you *have* to be safe!"

Jenna fumed. How many times had she been sidelined just because she had to be *safe*? She leaned forward – all the better to yell at Septimus and tell him she didn't care about being Queen, *so there* – and *The Queen Rules* dug into her. Angrily she pulled the book out of her pocket, intending to hurl it into the Moat below. But something stopped her. The little red book sat so naturally in her hand and felt so much a part of her that suddenly Jenna knew she could not throw it away – in fact, she could *never* throw it away. This fragile, worn, little red book contained her history. Whatever she thought of it, whether she liked it or not, this was who she was, who her family was, and she knew, as she looked down on to the Darkening Castle below, that this was where she belonged. Nothing she did would ever change that.

And so, sitting on a somewhat confused dragon, Jenna realised what the Day of Recognition actually meant. Somehow, without any official ceremony, procession or traditional hoo-ha, it had happened. She understood who she was and she accepted it. It was, she realised, recognition of something she had known for a while but had preferred not to notice. It was a bit late in the day, she thought, as she heard the chimes of the Drapers Yard Clock strike ten, but that was fine.

Septimus took Jenna's sudden silence to mean that she had stopped speaking to him in disgust.

"Landing!" he yelled.

"OK!" Jenna shouted back.

Surprised, Septimus turned around. "Really?" he shouted.

Jenna smiled. "Yep! Really!"

Septimus gave Jenna a huge grin of relief – he hated arguing with her – and once more Spit Fyre began his approach to Snake Slipway. The slipway was hemmed in on both sides by houses, some leaning in towards each other and none wanting their windows smashed by a misplaced dragon's tail. It was not an easy landing, even for a dragon used to the narrow confines of the Castle. With a loud snort of excitement – Spit Fyre liked a challenge – the dragon headed down.

It was a perfect landing. Spit Fyre settled lightly in the centre of the slipway and folded his wings with an air of satisfaction and the creaking sound of old leather. His Pilot and Navigator slipped down from their places and stood on the sleet-shined slipway.

"Spit Fyre," said his Pilot. "Stay!"

Spit Fyre regarded his Pilot quizzically. Why did his Pilot want him to Stay in this bad place? Had he done something wrong? His Navigator came to his rescue.

"You can't tell Spit Fyre to Stay, Sep."

"It's only for a few minutes, Jen. Then I'm going to get Mum."

But Spit Fyre's Navigator dug her heels in. "*No*, Sep. Supposing those Things come back? You have to take the Stay off. It's not fair."

Septimus sighed. Jenna was right. "OK. Spit Fyre, Stay replaced with StaySafe." He patted the dragon's nose. "OK?"

Spit Fyre snorted. He thumped his tail and sent a plume of Moat water up into the air. The dragon watched his Pilot and Navigator walk to a doorway a few yards up on the left where the slipway levelled out. His Pilot placed a key in the lock and turned it, then they disappeared inside and the door closed behind them.

Spit Fyre watched the door, waiting for them to come out again. And while he watched he stretched out his wings so that he was ready to take off quickly – just in case. He didn't like the slipway. It was narrow and full of hiding places on either side. Spit Fyre didn't like what was happening to the Castle either; he could smell the Darke, he could feel it coming closer. And then, suddenly, he saw a movement in the shadows. His Pilot's StaySafe kicked in and so, as a group of Things crept up on him in a pincer movement, knives at the ready, Spit Fyre raised his wings and, with one powerful downstroke, he was airborne. He looked down and saw the Things on the slipway staring up at him. A moment later there was a loud *splat* – a particularly large amount of dragon poop had scored a direct hit.

Jenna didn't like Marcellus's house very much. There was something about the smell of it that reminded her of a Time five hundred years ago.

"Do we *have* to come here?" she asked uneasily.

"Marcellus has a SafeChamber," said Septimus. "Where you can be, um, safe." He glanced around. The narrow hallway and the flight of stairs leading up to the next floor were ablaze with candles, as they always were, but a stillness hung in the air, and he knew the house was deserted. Septimus felt at a loss.

He realised he was also hoping for Marcellus's company – and advice. "He's not here," he said flatly.

Jenna was puzzled. "He must be. All these candles are lit."

"He always does that," said Septimus. "I've told him that one day he'll come back to find his house burned down but he doesn't listen."

"I don't want to stay here on my own, I really don't," Jenna said anxiously. "It's so creepy . . ."

"Let's go," said Septimus. "We'll sit it out on Spit Fyre and wait for him to come back."

"I'm not leaving the Castle," said Jenna, a warning in her voice.

"Neither am I. We'll just kind of hover. We'll be safe on Spit Fyre." Septimus opened the door and stepped outside. Jenna heard a sharp intake of breath.

"What is it?" she asked.

"Spit Fyre. He's *gone*."

❋ 33 ❋

THIEVES IN THE NIGHT

As Jenna and Septimus stood on the lonely slipway, the dark waters of the Moat to their right and the spreading Darkenesse of the Castle all around them, they heard an echoing, flip-flapping noise coming towards them.

"Quick, Jen. Let's get back inside."

Jenna nodded. The noise sounded horribly like an approaching Thing. Septimus was fumbling with the key when a voice called out, "Apprentice! Apprentice!"

The flustered figure of Marcellus Pye, with one shoe looking like a dog had got it, appeared from a gap between two houses and hurried towards them. "Thank goodness you are here." He bowed slightly to Jenna, as he always did, and then succeeded in annoying her – as he always did. "Princess. I did not recognise you at first. You do realise you are wearing the cloak of a true witch?"

"Yes. I do, thank you," said Jenna. "And before you ask, the answer is no, I will not take it off."

Marcellus surprised her. "I should hope not. It may prove useful. And you will not be the first Witch Princess in the Castle."

"Oh." Jenna was not entirely pleased. She had rather assumed that she *was* the first Witch Princess.

"Marcellus," said Septimus urgently. "Jenna needs to stay somewhere safe. I thought your SafeChamber –"

Marcellus did not let Septimus finish. "It is not safe here, Apprentice. Miss Djinn knows I have a SafeChamber – all Chambers are declared to the Chief Hermetic Scribe – and I fear our Chief Hermetic Scribe has already given away our secrets." Marcellus shook his head sadly. He hated to see what had happened to the Manuscriptorium. "There are Things abroad already," he continued. "They will come here soon enough, and Princess Jenna will be trapped like a rat. We must go somewhere the Darke Domaine will have trouble finding."

"But the Darke Domaine is spreading fast," said Septimus. "It will soon be *everywhere*. Jenna should leave the Castle."

"Sep, I'm actually still *here*," said Jenna, annoyed. "And I am *not* leaving the Castle."

"Quite right, Princess," said Marcellus. "Now, I believe that the Domaine will have some trouble getting into the Ramblings, and even once it's inside it will not find it easy to spread. So I suggest we head there and . . . what is that Young Army term, Apprentice?"

"Regroup?" Septimus offered.

"Ah, yes. Regroup. Ideally, what we need is an overlooked little fleapit down a dead end, with an outside window."

Jenna knew exactly where to find one. She pulled out the key that Silas had given her not so very long ago.

"What's that?" asked Septimus.

"It's a key, Sep," teased Jenna.

"I *know* it's a key. But where to?"

Jenna grinned. "An overlooked little fleapit down a dead end, with an outside window," she said.

★ ★ ★

Marcellus Pye closed the door of his house behind him with a sigh and looked up at his dark windows. Septimus had insisted he blow out all his candles and it had made him feel quite depressed.

"Come now, we must go," said Marcellus.

"I'll Call Spit Fyre," said Septimus. "Something must have spooked him. He can't have gone far."

Marcellus looked doubtful. He'd got along just fine without dragon flight for more than five hundred years and he wasn't in a hurry to change things. But Septimus was already letting out the ululating Call, which reverberated off the densely packed houses on Snake Slipway and made the Alchemist shiver. It was a primeval sound, Marcellus thought, one that went back way beyond Alchemie.

They waited nervously on the slipway, glancing at the shadows, imagining movements.

After a few minutes Marcellus whispered, "I do not believe your dragon is coming, Septimus."

"But he *has* to come when I Call," said Septimus, worried.

"Maybe he can't, Sep," whispered Jenna.

"*Don't*, Jen."

"I didn't meant that he was . . . well, I . . ." Jenna stopped. She could see she was only making things worse.

"Dragon or no dragon, we can wait no longer," said Marcellus. "With care we can travel short distances through the Darke Domaine. My cloak has certain … abilities, shall we say, and you, Apprentice, have a small tinderbox that may prove useful." Jenna shot Septimus a questioning look. "And you, Princess, will be protected well enough with your membership of . . ."

Marcellus peered at the markings on her witch cloak. "My, you don't do things by halves, do you? The Port Witch Coven! Now, we must go. We will travel by the Castle Canyons."

"Castle Canyons?" asked Jenna, who liked to think she knew most things about the Castle. "*I've* never heard of them."

"I suspect not many Princesses ever do. Although now you have other, er, allegiances, you might find that will change," Marcellus said with a smile. "The Canyons are not, shall we say, salubrious places. Those using them generally have reasons to hide. However, I know them well and we can slip through the night unnoticed. I am much practised at the art."

That did not surprise Jenna. Marcellus threw his long black cape around himself with a dramatic swirl and, equally theatrically, Jenna followed suit with her witch's cloak, pulling the hood over her head to cover her gold circlet. Compared with his companions, Septimus felt a little conspicuous in his Apprentice green. He followed in their footsteps, feeling like an apprentice thief shadowing his masters.

Almost immediately Marcellus dived into a tiny gap between the houses. An ancient sign half hidden behind some ivy announced its name: SQUEEZE GUTS OPE. With the rough bricks snagging at their cloaks, they threaded their way through the warren between the jumble of houses that were packed in behind Snake Slipway. Their footsteps made no noise as they trod on years of leaves, moss and the occasional soft mound of a small dead animal. Feeling like a small animal himself scuttling through its burrows, Septimus kept glancing up, hoping to see the sky. But the dark of the moon and the snow-laden clouds gave nothing away. Once or twice he thought he saw a star, only to be obscured by the black shape of a chimney or a twist of a roofline as he turned yet another corner. The only light came from the comforting glow of his Dragon Ring as he held his right hand out in front of him.

As they went deeper in, the Canyons narrowed, sometimes so much that they were forced to walk sideways, squeezing past towering walls that threatened to press them flat. Septimus had an image of them squashed between the walls like the dried herbs Sarah Heap kept between the pages of her herb book. He longed to be able to stretch his arms out wide in all directions without his knuckles hitting brick, to be able to run freely in any direction he wanted to, not crawl like a crab between rocks. With every step he felt as though he were going deeper into a place from which he would never escape.

Septimus tried to take his mind off the encroaching walls by looking out for lighted candles in windows but there were hardly any windows to see. The sheer sides of stone rising up on either side blocked any view, and few people had put a window in a wall that looked out on to another wall no more than an arm's length away. But once or twice Septimus saw the telltale glow of a candle way up above them, shining on to the opposite wall, and his spirits raised a little.

At last they followed Marcellus into a wider gap and the Alchemist raised his hand in warning. They stopped. At the end of the gap was a bank of Darke Fog – they had reached the edge of the Darke Domaine.

Jenna and Septimus exchanged anxious glances.

"Apprentice," said Marcellus, "it is time to open your tinderbox."

Jenna watched with great interest as Septimus took a battered tinderbox from his pocket and prised off the lid. She saw him draw something from it, but what it was, she could not tell. He muttered some strange words that she could not catch and threw his hands upwards. She got the impression that something floated down very slowly and settled on to him, but she couldn't be sure. He looked no different. In fact, it seemed more like a mime than anything else – the kind of thing they had had to do in drama classes in the Ramblings Little Theatre, which Jenna had always found rather embarrassing.

However, Marcellus and Septimus seemed satisfied, so Jenna guessed something must have happened. And then she did notice a change – the light from Septimus's Dragon Ring seemed more fleeting somehow, as if thin gauze was moving across it. And, when she looked at Septimus and tried to catch his eye, she realised that something about him eluded her. He was there, and yet he was not there. A little spooked, Jenna stepped back. Sometimes she felt Septimus was part of things that she would never fully understand.

Marcellus regarded his two charges closely. They were as prepared as they could ever be, he thought. Now they would have to put things to the test – it was time to step into the Darke Domaine. He beckoned them to the end of the passageway. They stopped where the Fog rolled in front of them, close enough to reach out and touch, and Marcellus said, "I will go first, then you two walk together. Keep a steady pace, breathe quietly. Keep your mind clear, for it will tempt you to stray from our path with beguiling thoughts of those you once loved. Do not react to anything and above all, *do not panic*. Panic draws Darke things to it like a magnet. Understood?"

Jenna and Septimus nodded. Neither could quite believe they were about to step into the shifting wall of Darkenesse of their own free will. Both Septimus's Darke Disguise and Jenna's witch cloak protected them from the beguiling thoughts that drew people into the Darke Domaine. It was odd, thought Jenna, that her witch cloak allowed her to see the Darke Domaine for what it truly was: a terrifying blanket of evil.

Once again they exchanged glances, then together they followed Marcellus into the Darke Fog.

Septimus's Darke Disguise felt like a second skin. He moved easily through the thick Darke Fog, but both Marcellus and Jenna struggled. Jenna's witch's cloak gave her less protection – it did not totally enclose her in the way Septimus's Darke Disguise did and it was not nearly as powerful. Marcellus's cloak gave even less protection – he did not dabble with the Darke quite as much as he liked people to think he did. But any remnants of Darke offer protection in a Darke Domaine and Marcellus and Jenna managed to struggle along, even though they felt as though they were wading through glue and breathing through cotton wool. Waves of fatigue washed over them, but by force of will they managed to keep going.

After some minutes they came to a halt – they had reached Wizard Way. Marcellus peered cautiously out. He looked right and left and right again in exactly the way Jenna remembered Sarah doing when they used to cross the Way when she was little. Then Jenna had known what Sarah was looking out for, but now she had no idea what it was Marcellus was watching for – or how he could possibly see anything. Marcellus beckoned them forward and they stepped out into Wizard Way.

It was not a good place to be. The Darke Domaine felt heavier here and it moved around them like a living thing. Sometimes they felt something brush past them, and once a

Thing's finger poked at Marcellus but he swept it off with a Darke curse and the Thing scuttled away. They walked steadily down the middle of the Way and concentrated on breathing slowly and calmly, in and out, in and out, as they measured their steps along the familiar – yet now so strange and frightening – Wizard Way.

As they walked on, Septimus began to get a strong sensation that there was something approaching behind them. It was a sense that he had learned to develop over his Apprentice years and he knew it was good. Remembering what Marcellus had said, he fought the urge to look back, but he could not rid himself of the feeling of a great creature bearing down on them fast. So fast that if they didn't jump out of the way right *now* . . . Septimus gave Marcellus and Jenna a hefty shove – not so easy in a Darke Domaine – and leaped to the side.

He was just in time. A huge black horse thundered past, his eyes wide and wild, mane streaming in the Darke and Lucy Gringe clinging on, screaming silent, terrified screams.

Thunder's flight had the effect of clearing a temporary path through the Darke. Marcellus quickly recovered himself and steered Jenna and Septimus into the horse's wake, where they moved quickly along the horse-shaped tunnel that Thunder had created through the swirling blackness. For Marcellus and Jenna it was a relief to be out of the weight of the Darke, although they knew it would not last long – the space was already being invaded by a dull murkiness. At the end of the tunnel they could see that Thunder had halted, and the muffled sounds of shouting drifted towards them.

Jenna risked an excited whisper to Septimus. "Mum . . . I can hear *Mum*."

Septimus was not sure it was Sarah. It sounded more like Lucy Gringe to him, and there was a deeper voice there too.

Thunder's tunnel was slowly collapsing under encroaching wisps of Darke Fog moving into the space like smoke from a fire burning something foul. The sounds at the end of the tunnel faded into ghostly whispers, but in those faraway echoes, Jenna was absolutely convinced she could hear Sarah's voice. Suddenly, much to Marcellus's disapproval, she broke into a run. She could not bear the sound of her mother being obscured by the Darke once more. She *had* to get to her this time.

Jenna flew along the space, forcing Septimus and Marcellus to follow the departing witch's cloak, which spread out behind her like a huge black wing. They arrived at a scene of which Septimus, let alone Marcellus, could make no sense at all.

At first all Septimus could see was Thunder, stamping and tossing his head, rolling his eyes from side to side – a terrified horse longing to flee. A man had hold of his mane and was talking to him in a low voice without much effect, it seemed to Septimus. On the other side of the horse, mostly obscured by Thunder's bulky body and starry horse blanket, he saw the hem of Lucy Gringe's embroidered robes and chunky boots and then he saw Jenna's witch's cloak – with four feet coming from beneath it. And then, as Thunder did a sudden turn, he saw Jenna. She was wrapped in Sarah's arms and had enfolded her mother in her cloak as if to never let her go. Lucy was also hanging on to someone . . .

"Simon!" gasped Septimus. He turned to Marcellus. "My brother. It *had* to be. Of course it did. *He's* behind all this. So that's what his creepy letter was about: *Beware the* Darke. I get it now."

Simon heard every word. "No!" he protested. "No, it's not that. It is *not*. I —"

"Shut up, you *toad*," snapped Septimus.

Marcellus did not know what was going on. But what he did know was that the middle of a Darke Domaine was not the place to have a family argument.

"Believe me, this is *nothing* to do with me," said Simon, half pleading, half angry at being blamed yet again for something he had not done.

"Liar!" exploded Septimus. "How dare you come here and —"

"Be silent, Apprentice!" snapped Marcellus.

Shocked at being spoken to in that way, for Marcellus was always scrupulously polite, Septimus stopped in mid-sentence.

Marcellus took advantage of the surprised silence. "If you value your lives, you will — all of you — do as I say," he said with great command. "Immediately."

The peril of their situation hit home. Everyone — even Simon — nodded.

"Very well," said Marcellus. "Jenna, you know where to go so you will lead the way with the horse. It will help that you will both clear the air a little." Simon went to protest but Marcellus stopped him. "If you wish to survive you will do as I say. Septimus, your mother is very weak; you will find your Disguise will stretch to two. It will shield her from the worst of it. I will follow with the young lady and with Simon Heap — for I presume you are he?" Simon nodded. "We shall move in this formation: one, two, three. It is the most efficient way to move through viscosity. We will go silently as one. There must be no dissent. *None whatsoever.* Is that understood?"

Everyone nodded.

And so like winter geese they set off in their V formation, Jenna with Thunder, Septimus and Sarah Heap sharing the Darke Disguise, followed by Marcellus, who had thrown his cloak around Simon on one side and Lucy on the other.

As they set off, Jenna muttered their destination under her breath. She didn't know why she did, but as soon as she had, Jenna felt sure that she would find the way. She moved quickly out of Wizard Way and into the alleyways that would take her to the nearest entrance to the Ramblings. Deep in the Darke Fog Jenna found that the silence suited her. It allowed her to concentrate, and there was something about the witch's cloak that gave her a feeling of safety within the danger that surrounded them. She moved easily through the Darke, and when she glanced around to check that everyone was still following her, she saw that, like Thunder, she was clearing a path for those behind. Not for the first time she wondered at her cloak's powers.

There was no one in the Castle that terrible night who moved through the Darke Fog with anything approaching Jenna's light-heartedness. Her happiness at finding Sarah safe overwhelmed everything. She hardly cared about the Darke Domaine or Simon's sudden, suspicious appearance. She had her mum back and that was all that mattered.

And every route she had learned for her Extramural Ramblings Certificate all those years ago led to the very place she was now headed: The Big Red Door, There and Back Again Row.

THE BIG RED DOOR

The Darke Domaine stopped at the Ramblings.

It had faded slowly. First they began to hear the sound of Thunder's hooves, muffled and distant but growing louder every step. Hazy shadows began to form recognisable shapes – Lucy first heard, then saw Marcellus's mangled shoe flapping on the paving stones – but they knew they had reached the boundary when they could at last make out the glimmer of a distant rushlight. As they stepped out of the Darke Fog, they found themselves in an alleyway not far from Ma Custard's Cake Stop. Feeling as though a great weight had been lifted from their shoulders, everyone exchanged strained glances – although only Lucy and Sarah met Simon Heap's eyes. No one spoke.

Free of the Darke Fog, Thunder snorted and pulled away from Jenna's grasp. As he headed noisily back to his master's side Jenna let go and, to her surprise, saw a rat clinging to Thunder's mane.

"Stanley?" she said, but the rat did not respond. Its eyes were shut tight and it was muttering something that sounded like, "Stupid, stupid *stupid* rat." It did not look happy, thought Jenna.

Marcellus looked about anxiously. The border of a Darke Domaine was not a place to relax – this was where outriders patrolled, extending its boundaries, pulling the Domaine ever outwards. He placed a finger on his lips for silence and, reverting to what Septimus called old-speak – as he did when a little tense – he whispered to Jenna, "Whither now, Princess?"

Jenna pointed at the lone rushlight, which illuminated the entrance to the Ramblings she had been heading for – a tumbledown archway covered in ivy and a purple flowering plant that grew out of untended walls in the Castle. The purple flowers were long gone in the dead of winter but the woody twigs of the plant hung down and brushed their heads as they stepped through the old stones into the hush of the Ramblings backwater.

Muttering, *"I knaht uoy, esaelp eriter,"* Septimus was busy returning his Darke Disguise to its tinderbox. It folded up as helpfully as his House Mouse and as thin as a piece of tissue paper. He pushed the lid on tight and placed the little box back in his deepest pocket, along with the precious key to Dungeon Number One.

"I'll put a SafeScreen on the arch," he said. "At least that will keep the *Darkenesse* out for a little while longer."

Marcellus disagreed. "No, Apprentice. We must leave no clue that we have come this way. We must leave it as we found it."

Freed from the Darke Domaine, the party split into its natural alliances, which meant that Septimus and Simon got as far away from each other as possible. Marcellus and Septimus led the way. Simon – grabbed by Lucy on one side and Sarah on the other – stayed back, hiding his awkwardness at being near

Jenna and Septimus by fussing with Thunder. Jenna hovered between the two groups like a magnet, attracted by the presence of her mother and repelled by the presence of Simon. Eventually, after two wrong turnings, Jenna joined Marcellus and Septimus and once again led the way.

The Ramblings was a strange place that night. Normally on the Longest Night it had a festive atmosphere. Doors would be flung open to reveal welcoming rooms with candles ablaze and tables piled high with delicacies from the Traders' Market. People would sit chatting with friends while children, allowed to stay up late and run free, played in the corridors. It was always a noisy, riotous time, fuelled by plates of sugared biscuits and bowls of sweets, which were traditionally left beside the numerous candles that roosted on any free perch in the passageways.

But as Jenna led the way through the empty corridors, the only sounds to be heard were low, worried conversations drifting through closed doors and the occasional wail of a disappointed child. It felt, she thought, as though everyone was waiting for the onslaught of a violent storm.

But despite the sense of trepidation pervading the place, the candles still shed their warm light on the newly swept passageways and the bowls of biscuits and sweets sat untouched in their niches, although not for long. Jenna, who had had nothing to eat since "Edifice" with Beetle, spied her favourite iced pink rabbit biscuits and grabbed a handful. Septimus was particularly pleased to find a whole bowl of Banana Bears, and even Marcellus permitted himself a small toffee.

And so they walked on through the deserted corridors, Thunder's hooves *clip-clopping* as they went. The sound of the hooves brought one or two worried faces to the tiny, candlelit windows that looked out on to the passageways, and once or twice a door was held open an inch or two and frightened eyes gazed out. But the door was soon slammed and the candles quickly snuffed out – no one seemed reassured at the sight of the ExtraOrdinary Apprentice in the company of a witch, an ancient Alchemist, and that disgraced Heap boy – what was his name?

With Thunder in mind, Jenna led them up what was known as a trolleyway – a sloping passage with no steps. Trolleyways were longer, although not always wider, than the normal passageways, which often had very steep flights of steps. They were, naturally, designed for trolleys – an everyday feature of Ramblings life and an essential piece of equipment for people who lived on the top floors. "Trolley" was a term that covered a multitude of wheeled carts, the number of wheels varying between two and six. Those on the lower floors considered them to be the bane of Ramblings life, especially late at night when rowdy groups of teens would take them to the top of the steepest trolleyway and hurtle down through the various levels. Two-wheelers were the most popular for this sport, as they were easier to steer and had the advantage of being able to use the handles as brakes – if you leaned back at the right moment. But that night there was no danger of being run down by a trolley rider yelling, *"Way! Way!"* as a warning. All trolley riders were behind closed doors, fearful, bored and having to be nice to their visiting aunts – while the visiting aunts were deeply regretting their decision to come to the Castle for the Longest Night festivities.

With Thunder's hooves slipping on the worn surface of the bricks, the group trooped up the final and by far the steepest incline and stepped thankfully out into a wide passageway known locally as Big Bertha. Big Bertha wound through the top of the Ramblings like a lazy river and many tributary passageways branched off from it. This was one of the most difficult areas of the Ramblings to understand – some of the corridors were dead ends but did not appear to be, while others looked like dead ends but were not. Most twisted and turned in such a way as to disorientate even the most experienced traveller.

But Jenna had got top marks in her Ramblings Certificate and now it showed. Holding the key to the Big Red Door in her hand as if it were a compass, she led the way straight across Big Bertha into a corridor that appeared to be a dead end but was not. The wall at the end was a screen that had the entrances to two passageways hidden behind it. Jenna skirted the wall – which sported a line of multicoloured pots, each containing a tall, thin candle stuck into a mound of boiled sweets – and took the right-hand entrance. It was a tight corner and Thunder had some trouble getting around it. Jenna wondered if Thunder might be a little spooked by the narrow confines, but for a horse that once lived in an old Land Wurm's Burrow, the Ramblings passageways were positively airy and spacious.

The passage led into a Well Hall – a circular space open to the sky. In the middle was the well, which was protected by a low wall and a wooden cover, on which stood three buckets of varying sizes. Above the well was a complicated pulley system that allowed heavy buckets to be easily drawn up from the huge fresh water cistern built into the foundations of the Ramblings. Rushlights cast a warm glow across the smooth, damp stones, which were warm enough to melt the occasional snowflake that drifted down. Set into the curved walls were some well-worn stone benches; pots with candles and wrapped sweets had been left on the benches and gave the Well Room a festive look. But even this popular meeting place was, like everywhere else, deserted.

Jenna waited by the well while everyone caught up. She caught Sarah's eye and smiled, hoping that Sarah recognised the place where she used to draw water and spend many hours chatting to her neighbours. But to Jenna's distress, Sarah just gazed blankly back.

"Nearly there," said Jenna, trying to keep cheerful.

"Hey, Jens, remember when you dropped your bear down the well and I fished it out in a bucket?" said Simon.

Jenna ignored him. She didn't think Simon had any right to use the old name he used to call her by before he kidnapped her and planned to kill her – no right at all. She spun on her heel and strode off into a narrow whitewashed corridor, which was lined with an array of multicoloured candles. After a minute or so the party emerged once again into Big Bertha, having cut off a huge loop. They went around one more bend and then Jenna turned down a wide alleyway, which proclaimed itself There and Back Again Row. A few moments later she was standing outside the door to the room where she had lived for the first ten years of her life.

It looked different. No longer a scuffed and dismal black, the door was now painted bright, shiny red, just as it had been in what people still called The Good Old Days. In her hand Jenna held the precious key that she remembered Silas lock-ing the door with every night, and which had hung on a high hook on the chimney the rest of the time. No one but Silas or

Sarah had been allowed to touch the key because – as Silas had informed everyone one night when its hook had fallen out of the wall and Maxie had hidden the key under his blanket – it was a precious Heap heirloom. The Big Red Door, complete with lock and key (with *Benjamin Heap* inscribed on the bow) was the only thing that Silas's father had left him.

Jenna knew exactly what to do with the key. She handed it to Sarah.

"You open it, Mum," she said.

Sarah took the key and looked at it.

Jenna watched Sarah anxiously. She glanced up and saw that everyone else was watching too. Even Marcellus. It felt like an eternity while Sarah Heap stared at the big brass key lying on her palm. And then, very slowly, recognition dawned in Sarah's eyes and the corners of her mouth flickered into the beginnings of a smile.

Hesitantly Sarah placed the key in the lock. The door recognised Sarah, and when she began, very weakly, to turn the key, the lock did the rest for her and the door swung open.

❖ 35 ❖

THE LONGEST NIGHT

A large variety of animals had spent time – sometimes their whole lives – in the room behind the Big Red Door, but Thunder was the first horse. Sam had once brought a goat in but only for a few seconds. Sarah Heap did not, in those days, *have things with hooves* in her room. But this time Sarah had no problems with hooves. She was perfectly happy to have a huge black horse standing in the corner while her Simon fed him some withered apples that he had found in a bowl on the floor.

Sarah was amazed at the transformation of her old home. As she stood gazing about her, taking in all the changes that Silas had secretly made over the previous year, happy memories came flooding back and began to displace the heaviness and gloom that the Darkenesse had left within her. *Now* she understood why Silas was always disappearing.

Neither Jenna nor Simon had been back to their old home since their hurried departure on Jenna's tenth birthday, and now they hardly recognised the place. Gone were the piles of books, clutter, bedding and general household "jumble-junk", as Silas had called it. Now there were rows of neat – albeit home-made – bookshelves carrying all the Magyk books that Silas had once saved by hiding them in the attic. The fireplace in the central chimney was swept and laid with large logs; the pots hanging on the chimney were clean and lined up in order of size; the worn wooden floor was covered with rugs (some of which Jenna recognised from the Palace) and scattered with cushions, ready for the chairs that Silas was planning to make.

For Septimus it was a strange feeling to be in the very place where he had been born and yet had spent no more than the first few hours of his life. He stood awkwardly on the threshold. He saw Simon with his arm around Lucy pointing something out to her from the mullioned window that overlooked the river and Septimus realised why he felt so uncomfortable. Simon was at home; this was where he had belonged. It was he, Septimus, who was now the outsider.

Sarah Heap saw her youngest son at the doorway, looking as if he was waiting to be asked in. The sight of him cleared the very last remnants of the Darkenesse from her head. She walked over to Septimus, put her arm around his shoulders and said, "Welcome home, love." Sarah drew him inside and closed the door.

A strange feeling welled up inside Septimus – he didn't know whether he wanted to laugh or cry. But he did know that he felt like a weight he had been carrying on his shoulders without even realising it had suddenly been lifted off. It was true – he was home.

The Longest Night drew on. Outside the Ramblings the Darke Domaine grew stronger as it spread through the Castle, drawing energy from all those trapped within it. The only spaces that remained clear were the Wizard Tower, protected by its dazzling SafeShield, the Sealed Hermetic Chamber, in which

Beetle sat like a butterfly in a chrysalis, a tiny SafeChamber deep within Gothyk Grotto – and the Ramblings.

The Ramblings had been inhabited for a very long time. It went back to the days when many Castle inhabitants practised a little amateur Magyk of their own, and so there were many remnants of SafeScreens, PassageProtectors, Blessings, HappyHomes and all kinds of spells for good things still hanging around the entrances. The Magyk was faint, but its cumulative effect over the years had soaked into the old stones and was enough to halt the Darke Domaine at every single archway, gate, door and window that led into the Ramblings. It was not, however, strong enough to hold out against the determined assault that now began.

At the ivy-covered archway near Ma Custard's – and at each and every Ramblings entrance – the ragged shadow of a Thing walked out of the Darke Domaine. The Thing stepped through the archway, forcing its way through the ancient echoes of Magyk. With it came the first tendrils of Darkenesse, smothering the rushlight with a soft *hissssss* as they went swirling into the corridor. The Thing – which happened to be the one that Spit Fyre had hurled into the river – dripped along the stone flags, sending the candles sputtering out and drawing the eddying blackness behind it. As it passed by the rooms and apartments, the Darke Domaine went creeping under the doors and through the keyholes, and the fearful voices within were stilled. Sometimes there was a scream or a shout of joy as someone thought they were about to meet a long-lost love, but these were soon cut short and followed by silence.

On the top floor of the oldest part of the Ramblings, in the room behind the Big Red Door, Sarah Heap was getting ready for a siege. Against all protests she was about to go and fetch water from the Well Hall.

"I'll come with you," Septimus and Simon said at the same time – and then glared at each other.

Sarah regarded her oldest and youngest sons. "You can *both* come, but I'm not having you squabbling all the way to Well Hall and back," she said sternly. "Understood?"

Septimus and Simon grunted assent and then frowned, annoyed at sounding so similar.

Flanked by her oldest and youngest sons, both now taller than she, Sarah set off for the once familiar trip to the well. As she walked between them, moving swiftly along the silent passageways, she could hardly believe what was happening. It was all her dreams come true. No matter that her sons refused to speak to each other, or that terrible things were happening in the Castle right then – and no doubt would soon reach them too. She had, for a few precious minutes, her boys back. Not all her boys, it was true, but she had the very two of whom so many times she had despaired of ever seeing again – and indeed had often believed dead.

Sarah's moment of contentment did not last long. As they made their way back from the Well Hall, each carrying two heavy pails of water, they saw a telltale eddy of Darkenesse appear around the far corner of Big Bertha. Quickly they hurried into There and Back Again Row and the Big Red Door threw itself open. They rushed in and the door immediately slammed itself shut. Sarah shoved the key in the lock and turned it.

"It needs an Anti-Darke," Septimus said. "I'll do one."

Sarah didn't like Anti-Darkes. She had grown up in a family

that contained both witches and wizards and she was not happy hearing the word "Darke" spoken in her home, even when it was partnered by the word "Anti". Sarah subscribed to the witch view on words – *a deed named was a deed claimed*. "No, thank you, love," she said. "We'll be safe without. The door has its own Magyk."

Marcellus, who had been feeling rather useless since they had arrived in the room, was glad to weigh in with some advice. "We need all the protection we can get, Mistress Heap," he said. "My Apprentice is right."

Both Simon and Sarah shot Marcellus a questioning look. "*Your* Apprentice?" said Sarah.

Marcellus decided not to – as Septimus would have said – *go there*. "I would go as far as to say that an Anti-Darke may be essential for our survival," he said.

Simon could hold back no longer. "That is true," he said. "What we need is a fluid Anti-Darke combined with a powerful SafeScreen. Once those are in place we must have an effective Camouflage – *that* is crucial."

Septimus gave a snort of derision. Did Simon really expect him to take the advice of the very person who had caused this whole thing to happen?

Simon misunderstood the snort. He tried to explain. "Look, you can do the most powerful Anti-Darke in the world, but it's no good if it's visible. A Darke Domaine will just hammer away at it until it's gone. And sooner or later it will be. Trust me, I know."

"Trust *you*?" spluttered Septimus – worried by the fact that he had actually agreed with everything Simon had said. "You must be joking."

The argument continued.

Sarah tried to ignore her sons. She wanted them to sort things out between them and she hoped that the knowledge that a Darke Domaine was coming their way would concentrate their minds. She busied herself checking all the preserved and dried food that Silas had piled up in the larder – and she told Septimus and Simon to *stop bickering*. She calmed Thunder by blowing on his nose and whispering to him – and she told Septimus and Simon that there was to be *no arguing about anything*. She began sweeping up some wood shavings that Silas had left behind – and she told Jenna to *keep out of other people's quarrels*. She told Lucy to *let Jenna be*. And then, when a full-on fight, with Jenna and Septimus on one side and Simon and Lucy on the other, seemed inevitable, Sarah's patience ran out.

"*Stop* it, all of you!" she yelled, banging the end of her broom on the floor. "Stop it *right now!*"

The melee by the door paused and they looked at Sarah, surprised.

"I will have *no* angry words in this room, do you understand?" Sarah told them. "I don't care what any of you have done in the past, I don't care how stupid or misguided or just plain bad you have been – and some of you have been all of those – because you are my children. *All* of you. And yes, Lucy, that includes you too now. Whatever any of you have done, however much you have hurt each other in the past, when you are in this room you will put that to one side. You will behave towards each other as brothers and sisters should. *Is that understood?*"

"Well said," murmured Marcellus.

Jenna, Septimus, Simon and Lucy looked dumbfounded. They nodded sheepishly. Simon and Lucy went and sat by the fire, leaving Septimus to do the Anti-Darke his own way, which was also, Simon noticed, *his* way.

Jenna went over to the window. An unusually quiet rat was sitting on the window sill, gazing out.

"Hello, Stanley," she said.

"Hello, your Majestyness," Stanley replied with a heavy sigh.

Jenna followed his gaze to the river. Across the water the lights of the Grateful Turbot Tavern could just be seen flickering through the trees, and far below the indigo ribbon of the river flowed slowly past.

"It's clear out there," said Jenna. "Isn't it lovely? No Darke stuff."

"Only a matter of time," Stanley replied gloomily.

The flap of a wounded shoe sounded behind them. Marcellus joined them at the window. "Not so," he said. "A Darke Domaine is stopped by flowing water, especially by that which is influenced by the tides of the moon."

"Really?" said Jenna. "So ... outside here, outside this window, will stay safe?"

Marcellus peered down. It was a precipitous drop straight down to the water's edge. "I believe so," he said. "The river runs close here."

Jenna knew all about that. She had watched the river from her own little window in her cupboard for as long as she could remember. "It comes right up to the walls," she said. "There's no bank at all, just some pontoons for boats to tie up to."

"Then there is nowhere for the Domaine to go," said Marcellus.

"In that case," said Stanley, who had been listening with great interest, "I'll be off."

"You're *going*?" asked Jenna.

"I must, your Majestyness. I've got four ratlets out there all alone. Goodness knows what's happening to them."

"But how're you going to get down?" Jenna looked out of the window. It was a very long way down indeed.

"A rat has its ways, your Royal Personageness. Besides, I do believe I can see a drainpipe. If you'd be so kind as to open the window, I'll be off."

Jenna looked at Marcellus questioningly. "Is it safe to do that?" she asked.

"It is, Princess – for the moment at least. Of course, we do not know what will trickle down from the roof later. If the rat needs to go, it had better go now."

Stanley looked relieved. "If you'll do the honours, Sir, I'll go right away," he said.

Marcellus looked puzzled. "What honours?"

"He means open the window," explained Jenna, who had spent enough time with Stanley to be able to translate.

Marcellus pulled the window ajar and a gust of cold fresh air blew into the room.

"What are you *doing*?" cried Sarah, aghast. "You'll let it all in. Close the window now!"

Quickly the rat hopped on to the sill and peered down, trying to work out the best way down the sheer rock face of the Ramblings.

"Stanley, please, could you –" Jenna began as Sarah came hurtling across the room, still holding her broom.

"Could I *what*?" asked Stanley edgily, eyeing Sarah with the suspicion of a rat used to trouble with brooms.

"*Find Nicko* – Nicko Heap, at Jannit's boatyard. Tell him what's happening. Tell him where we are. Please?"

Sarah slammed the window shut.

On the other side of the glass, Jenna saw Stanley's little rat mouth open wide in surprise as he tumbled away into the night.

"Mum!" yelled Jenna. "What are you doing? You've *killed* him."

"Better a rat than all of *us*, Jenna," said Sarah. "Anyway, he'll be all right. Rats always land on their feet."

"That's *cats*, Mum, not rats. Oh, poor Stanley!" Jenna peered down but she could see no sign of him anywhere. She sighed. She didn't understand her mother, she really didn't. She would happily send a rat hurtling to its doom and yet risk her life for a duck.

"He'll find something to catch hold of, Princess," said Marcellus. "Don't you worry."

"I hope so," said Jenna.

Stanley's eviction upset everyone – including Sarah. She hadn't meant for the rat to fall. In her panic to close the window, she hadn't registered the fact that Stanley was on the *outside*. But Sarah was not going to admit to that. She needed to keep control of things, and if people thought she was tough enough to throw out a rat to its possible demise, then that was no bad thing.

Sarah set about organising everyone, and soon there was a fire blazing and a fragrant stew bubbling in the pot hanging above it. A stew, Lucy noted, as far removed from her mother's as to be worthy of a different name. At the thought of her mother, Lucy sighed. She hardly dared think what was happening to her parents just then – or to Rupert in the boatyard. In fact, it was all so frightening that Lucy hardly dared think at all. She sat close to Simon beside the fire and held him tight. At least Simon – bruised and battered though he was from the Fetch – was safe.

Simon drew Lucy close to him. "They'll be OK, Lu," he said. "Don't you worry."

But Lucy did worry. And so did everyone else behind the Big Red Door.

The walls at this point of the Ramblings went straight down into the river but, luckily for Stanley, far away in the Port the tide was going out, and the river even as far up as the Castle was affected by the tides. At the bottom of his controlled descent Stanley clambered down the huge blocks of slimy green stone that formed the base of the Ramblings (and spent most of their time under water), slipped off and landed in the river mud with a faint *plop*.

The rat now began the long trek home. He skirted the Castle walls, hopping up on to the riverbank when he could, leaping over rocks, rotting hulks and mud flats when he couldn't. It was a dismal and occasionally frightening journey. Once Stanley thought he heard a distant roar come from deep within the Castle and the sound unsettled him, but it was not repeated and he began to think he had imagined it. As Stanley travelled onwards he could not help but glance up at the Castle, searching for a lighted window to raise his spirits. But there were none. He had left the only one far behind him, and he began to wonder if even that was now Darke. The darkness frightened Stanley. He had never paid much attention to the Castle lights before; rats did not understand humans' love of light and flames. They preferred shadows where they could run unseen; light meant danger and usually someone wielding a broom – or worse. But that night Stanley began to appreciate the human love of light. As he hopped through yet another patch of sticky, fishy mud he realised that, in the past, when he had looked up and seen lights in windows, he had known that behind each flickering candle flame there was the person who had lit it – someone who was in the room, busy by the light of the candle. It meant, thought Stanley, *life*. But now, with every window dark, it felt as if the Castle was empty of all human life. And without humans, what is a rat to do?

And so it was a rat filled with foreboding that finally scaled the outside wall of the East Gate Lookout Tower – headquarters of the Message Rat Service and home to Stanley and his four teenage ratlets. Stanley peered in through the tiny, arrow-slit window and saw nothing. But he smelled something. His delicate rat nose smelled the Darke – a sour, stale smell with a touch of burned pumpkin about it – and he knew he was too late. The Darke Domaine had invaded his home and somewhere inside were the four foundling ratlets whom Stanley loved more than anything else in the world.

Florence, Morris, Robert and Josephine – known to all but Stanley as Flo, Mo, Bo and Jo – appeared to any other rat to be four scrawny, awkward teen ratlets, but to Stanley they were perfection itself. They had been no more than a few days old when he had found them abandoned in a hole in the wall on the Outside Path. Stanley – who had never been remotely interested in babies – had scooped up the blind and hairless ratlets and taken them home to the East Gate Lookout Tower. He had loved them as his own; he had fed them, picked off their fleas, worried about them as they first went out scavenging alone, and recently he had begun to teach them the basic skills of a Message Rat. They were his whole life – they were the bright and starry future of the Message Rat Service. And now they were gone. Stanley dropped down from the window, utterly desolate.

"Ouch! Watch it, Dadso!" a young rat squeaked.

"Robert!" gasped Stanley. "Oh, thank goodness . . ." He felt quite overcome.

"You're heavy, man. You're squashing my tail," said Bo gruffly.

"Sorry." Stanley shifted his weight with a groan. He was getting too old to fall a hundred feet and not notice it.

"You all right, Da?" asked Flo.

"Where you been?" This from Jo.

"*Oh, Da!* We thought it had got you." A hug from Mo – always the emotional one – made Stanley's world feel right once more.

The five rats sat in a despondent line on the Outside Path, which was no more than a narrow ledge below the East Gate Lookout Tower. Stanley recounted the events of the past few hours.

"It's bad, Da, isn't it?" Mo said after a while.

"Doesn't look good," said Stanley gloomily. "But, according to that Alchemist chappie, we'll be all right here – we're outside the walls. It's all those poor rats trapped in the Castle I worry about." He sighed. "And I'd only just got the Service fully staffed."

"So where to now, Dadso?" asked Bo, kicking his feet impatiently on the stones.

"Nowhere, Robert, unless you want to swim the Moat. We'll sit the night out here and see what the morning brings."

"But it's so *cold*, Da," said Flo, looking mournfully at the tiny flakes of snow drifting down.

"Not half as cold as it is inside the Castle, Florence," said Stanley severely. "There's a stone missing from the wall a bit farther along. We can spend the night in there. It's good training."

"For *what*?" moaned Jo.

"For becoming a reliable and effective Message Rat, that's for what, Josephine."

This was met by a barrage of groans. However, the ratlets made no further protests. They were tired, scared and relieved to have Stanley back safe. Led by him, they trooped along to the space in the wall and, reverting to babyhood, they fell into a rat pile – exactly as they had been when Stanley had found them – and resigned themselves to an uncomfortable night. When Stanley was sure they were settled he said, very reluctantly, "There's something I have to do. I won't be long. Stay there and *don't move an inch*."

"We won't," they chorused sleepily.

Stanley set off along the Outside Path towards Jannit Maarten's boatyard, muttering grumpily to himself.

"You really should know better by now, Stanley. *Do not mess with Wizards*. Or Princesses. Not even just *one* Princess. One Princess is as bad as at least half a dozen Wizards. Every time you get involved with a Princess or a Wizard – especially the Heaps – you end up on some wild goose chase in the middle of the night when you could be tucked up nice and warm in your bed. When will you ever learn?"

Stanley scurried along the Outside Path. Soon he was having second, third and fourth thoughts about the wisdom of his journey.

"What are you doing, you stupid rat? You don't have to go off and find yet another no-good Heap. You never actually *said* you would, did you? In fact, you didn't actually have a chance to *say* anything, did you, Stanley? And why was that? Because if you just cast your mind back, mouse-brain, that no-good Heap's own *mother* tried to kill you. Have you forgot already? And in case you hadn't noticed, it's freezing cold, this path is a death trap, goodness knows what is going on in the Castle and you really shouldn't leave the ratlets outside on their own; aren't they just as important as a bunch of troublesome Wizards *ohmysaintedauntiedoriswhatisthat?*"

A roar — wild and rough-edged — broke through the silence. This time it was close. Too close. In fact, it sounded as though it was right above him. Stanley shrank back against the wall and looked up. There was nothing to see but the deep, dark night sky, scattered with a few clouded stars. The Castle Walls reared up high behind him and above them, Stanley knew, were the tall, thin houses that backed on to the Moat. But without even a glimmer of light the rat could see nothing.

As Stanley waited, wondering if it was safe to move, he realised that he could see something. On the still surface of the Moat, just around the next bend, a faint reflection of light caught his keen rat eye. It was, he figured, coming from the very place he was heading: Jannit Maarten's Boatyard. The glimmer of light raised Stanley's spirits considerably. He decided to carry on with his mission — even if it did involve a no-good Heap.

A few minutes later Stanley leaped lightly down from the Outside Path and ran across the boatyard, dodging between the tangle of boat clutter that inhabited Jannit's yard, heading for the wonderful sight of a lighted window. Granted it belonged to the Port barge and was, strictly speaking, a lighted porthole, but Stanley didn't care. Light was light, and where there was light there was life.

The hatch to the cabin-with-the-porthole was locked and barred but that did not deter a Message Rat. Stanley bounded on to the cabin roof, found the air vent – an open tube shaped like an umbrella handle – and dived in.

Nicko had never heard Jannit Maarten scream before. It was actually more of a loud squeak – short, sharp and very high-pitched. It didn't sound like it had come from Jannit at all.

"Rat, rat!" she yelled. She leaped to her feet, picked up a nearby spanner – there was always a spanner near Jannit – and smashed it down. Stanley's split-second reactions were severely tested. He leaped aside just in time and, waving his arms in the air, he squeaked, "Message Rat!"

Spanner raised for another swipe, Jannit stared at the rat that had suddenly landed in the middle of the table, only just missing the lighted candle. Stanley watched the spanner with particular interest. Everyone else around the table watched Stanley.

Jannit Maarten – wiry, with a wind-browned face like a walnut and iron-grey hair in a sailor's pigtail – was a woman who looked like she meant business. Very slowly she put the spanner down. Stanley, who had been holding his breath, exhaled with relief. He looked up at the expectant faces surrounding him and began to enjoy the moment. This was what Message Ratting was all about – the drama, the excitement, the attention, the *power*.

Stanley surveyed his audience with the commanding, confident eye of a rat that knows it will not, for the next few minutes at least, be swiped at with a spanner. He looked at the recipient of his message, Nicko Heap, just to check it was really him. It was. He'd recognise Nicko's tiny sailor's plaits woven into his straw-coloured hair anywhere. And those Heap bright green eyes too. Next to him was Rupert Gringe, his short hair shining carroty in the candlelight, and for once he was not scowling. In fact, Rupert actually had a smile on his face while he looked at the slightly plump young woman sitting close beside him. Stanley knew *her*, all right. She was the skipper of the Port barge. She had red hair too, a good deal more of it than Rupert Gringe. And she too had a smile, and in the candlelight she even looked quite friendly, although Stanley was not convinced. The last time he'd seen her she'd hurled a rotten tomato at him. Better than a spanner, though ...

Nicko cut through the rat's musings. "Who's it for then?" he said.

"What?"

"The *message*. Who is it for?"

"Ahem." Stanley cleared his throat and stood up on his back legs. "Please note that due to the current, er ... situation ... and circumstances pertaining thereto, this is not delivered in Standard Message Form. Therefore no responsibility can be accepted for the accuracy or otherwise of this message. A fee is not payable but a box for contributions towards the new drains at the East Gate Lookout Tower may be found at the Message Rat Office door. Please note that no money is kept in the box overnight."

"Is that it?" asked Nicko. "You came to tell us about the *drains*?"

"What drains?" said Stanley, whose mouth so often ran ahead of his thoughts. And then, when his thoughts caught up, he said rather snappily, "No, of course I didn't."

"I know which rat you are," said Nicko suddenly. "You're Stanley, aren't you?"

"Why do you say that?" asked Stanley suspiciously.

Nicko just grinned. "Thought so. So, Stanley, who is the message for?"

"Nicko Heap," Stanley replied, feeling slightly offended, although he was not sure why.

"Me?" Nicko seemed surprised.

"If that is you, yes."

"Of *course* it's me. What's the message?"

Stanley took a deep breath. "*Find Nicko* – Nicko Heap, at Jannit's boatyard. Tell him what's happening. Tell him where we are. *Please.*"

Nicko went pale. "Who sent it?"

Stanley sat down on a pile of papers. "Well, I wouldn't go running messages like this for just *anyone*, you know – especially given the present, er . . . situation. However, I do consider that I am, to some extent at least, not a mere messenger but operating in the capacity of a personal representative of – *oof*!"

Nicko's finger jabbed the rat's ample stomach. "Ouch! That hurt," protested Stanley. "There is no need for violence, you know. I only came here out of the goodness of my heart."

Nicko leaned across the table and stared eyeball to eyeball with the rat. "Stanley," he said, "if you don't tell me who sent the message *right now* I shall personally throttle you. Got that?"

"Yep. Okey-dokey. Got that."

"So who sent it?"

"The Princess."

"Jenna."

"Yes. *Princess* Jenna."

Nicko looked at his companions, the light from the single candle in the centre of the table throwing glancing shadows across their worried faces. For a few minutes Stanley's antics had distracted them from what was happening outside – but no longer. Now all their worries for their families and friends in the Castle came flooding back.

"OK," said Nicko slowly. "So ... tell me. Where is Jenna? Who is 'we'? Are they safe? When did she send the message? How did you –"

It was Stanley's turn to interrupt. "Look," he said wearily. "It's been a long day. I've seen some nasty stuff. I'll tell you about it, but a cup of tea and biscuit first would work wonders."

Maggie went to get up but Rupert stopped her. "You've had a long day too," he said. "I'll do it."

Silence fell, broken only by the gentle hiss of the little stove – and the sudden, terrifying roar of something outside, deep in the Darkenesse.

The night wore on in the room behind the Big Red Door, its occupants sleeping fitfully on the odd assortment of cushions and rugs. They were rudely awoken twice by Thunder – who was not named just for the stormy colour of his coat – but after protests and much fanning of the air, everyone managed finally to drift off once again.

Jenna had appropriated her old box bed in the cupboard, which still had the rough, threadbare blankets of her childhood. They were very different from the heirlooms of fine linen and soft furs that covered her four-poster bed in the Palace, but Jenna loved her old blankets and box bed as much as she ever did. She kneeled on the bed and peered out of the tiny window for some minutes, looking up at the stars and down at the river far below, just as she had always done before she went to sleep. But the combination of the Dark of the Moon – which she sleepily remembered Aunt Zelda explaining to her one night on the Marram Marshes – with the thick, snowy clouds that covered most of the stars, meant she could not see much at all. Her cupboard was colder than she remembered but before long Jenna too was asleep, curled up on the bed (which she had to be, because the bed was too short for her now), covered in the rough blankets, her fine fur-lined Princess cloak and her newly acquired Witch cloak. It was an odd combination but it kept her warm.

Septimus and Marcellus took turns through the night watching the door – two hours watching, two hours sleeping. When at about four in the morning the Darke Fog rolled down There and Back Again Row and pushed against the Big Red Door, Septimus was on watch. He woke Marcellus and together, on tenterhooks, they watched the door. The door tightened its hinges and long minutes passed, but the Darke Domaine did not get in.

The reason for this was not only Septimus's Magyk; it was also the Big Red Door itself. Benjamin Heap had suffused the Big Red Door with Magykal SafeScreens of his own before he gave it to his son, Silas. It was his way of ensuring that his son and grandchildren would be protected after he had gone. Benjamin's SafeScreens could not stop anything or anyone who had been invited in (like the midwife who had stolen Septimus) but they were pretty good at stopping anything that the Heaps had not invited over the threshold. Benjamin had never told Silas this, for he did not want his son to think that he doubted his Magykal powers – even though he did. But Sarah Heap had guessed long ago.

And so the Darke Domaine began its unrelenting onslaught – just as it was doing in the three other places in the Castle that had protected themselves: the Wizard Tower, the Hermetic Chamber – and Igor's own secret SafeChamber in Gothyk Grotto, which, in addition to Igor, contained Marissa, Matt and Marcus. But those behind the Big Red Door were safe for the moment. And when the light of the rising sun began to shine through the dusty mullioned window, Septimus and Marcellus relaxed their guard and fell asleep beside the glowing embers of the fire.

Sarah Heap woke with the sun as she always did. She stirred awkwardly, her neck stiff from the night spent on a threadbare rug with only a rocklike cushion for a pillow. She got up and walked stiffly over to the fire, stepping over Marcellus, and gently placing a pillow beneath Septimus's head. Then she added some logs to the embers and stood, arms wrapped around herself, watching the flames begin to wake. Silently she thanked Silas for all the stores he had laid in: logs neatly stacked under Jenna's bed, blankets, rugs and cushions, two cupboards full of jars of preserved fruit and vegetables, a whole box of dried WizStix, which would become strips of tasty dried fish or meat when reconstituted with the correct Spell (the tiny, sticklike Charm for which Silas had thoughtfully left tucked beside them). Plus, Silas *had mended the loo*. This had been the bane of Sarah's life when the Heap family had lived there. Plumbing was not one of the Ramblings' strong points and the lavatories – little more than huts perched precariously on the outside walls – were always messing up. But now, at long last, Silas had fixed it. All this, along with a late-night discovery of a WaterGnome hidden in the back of the cupboard, made Sarah think of Silas with wistful affection. She longed to thank him and apologise for all the times she had complained about him disappearing without saying where he was going. But most of all, she wished Silas knew that she was safe.

Sarah got out the WaterGnome and stood it on top of the cupboard where she had found it. She smiled; she could see why Silas had hidden it – it was one of the rude ones. But none the worse for that, Sarah thought, as the Gnome provided a stream of water for the kettle. Water was the thing she had been most worried about – hence the risky trip to the Well Hall. But now, thanks to Silas, they had a reliable supply.

Sarah hung the kettle over the fire and sat to watch it boil, remembering how she used to do this every morning. She had loved those rare moments to herself when all was quiet and peaceful. Of course when the children were very little she often had one or two of them sitting sleepily at her feet, but they were always quiet – and once they were older none of them ever woke up until she banged on the breakfast porridge pan. Sarah remembered how she would take the kettle off the fire just before it began to whistle, brew herself a cup of herbal tea and sit quietly watching the sleeping forms strewn around the floor – just as she was doing now. Except, she thought wryly, as Thunder made his presence known in his own special way, she wouldn't have been staring at a fresh pile of horse poop.

Sarah got the shovel, opened the window and launched the steaming pile into the air. She leaned out and breathed in the sharp, fresh morning air, which was dusted with a scent of snow and river mud. Happy memories of Mid-Winter Feast days with Silas and the children came flooding back – along with a memory of one much less happy day fourteen years ago. She turned and looked at the sleeping form of her youngest son and thought that, whatever happened, he had now at last spent a night in the room he should have grown up in.

Sarah watched the pale, wintry sun edging up above the distant hills, shining weakly through the bare branches of the trees on the opposite side of the river. She sighed. It was good to see daylight once more – but who knew what the day would bring?

It brought another fight between Septimus and Simon.

Septimus and Marcellus had retreated to a quiet corner by Silas's bookshelves and were looking through his old Magyk books, searching for anything written about Darke Domaines. They found nothing of use. Most of Silas's books were common textbooks or cheap versions of more arcane books with pages missing – always the pages that promised something interesting.

Septimus, however, had just found a small pamphlet hidden inside an ink-spattered copy of *Year III Magyk: Advanced Bothers*, when Simon wandered across to see if any of his old favourites were still on the shelves. He glanced down and saw the title of the pamphlet: *The Darke Power of the Two-Faced Ring*.

A dangerous and deeply flawed device, historically used by Darke Wizards and their acolytes, Septimus read. *Traditionally worn on the left thumb. Once put on, the ring will travel in only one way and so cannot be removed except over the base of the thumb. The faces are thought to represent those of the two Wizards who created it. Each Wizard desired to possess the Ring and they fought to the death over it. (See this author's pamphlet on the formation of the Bottomless Whirlpool. Only six groats from Wywald's Witchery.) After this the Ring passed from Wizard to Wizard, wreaking havoc. It is thought to have been instrumental in the Slime Plague at the Port, the horrific Night River Serpent*

> *attacks at the Ramblings and very possibly the Darke*
> *Pit over which the Municipal rubbish dump was even-*
> *tually built. The Two-Faced Ring possesses Incremental*
> *Power — each wearer attains the Darke power of all the*
> *previous wearers. This power reaches its full potential*
> *only after it has been worn for thirteen lunar months.*
> *Although many say that the Two-Faced Ring is still in*
> *existence, the author does not believe this to be the case.*
> *It has not been heard of for many hundreds of years*
> *now, and the likelihood is that is has been irretrievably*
> *lost.*

"Interesting," said Simon, reading over Septimus's shoulder. "But not entirely accurate."

Septimus's reply was short and to the point. "Go away," he said.

"Ahem." Marcellus coughed ineffectively.

"I am only trying to help," said Simon. "We all want to find a way to get rid of this Darke Domaine."

"*We* do," said Septimus, looking pointedly at Marcellus. "I'm not so sure about *you*."

Simon sighed, which annoyed Septimus. "Look, I don't do that stuff any more. I really and truly *don't*."

"Ha!" said Septimus scornfully.

"Now, now, Apprentice. Remember what you promised your mother."

Septimus ignored Marcellus.

"You just don't get it, do you?" Simon sounded exasperated. "I made a mistake. OK, it was a really bad mistake, but I am doing my best to put things right. I don't know what more I can do. And right now I could be really useful. I know more about this . . . *stuff* than both of you put together."

"I'll bet you do," snapped Septimus.

"Apprentice, I do think you should calm down and –"

Simon exploded. "You think just because you're Marcia's precious little Apprentice you know it all, but you *don't*."

"Don't patronise me," said Septimus.

"Boys!" Suddenly Sarah was there. "Boys, *what* did I tell you?"

Septimus and Simon glared at each other. "Sorry, Mum," they both muttered between clenched teeth.

It was Marcellus who was the go-between. To a seething Septimus he said, "Apprentice, these are desperate times. And desperate times call for desperate measures. We need all the help we can get. And Simon has a great advantage; he knows the Darke and –"

"Too right," Septimus muttered under his breath.

Marcellus ignored the interruption. "And I do believe that he has changed. If anyone knows a way to defeat this Darke Domaine, it will be him *and there is no need to make that kind of face, Septimus.*"

"Huh."

"We must do all that we can. Who knows how long we can keep the Darke Domaine out of the room? Who knows how long the poor people in the Castle can survive inside the Domaine? And indeed, who knows how long the Wizard Tower can hold out?"

"The Wizard Tower can hold out for ever," said Septimus.

"Frankly, I doubt it. And what would be the point if it did? Soon it will be nothing more than an island marooned in a

Castle of death."

"No!"

"Mark my words, Apprentice, the longer the Darke Domaine is in place, the more likely this is to be the case. Most people will survive for a few days. Others, perhaps those less lucky, will survive for longer but be driven mad by their experiences. We have a duty to do our utmost to prevent this. Do you not agree?"

Septimus nodded. "Yes," he said heavily.

Marcellus arrived where Septimus knew he'd been heading. "To this purpose I believe we should enlist the help of your brother."

Septimus could not bear the thought. "But we can't trust him," he protested.

"Apprentice, I truly believe we can trust him."

"No, we can't. He *knowingly* messes with the Darke. What kind of person does *that?*"

"People like us?" Marcellus said with a smile.

"That's different."

"And I believe your brother is different too."

"Too right."

"Apprentice, do not deliberately misunderstand me," Marcellus said sternly. "Your brother has made mistakes. He has paid – and indeed still is paying – a high price for them."

"And so he should."

"You are being a little vindictive, Apprentice. It is not an attractive quality in one with so much Magykal ability as you. You should be more magnanimous in your victory."

"My *victory?*"

"Ask yourself who anyone would rather be – Septimus

Heap, ExtraOrdinary Apprentice, loved and respected by all in the Castle, with a brilliant future ahead of him, or Simon Heap, disgraced, exiled and living a hand-to-mouth existence in the Port with little to hope for?"

Septimus hadn't thought of it like that. He glanced over to Simon, who was alone, staring fixedly out of the window. It was true; he wouldn't swap places with Simon for anything.

"Yeah," he said. "Yeah. OK."

And so it was that, much to Sarah Heap's surprise and joy, her youngest and eldest sons spent the next few hours sitting together at the foot of Silas Heap's bookshelves, in deep discussion with Marcellus Pye – about whom Sarah had had a complete reversal of opinion. Occasionally one would take down a book from the shelves, but for the most part they sat quietly and apparently companionably together.

By the nightfall both Septimus and Marcellus Pye had learned a lot from Simon: How Simon had last seen the Two-Faced Ring on the slimy bones of his old Master, DomDaniel, as they were about to strangle him. How he had trapped the bones into a sack and thrown them into the Endless Cupboard in the Observatory. How Merrin must have somehow retrieved the ring from the slimy thumb bone of DomDaniel – the thought of which made them all shudder.

Septimus thought that if they got hold of Merrin and took the ring off him the Darke Domaine would disappear, but Simon had explained that once the Darke Domaine was in place it would take more than that to get rid of it – it would take the most powerful Magyk possible. When he mentioned the Paired Codes, Marcellus reluctantly recounted what had happened and a gloom fell.

"There is another way," said Simon after a while. "Apprentices to the same ExtraOrdinary Wizard share a Magykal link. Alther and Merrin were both Apprenticed to DomDaniel. And Alther is the most senior. There is a slim chance that he could UnDo the Darke Domaine, as it is the work of a more junior Apprentice. But . . ."

Septimus was listening with interest. "But what?" he asked. It was the first question he had asked Simon that was not an accusation too.

"But I am not sure if it works for ghosts," said Simon.

"It might though?"

"It might. It might not."

Septimus made up his mind. He would go to the Darke Halls and find Alther. It didn't matter whether Alther had the power Simon thought he had or not. Alther would know what to do, he was sure of that. He was their only hope.

"Marcellus," Septimus said. "You know how you said there were other Portals into the Darke Halls?"

"Yeess?" Marcellus knew what was coming.

"I want to find the most effective one. I shall go and bring Alther back."

Simon was horrified. "You can't go to the Darke Halls!"

"Yes, I can. I was going there anyway before all this happened."

Simon looked very concerned. "Septimus, be careful. That's why I wrote to you – apart from saying sorry for, um . . . trying to kill you. Which I am. I *really* am. You know that, don't you?"

"Yes, I think I do," said Septimus. "Thanks."

"Well, the last thing I want is for my little brother to get enmeshed with the Darke. It pulls you in. It changes you. It's a terrible thing. And the Darke Halls are the Darkest place of all."

"Simon, I don't *want* to go, but that's where Alther is," said Septimus. "And if there's a chance he can help, then I want to take it. Anyway, I promised Alice I'd bring him back. And a promise is a promise."

Simon threw in his last card. "But what would Mum say?"

"Say about what?" Sarah – who had ears like a bat when it came to her children discussing her – called out from the other side of the room.

"Nothing, Mum," Simon and Septimus chorused in reply.

In the shadows of the bookshelves, Marcellus produced his pocket version of the almanac section of his book, *I, Marcellus*, and turned to the chapter headed Portal *Calculations: Coordinates and Compass Points*.

Night fell. Septimus Called yet again for Spit Fyre, although he now no longer expected his dragon to answer. The empty silence that followed his Call upset Septimus, but he tried not to let it show.

Sarah cooked up another stew, helped by Lucy, who wanted to know how to make a stew that was actually edible. After supper Septimus, Simon and Marcellus returned to the bookshelves and, fortified by Sarah's stew, finished the first set of calculations, which showed where the Portal to the Darke Halls was – give or take half a mile. No one was very surprised at the result.

The evening drew on and a north-east wind began to blow up. It shook the window pane and sent icy draughts into the room. The occupants wrapped themselves in blankets and settled down for the night. Soon the room behind the Big Red Door fell quiet.

Shortly after midnight, on the other side of the Big Red Door, a Thing arrived. It regarded the door with interest. It placed its ragged hands on the shiny red wood and winced as they touched the Camouflaged Magyk that covered the surface. Unnoticed by Marcellus – who was meant to be keeping watch but had actually dozed off – the door shuddered slightly and tightened its hinges.

The Thing sloped off down the corridor, muttering Darkely to itself.

❋ 38 ❋
THE PIG TUB

Nicko had set off to rescue Jenna and her companions from the Ramblings as soon as Stanley had left. He had not wanted to take the Port barge but he'd been outnumbered – even Jannit had agreed with Rupert and Maggie. She had told him that the Heaps were not the only ones to need rescuing; there would be others, surely, and they must take the biggest boat they could. Besides, what else did they have that was suitable? It was the depths of winter. Most of their boats were out of the water and sitting on props in the boatyard. Nicko had agreed reluctantly but before long he was regretting his decision. The Port barge – or the Pig Tub, as he soon began to refer to it – was nothing but trouble.

Right from the beginning progress had not been easy. They had to go the long way round because, for the Port barge, the Moat was not navigable past the boatyard. Added to that, the wind was against them and the long, unwieldy boat, which could not easily sail in the narrow confines of the Moat, needed to be poled along by Rupert and Nicko. This involved them standing on either side of the barge, pushing long barge-poles through the water. Progress was made a little easier by the falling tide, which was flowing their way, but it was still painfully slow and gave them plenty of time to stare at the Darkened Castle.

"It's like everyone has ... gone," Maggie whispered to Rupert, not liking to say "died", which was what she meant. She didn't see how anyone trapped in the Castle could survive and thought that the sooner she and Rupert got away to the Port, the better.

Nicko had pushed the oar through the water with all his might, propelling the barge inch by frustrating inch towards Raven's Rock, longing for the moment when they were out in the wide river with the wind in their sails. And then, just before the Moat joined the river, they ran aground on the Mump – the notorious mudbank at the entrance to the Moat. Nicko couldn't believe it.

Despite desperate efforts with the grounding poles, made specially to push a barge off a mudbank, nothing they could do would shift the "stupid Pig Tub idiot boat", as Nicko put it. She was stuck fast.

Maggie was horribly embarrassed. A skipper going aground was hard to live down. At least she did not have a boat full of passengers and livestock with whom she would be marooned for six interminable hours, enduring their complaints, moans, barks and brays with no means of escape. With any luck, no one would get to hear of this. And Port barges were made to sit on mud, so there was no harm done.

But for Nicko and Rupert, there *was* harm done. They stared disconsolately over the side at the thick, muddy water, knowing that every minute marooned on the mudbank meant another minute of danger for Jenna, Sarah, Septimus and Lucy (they had forgot about Marcellus, and neither of them cared if Simon was in danger). Although neither said it, Nicko and Rupert had no idea if they were even still alive. All they had was hope, which faded as the tide fell.

And then they had nothing to do but sit and stare at the Castle – and try not to think about what creature could be making the spine-chilling roar that echoed across the Walls every now and then and made the hairs on the backs of their necks stand on end. The only consolation was that, from where they were stranded, they could now see the indigo and purple glow of what Nicko told Rupert must be the Wizard Tower SafeShield.

At midnight, down in the Port, the tide turned. Salt water began to creep into the empty gullies in the sand and it began to rise once more in the sleeping harbours and push its way back up the river. At about three in the morning the Port barge shifted. To the accompaniment of another spine-chilling roar from inside the Castle, Nicko and Rupert got out the grounding poles and pushed with all their strength, knowing that this time they would get free. Ten minutes later they were sailing – slowly – towards the river. According to Jannit they were a little too close to Raven's Rock; Maggie pushed the huge tiller across to the right, but the boat seemed sluggish – and as they sailed beneath Raven's Rock they hit something.

Jannit knew at once that they'd hit one of the Beaks – a line of small rocks that came out from Raven's Rock and were not visible after mid-tide. Maggie was distraught. It didn't help that Jannit had said she'd *told* her they were going too close and that Maggie had snapped she *knew that, thank you, Jannit*.

Rupert and Nicko took a spare sail and rushed below. Water was pouring into the cargo hold; Rupert was horrified, but

Nicko knew that water coming in often looked worse than it really was. He and Rupert rammed a heavy canvas sail into the gash in the hull and found to their relief that the hole was barely bigger than Rupert's fist. The gush stopped and the red sail darkened as it grew wet. The water still came in but slowly now, dripping from the canvas at a speed that allowed Nicko and Rupert to bail it out with a bucket.

A holed boat must be got to shore as soon as possible. They decided to take the Port barge to the nearest landing stage on the Castle side – no one wanted to risk tying up on the Forest side at night. While Rupert and Nicko poured buckets of river water over the side, Maggie and Jannit, both pulling hard on the unusually stiff tiller, took the barge across to the Palace Landing Stage. As they got closer they saw that the normally brightly lit Palace – a landmark for returning mariners – was utterly dark.

"It's as if it isn't there any more," whispered Jannit, staring across to where she knew the Palace should be and seeing nothing but blackness.

By the time they drew near to the Palace Landing Stage – which, unlike anything behind it, was still visible – everyone was having second thoughts about the wisdom of getting any closer. Nicko shone one of the powerful boat lanterns across to the bank but he could see nothing. The light petered out just behind the landing stage on what looked like a fog bank, but different. Fog had a brightness to it and bounced light back. This Fog drew in the light and killed it, thought Nicko with a shiver.

"I don't think we should get any closer," he said. "It's not safe."

But Maggie, worried about her boat sinking, didn't think

the river was exactly safe either. She pushed the tiller hard to the right – the barge was being particularly contrary – and headed for the landing stage.

Suddenly a ghostly voice drifted across the water.

"Beware, beware. Come no closer. Flee . . . flee this place. This terrible place of dooooooooom."

White-faced in the light of the lantern, they looked at each other.

"I *told* you," said Nicko. "I told you it wasn't safe. We have to go somewhere else."

"All right, all right," snapped Maggie, who no longer had any confidence in her own decisions. "But where? It's got to be close. Supposing everywhere is like this – what do we do then?"

Nicko had been thinking. He knew from Stanley that this was a Darke Domaine. Nicko hadn't taken much notice of his Magyk classes at school – in fact, as soon as he was old (and brave) enough he had cut them to go to the boatyard – but he did still remember a few Magykal rhymes. The ones he thought of were:

> A *Darke Domaine*
> *Must remain*
> *Within the bounds of water.*

and:

> *The Castle Walls are tall and stout,*
> *They are built to keep the Darkenesse out.*
> *But if the Darkenesse grows within,*
> *The Castle Walls will keep it in.*

"Everywhere *won't* be like this," said Nicko in answer to Maggie's question. "This Darke stuff is stopped either by the water or by the Castle Walls. That's why we were all right in the boatyard, because we're outside the walls. So I reckon if we go up to Sally Mullin's place we'll be OK; she's outside the Castle Walls. We can tie up at the New Quay just below Sally's pontoon and we'll be safe. Then Rupert and I can find another boat. OK?"

Maggie nodded. It was as OK as anything was likely to be right then – which was not, in her opinion, saying a lot. But she and Jannit set the sails and turned the Port barge out into the river.

It was then that they discovered that the rudder was jammed. The barge had not escaped unscathed from being grounded; it now insisted on turning steadily right, which was probably why she had hit the Beaks, Maggie realised. The barge now refused to turn left up to the New Quay. To everyone's dismay, it drifted inexorably into the Raven's Rock Run until it was taken by the reverse current and pulled through the deep, choppy waters at the base of the rock so that it was now heading rapidly away from the Castle. Desperately they tried to steer out of the Run using the barge oars as rudders, to no avail. The Pig Tub made a beeline for the Forest and as they neared the overhanging banks tangled with trees, they began to hear the frightening grunts and screeches of the Forest night creatures. But at least, Nicko pointed out, they could hear something *normal*. It was better than the awful silence of the Castle punctuated by that weird roar.

They were lucky. Once more they ran aground, this time on a shingle bar some yards out from the bank, which left a comfortable stretch of water between the barge and the Forest. Maggie, at her insistence, kept watch. "I'm skipper," she said firmly when Rupert objected. "Besides, you three will be busy working on the rudder tomorrow. You need to sleep."

Nicko, Rupert and Jannit spent most of the following day fixing the rudder. It would have been a quick and easy job in the boatyard, but without the right tools it took much longer. It was also much wetter and colder than it would have been in the boatyard, and even Maggie's steady supply of hot chocolate did not stop tempers fraying by the afternoon.

The winter sun was low in the sky when the repaired Port barge finally floated off the shingle bank and headed upriver towards the New Quay. As the barge rounded Raven's Rock they saw the Darkened Castle in daylight for the first time. It was a shock. At night the only visible sign of the Darke Domaine was the absence of the normal night-time lights, but the daylight showed the full scale of the disaster that had overwhelmed the Castle. A great black dome of cloud squatted within the Castle Walls, obscuring the usual cheerful sight of the higgledy-piggledy rooftops and chimneys and the occasional turret or tower that would greet any boat as it rounded the bend at Raven's Rock. It was, thought Nicko, like a dark pillow pushed on to the face of an innocent sleeper. But still, shining above the Fog – just – like a brilliant beacon of hope, was the Wizard Tower. Wreathed in its shimmering Magykal haze, it sent out a defiant blaze of indigo and purple. Nicko and Rupert exchanged strained smiles – all was not yet lost.

As they drew near to the New Quay they saw the welcoming lights of Sally Mullin's Tea and Ale House glowing in the gathering twilight and Nicko knew that he was right about the Darke Domaine. Sally Mullin's was safe. As they got closer, they saw through the steamed-up windows of the long, low wooden building that the place was packed with those lucky enough to have escaped and their spirits lifted – they were no longer the only ones.

But as the Port barge drew alongside the New Quay, a fearsome roar from the Castle – louder than they had ever heard before – sent the hairs on the backs of their necks prickling. Once more Rupert and Nicko exchanged glances, but this time without a trace of a smile. There was no need for words; they both knew what the other was thinking – how could anyone survive inside *that*?

Jenna appeared at her cupboard door, hair awry, witch's cloak up to her chin against the cold. "What is it?" she asked sleepily, half knowing already what the answer was.

"It's coming in," said Septimus. As if on cue, a spurt of Darkenesse puffed through the keyhole with such force that it looked as though it had been blown in with a pair of bellows.

"We must leave at once," said Marcellus. "Sarah, is everything ready?"

"Yes," said Sarah sadly.

As part of the previous day's preparations, a huge coil of rope lay on the floor below the window. One end of the rope was tied around the central mullion of the window; it then snaked back across the room, looped around the base of the huge stone chimney that went up through the middle of the room, where it was secured with an impressive knot. Sarah pulled open the window and a freezing blast of air blew in, taking her breath away. It was not a night to be out, let alone a night to be climbing nearly a hundred feet down an exposed north wall, but they had no choice. With Jenna's help Sarah picked up the coil of rope and together they heaved it out of the window into the night. They jumped back and watched the loop around the mullion tighten as the rope hurtled down to the river far below.

Simon went over to Thunder. "Goodbye, boy," he whispered. "I'm sorry . . . so sorry." He put his hand in his pocket and felt for his last peppermints. Thunder nuzzled at his hand and then rubbed his nose against Simon's shoulder. Breaking his promise to Lucy not to do any more Darke stuff, Simon did a Sleep Spell laced with just enough Darke to give Thunder a chance of surviving. As the horse settled down on to Sarah's best rug and his eyes closed, Simon gently placed a blanket over him.

The previous day, when they were making plans to escape, they had decided to leave in order of their importance to the safety of the Castle. That had made Simon third to last – Sarah had been next and then Lucy had been last, but Simon had insisted on going last. There was no way he was going to leave Lucy and his mother alone to face the Darke. As Septimus and Marcellus stood at the window, Simon sat beside Thunder and wondered if they would be spending their time together in the Darke Domaine.

Another smoky tendril came slithering under the door.

"Time to go, Apprentice," said Marcellus.

Septimus steeled himself. He took a deep breath and looked down. He saw the rope snaking down the rough stones of the Ramblings wall and disappearing into the night. The previous afternoon he had Transformed it from three rugs, two blankets and a pile of old towels. He had never Transformed anything into something so *continuous* before and, as he peered out of the window and tried – unsuccessfully – to see the ground, he hoped he'd done it right.

Sarah was fussing, anxiously checking the knots. She was confident that even if the mullion did not hold their weight, the chimney would – but she was not so sure about the knots. She just hoped she'd got them right. If only Nicko was here, she thought, he'd know how to do them. A pang of concern shot through her at the thought of Nicko, but she pushed it away. Time enough to worry about Nicko when they'd all got out safely, she told herself.

"I'll just Call for Spit Fyre one more time," said Septimus, putting off the terrifying moment of climbing out.

Marcellus glanced anxiously back at the door. A long stream of Darke Fog was curling beneath it and creeping across the floor towards the fireplace.

"No time now," said Marcellus. "Do that when we've got down there."

Shakily Septimus took hold of the rope. His hands were clammy but he had made the rope rough and thick for a good grip. He climbed up on to the window sill and as he swung his legs over the side, Septimus felt a shiver of vertigo run through him – there was nothing between his feet and the river far below.

"Be careful, love," said Sarah, raising her voice against a sudden gust of wind. "Don't go too fast – far better you get down safely. When you've got to the bottom, give the rope three tugs, then Jenna will go."

With his arm around his Sleeping horse, Simon watched his youngest brother inch out into the night until all he could see were Septimus's hands gripping the rope and his curls blowing wildly in the wind.

Septimus began his descent. He knew that to give everyone a chance of getting out he had to put his fear of heights to one side and concentrate on getting quickly down the rope. It was not easy. The wind kept pushing him against the wall, banging him against the protruding stones, taking his breath away and disorientating him. It was only when – terrifyingly – his grip slipped and he found himself almost at right angles to the wall that Septimus discovered that if he deliberately leaned out from the rope, the wind buffeted him less and he could almost walk down the rough stones, many of which stuck quite a long way out and gave good footholds.

Septimus's descent continued until he stepped on the bush that had saved Stanley. The sudden change of foothold panicked him and he very nearly let go of the rope. But as he steadied himself and got his breath back he realised he could smell the river and hear the lapping of water. He speeded up and soon, like Stanley before him, he had landed on the mud. He gave three quick tugs of the rope and leaned against the Ramblings wall, shaking. *He had done it.* He felt the rope move in his hands and knew that Jenna was on her way down.

It was not long before Jenna landed beside him, breathless and exhilarated. Unlike Septimus, she had loved the excitement of the descent. They stood, looking up to the only lighted window in the entire Ramblings wall and saw another figure climb out. The figure moved quickly down, and Septimus was surprised at how agile Marcellus was – but a scream when the figure met the spiky bush growing from the wall told them it was Lucy, not Marcellus as they had all agreed earlier.

"He made me go first," said Lucy breathlessly, as she tugged the rope. "He said he'd lived long enough already. And he said Simon must come next."

"Simon!" spluttered Septimus. "But we need *Marcellus*."

Lucy said nothing. She looked up and did not take her eyes off Simon as he descended the rope, fast and easily. Soon he was beside them. Quickly he gave the rope three tugs and looked up anxiously at the window.

"The door's not going to hold much longer," he said. "They're going to have to get a move on."

It was too much for Jenna. She had waited once for her mother outside a room filling with Darkenesse and once was enough. She couldn't stand the thought of doing it again.

"Mum!" she called up. "Mum! Hurry up! Please, *hurry!*"

But no one came.

Up in the room behind the Big Red Door, two people who should have known better were arguing about who was leaving next. Sarah looked around the room she loved – that she now knew Silas loved too – and she dithered. No matter that Benjamin Heap's door was changing as she looked at it, the red paint blackening as though a fire was raging on the other side. No matter that wisps of Darke Fog hung in the room like storm clouds heralding the arrival of a hurricane – Sarah would not budge. She was determined to be the last to leave.

"Marcellus. You must go first."

"I will not leave you here alone, Sarah. Please, go."

"No. *You* go, Marcellus."

"No. *You.*"

It was Benjamin Heap's door that settled it. There was a sudden *craaaaack.* A panel split and a long stream of Darkenesse poured in. In a moment the fire in the hearth was out.

"Oh, that poor horse," said Sarah, still dithering.

"Sarah, *get out*," said Marcellus. He grabbed her hand and pulled her to the window. "We *both* go," he said.

Sarah gave in. Surprisingly agile, she clambered out of the window and swung herself on to the rope – she had not lived in Galen's tree house for nothing. Marcellus followed. He slammed the window shut, jamming it on the rope. Then he, too, easily began the descent, which was nothing compared to the tall chimney in the Old Way that he had regularly climbed in his old age. Far below Septimus, Jenna, Simon and Lucy looked at each other in relief.

Sarah and Marcellus made good progress, slowed only by Stanley's bush, which Sarah irritably kicked at. It was the last straw for the bush, and it went tumbling in a shower of stones, which scattered the watchers below. When they looked back up, the light

in the small mullioned window had gone out. The great rock face
wall of the Ramblings was now completely in Darkenesse.

At last Sarah stepped unsteadily on to the ground. Jenna
flung her arms around her.

"Oh, *Mum*."

Marcellus pushed away from the wall and jumped athleti-
cally – he hoped – away from the knot of people gathered
around Sarah. He landed with a *splat*. "Eurgh," he muttered.
"Wretched horse."

"You only *just* made it," Septimus told him disapprovingly.
He thought Marcellus should have stuck to the agreed order
of leaving.

"Indeed," said Marcellus, inspecting his ruined shoe.

Marcellus's casualness annoyed Septimus. "But we decided
the order we would leave for a reason. It was important – for
the whole Castle," he persisted.

Marcellus sighed. "But things that are right in the cold light
of reason may feel very wrong when faced with reality. Is that
not so, Simon?"

"Yes," said Simon, remembering the Thing strangling Sarah.
"Yes, it is."

"It's my fault," said Sarah. "I wanted to be last – like a captain
leaving her ship. Anyway, it doesn't matter; we're all safe now."

"It doesn't *feel* very safe," said Lucy, saying what most of
them were thinking. She looked at Jenna accusingly. "You said
there were always boats here. But I can't see any."

Jenna looked along the strip of mud that ran between the
edge of the river and the sheer walls of the Ramblings. She
didn't understand it. There were always little boats tied up on
the numerous outhauls – lengths of rope that snaked out from

rings in the walls to weights sunk on to the riverbed. But now there were none.

Lucy was getting agitated. "What are we going to *do*? The water's coming up and *I can't swim*."

"It's OK, Lucy," said Septimus, sounding more confident than he felt. "I'll Call for Spit Fyre now. He'll probably come now that we're away from the Darke."

Septimus took a long, deep breath and gave the loudest dragon Call he had ever made. The piercing, ululating sound bounced off the Ramblings walls and echoed across the river, and as the last faint whispers died away, his Call was answered – not by the hoped for sound of dragon wings beating the air, but by the answering cry of a monster within the Castle.

"Sep . . . what have you Called?" whispered Jenna.

"I don't know," whispered Septimus in reply.

Spit Fyre did not come, and Septimus dared not Call again. The thin strip of mud between the sheer walls of the Ramblings and the broad band of the deep, cold river was a temporary refuge only. They knew that as the tide came in it would slowly disappear. They gazed longingly over to the safety of the opposite bank. Far away to the right, flickering through the bare branches of the winter trees, were the distant lights of a farmhouse. Upstream to the left was a glow of firelight in the downstairs window of the Grateful Turbot Tavern. Both were unreachable.

"We'll have to walk down to Old Dock," said Septimus. "See if we can find a boat there."

"One that isn't half sunk already," said Jenna.

"Do you have any better ideas?" demanded Septimus.

"Stop it, you two," said Sarah. "I don't think anyone *does* have any better ideas – do we?"

There was silence.

"Old Dock it is," said Sarah. "Follow me."

Sarah led the cold, tired group along the mud. But whereas Stanley, with the lightness of a rat, had scampered over the top of the mud, it was not so simple for humans. Their feet sank deep into the gloop and they stubbed their toes on hidden rocks and tripped over the empty outhauls. As they struggled on through the freezing mud, they saw countless open windows from which abandoned knotted sheets and makeshift ropes dangled – and they now understood why all the boats had gone. Even the floating pontoons had been unhitched and pressed into service; there was nothing left afloat on their side of the river.

Finally they arrived at the Underflow, an underground stream that ran from below the Castle. Sarah, not realising where she was, took a step forward into the dark and fell into deep, fast-flowing water.

"Agh!" Sarah gasped with shock as she was swept out into the river.

There was a loud splash and a scream from Lucy. Simon surfaced in the river, spluttering – then he turned and swam into the darkness after Sarah.

"Simon!" yelled Lucy. "Aaaaaaaaaaaaaaaaaagh! *Simon!*"

Jenna, Septimus and Marcellus stood, shocked, on the muddy bank of the Underflow. They stared into the night but could see nothing. Lucy stopped screaming, and the sounds of Simon swimming receded. Chilled by the freezing wind, they listened in silence to a few faint splashes coming from somewhere in the middle of the river.

✳ 40 ✳
ANNIE

Sally Mullin had insisted that Nicko take her new boat, *Annie*.

"I hope she gives you as much luck as my *Muriel* did," she had said. "Just don't turn her into canoes this time."

Nicko had promised. *Annie* – a wide, generous boat with a cosy cabin – was far too good to turn into anything else.

After helping Jannit and Maggie to safely dock the Pig Tub, Nicko and Rupert had not set off until way past midnight. They sailed up the river, heading towards the Ramblings on the north side of the Castle. It was slow progress at first because the blustery north-east wind was against them, but they followed the river around as it hugged the Castle walls, and slowly *Annie's* position to the wind altered and she picked up speed.

It was a miserable journey. The eerie sight of the desolate, Darkened Castle made both Rupert and Nicko doubt that they would find anyone safe in the Heaps' room at the top of the Ramblings. And when, once again, the terrifying roar echoed across the river, they began to dread what they would find.

"What *is* it?" Rupert whispered.

Nicko shook his head. Right then he didn't want to know.

As they sailed towards Old Dock, a knot began to tighten in Nicko's stomach. This was the place where it was first possible to see the Heaps' tiny, arched mullion window at the very top of the Ramblings. Nicko always looked up when he passed – and felt a small tug of nostalgia for times gone by – but now he did not dare. He kept his eyes fixed on the dark water of the river because every moment he did not look was another moment of hope. A quick flurry of tiny snowflakes blew into his eyes and Nicko rubbed them away, glancing up as he did so. *There was no light.* The sheer wall of the Ramblings reared up like a cliff face and, just like a cliff face, it was totally dark. A wave of desolation swept over Nicko; he slumped down and stared at the tiller. It was then that he heard a splash.

"Just a duck," said Rupert in response to Nicko's questioning glance.

"Big duck," said Nicko. He stared towards the Ramblings side where the splash had come from, for some reason his hopes beginning to rise. Then came another splash and a scream cut through the air.

"Lucy!" Rupert gasped. "That's *Lucy*." No one screamed like his sister.

Nicko had already turned *Annie* towards the splashing. Rupert took the boat lamp out from under its cover and played its light across the water, searching.

"I can see her!" he shouted. "She's in the water. Lucy! Lucy! We're coming!" He threw the ladder over the side.

Beside the Underflow the stranded group heard shouts from the river and saw a light suddenly appear from the darkness. In the wildly swaying beam of light they saw Sarah being pulled from the water and then Simon's head bobbing at the foot of the ladder. A curse travelled across the water, followed by a voice saying, "It's your dingbat brother."

"Which one?" came the reply that they all recognised as belonging to Nicko.

"What does he mean, *which one?*" muttered Septimus.

It took a few trips in *Annie's* coracle to pick up Jenna, Septimus, Lucy and Marcellus. But eventually everyone was on board, a little wetter than they would have liked, but not – as Jenna pointed out – as wet as they would have been if Nicko hadn't turned up.

Nicko could not stop grinning as he hugged his brother – *not* the dingbat one – and his sister.

"Did Stanley tell you where we were?" asked Jenna, gratefully wrapping herself in one of the many blankets that Sally Mullin had provided.

"Eventually," said Nicko. "That rat does go on. Anyway, we decided we'd sail around and wait below. I reckoned sooner or later you'd look out and see us, Jen." He smiled. "Seem to remember you were always gazing out of the window when you were little."

"Good old Stanley," said Jenna. "I do hope his ratlets are OK."

"His what?"

Jenna's answer was cut short by another bleak roar echoing across the water.

"His – oh, Nicko, Sep, oh – look at *that* . . . what *is* it?"

Illuminated by the glow from the Wizard Tower SafeShield, a monstrous shape could be seen inside the Darke Fog.

"It's *massive* . . ." Jenna breathed.

The creature opened its great mouth and sent another bellow across the river.

"It's . . . a *dragon*," gasped Nicko.

"About ten times bigger than Spit Fyre," said Septimus, who was feeling extremely worried about his dragon.

"It would eat Spit Fyre for breakfast," said Nicko.

"Nicko, *don't!*" protested Jenna.

But Nicko had voiced the very thing that was worrying Septimus.

They stared across the water, watching the monster. It appeared to be trying out its wings – of which it had six. It rose a little into the air and then fell back with what sounded like a roar of frustration.

"Six wings. A Darke dragon," muttered Septimus.

"That's not good," said Nicko, shaking his head.

Marcellus joined them. "Things are worse than we feared. No one is safe in the Castle with that thing on the loose. How fast can this boat go, Nicko?"

Nicko shrugged. "Depends on the wind. But it's blowing up a bit. We can get to the Port not long after dawn if we're lucky."

"The *Port*?" asked Marcellus, puzzled. He glanced at Septimus. "You have not told him, Apprentice?"

"Told him what?" asked Nicko suspiciously.

"That we're going to Bleak Creek," said Septimus.

"Bleak Creek?"

"Yes. Sorry, Nik. We have to get there. Fast."

"Jeez, Sep. Isn't it bad enough for you here? You want *more* Darke stuff?"

Septimus shook his head. "We have to go. It's the only hope we have to stop what's happening here."

"Well, you're not taking Mum," said Nicko.

Sarah's bat ears were working well. Her head appeared in the lighted hatch. "Not taking Mum where?"

"Bleak Creek," said Nicko.

"If that's where Septimus needs to go, then that's where I'll go too," Sarah said. "I don't want you wasting any time on me, Nicko. Just do what Septimus asks you — and Marcellus too."

Nicko looked surprised. "OK, Mum. Whatever you say."

They sailed past the reassuringly normal lights of the Grateful Turbot Tavern and then *Annie*'s mast scraped under the One Way Bridge, setting Nicko's teeth on edge. As they began to round the first bend, everyone gathered on deck to catch a last glimpse of the Castle. The only sound was the creaking of *Annie*'s ropes and the swash of the water as she sailed briskly along. Her passengers were grimly silent. They looked back at the dark shape of the Castle that had been their home and thought about all the people left behind. Lucy wondered if her mother and father were still alive — How long could you survive in a Darke trance? Simon had told her he'd once been in a trance for forty days and had been OK at the end of it. But Lucy knew Simon was different. She knew he'd practised all kinds of Darke things, even though he didn't like to talk about it. But her parents didn't have a clue about stuff like that. Lucy imagined them collapsed outside the gatehouse, snow covering them as they slowly froze. She stifled a sob and rushed below. Simon went after her.

As they drew farther away, the Wizard Tower became visible — but only just. The Darke Domaine was rising higher and only the top two floors of Marcia's rooms and the Golden Pyramid were now clear of the Fog. The indigo and purple

SafeShield still shone brightly, but every now and then there was a new colour visible – a faint flash of orange.

Sarah and Jenna took comfort from the lights. They thought of Silas somewhere in the Tower, adding his – admittedly small and somewhat unreliable – share of Magyk to the Wizard Tower's defences. Septimus and Marcellus, however, took no comfort at all.

Marcellus drew Septimus away from the others. "I assume you know what that orange flash means, Apprentice?" he asked.

"The SafeShield is in distress," Septimus said. He shook his head in disbelief. "That's not good."

"No, it's not," said Marcellus.

"How long do you think we've got until it . . . fails?" asked Septimus.

Marcellus shook his head. "I don't know. All we can do is make haste to Bleak Creek. I suggest you get some rest."

"No. I'll stay up. We still have to work out *exactly* where in Bleak Creek the Portal is," said Septimus.

"Apprentice, you must sleep. You have a task ahead of you for which you will need all your powers. Simon and I will do the final calculations – *no protests, please*. He is proving a most able mathematician."

Septimus hated the thought of sleeping while Simon took his place at Marcellus's side. "But –"

"Septimus, this is for the good of the Castle, for the survival of the Wizard Tower. We must all do what we can – and what you can do now is *sleep*. Come away from the Tower, it does no good." Marcellus put his arm around Septimus's shoulders and tried to steer him towards the cabin.

Septimus resisted. "In a minute. I'll come in a minute."

"Very well, Apprentice. Do not be long." Marcellus left Septimus alone and went below.

Septimus longed for a glimpse of Marcia. He wanted to see her face at the window, to know that she was all right. "Nicko, do you have a telescope?" he asked.

Nicko did have a telescope. "Tower looks good, doesn't it?" he said, handing it to him. "I like the orange."

Septimus made no reply. He focused the telescope on the Wizard Tower and silently added his own Magnification. The top of the Tower that was peeping up over the Fog sprung into sharp focus. Septimus gasped. It seemed so close that he felt he could reach out and touch it. Eagerly he searched out Marcia's study window, which he thought should just be visible. It was. And not only was the study window visible but so were Marcia's head and shoulders, silhouetted against the lighted window. It looked as though she was staring out of the window straight at him. Feeling a little silly Septimus waved, but almost immediately Marcia turned away, and Septimus knew that she had not seen him at all. Feeling suddenly lonely, Septimus longed to talk to Marcia. He longed to tell her that there was still hope, to say, "Hold on as long as you can. Don't give up. Please don't give up."

Jenna's voice broke into his thoughts. "Let me have a look, Sep. Please. I want to see ... well, I want to see if I can spot Dad anywhere."

Reluctant to let go of what felt like a link to the Wizard Tower, Septimus swung the telescope upwards for a quick last glance at the Golden Pyramid. He gasped in surprise. Sitting on the flattened square at the very top of the pyramid was the unmistakable shape of Spit Fyre.

"What is it, Sep?" asked Jenna, worried.

Septimus handed her the telescope with a broad smile. "Spit Fyre. So that's why he never came. Somehow he's got inside the SafeShield. He's sitting on top of the Golden Pyramid."

"Wow. So he is," said Jenna. "Clever dragon. No one can get him there."

"For now," said Septimus. He went over to the hatch. "I'm going to get some sleep, Jen."

Jenna sat on the cabin roof, playing the telescope over the few visible windows in the Wizard Tower until *Annie* eventually rounded the bend and the Castle disappeared from sight. But she saw no sign of Silas.

The next morning the wintry sun rose to reveal an unfamiliar landscape. On either side of the river were empty fields dusted with frost and dotted with sparse trees stretched out to a range of blue hills on the horizon. The land seemed deserted, with not a farmhouse in sight.

The inside of *Annie's* cabin was warm but cramped. Nicko, Jenna, Rupert and Lucy were up on deck, leaving Sarah some space in the tiny galley to prepare a huge plate of scrambled eggs for breakfast. Marcellus and Simon were at the chart table with their set squares and protractors, making their final drawings from the almanac's coded coordinates of the Portal to the Darke Halls. Septimus was still asleep, tucked into a quarter berth, with only his tangled curls visible above his cloak and one of Sally's blankets. No one was in a hurry to wake him.

Eventually the mouthwatering smell of the eggs drifted into his dreams and Septimus opened his eyes blearily.

Simon looked up, his eyes red-rimmed with fatigue. "We've worked out where the Portal is," he said.

Septimus sat up, remembering with a sinking feeling what he was going to have to do that day. "Where?" he asked.

"Have some breakfast first, Apprentice," said Marcellus. "We'll discuss it afterwards."

Septimus knew it was bad news. "No. Tell me now. I need to know. I need to ... to get ready."

"Septimus, I'm so sorry," said Marcellus. "It's in the Bottomless Whirlpool."

BLEAK CREEK

Bleak Creek was a dank and dismal place. Haunted by the ghost of the *Vengeance,* a Darke ship once berthed there, its waters lay deep and still, trapped between two rocky hillsides. A few stunted trees half-heartedly clung to the gaunt slopes but most had stopped bothering and had fallen into the water, where they lay rotting, providing a perfect breeding ground for the infamous Bleak Creek water snake – a nasty black squidge of venomous slime – and its equally lovely parasite, the Long White Leech. In the summer swarms of biting gnats patrolled the banks of the creek, but in the winter they were gone, thankfully. Their absence was more than compensated for by the tiny Jumping Log Beetles, which ventured on to the land once the water grew cold. Log Beetles could jump as high as six feet and would fasten their pincers into any flesh they could find and begin to chew. The only way to remove them was to snap their heads off and wait for the pincers to die. Some heads could keep chewing for days until they fell off.

Dotted among the sharp rocks that littered the hillsides were a few stone hovels built by ancient hermits, misfits and the odd person who had wanted a house by the water but had clearly suffered from a total lack of common sense. These piles of stones were deserted now, although Septimus knew that at least one was Possessed.

Not surprisingly Bleak Creek did not receive many visitors, although this was not necessarily due to its ghostly ship or even to the hostile wildlife and the pungent smell of decay that hung in the air. It was because its entrance was guarded by the notorious Bottomless Whirlpool.

Every Castle child knew the story of the Bottomless Whirlpool. How it was created during a great battle between two Wizards in ancient times; how it was said that each Wizard had stirred up the waters into a frenzy in an effort to drown the other; that they had circled one another, faster and faster, until they had both been sucked into the depths and were never seen again. Everyone knew that the whirlpool went down into the very centre of the earth, and some believed that it went right out to the other side.

There were occasional day trips from the Castle to see the Bottomless Whirlpool. These were often a thirteenth-birthday present. After sailing into Bleak Creek to try and spot the *Vengeance*, the boats – full of new teens screaming with excitement – would circle the whirlpool. However, these trips were run by experienced skippers who knew the safe distance from the whirlpool and who could tell the early warning signs that a boat was being dragged towards it. It was only the biggest, heaviest ships – as the *Vengeance* had once been – that could pass close by.

Nicko knew for sure that *Annie* was not one of these. He also knew that he was not one of those skippers who understood the safe distance from the whirlpool, although he hoped that he could tell the signs that they were being dragged too close. And so, as the forbidding rocky outcrops that heralded the entrance to Bleak Creek came into view, Nicko began to feel nervous – but not as nervous as Septimus.

Septimus was sitting alone in the prow of the boat, just behind the bowsprit and its large red sail that billowed in the wintry wind. He had never – not even on the Do-or-Die Night Exercises in the Forest – felt so scared. He glanced down at a small sheet of paper covered with Marcellus's neat handwriting that set out some bullet-pointed questions and answers, which he was trying to fix in his head. They were not unlike the Young Army Pre-Exercise Pointers (or PEPs) that the boys had had to memorise and then chant before each expedition. This sense of déjà vu added to Septimus's feeling of doom, but it also meant that he fell back into his old Young Army ways of focusing on survival – and nothing else. And so, as he sat behind the bowsprit, Septimus gazed out at the iron-grey water and chanted under his breath, learning the responses he must use when challenged by anything Darke.

"*Who be you?* Sum."

"*How be you?* Darke."

"*What be you?* The Apprentice of the Apprentice of the Apprentice of DomDaniel."

"*Why come you here?* I seek the Apprentice of DomDaniel."

Septimus was so absorbed that he did not notice Jenna and Nicko slipping into the spaces on either side of him. They waited patiently until he had stopped muttering and then Jenna spoke.

"We are coming with you," she said.

Septimus looked shocked. *"What?"*

"Nik and I . . . we have decided to come with you. We don't want you to go alone," said Jenna.

This had the opposite effect to what Jenna had intended – Septimus suddenly felt totally alone. He realised that they had no idea about the utter impossibility of their request. He shook his head.

"Jen, you can't. It's not possible. Believe me."

Jenna saw the look in Septimus's eyes. "OK . . . I believe you. But if we can't come with you, then I at least want to know where you are going. Marcellus knows, even *Simon* knows, so I think Nik and I deserve to know too."

Septimus did not reply. He stared out at the water and wished that Jenna and Nik would leave him alone. He needed to disconnect.

But Jenna would not let him. She reached beneath her witch's cloak, took out *The Queen Rules* and opened it at a page she knew well. She thrust it under Septimus's nose.

"Look," she said, stabbing her finger at a grubby, well-worn paragraph.

Reluctantly Septimus squinted at the tiny type. Then he gave in. He got out his birthday present from Marcia and moved the Enlarging Glass across the page. He read:

"The P-I-W has a Right To Know all facts pertaining to the security and wellbeing of the Castle and the Palace. The ExtraOrdinary Wizard (or, in absentia, the ExtraOrdinary Apprentice) is required to answer all the P-I-W's questions truthfully, fully and without delay."

With his head full of what he had to do, Septimus didn't immediately recognise what he was looking at – and then it came back to him. He remembered the morning of his birthday, which seemed so far away now. He smiled as he recalled

Marcia's comment about "the wretched red book with its tiddly-squiddly type, the bane of every ExtraOrdinary Wizard's life". So *this* was what she had meant. And in remembering the Wizard Tower and the Castle as it had been, and with Marcia's beautiful birthday gift in his hand, Septimus somehow felt less alone. He felt part of everything once more and he also, he realised, felt relieved. He *wanted* to tell Jenna where he was going, he wanted her to be part of what he was doing. Even though she couldn't come with him, she could be thinking of him while he was there, wishing him safely through the Darke Halls to the other side. Septimus wasn't sure that he should be telling Nicko too, but he no longer cared about *should* or *shouldn't*.

And so, as they drew near to Bleak Creek and they saw the telltale chop of the water that heralded the Bottomless Whirlpool, Septimus told Jenna and Nicko how he was going to find Alther and bring him back to the Castle through Dungeon Number One. He told them not to worry because he had the Darke Disguise. And even though he didn't believe it, he told them that he would be fine and he would see them soon. When he had finished talking, Nicko and Jenna were silent. Jenna wiped her eyes with her sleeve and Nicko coughed.

"We'll be there waiting, Sep," said Jenna.

"Outside Dungeon Number One," said Nicko.

"No. You can't do that."

Jenna put on her best Princess voice. "Nicko and I *will* be waiting for you at the entrance to Dungeon Number One. *No, don't say anything, Sep*. We can get through the Darke with my witch's cloak. You are not in this alone. Got that?"

Septimus nodded. He did not trust himself to speak.

A shout from Rupert broke the moment. "Nik – she's beginning to go!"

Nicko leaped up. He could feel the pull of the current beneath them and the flapping of *Annie*'s sails told him that the boat's prow was being pulled into the wind and she was losing way – they were heading towards the wisp of spray that marked the Bottomless Whirlpool. Nicko raced back to the stern. He grabbed the tiller from Rupert – who was not a natural sailor – and yelled, "Oars! Everyone, get the oars!"

Annie's four long oars were snatched off the roof. Standing along the sides of the boat, Sarah, Simon, Lucy and Rupert dug them into the water. Frighteningly slowly, the boat's progress towards the Bottomless Whirlpool halted.

Septimus got to his feet. "I have to go, Jen," he said. "I'm putting everyone at risk."

"Oh. Oh, *Sep*."

Septimus hugged Jenna and quickly stepped back. "That witch's cloak is really . . . *zingy*. It buzzes when I touch it."

Jenna was determined to be positive. "Good. That means it's full of, er, witch stuff. It will get me and Nik through the Castle."

"Right." Septimus forced a smile. "I'll see you there, then."

"At the door to Dungeon Number One. We'll wait for you. We'll be there, I promise."

"Yeah. OK. I'll go and find Marcellus now."

"Yep. See you, Sep."

Septimus nodded and picked his way back along the deck, past Simon and Lucy, who were sitting like gloomy seagulls on the cabin roof.

"Good luck, Sep," said Lucy.

"Thanks."

Simon held out a small, black metallic Charm. "Take it, Septimus. It will guide you through."

Septimus shook his head. Right then it was hard to turn down any offer of help, even from Simon. But he was determined. "No thanks. I don't take SafeCharms from anyone."

"Then take some advice – always take the left."

Septimus reached the cockpit of the boat, where Marcellus had just emerged from the cabin.

"It is time, Apprentice," Marcellus said, with an anxious glance at Sarah. He had just had a fraught conversation with her, trying to impress upon her how she must let Septimus go without upsetting him. He wasn't sure that Sarah was going to manage it.

But Sarah did – just. She enveloped her youngest son in a desperate hug. "Oh, Septimus! Be careful."

"I will, Mum," said Septimus. "I'll see you soon. OK?"

"OK, sweetheart." With that Sarah rushed down into the cabin.

Nicko and Rupert hauled the little coracle down from the mast and dropped it over the side, hanging on to its rope. The flimsy round boat made of willow and skin bobbed lightly on the water like a leaf. Aware that everyone – except Sarah – was watching him, Septimus gave a tight smile and climbed down the ladder into the coracle. Nicko handed him the single paddle. "OK?" he said hoarsely.

Septimus nodded.

With every instinct telling him that he was *killing his little brother*, Nicko threw the rope into the coracle and set it free.

At first it drifted aimlessly, bobbing merrily as if out for a summer's day paddle on a gentle lake. And then it began to turn, slowly at first, as though it had caught a gentle breeze. Moving steadily towards the wisp of steam at the centre of the whirlpool, the coracle began to pick up speed and, like a fairground ride from which there is no return, to spin ever faster as it was drawn inexorably towards the edge of the vortex.

And then it reached the point of no return. With a suddenness that drew a gasp of dismay from everyone on *Annie*, it was whirled into the slipstream of the vortex. Spinning like a top as it raced around in ever decreasing circles, Septimus's green cloak was the pivot around which his tiny black craft spun. There was a final acceleration as it tipped into the centre of the whirlpool and was gone.

The creek was still. *Annie* was silent. No one could believe what they had just done.

✳ 42 ✳

THE DARKE HALLS

Septimus timed his Darke Disguise perfectly. As the coracle tipped into the centre of the whirlpool he muttered "ehtolc Sum" and felt the coldness of the Darke veil spread over him like a second skin. After that things were not quite so perfect.

Septimus was sucked into the roar of the whirlpool, whirled around like a piece of flotsam and pulled into its maw. Down, down, down he fell, whirling so fast that all his thoughts spun into a tiny dark place in the middle of his mind and he knew nothing except the roaring of water and the relentless pull of the vast emptiness below.

At that point, without a Darke Disguise Septimus would, like most of the whirlpool's previous victims, have drowned. He would have taken one last breath, filled his lungs with water and been pulled through a hole in the riverbed into a great underwater cave that was hollowed out in the bedrock like the inside of a hundred-foot-long egg. Here, for a few weeks, he would have circled until, one by one, his bones dropped and mingled with the pile of clean, white, delicate sticks scattered on the smooth cave floor – all that remained of those who had travelled the Bottomless Whirlpool over the many centuries that had elapsed since the Great Fight of the Darke Wizards.

The Darke Disguise did not spare Septimus the hole in the riverbed – through which he was sucked like a noodle into a greedy mouth – or the swash of the cave below. But it protected him like a glove and gave him the Darke Art of Suspension Underwater – something that Simon had spent many uncomfortable months with his head in a bucket learning to perfect. As Septimus swirled slowly around the underwater cave his thoughts unwound; he opened his eyes and realised that he was still alive.

The Darke Art of Suspension Underwater imparted an oddly distancing effect. The reason for this was to allay panic and so to conserve oxygen, although Septimus – indeed, most practitioners of the Art – did not realise this. It also allowed the eyes to see perfectly through the normal watery blurriness and this made moving underwater feel closer to flying than swimming. And so, as Septimus swam along with the circular currents of the egg-shaped cave, he found to his surprise that he was actually enjoying the sensation of being underwater. His Dragon Ring glowed brightly, turning the water around him a beautiful milky green and, when he drifted near the walls of the cave, the light made the crystals in the rock glitter as he passed.

But the Darke Art of Suspension Underwater does not last for ever. After some long, hazy minutes, Septimus began to feel breathless and twitchy. Pushing aside the early signs of panic, he swam upwards towards what he hoped was the surface and some air to breathe, only to hit his head with a painful *crack* on the roof of the cave. The panic welled up. There was no surface – *there was no air*.

Septimus sank a little and, holding his Dragon Ring out in front of him, he swam fast, looking upwards, hoping to see some kind of space where he could draw a breath. Just one deep, beautiful breath of air was all he needed ... *just one*. He was so busy looking up that he almost did not notice a flight of steps cut into the rock in front of him. It was only when the light from his Dragon Ring showed a strip of lapis lazuli set into the edge of a step, and above it another, and then another, that he realised he had found his way out. Eagerly his hands followed the steps up to an underwater gap in the rocky roof, through which they disappeared. Desperate now to take a breath, Septimus pulled himself up through the rock and emerged gasping into the freezing air of the Darke Halls.

The cold shocked him. His teeth chattering, water cascading off him, Septimus got shakily to his feet. In his preparation for his Darke Week, he had read ancient descriptions of what many now thought was no more than a mythical place beneath the earth, but he knew now they were true. All described what he was experiencing: a musty smell of earth and the stifling feeling of being pressed down by the surrounding rock and, accompanying everything, an eerie wail that seemed to drill into his bones. They had also described an overwhelming fear, but Septimus, insulated by the Darke Disguise covering him from head to toe, felt no fear – just elation at being alive and able to breathe once more.

Septimus drew in a few more luxurious deep breaths and took stock. Behind him was the egg-shaped hole in the ground through which he had just emerged; the faint light from his Dragon Ring caught the glint of gold from the lapis lazuli strip on the top step. In front of him was the unknown: a deep, thick darkness. Septimus had no landmarks, nothing to navigate by, just the sensation of a colossal empty space. All he had to go on was Simon's advice. And so he took it. He turned left and began to walk.

As he got into his stride, Septimus's mind began to emerge from the state of panic into which it had descended during his last few seconds underwater and he began to think clearly once more. According to Marcellus, all he had to do was walk through the Darke Halls until he reached the lower entrance to the antechamber to Dungeon Number One. It was there, Marcellus had said, that he was most likely to find Alther. *He has not long been* Banished, *Apprentice. He is unlikely to have yet roamed far.* Marcellus had even described the entrance to him – in such detail that Septimus suspected that the Alchemist had actually seen it for himself. A portico, he had called it: a square-cut doorway flanked on either side by ancient lapis pillars. Marcellus had calculated it to be about a seven-mile walk, which was the distance as the crow flies from the Bottomless Whirlpool to the Castle.

Septimus set a brisk pace. Seven miles at that speed should take him about two hours, he calculated. It was a monotonous journey. He saw very little except the pressed earth floor beneath his feet, and when he held his Dragon Ring out in front of him he saw nothing but the circle of light. It was a little disorientating, but he walked with a feeling of excitement – *Alther was near.* Soon he would see him and say, "Oh, *there* you are, Alther," as though he'd bumped into the ghost while strolling down Wizard Way. He tried to imagine what Alther would say and how pleased the ghost would be to see him. To prepare for that moment, Septimus went over in his mind the Banish Reverse that Marcia had taught him. It was complicated and, like the Banish itself, it must last for precisely one minute and be completed without hesitation, repetition or deviation.

Septimus walked on, his boots thudding dully against the earthen floor. He had the sensation of moving through a massive space, but not an empty one. All around him was a dismal wailing as if the wind was crying out in despair and loss. As he pushed through the dank, earthy atmosphere, small gusts of air brushed past him, some warm, some cold and some with a feeling of intense evil that took his breath away and reminded him that he was in a dangerous place.

After some time – surely much longer than an hour and a half – Septimus began to suspect that the Darke Halls were a whole lot bigger than he or Marcellus had thought. One of the ancient writers had called them "The Infinite Palaces of Wailing". Septimus had noted the Wailing but had paid little attention to the Infinite Palaces bit. But the cavern he had been walking through was surely as big as a dozen Castle Palaces – and it showed no sign of ending. The enormity of his task suddenly hit him. There were no maps to the Darke Halls; everything they knew was based on legends or on the writings of a handful of Wizards who had ventured there and returned to tell the tale. Most of these had drifted quickly into madness – not the most reliable of sources, thought Septimus, as his weary feet ploughed onwards.

And so it was with huge relief that Septimus at last saw a landmark appearing out of the gloom – a great square-cut gap in the rock, flanked on either side by two lapis lazuli pillars. It was exactly as Marcellus had described the entrance to Dungeon Number One. With his spirits soaring Septimus hurried towards it. Now all he had to do was to walk through and find Alther on the other side.

As he got closer to the portico Septimus noticed something white at its foot, and as he drew nearer still, he saw what it was. Bones. Clean and completely white – except for a thin brass ring with a red stone on the left little finger – the skeleton was sitting propped against the wall, the skull tipped at a jaunty angle towards the pillars as if pointing the way through.

Feeling it was wrong to pass casually by, Septimus stopped beside the bones. They had belonged to someone small, probably no taller than he had been a year ago. They looked fragile, sad and lonely, and Septimus felt a wave of sympathy for them. Whoever they had been had somehow survived the Bottomless Whirlpool only to find a haunted, freezing desert awaited them.

A sudden wail of wind blew through the portico and chilled him, even through the Darke Disguise. A bout of shivering overtook Septimus and he decided it was time to go through to the antechamber to Dungeon Number One; time to find Alther and do what he had come to do. He nodded respectfully to the bones and stepped through the portico.

The antechamber to Dungeon Number One was not what Septimus had expected – it seemed much the same as the empty space he had been walking through before. And there was no sign of Alther – there was, in fact, no sign of any ghosts at all. According to the texts, the antechamber was the most haunted place on earth, mostly by the ghosts of those thrown into the dungeon over the centuries. One of the great fears that Dungeon Number One held was the knowledge that those who died there were never seen as ghosts. All fell victim to the thrall of the Darke Halls and spent their entire ghost-hood below the ground, with no possibility of ever seeing the people or places they had once loved ever again. Many quite reasonably preferred to stay with the company of other ghosts rather than roam the "Infinite Palaces of Wailing".

The antechamber to Dungeon Number One was described as a circular walled chamber lined with black bricks, the same as those used to build the little round brick pot that marked the top entrance to the dungeon. And if those descriptions were right – and Septimus believed they were – then he was most definitely not in the antechamber to Dungeon Number One.

Septimus felt near to despair. If he was not in the antecham-ber, where was he? Unbidden the answer came to him – he was lost. Totally and utterly lost. Far more lost than he had been during the night he had spent in the Forest with Nicko a few years back. To stop himself sliding into panic Septimus thought about what Nicko would say right then. Nicko would say that they must keep going. Nicko would say that sooner or later they would come to Dungeon Number One, that it was only a matter of time. And so, taking an imaginary Nicko with him, Septimus set off once more into the Darke.

Almost immediately he was rewarded with the sight of three plain, square entrances set into the smooth rock wall. Septimus stopped and considered what to do. He remembered Simon's advice and Marcellus's words came back to him: *Apprentice, I truly believe we can trust him.*

Septimus stepped through the left-hand entrance.

Another empty space full of wailing and fear met him. Imagining Nicko by his side, Septimus walked quickly on and before long he came to two more porticos standing side by side. Once again he took the left one. It led him into a long, winding passageway down which a foul wind funnelled. It screamed at him, buffeting him and at times throwing him against the walls, but Septimus pushed on, and at last he stepped out of the passageway and into yet another empty cavernous space where, once again, he turned left.

Another tedious hour of walking followed. By now Septimus was footsore and weary, and the Darke Disguise felt as though it was wearing thin. The chill of the air was striking deep into him, and he could not stop shivering. The wailing was at times so loud that he felt he was losing touch not just with his own thoughts but with who he was – with *himself*. A deep, dark fear began to seep into him, a fear that even the imaginary Nicko could not keep out. But Septimus struggled on. It was either that, he told himself, or sit down and become another pile of bones.

Eventually he was rewarded by the sight of a distant portico. As he drew nearer his spirits rose cautiously. Surely *this* was the entrance to the antechamber – it fitted the description exactly. He picked up speed, but as he came closer he saw something that sent him very nearly over the edge of despair. He saw a small skeleton propped up against the side of the lapis pillar.

Septimus stopped dead. He felt sick. What were the chances of *two* skeletons sitting beside two identical porticos? He walked slowly forward until he was standing in front of the skeleton. It was small, delicate, and its skull nodded jauntily at the pillar. Septimus forced himself to look at its left hand. On the little finger was a cheap brass ring with a red stone.

Septimus sank to the ground – he had come full circle. He leaned back against the cold lapis and stared into the darkness in despair. Simon had deceived him. Marcellus was a fool. He would never find Dungeon Number One. He would never find Alther. He would be here for ever, and one day some unfortunate traveller would find *two* sets of bones propped up beside the arch. Now he understood why the skeleton was there. Whoever it had once been had also gone around in circles – how many times? Septimus looked up and found that he was eye to eye with the skull. Its teeth seemed to smile at him conspiratorially, the empty eye sockets to wink, but after the vast desert of empty spaces the bones felt like company.

"I'm sorry you didn't make it," he said to the bones.

"No one makes it on their own," came a whispering reply.

Septimus thought he was hearing his own thoughts. It was not a good sign. But even so, just to hear the sound of a human voice, he said, "Who's there?"

He thought he heard a faint reply that blended into the wail of the wind. "Me."

"Me," Septimus muttered to himself. "I *am* hearing myself."

"No. You hear *me*," said the whisper.

Septimus looked at the skull beside him, which returned his gaze mockingly. "Is it *you?*"

"It *was* me," came the reply. "Now it is not. Now it is bones. *This* is me."

And then something made Septimus smile for the first time since he had left *Annie*. A small figure began to materialise – the ghost of a girl aged no more than ten, he guessed. She looked like a miniature version of Jannit Maarten. She had the same wiriness about her and wore a child's version of Jannit's work clothes – a rough sailor's smock, cut-off trousers and her hair in a small, tight plait down her back. Septimus was almost as pleased to see her as he would have been to see Alther.

"Now you see me?" she asked, her head tilted to one side in an echo of her skull.

"Yes, I see you."

"*Now* I see you. But I could not before you spoke. You look . . . funny." The ghost extended what Septimus could see had once been a very grubby hand. "You must get up," she told him. "If you do not get up now, you will never get up. Like me. Come."

Wearily Septimus got to his feet.

The ghost looked up at him, excited. "You are my first Living. I watch from the shore. I saw those wicked people cast you adrift. I saw you go in," she chattered with the pent-up energy of a Living girl herself. "I followed." She saw Septimus's questioning glance. "Yes, through the whirlpool. It is Where I Have Trod Before."

Septimus felt he had to clear the name of all those on board *Annie*. "They did not cast me adrift. I came here on purpose, because I have to find a ghost. His name is Alther Mella. He wears ExtraOrdinary Wizard robes with a bloodstain over his heart. He is tall with white hair tied back in a ponytail. Do you know him?"

"No, I *don't*." The little girl sounded indignant. "The ghosts here are bad. Why would I want to know any of them? I only came back to this horrible place so that I can save you. Come on, I'll show you how to get out."

It took all Septimus's willpower to refuse her offer. "No, thank you," he said regretfully.

"But that's not *fair*. I have come here to *save* you!" The ghost stamped her foot.

"Yes, I *know*," said Septimus, a trifle irritably. He had prepared for many things in the Darke Halls but dealing with a little girl in a bad temper was not one of them. "Look, if you really want to save me then show me the way to Dungeon Number One. You do know the way?"

"Of course I do!" the ghost said.

"So please . . . will you show me?"

"No. Why should I? It's a horrid place. I don't like it."

Septimus knew she had him in her power. He took a deep breath and counted to ten. He could not afford to say something wrong. He had to find a way to persuade her to show him the way to Dungeon Number One.

Suddenly the ghost reached out and he felt the cool waft of her touch across his Dragon Ring. "This is pretty. I have a ring." She waggled her little finger with its cheap brass ring. "But it is not as pretty as this one."

Septimus was not sure whether he should agree with her or not, so he said nothing.

The ghost looked up at him earnestly. "Your pretty dragon. You wear it on your *right* hand."

"Yes, I do."

"On your *right* hand," she repeated.

"Yes. I *know*." Septimus was exasperated. He had had enough chit-chat about rings.

And then, to Septimus's dismay, she said, "You are a silly boy. You want to stay here, but I don't. I am going now. Goodbye."

And she was gone.

Septimus was alone once more. The little skull looked up at him and grinned.

❊ 43 ❊

DUNGEON NUMBER ONE

Septimus sat next to the pile of bones feeling bad. Really bad. Really, *really* bad. He thought of Beetle, Sealed into the Hermetic Chamber, and himself marooned in the Darke Halls and he knew that there was no hope left for either of them.

He stretched out his hands and looked at his Dragon Ring, the only thing he had left for company. He saw the warm yellow glow and the green emerald eye and he thought it was true; it *was* a pretty ring. And suddenly something clicked – he understood the little ghost's chattering about the ring. He wore his Dragon Ring on his right hand – he knew he did. He could even *feel* it on his right hand, on the index finger, where it always was. And yet, when he looked at his hands, the ring appeared to be on his *left* index finger. Septimus stared at his hands, uncomprehending. And then he understood. *That was it.* The ghost had been giving him a clue – in the Darke Halls everything was Reversed, so when he had thought he was taking the left turning, he had in fact been taking the right. So maybe Simon had not deceived him after all. Maybe . . .

Septimus leaped to his feet and, with renewed hope, he set off once more. He took the apparent right-hand entrance of the first three and found himself in yet another great Hall.

He speeded up, almost running in his wish to discover if this really was the secret to finding his way to Dungeon Number One. After choosing an apparent right-hand passageway leading from a small archway that very soon divided into two flights of steps – of which he took the right-hand flight – he pushed open a heavy door and found himself in a huge cavern that was actually *lit*. Great torches flared from niches carved into the smooth rock walls, illuminating the soaring heights of the Hall, casting long shadows across the smooth rock floor. Septimus felt like yelling with joy. He was getting somewhere now, he *knew* he was.

As he jogged along he began to encounter Things, Magogs, Wizards, Witches and all manner of misshapen creatures – and he was glad to see every single one. Each and every one passed him by and paid him no attention. His Darke Disguise still did what it was meant to do – it presented Septimus as something Darke, something that was one of them.

Septimus reckoned he must now be walking beneath the Castle. He began to pass by archways protected by metal grilles, which he suspected led into secret entrances somewhere in the Castle – entrances that even Marcia did not know about. There was a buzz of excitement in the air, which Septimus guessed was to do with the Darke events far above in the Castle itself. He passed by two Wizards who had left the Wizard Tower in disgrace a few years ago and heard one say excitedly, "Our time has come."

And then, at last, he saw ahead of him a portico. Gold streaks in the lapis lazuli of its pillars glistened in the light of the torches and Septimus knew that this was the one that would take him into the antechamber to Dungeon Number One.

Some minutes later, feeling so excited that he could hardly breathe, Septimus reached the portico.

As he went to step through, Tertius Fume – self-appointed busybody who terrified many of the ghosts – accosted him with a touch so cold that it felt burning hot. Septimus stopped, his heart beating fast. This put the Darke Disguise to its greatest test so far. Surely Tertius Fume would recognise him?

It appeared the ghost did not. He glared at Septimus with his piercing, goatlike eyes and demanded, *"Who be you?"*

Septimus was ready. "Sum."

"How be you?"

"Darke."

"What be you?"

"The Apprentice of the Apprentice of the Apprentice of DomDaniel."

Tertius Fume looked surprised. He stopped his questioning and tried to work out who exactly Septimus was. Septimus took advantage of the ghost's confusion and stepped through the entrance. He was probably the first person to feel utter delight at finding himself in the large, round chamber lined with black bricks, stuffed full of depressed ghosts. Now all he had to do was to find one ghost in particular.

Septimus scanned the room and his heart leaped. There was Alther, sitting motionless on a stone bench set into the wall, his eyes closed.

Tertius Fume had given up trying to work out who Septimus was – there were too many possibilities. The ghost followed him into the antechamber.

"Why come you here?" he demanded.

Septimus ignored Tertius Fume and began to make his way over to Alther. Tertius Fume followed like a storm cloud as Septimus dodged from side to side to avoid Passing Through the throng of ghosts. Eventually, with a feeling of elation, Septimus reached Alther's side. He had imagined this moment many times as he had travelled through the Darke Halls. He had longed to see Alther's expression as the ghost looked up and Saw through his Darke Disguise to the person he really was. But to his disappointment, nothing happened – Alther did not react. He seemed oblivious to his surroundings. His eyes remained closed and he sat still as a statue. Septimus knew that Alther had gone somewhere deep within himself.

Mindful of Marcellus's instructions to speak only the set responses in the presence of the Darke – and with Tertius Fume hovering at his shoulder, he was certainly in *that* – Septimus stood wondering how to reach Alther. Tertius Fume solved his problem.

"Why come you here?" he demanded once again.

Loudly, hoping that Alther would recognise his voice, Septimus said, "I seek the Apprentice of DomDaniel."

The moment that Alther recognised him was one of the best moments in Septimus's life. Alther's eyes opened slowly and Septimus saw recognition dawn. But Alther did not move an inch. His glance flicked sideways, took in Tertius Fume, and closed again. Septimus was elated. Alther understood. Alther was with him once again.

Tertius Fume did not notice Alther's awakening, as he was too busy scrutinising the newcomer. There was, he was sure, something odd about Sum – but what it was, he could not tell. The ghost gave Septimus a goaty gloat of a smile and replied,

"Then, Sum, you are in the wrong place. The Apprentice of DomDaniel is doing well – surprisingly well, I hear – above."

Septimus bowed and smiled in reply.

Tertius Fume mockingly returned the bow and drifted away.

Septimus sat down beside Alther. He knew Tertius Fume was suspicious and he had to work fast. He got straight to the point. "Marcia has given me the Revoke for the Banish. I have come to deliver it." He glanced at the ghost. To any onlooker, Alther looked the same. He was sitting stone still with his eyes closed. But Septimus could tell that the ghost was poised like a cat waiting to pounce. He was ready to *go*.

Septimus took a deep breath and in a low monotone, he began the Revoke. He longed to rush through the words and get it over with before Tertius Fume noticed what was happening, but he knew he could not. The Revoke must mirror the original form of the Banish. It must last, to the microsecond, the same amount of time. It must begin at the end of the Banish and end at the beginning.

Five and a half seconds before the end of the Revoke, Tertius Fume finally put two and two together. From a shortlist of seven, he had worked out who Septimus was. He was across the antechamber in a flash, Passing Through any ghost that got in his way. If it hadn't been for a particularly grumpy ghost – an unlucky bricklayer who had fallen into Dungeon Number One while repairing the wall – Tertius Fume would have been at Septimus's side in time to disrupt the Revoke. But thanks to the bricklayer, he arrived at the very moment the last words – "Overstrand Marcia I" – were being spoken.

Like a coiled spring, Alther leaped to his feet. In a most unghostly fashion, he grabbed Septimus by the hand and headed for the Darke vortex that spun in the very centre of the antechamber. Tertius Fume raced after them but he was too late. Septimus and Alther were sucked into the vortex, but the still-Banished Tertius Fume was thrown clear and sent spinning across the antechamber like any new ghost hurled from Dungeon Number One.

Septimus and Alther were free. Together they crashed up through the layers of bones and despair, burst out through the sludge and slime, and hurtled into the chimney of Dungeon Number One. Septimus was propelled upwards with the force. High above him he saw the iron rungs of the ladder that he must reach. Up, up he went, but just as he was within an arm's length of the lowest rung he felt his momentum fade and Septimus knew that he would not reach it. Soon he would drop back into the mire at the bottom of the dungeon – the mire from which few escaped. Dismayed, Alther saw gravity begin to take its hold on Septimus.

"Flyte, Septimus! Think Flyte!" the ghost urged, hovering beside Septimus. "Think it, be it, do it. Flyte!"

And so, remembering a time on the edge of an icy cliff beside an abyss, Septimus thought of his ancient Flyte Charm – now languishing in the bottom of a pot in the Manuscriptorium Vaults – and he felt gravity loosen its hold and allow the momentum to continue. The next moment his hand had clutched the icy iron rung at the foot of the ladder and Septimus knew he was safe.

Alther kept pace with Septimus as he climbed the rungs. Far below the howl of the vortex grew ever fainter as he struggled upwards and now, at last, he could see the thick iron door at the top, streaked with rust. On the very top rung Septimus halted and, clinging on with one hand, he fumbled in his buttoned pocket for the precious key. It took him many long, tired minutes to undo the buttons, but finally he took out the key, looped its cord around his wrist for safety, pushed it into the lock and turned it.

The door swung open and the Darke Fog tumbled in fast, taking Septimus by surprise and knocking him backwards. He would have fallen had not two pairs of strong arms grabbed him and dragged him out of the door like a sack of potatoes.

"*Sep*! You're safe! And Uncle Alther! Oh, *you're both safe*!" Jenna's voice was distant in the Darke Fog but there was no mistaking the laughter and relief in it.

Septimus sat propped up against the little brick cone of the top of Dungeon Number One, too tired to do anything but smile. Jenna and Nicko, both swathed in the voluminous witch's cloak, regarded him with answering smiles. There was nothing anyone needed to say – they were all together again.

But Alther had something to say. "Hmm," he murmured. "You've let the old place get into a bit of a state while I was away."

44

The sick-bay Apprentice knocked timidly on the large purple door that guarded Marcia's rooms. The door was on high alert. It did not recognise Rose so it stayed firmly closed and it was Marcia herself who let Rose in. Rose felt quite overwhelmed to be standing in the ExtraOrdinary Wizard's rooms and for a moment forgot what she was meant to say.

"Yes?" asked Marcia anxiously.

"Um ... excuse me, Madam Overstrand, the duty Wizard says that there is nothing more we can do. She respectfully asks to return the patient at your earliest convenience."

Marcia sighed. She could do without this. "Thank you, Rose. Would you be so kind as to tell the duty Wizard that I shall collect her at the end of my rounds?"

Some minutes later Marcia emerged from her rooms and set off down the stairs, which were now on permanent energy-saving Snail mode. Determined now to keep the Wizards' spirits up, Marcia breezed through the Wizard Tower like wildfire. To keep the Living SafeShield going in the face of the continuing onslaught of the Darke, she needed every Wizard to concentrate on their Magyk. The frequent flashes of orange light that came through the windows were a constant reminder

that the Magykal energy was draining away. Marcia wasn't sure
if the Tower could hold out much longer, and she was afraid
that many Wizards felt the same. But she had to make them
believe it was possible.

As she went around spreading encouragement, Marcia felt
the air begin to buzz with Magyk once more. It was exhilarat-
ing, like walking through the aftermath of a storm, with the air
fresh and tingling and dusted with faint sparkles of light rain
drifting in the breeze. Gone was the gossip, the bickering and
the petty rivalries that always bubbled below the surface of the
Wizard Tower – now everyone was working together.

Marcia moved quickly through the Tower. Most Wizards
and Apprentices chose to be in a public part of the Tower;
few wanted to be alone at such a time. They were scattered
about, each focusing on their Magyk in ways that were best for
them. Many paced the Great Hall, murmuring quietly, so that
a purposeful hum rose up through the Tower. Others sat by a
window and stared intently at the indigo and purple lights of
the SafeShield, trying not to wince when a flicker of orange
disrupted them.

Having made a point of being seen by as many Wizards as
possible, Marcia took the stairs to the sick bay. First she slipped
into the DisEnchanting Chamber to see Syrah Syara. Marcia
stood for a moment saying a silent goodbye – just in case.
She knew that Syrah, still deep in DisEnchantment, would not
survive for long if the Darke Domaine entered the Tower.

Marcia emerged shakily to find Jillie Djinn waiting for her
at the duty Wizard's desk like a parcel in lost property.

"The duty Wizard sends her apologies but she has just been
called to an emergency," said Rose. She fished out a large

ledger from underneath the desk. "Um, Madam Overstrand, would you mind signing for the return of the Chief Hermetic Scribe, please?"

Marcia signed somewhat unenthusiastically for Jillie Djinn.

"Miss Djinn is ready to go now," Rose said.

"Thank you, Rose. I'll take her upstairs."

Stopping on every floor and encouraging Wizards as she went, Marcia made her way slowly back up to the top of the Wizard Tower with Jillie Djinn following her like a little dog.

Once the big purple door had closed behind her, Marcia's upbeat manner evaporated. She sat Jillie Djinn on the sofa and then slumped down on to Septimus's stool beside the fire. She took down a small silver box from the chimneypiece and opened it. Inside lay the Wizard Tower half of the Paired Code – a thick, shiny silver disc with a circular indentation in the centre. The disc was covered with closely packed numbers and symbols; each one was joined to a finely etched line that radiated from the centre.

Marcia stared at it for some minutes, thinking what might have been if only she had the Manuscriptorium half of the Code. The silver disc taunted her. *Where is my other half?* it seemed to say. Marcia fought down a desire to Transport out of the Wizard Tower and hunt down Merrin Meredith – how she longed to get her hands on him. But Marcia knew that any Magyk that breached the SafeShield would let the Darke come streaming in – and it would be the end of the Wizard Tower. She was a prisoner of her own defences.

Angrily Marcia looked up and glared at Jillie Djinn – the Chief Hermetic Scribe was, in her opinion, guilty of gross negligence. If she had not nurtured that snake Merrin Meredith in the Manuscriptorium, none of this would have happened. Marcia shut the silver box shut with a crisp *snap*. Jim Knee jumped. With a loud *snurrrrf* the jinnee turned and made himself comfortable on the grubby shoulder of Jillie Djinn. The Chief Hermetic Scribe did not react. She sat staring into space, white-faced, vacant. A sudden flash of orange lit up jinnee and Djinn, making them look eerily like wax dummies.

At the sight of them a great wave of despair overwhelmed Marcia – not since the night Alther and Queen Cerys were shot had she felt so alone. She wondered where Septimus was now and imagined him lying in a Darke trance in an empty alleyway somewhere, freezing in the snow. Marcia blamed herself. It was *her* intransigence that had driven Septimus to Marcellus that afternoon, just as it was *her* stupid mistake that had Banished Alther. And now she was going to be the ExtraOrdinary Wizard who lost the Wizard Tower to the Darke. It would be *her* name reviled in the future, known only as the last ExtraOrdinary Wizard who had squandered all the precious history and knowledge that was gathered in this beautiful, Magykal space. Marcia Overstrand, seven hundred and seventy-sixth ExtraOrdinary Wizard – the one who threw it all away. Marcia let out a sound somewhere between a groan and a sob.

At the top of the Wizard Tower was a large and very ancient Dragon Window that led into Marcia's sitting room. Outside the window was a wide ledge made for the perching of dragons, which was also useful for the perching of ghosts who were unused to exercise. Feeling thankful that as an

Apprentice he had once – *very* briefly – climbed out on to the ledge for a dare, Alther hovered there while he recovered enough strength to DisCompose himself and go through the window. He peered through the glass but could make out very little. The room was dim, lit only by firelight. There was, he thought, a figure sitting by the fire with her head in her hands, but it was hard to tell.

Some minutes later Alther had regained enough strength to DisCompose. He took the ghostly equivalent of a deep breath and walked through the Dragon Window.

Marcia looked up. Her glistening green eyes widened and her mouth fell open. She did not move.

"Marcia . . ." said Alther very gently.

Marcia leaped to her feet and squealed – there was no other word for it. "Alther! *AltherAltherAlther!* It's you. Tell me, it *is* you?" She raced across the room and, forgetting that he was a ghost, she hurled herself at him, Passed Through and cannoned into the Dragon Window.

Alther reeled with the shock of being Passed Through and fell back beside Marcia.

"Oh, Alther!" she gasped. "I'm *so* sorry. I didn't mean to do that. But . . . oh, I can't believe you're here. Oh, you don't know how *pleased* I am to see you."

Alther smiled. "I think I do. Probably as pleased as I am to see you."

Up in the Pyramid Library a windswept Marcia closed the tiny window that led out on to the Pyramid steps. She looked amazed. "I saw his tail! What, for goodness' sake, is he doing up there?"

"Keeping safe, I suppose. He must have found the expansion point where the SafeShields meet and slipped in," said Alther. "I am guessing that *is* where they meet?"

Marcia nodded. "I've not had much luck with sticking things together recently," she sighed.

"No defence is ever impregnable, Marcia. You seem to have done a pretty good job to me. Besides, a dragon may slip in and out of a SafeShield in a way that a Wizard cannot." He paused. "I am sorry I cannot be more help, Marcia. Septimus thought I could UnDo the Darke Domaine because unfortunately, Merrin Meredith and I were both Apprenticed to the same Wizard."

"Heavens, so you were. I'd never thought of it like that," said Marcia.

"I try not to myself," said Alther. "Septimus had hoped that the more senior Apprentice could fix the junior's mess. But as I am no longer Living the rules don't apply. I only wish they did." Alther sighed. "So it is down to you, Marcia. Your dragon awaits. As indeed does your Apprentice."

"And that little piece of vermin."

"Indeed, although I doubt Merrin Meredith is exactly *awaiting* you."

A few minutes later Marcia closed the Dragon Window with a bang.

"*He won't come.* The wretched beast is *ignoring* me!"

"Well, if the dragon won't come to the ExtraOrdinary Wizard, the ExtraOrdinary Wizard must go to the dragon," said Alther.

"What – *up there*? At the top of the pyramid?"

"It can be done," said Alther, "take my word for it. I wouldn't recommend it, but desperate times call for ..."

"Desperate measures," said Marcia, steeling herself.

Some minutes later, if anyone had been able to see through the Darke Fog they would have picked out the arresting sight of Marcia Overstrand climbing shakily up the stepped sides of the Golden Pyramid on top of the Wizard Tower. The wind blew her purple cloak out behind her like the wings of a bird as she moved through the fuzz of Magyk beneath the Magykal indigo and purple lights, following the fainter figure of a ghost – similarly clad in purple – who was guiding her up towards a dragon that roosted on the flat square at the very top of the pyramid.

As soon as Marcia reached the dragon's tail she grabbed hold of one of the spines. "Got you!" she gasped.

Spit Fyre raised his head sleepily and looked around. *Bother,* he thought, *it's that irritating one in purple again.* Spit Fyre's Pilot had never told him to come when the Purple One Called, but he had instructed him to let the Purple One fly him. She wasn't very good at it from what he could remember.

Spit Fyre patiently allowed Marcia to clamber into the Pilot Dip and waited while she Reversed her cloak to give some protection from the Darke Domaine. When she told him "Spit Fyre, follow that ghost", he stretched out his wings and, with great control, he flew slowly upwards, following Alther as the ghost headed up towards the tiny expansion gap where the four SafeShields joined. As he approached, Spit Fyre performed a rare arrow manoeuvre – he folded his wings close to his body and then flipped into a completely vertical position, leaving Marcia to use the Panic Spine for what it was meant for – hanging on in a panic. With his nose pointing up to the sky, like a dragon-shaped bolt from a crossbow, Spit Fyre shot through the expansion gap at a tremendous speed and left it as undisturbed as he had done when he had arrowed in two days earlier.

Ghost and dragon flew off through the Darke Fog, heading for the Maker's Mile Tally Hut.

Down below in Marcia's rooms, the big purple door recognised Silas Heap. It opened and Silas stepped inside.

"Marcia?" he whispered.

There was no reply. The firelight flickered, casting weird shadows on the wall of . . . a dwarf and . . . someone balancing a pile of doughnuts on his head?

Silas felt a little spooked. "Marcia – are you there? It's only me. I came to see if you were all right. I . . . well, I thought you looked a bit lonely. Might need some company? *Marcia?*"

There was no reply. The bird had flown.

45

DRAGONS

"It's so lovely out." The Witch Mother's voice carried like a bell through the Darke. From the cover of the Maker's Mile Tally Hut, Jenna, Septimus and Nicko watched the five shadowy figures of the Port Witch Coven stroll by, as carefree as if they were out for a walk on a summer's day. A slightly less carefree figure – Nursie under a Darke blanket – scuttled behind them.

"There goes your Coven, Jen," whispered Septimus.

"Stop it, Sep," hissed Jenna. The sight of the five misshapen shadows trolling past made her remember how scared she'd been in Doom Dump. She suddenly felt a little less fond of her witch's cloak as they watched the witches disappear jauntily down the Ceremonial Way.

Jenna, Septimus and Nicko were waiting for Spit Fyre. They had chosen somewhere out of the way where the dragon could easily land. Alther had gone to collect Spit Fyre; he had promised to be as quick as he could, but they all knew so much could go wrong. Every minute in the Tally Hut felt like an hour, but the moment when they saw the shadow of a dragon hovering above felt like for ever. No one – not for one second – thought it was Spit Fyre.

So different from the elegant Spit Fyre in flight, the six-winged Darke dragon descended clumsily through the Fog and, after three attempts, landed with a resounding *thud* on the raised circle that marked the centre of the Makers' Mile. It shook the Tally Hut to its foundations.

Jenna, Septimus and Nicko shrank back into the depths of the hut, convinced that the dragon Knew they were there. The frantic beating of its wings during its landing attempts had cleared away the Fog and they could see the Darke dragon frighteningly clearly. Its massive size was the first shock – it made Spit Fyre seem like a delicate dragonfly in comparison. The dragon squatted awkwardly, shifting its bulk from one tree-trunk leg to another, while a white forked tongue flicked in and out of its red slash of a mouth. It shook its lumpen head and rolled its eyes – all six of them – as it looked around. The eyes were arranged so that the dragon had virtually 360-degree vision – its blind spot was a mere ten degrees compared with the standard dragon blind spot of ninety degrees. The all-seeing eyes swivelled like glistening red ball bearings as the dragon surveyed the ramshackle remains of the market. Pointed spines barbed like fish hooks ranged down the dragon's back, and its four huge feet were equipped with curved black talons, each one shaped like – and as sharp as – a scimitar. It was a terrifying sight, but the most horrifying thing of all was that one talon had speared a scrap of blue cloth, which had something red and meaty stuck to it. Jenna covered her face. That, she thought, had once been someone, someone who lived in the Castle – someone like her.

A sharp nudge from Septimus made Jenna look up again.

"Look," whispered Septimus. "In front of the Pilot Spine. *There's someone there.*"

The Darke dragon's Pilot Spine was, like Spit Fyre's, the tallest of all the spines. But unlike Spit Fyre's, which was solid and straight, with a rounded top, it curved forward with a razor-sharp barb on the end of it. Sitting in the Pilot Dip was a figure swathed in grubby scribe robes. Jenna knew exactly who it was.

"*Merrin Meredith,*" she whispered.

"Yeah," said Septimus. "He's got serious now, hasn't he? He's not just an irritating little tick any more – he's for real."

"I can hardly believe it," whispered Jenna. "He's so pathetic, but he's caused all *this* to happen."

"It's the Darke, Jen. He's got that ring and now he's got its power. And he's so stupid, he doesn't care what he does with it. He just wants to destroy everything."

"You in particular."

"Me?"

"Beetle said he was ranting on about you, Sep. You know, about how he was Septimus Heap first. How he was going to get you. Then he'd be Septimus Heap. With a ten-times-better dragon."

"Yeah. Well, he's got a ten times *bigger* one, that's for sure."

"Not better though."

"No way. Spit Fyre's the best."

Suddenly the Darke Dragon raised all six wings and brought them down fast; a terrific rush of wind swooshed into the Tally Hut along with a foul smell that sent the occupants reeling. It also dispersed the re-gathering Fog and gave them a clear view of what happened next. The dragon shuffled awkwardly around and began a lumbering run down the broad space of the Ceremonial Way, its wings rising and falling like black sails.

They watched it go, getting faster and faster until it reached the Palace gates, where it finally took off, rose slowly into the Fog and disappeared into the night.

"Phew," breathed Nicko. "It's gone."

"I was so scared Spit Fyre would come while that thing was here," whispered Jenna.

Septimus nodded. He had been too, although he had not dared to think it. He believed what Aunt Zelda always said: *the thought is the seed for deed.*

But a few minutes later something happened that Septimus had definitely not thought of: the Darke dragon came back. It landed with a thud, the Tally Hut shook, the red eyes swivelled and everyone held their breath. And then once more it lumbered into a turn and galumphed down the Ceremonial Way until at last it took off. Three times the Darke dragon came back and each time the occupants of the Tally Hut prayed that Spit Fyre would not choose that moment to arrive. Each time they became more frightened, convinced that the dragon knew they were there – why else would it keep returning? It was not until the third time when the dragon was a little more skillfully heading into his take-off that Jenna realised what was going on.

"He's practising," she whispered. "It's the only space in the Castle where a dragon that big can land and take off."

And they all knew what the dragon was practising for – the assault on the Wizard Tower.

A few minutes after the Darke dragon had taken off for the fourth time, the smaller, more delicate – and infinitely more welcome – two-winged shape of Spit Fyre came down through the Fog, heralded by the swooping figure of Alther, arms outstretched in his favourite flying mode.

Spit Fyre landed lightly on the very spot the Darke dragon had so recently vacated. He sniffed the air uneasily, in the way a house cat might sniff a pile of lion poo left outside its cat flap. The next thing Spit Fyre knew, three figures were hurtling towards him, one of which was his Pilot. Spit Fyre felt relieved. It had been a nightmare flying with The Purple One. Now she would get off and let his Pilot sit in his rightful place.

The Purple One, however, did not get off.

Pleased as he was to see Marcia once again, Septimus was not prepared to let her fly Spit Fyre. They needed to get away fast and he doubted her ability to do it. He got to the point right away.

"Get off!" he yelled through the weight of the Darke Fog.

"Hurry up, Marcia," said Alther, who shared Septimus's opinion of Marcia's flying skills. "Get off and let the Pilot fly his dragon."

"I'm *getting* off. My cloak's caught. Oh, these *stupid* spines . . ."

Septimus was hopping from one foot to another in impatience. He yanked the Reversed cloak off a small spine and Marcia clambered down. She surprised Septimus with a fierce hug, helped him up to his seat in front of the Pilot Spine and then took Jenna's place behind him in the Navigator seat. Jenna stifled her irritation – this was neither the time nor the place to argue about where she sat – and she and Nicko squeezed on behind Marcia.

Septimus took Spit Fyre up fast with Alther keeping pace alongside. Marcia tapped him on the shoulder.

"Manuscriptorium!" she yelled into the clear air created by the beating of Spit Fyre's wings.

Septimus wanted to get Spit Fyre out of danger. He most definitely did not want to fly to the Manuscriptorium. "Why?" he yelled.

"Merrin Meredith. Code!"

"Merrin Meredith's *cold*?"

"Not cold, Code! Paired Code. He's got it! He's at the Manuscriptorium!"

Now Septimus understood.

"He's not there!" he yelled. At that moment a massive shadow cruised overhead, accompanied by a foul downdraught of air. "He's up there!"

They all looked up. The wake of the Darke Dragon cleared the Fog just enough for them all to see the cruel talons, black and bloodied against the white underside of its belly. For the first time ever Septimus heard Marcia say a very rude word.

"I'm taking Spit Fyre out after that *thing*," said Marcia. "I'll get Merrin Meredith if it's the last thing I do."

Septimus thought it probably would be.

"Septimus, fly Spit Fyre back to the Wizard Tower at once. Land him on the dragon platform. You three can get off."

Septimus had no intention of getting off his dragon, but he knew better than to argue just then. He turned Spit Fyre around and headed back to the Wizard Tower. Spit Fyre arrowed through the join and took them into the bright, buzzing, Magykal air that surrounded the Wizard Tower. He landed perfectly on the dragon ledge.

"Wait there, I'll open the window," said Marcia, slipping down from the Navigator seat. She ushered Jenna and Nicko inside and stood waiting impatiently for Septimus to relinquish his place in the Pilot Dip.

"Hurry up, Septimus. Let me get on."

Septimus did not move.

"Septimus, get off. I am ordering you!"

"And I am refusing," said Septimus. "*I'll* get him."

"No, Septimus. Get off at once."

The stalemate might have lasted a while had not the orange warning lights zipping up and down the outside of the SafeShield suddenly stopped flashing.

Marcia gasped. "The SafeShield's failing! Septimus, get off! Now!"

The blue and purple skin of the SafeShield began to take on a dull, reddish hue. A movement above caught Septimus's eye – tendrils of Darke Fog were beginning to drift down through the join. Suddenly a great curved black claw reached down through the gap.

Septimus knew what he had to do.

"Up, Spit Fyre," he said. "Up!"

Before Marcia could do anything to stop him, Pilot and dragon flew up through the dim glow of the failing Magyk to meet dragon and pilot.

46

SYNCHRONICITY

Septimus and Spit Fyre burst through the top of the SafeShield and Spit Fyre's nose spine slammed into the Darke dragon's soft white underbelly with a jarring thud. Spit Fyre was sent reeling backwards, but the Darke dragon seemed no more upset than if it had been stung by a wasp.

Spit Fyre recovered fast and snorted with excitement. He was at the age when, in ancient times when the world was full of dragons, he would have been looking for his first fight. In those days the dragon community would not have regarded him as an adult until he had fought another dragon – and won. And so, deep down in his dragon brain, Spit Fyre *wanted* a fight.

So did the Darke dragon's pilot. Merrin leaned out between the bristling spines, his eyes wild with excitement. Using a popular Castle insult for Apprentices, he yelled, "I'll get you, caterpillar boy!"

"No chance, rat face!"

Merrin pointed his left thumb at Septimus like a pistol. "You're *dead*. And your toy dragon. Yeah!"

In answer Septimus and Spit Fyre shot up past the Darke dragon before it had time to register what was happening.

They whizzed by so close that Septimus could see Merrin's spots blazing out of his pale face and the look of hatred in his eyes – which shocked him more than the close-up view of the Darke dragon. As Spit Fyre shot past, Septimus made a very rude sign at Merrin. He left behind a stream of obscenities haemorrhaging into the Darke Fog.

Septimus and Spit Fyre stopped at the very edge of the Fog and looked back. Far below them, at the bottom of the clear tunnel of air that their wake had created, they saw the huge bulk of the Darke dragon. Behind it they could see the fading blue and purple Magykal glow of the Wizard Tower changing slowly to a dull red.

As they hovered above the Darke Domaine, suspended between the stars and the blanket of silence below, a stillness spread through Septimus and his dragon and together they entered a state that is much sought after by dragon Imprintors but rarely achieved. It is known in dragon manuals (see *Draxx*, page 1141) as Synchronicity. Dragon and Imprintor became One, thinking and acting in perfect harmony. They hovered for a moment on the edge of the Darke Domaine and looked down at the Darke dragon far below at the end of the trail They had left in the Fog. They knew they must use the line of sight while they had it.

Suddenly They tipped forward and went into a nosedive. Septimus slammed into the broad, flat spine in front of him and wedged there, exhilarated as the air rushed past. They hurtled down like a bullet falling to earth and saw Merrin looking up, yelling and kicking at his dragon. In a beautifully controlled movement, the Synchronised pair decelerated, swooped to the left and headed for the rear set of the Darke dragon's wings.

Their nose spine ripped through them. In a shower of splintering wing bones and folds of foul flapping skin they shot out the other side, wheeled around and stopped to view their handiwork.

The Darke dragon tumbled out of control. Its pilot's terrified screams were absorbed by the Fog as it catapulted down towards the Wizard Tower. With a dull *boom* that travelled through the Fog like distant thunder, the Darke dragon slammed against the failing SafeShield, sending sparks of Magyk into the air and setting off a chain of red distress lights that rippled down to the ground like a lightning strike. Tail flailing, its four undamaged wings beating frantically, the Darke dragon bounced off the SafeShield and fell towards the rooftops of the houses that looked out over the Wizard Tower courtyard. The Synchronised ones watched triumphantly – They hadn't dreamed it would be this easy to get rid of the Darke dragon.

It wasn't. Four wings are enough to fly a dragon – even one as cumbersome as the great beast that Merrin had Engendered. In a hail of smashed chimney pots and roof tiles, his dragon righted itself, perched for a moment on a roof, and, as the rafters caved in under its weight, it rose up into the air, and its six eyes locked on to Spit Fyre. The next moment the Darke dragon was heading straight for Them, mouth wide open, revealing three rows of long, tightly knit teeth like needles.

They waited, daring the dragon to come dangerously near. And when it was so close They could see the tiny black pupils in all six red eyes (but neither of the pilot's – he had his eyes tightly closed) They shot around behind the monster's tail into the ten-degree blind spot, arrowed down underneath the white belly, and then zoomed up in front of the boxy head

– which was still staring upwards, wondering where They had gone. And then They swiped it hard on the nose with the barb of Their tail. *Wap*. Dragons' noses are a sensitive spot and a roar of pain followed Them as They shot out of reach once more.

"I'll get you for that!" They heard Merrin shouting as They zoomed around in a tight circle, way out of reach.

"You wish!" They yelled.

And so They taunted the Darke dragon and its pilot: diving down, flying circles around it, swooping out of sight only to reappear in exactly the opposite direction from where the dragon was looking. They landed sideswipes with Their tail; They stabbed the underbelly with Their nose spine; They even caught the tops of another two wings in a short burst of Fyre that They managed to summon from an empty fire stomach. The Darke dragon responded to every move – but about five seconds too late. Often it was countering the last attack while the next one was underway, and before long the monster was bellowing with fury and frustration and its pilot was whimpering in terror.

After some minutes, breathless and buzzing with excitement, they swooped up through the Darke Fog for a brief consultation. Hovering on the very edge of the dome of the Darke Domaine, buffeted by the breeze, They breathed in fresh night air untainted by the Darke. Above Them shone a glitter dust of stars and below them the tendrils of Fog waved like seaweed in an ocean current. They felt exhilarated, on top of the world.

But far below the Darke dragon still lurked. They decided it was time to lure the monster out of his Domaine. They figured that the dragon was now so frantic to get hold of Them that it would follow Them anywhere. They took a deep breath of clear air, then dropped down into the Fog once more. They saw the six blazing red pinpoints of Their quarry's eyes – and headed straight for them.

Taking care that the Darke dragon always had Them in his line of sight, They began a cat-and-mouse game with Merrin and his monster, venturing temptingly near for swipes of the scimitar claws – but never quite near enough to make contact. Once or twice the claws came a little too close for comfort and They felt the breeze ruffle Their hair as the blades flew past Their head. And so, taunting and teasing, parrying and feinting like a skilled swordsman, They lured the Darke dragon onwards and upwards – with no resistance from its whimpering pilot.

They shot out of the Darke Fog like a bullet. Focused only on the tempting barb of Their tail, which was less than a wing's breadth in front of its nose spine, the Darke dragon followed. It hit the cold clear air like a wall. Stunned, it stopped dead. For the first time in its short and nasty life it was without a Darke safety net – there was nothing but the cold black river running below. Its pilot opened his eyes, looked down and screamed.

Feeling its powers begin to trickle away, the Darke dragon threw back its head and bellowed with distress. Released from the muffling effect of the Darke Domaine the noise was loud and terrible. It sounded out across the countryside and sent people for miles around diving for cover under their beds. Far below, in Sally Mullin's Tea and Ale House, Sarah Heap and Sally Mullin looked anxiously out into the night.

"Oh, Sally," whispered Sarah. "It's so *awful* . . ."

Sally put her arm around Sarah's shoulders. There was nothing she could say.

Outside, beside the newly returned *Annie*, Simon Heap was pacing the pontoon with Marcellus Pye. Simon had been telling Marcellus that he had decided to go into the Castle. He had so much to offer, so much knowledge of the Darke. At last he had an opportunity to put it to use for *good* – and that was what he intended to do. But Marcellus had not heard a word Simon said. His last sight of Septimus in the little coracle spinning into the whirlpool haunted him; it played over and over in his head and he could not escape it. The more he thought about it, the more Marcellus doubted Septimus had survived. He had led his dearest Apprentice to his death. Marcellus felt utterly wretched.

The Darke dragon's roar cut through his thoughts. Marcellus looked up to see Spit Fyre, illuminated by the lights shining from Sally Mullin's Tea and Ale House, dropping out of the night sky. The dragon had come to exact revenge and Marcellus didn't care. He deserved it.

Sally Mullin saw Marcellus looking up into the sky. "Something's going on up there," she whispered.

"I wish Simon would come inside," Sarah said. "I wish . . ." But right then Sarah wished for far too many things to even begin, although at the top of the list was a wish to see Septimus again. To take her mind off the hundred awful things that Sarah had imagined might have happened to Septimus, she watched Marcellus.

"He's a bit of a drama queen, isn't he?" Sally whispered mischievously, hoping to cheer Sarah up.

Right then Marcellus did look rather dramatic. The light from the lamps in Sally's long line of windows caught the gold embellishments on his cloak as he raised his arms up in the air, hands outstretched. They saw him suddenly spin around and shout something to Simon, who came running.

"What *is* going on?" muttered Sally. "Oh! Oh, my goodness. Sarah! Sarah! It's your Septimus. Look!"

Sarah gasped. Hurtling towards the river and – she was convinced – to certain death, was her youngest son on his dragon. And when she saw the horrific shape of the Darke monster that was chasing Them, Sarah screamed so loudly that Sally's ears rang. Sarah and Sally watched the Darke dragon diving like a hawk after a sparrow, its razor claws poised and ready to grab, and when it drew so close to Spit Fyre that it must surely tear the dragon and its rider to pieces any moment, Sarah could bear it no longer – she gave a cry of despair and buried her head in her hands.

A few feet above the surface of the river the Synchronised pair suddenly – as planned – changed course, but in the moment They slowed, the longest claw on the Darke dragon's right foot made contact with Their head. Sally suppressed a scream. It would not do Sarah any good right now. She watched Spit Fyre reel back, wings frantically beating the air. Seconds later a massive plume of river water rose into the air.

The Darke dragon hit the surface and sank like a house.

Sally Mullin gave a great whoop of excitement. "You can look now," she told Sarah as Spit Fyre flew back shakily just above the surface of the river. "They're all right." Sarah burst into tears. It had all been too much.

Sally comforted Sarah while keeping one eye on events outside. When she saw Septimus jump into the middle of the fast-flowing river she decided not to tell Sarah.

The freezing water took Septimus's breath away. He swam quickly towards Merrin, who was flailing about in the water, yelling, "Help me! Help me! I can't swim! Help!" This was not strictly true, for Merrin could doggie paddle a few yards, although not enough to reach safety from the middle of the river.

Septimus was a strong swimmer and after the night exercises in the Young Army, swimming in the river did not frighten him. He grasped Merrin around the chest from behind and began the slow swim to the safety of Sally Mullin's pontoon. Above him Spit Fyre, dripping blood from a deep tear on the top of his head, circled anxiously, but on instructions from Septimus he flew off and landed on the wide stones of the New Quay. The current in the river was sweeping Septimus past Sally Mullin's pontoon and he knew better than to fight it. He swam diagonally across, heading always for the bank, with Merrin a dead weight in his arms.

Simon watched anxiously. He reflected that not so long ago he would have been pleased to see his youngest brother struggling in the icy river, and he felt ashamed of his old self. He saw where the current was taking Septimus and his burden, so he set off down to the next easy landfall, the New Quay where Spit Fyre had just landed. As Simon jogged down the path he heard a yell from the water followed by some wild splashing. He raced to the quay and saw Septimus struggling with Merrin some yards away – the exact distance, in fact, that Merrin could swim.

Merrin appeared to have miraculously recovered and was now pushing Septimus below the water. Septimus struggled, but the delicate fabric of his Darke Disguise was torn and ragged and it was no match for the power of the Two-Faced Ring, which strengthened tenfold any attempt at murder. As Merrin pushed the spluttering and fighting Septimus once more beneath the water, Simon dived in.

With the power of the Two-Faced Ring – and Merrin himself – fully occupied in drowning Septimus, Simon's old-fashioned punch to Merrin's head had the desired effect. Merrin let go of Septimus, took in a huge mouthful of water and began to sink. Septimus looked at his rescuer, shocked.

"You OK?" asked Simon.

Septimus nodded. "Yeah. Thanks, Simon."

Merrin gave a gurgle and slipped beneath the water.

"I'll get him," gasped Simon, teeth chattering as the icy cold began to take effect. "You get to the steps."

But Septimus did not trust Merrin. He swam alongside Simon as he towed Merrin back and when they reached the New Quay, Septimus helped him haul Merrin out of the water and up the steps. They lay Merrin facedown on the stones like a dead fish.

"We'll have to get the water out," said Simon. "I've seen them do it at the Port." He kneeled beside Merrin, placed his hands on Merrin's ribcage and began to push gently but firmly. Merrin coughed faintly. Then he coughed again, spluttered and suddenly retched up a huge amount of river water. Something went *clink* on to the stone. At Septimus's feet lay a small silver disc with a raised central boss. Trying not to think about where it had just come from, Septimus picked it up. It lay heavy in his palm, glinting in the light from the single torch burning on the quay.

"It must have hurt swallowing that," he said.

Simon, however, was not surprised. When Merrin had been Simon's assistant at the Observatory he had swallowed a variety of metal objects. But that was not a time in his life Simon wanted to remember – or wanted Septimus to remember either. So he said nothing.

At their feet Merrin stirred. "Give it back," he moaned weakly. "It's *mine*."

Both Septimus and Simon ignored him.

Simon looked at the disc lying in Septimus's palm. "It's the Paired Code!" he said excitedly. "We must get this to Marcia at once."

Septimus did not like the sound of "we". "*I'll* take it," he said, putting the disc into his Apprentice belt.

"But *I* know how to use it," protested Simon.

Septimus was dismissive. "So does Marcia," he said.

"How can she? She doesn't know where to begin." Simon sounded exasperated.

"Of course she does," snapped Septimus.

The sound of running footsteps broke up the argument. Sarah, Sally and Marcellus were racing down to the New Quay. Not wishing to become embroiled in a reunion just then, Septimus gave them a hasty wave and, clutching the Paired Code, he ran off towards Spit Fyre, who looked triumphant. He had won his first fight. He was now a fully fledged, adult dragon.

A few seconds later Septimus and Spit Fyre were airborne. Drops of dragon blood marked their flight path all the way to the Wizard Tower.

Speechless with frustration, Simon watched Spit Fyre and his pilot disappear up over the Darke Fog.

"Simon." Sarah gently touched his arm. "Simon love, you're frozen. Come inside. Sally's got the fire lit."

Simon felt grateful that she hadn't even mentioned Septimus. He looked at his mother, who was herself shivering despite one of Sally's blankets thrown around her shoulders. He felt so sad for her, but right then there was nothing he could do about it – except what he was about to do.

"I'm sorry, Mum," he said gently, "I can't. I've got to go. You go back with Sally. Tell Lucy I . . . I'll see you all later." And he walked briskly away, striding up the well-worn path to the South Gate.

Sarah watched him go without a protest, which worried Sally. Sarah seemed defeated, she thought. Sally led her friend back to the café and sat her down beside the fire. Lucy, Rupert and Maggie gathered around her but Sarah neither moved nor spoke for the rest of the night.

Marcellus Pye put the shivering, bedraggled Merrin in one of Sally's more dismal, windowless bunkhouses with a pile of dry blankets. As he went to lock the door his prisoner glared at him.

"L-Loser!" Merrin spat, his nose streaming as his cold returned with a vengeance. "Your st-stupid little key won't keep *m-me* in." He jabbed his left thumb at Marcellus. The green faces on the Two-Faced Ring shone malevolently. "H-He who wears *this* is indestructible. *Atchoo!* I wear it, therefore *I* am indestructible. *I* can do what I like. *B-Buckethead!*"

Marcellus did not deign to reply. He closed the door and locked it. He looked at Sally's flimsy tin key and reflected that even without the power of the Two-Faced Ring, Merrin could probably get out – but for the moment, freezing cold and in shock from nearly drowning, he didn't think Merrin was in a state to do anything.

On the chilly footpath outside the bunkhouse, Marcellus kept guard, pacing up and down to keep warm, his shoes flip-flapping on the frosty stone. Over and over again, Merrin's defiant words came back to him. Unlike much of what Merrin said, they were true. While he wore the Ring, Marcellus knew that Merrin himself was indeed indestructible – and free to wreak havoc. There was no doubt in Marcellus's mind that while Merrin had the ring, the Castle and all who lived there were in grave danger.

Marcellus thought of the shivering, sniffling boy alone in the bunkhouse. A feeling of pity flashed through him but he pushed it to one side. He made himself remember the Two-Faced Ring glinting on the taunting thumb and he knew that as soon as Merrin recovered he would be wreaking revenge. There was little time to lose – something had to be done. Fast. *Now*.

Marcellus walked briskly up the steps to the Tea and Ale House. He wondered how sharp Sally's kitchen knives were . . .

✳ 47 ✳

THE GREAT UNDOING

Marcia was about to put the Paired Code together. Her tiny study was packed and the atmosphere was electric. Even Nicko, who was not hugely interested in Magyk, was watching intently.

The tiny study window glowed an eerie red with the dimming of the SafeShield, but the study itself was bright with the light from a forest of candles dripping from a tall candelabrum set on Marcia's desk. Two books – *The Undoing of the Darkenesse* and *The Darke Index* – lay open on Marcia's desk. In the shadow of the books a small silver box and a tiny silver disc rested on a piece of purple velvet.

Alther had a bird's-eye view. To avoid the danger of being Passed Through, the ghost was sitting on the top step of a library ladder. He was watching the process with great interest. The use of the Paired Code was something Alther had known about in theory only. In his time as ExtraOrdinary Wizard both books that held the keys to deciphering the Code had long been lost. Marcia had found *The Undoing of the Darkenesse* in Aunt Zelda's cottage a few years back and she knew that somewhere within its pages lay The Great UnDoing – the legendary Anti-Darke incantation that practitioners of the Darke feared above all else. But its words were spread randomly throughout the book; to find them, the index to the book – *The* Darke *Index* – was required.

However, it was not that simple. Uncovering The Great UnDoing required more than merely using an index – it required using the correct pages of the index. This was where the Paired Code came in. In order to know which sections of *The* Darke *Index* gave the right sequence of page and word numbers in *The Undoing of the* Darkenesse, the Paired Code had to be read. Correctly.

And now that was about to happen. Under the rapt attention of Silas, Septimus, Jenna and Nicko – and the perching Alther – Marcia began to put the Paired Code together.

Marcia lifted out the Wizard Tower half of the Code and placed it on the velvet square on which its Pair – recently used to much less salubrious surroundings – lay waiting. She picked up the much smaller Manuscriptorium Code and placed its boss into the central indentation of the Wizard Tower Code. There was a brilliant blue spark and suddenly the Manuscriptorium Code was floating a fraction of a millimetre above the Wizard Tower Code. The Manuscriptorium Code now began to spin. Slowly at first, then faster and faster it went until it was no more than a flash of spinning light. There was a sharp *click* and the spinning disc stopped dead.

Everyone craned their heads for a closer look. The discs seemed to have fused into one and it was clear that the lines that radiated out from the Manuscriptorium Code joined up with some of those on the Wizard Tower Code. Each one of these led to a symbol. There was an awed hush. These were the symbols that would begin The Great UnDoing that would UnDo the Darke Domaine and set the Castle free.

Marcia got out her Enlarging Glass and peered at the symbols.

"Ready, Septimus?" she asked.

In his hand Septimus had his precious Apprentice diary, his pen poised at the top of a clean page. "Ready," he said.

The red glow from the failing SafeShield was beginning to fill the study, drowning out the candlelight. It fell on the smooth, blank page of Septimus's diary and cast threatening shadows across the room. Septimus knew it would not be long before the SafeShield was breached – it could happen any minute now, he thought. He waited, poised to write down the sequence of symbols that would lead them to The Great UnDoing. Why didn't Marcia begin reading out the symbols? There was no time to lose.

Jenna had guessed why but she hoped – desperately – that she was wrong. Unable to bear the suspense, she decided to test out her new *Right to Know*.

"But, Marcia, how do you know which symbol to start with?"

Aware that she now had to answer all the Princess-in-Waiting's questions "*truthfully, fully and without delay*", Marcia looked up at Jenna and met her gaze.

"I don't," she said.

The little room fell horribly quiet as the implications of Marcia's reply sank in.

Simon pushed his way through the Darke Fog, terrified that at any moment a Thing would recognise him. He'd been lucky on the South Gate. The Thing on guard had done no more than stretch out a bony arm and pull him in without even looking at him. He knew he might not be so lucky next time. Simon wished that Lucy had not made him throw away his Darke Robes – "disgusting old things", she had called them. Right now he could have done with them. Without their protection, the Darke Fog was suffocating – far worse than it had been in the Palace when it was still new. Now it had gained strength from all those it had overcome and it pressed down on Simon like a smothering pillow, closing off his ears and eyes, making each breath a huge effort.

Feeling as though he were walking underwater in lead boots, Simon struggled up Wizard Way, heading for the telltale red light of the Wizard Tower's failing SafeShield. As he waded past the Manuscriptorium he saw dim shadows of Things emerging and heading for the Great Arch, where they were gathering, waiting for the moment when the Barricade would fail. In a nightmare of slow motion Simon crossed to the other side of the Way and pushed on down the narrow lane that ran around the Wizard Tower courtyard wall. He was heading for the ExtraOrdinary Wizard's Hidden side gate, which was not visible from the outside and so, he hoped, would not attract the attention of any Things.

When Simon arrived at the lintel that marked the presence of the Hidden gate his head was spinning and he felt as though the Fog was inside his brain. He longed to rest his heavy limbs, to lie down for a moment, just a moment . . . he leaned against the wall and felt not stones but wood and a latch beneath him. Slowly his eyes closed and he began to slide to the ground.

Strange things happen in the dying phases of a Living SafeShield. The separate components begin to make their own decisions. So when Simon slid down the Hidden gate it Knew it needed to let him in. It swung open and he half rolled in. The gate did a nifty flick, pushed him inside and closed as fast as it could. A few tendrils of Fog curled in with him but stopped when the gate became one with the wall once more.

The clear air inside the Wizard Tower courtyard soon woke Simon up. He got shakily to his feet and took a deep breath. He looked up at the Tower rearing high above him, almost dark now – the only light the red of the dying SafeShield – and he felt quite overawed. Shakily he headed across to the wide marble steps that led up to the silver doors that guarded the Tower.

Once again the Living SafeShield recognised help when it saw it. The tall silver doors opened noiselessly and Simon, heart beating fast, stepped into the Great Hall. As the doors swung closed, Simon took stock. He could hardly believe that he was actually inside Wizard Tower. For so long he had dreamed that one day he would set foot in the Tower and rescue it from danger, and now that that was exactly what he was doing, it did not seem real.

But things in the Wizard Tower had changed. Simon had not been in the Great Hall since he was a boy. He remembered it as a bright, joyful place buzzing with Magyk, with beautiful pictures flitting across the walls and a fascinating floor that wrote your name when you stepped on it. He had loved the mysterious smell of the Magyk and the sharpness of the air, and the purposeful hum of the gently turning silver spiral stairs. And now it was all very nearly gone.

The lights were low and dull, the walls dark, the floor blank and the silver spiral stairs were Stopped. Everything was winding down. Shadowy figures of Wizards and Apprentices were scattered about the Great Hall, the younger ones wandering anxiously to and fro, the older ones slumped with exhaustion as they concentrated on the uphill struggle of adding their tiny piece of Magykal energy to the SafeShield.

Hildegarde stepped out of the shadows. Pale and drawn, with dark circles under her eyes, she watched Simon walk to the stairs. She did not stop or question him. It was a waste of energy. If the Tower had let him in, he was here for a reason. She just hoped it was a good one.

Simon ran up the Stopped stairs. Up through the darkened floors he occasionally heard a weary murmuring of a Magykal chant, but mostly he found nothing but silence. Outside he could see the red light fading fast and he knew that once it had gone, the Darke Domaine would enter the Wizard Tower. Simon did not know how long that would take but he guessed it was minutes rather than hours.

On the twentieth floor he jumped off the stairs, ran along the broad corridor that led to the ExtraOrdinary Wizard's purple door and threw himself against it.

Inside the study Marcia was dictating the symbols that the lines on the Manuscriptorium Code had picked out. She had decided that the only thing to do was to begin with each one in turn. There were forty-nine matches. This meant there were forty-nine words in The Great UnDoing – and forty-nine possible beginnings, of which there was no way of telling which was the right one. As The Great UnDoing was an ancient incantation, Marcia knew that it would not necessarily make any sense, so there would be no clue as to what might be the first word. It was a huge risk, but she had no alternative. It was just possible they might find the correct order right away.

It was the only chance they had and Marcia knew she had to take it.

And so she was rapidly dictating. "Zero, star, three, Magyk, labyrinth, gold, Ankh, square, duck – yes, I *did* say duck – two, twin, seven, bridge – *oh!*" Marcia looked up suddenly.

"My door ... it's let someone in," she whispered. "There's Darke on them. From *outside*."

There was a sharp intake of breath. "I'll go and check it out," said Silas, heading for the study door.

"Silas, wait." Alther got up from his perch. "*I'll* go. Bar the door when I've gone."

"Thank you, Alther," said Marcia as the ghost quickly DisComposed himself and walked through the door. "Now, where were we? Oh, goodness, I don't know. Septimus, I'll start again. Zero, star, three, Magyk, labyrinth, gold, Ankh, square, duck, two, twin, seven, bridge, spiral, four, ellipse, plus, tower – *Alther, is that you?*"

"Yes. UnBar the door please, Marcia. Quickly. I have someone to see you."

Everyone exchanged questioning glances. Who could it be?

Alther ushered in Simon to a stunned silence. "Before you say anything, Marcia, this young man has some important information. He knows where to begin."

"*He does?*" Marcia frowned. "Alther, there are other Invocations on this Code – and some are downright dangerous. How can I be sure he will tell me where to begin the *correct* one?"

Septimus, Nicko and Jenna looked at each other. *Other invocations?* So Marcia was gambling that they would reach the right one first. Things were even worse than they had thought.

"I've known him since he was born," said Alther. "I believe you can trust him."

"You *can* trust me. I promise," said Simon quietly.

Marcia looked at Simon. He was soaking wet, trembling with cold, and there was desperation in his eyes – a desperation that mirrored exactly what she was feeling that very moment. She made her decision.

"Very well, Simon," she said. "Would you show us where The Great UnDoing begins?"

And so Simon found himself somewhere he had never thought possible. At the top of the Wizard Tower, sitting at the desk of the ExtraOrdinary Wizard, surrounded by fabled Magykal books and objects – including, he noticed, his very own Sleuth. And now, watched by his father and his youngest brother, he was about to tell the ExtraOrdinary Wizard something that would save the Castle.

"The starting point is given in the index of *The Darke Index*," he said.

With trembling hands Simon picked up the book. For a moment it felt like an old friend, until he remembered that, in truth, it was an old enemy. The countless cold, lonely and sometimes terrifying nights he had spent reading it came back to him and he remembered the last time he had held it when, in an early attempt to give up the Darke, he had stuffed it into the back of a cupboard and locked the door. He had never dreamed that the next time he held it he would be in the Wizard Tower.

Gingerly he opened *The Darke Index* at the inside of the

back cover. Muttering a short incantation, he ran his finger across the well-worn endpaper and, as he did so, letters began to appear beneath his fingers.

An irritated *tut* came from Marcia. A simple Reveal – why hadn't she thought of that?

Beneath Simon's moving finger an alphabetical list began to Reveal itself. His finger slowed at G and everyone waited, but The Great UnDoing was not listed. Simon's finger slowed at the T but The Great UnDoing was not there. A palpable lack of confidence began to fill the little room and when Simon reached the letter U his hand began to shake. Suddenly "UnDoing. Great. The." appeared. Smiling with relief, Simon handed the Revealed index to Marcia.

"'UnDoing. Great. The. Begin with Magyk, end with Fyre,'" she read aloud. "Thank you, Simon."

Simon nodded. He did not trust himself to speak.

Marcia sat down. She put her spectacles on and opened *The Darke Index*. "Now, Septimus, read the symbols out to me again, beginning with Magyk. Slowly, please."

And so Septimus went through the list. At each symbol he paused while Marcia quickly leafed through the pages, grubby and grease-stained from Merrin's sticky hands. Each page had one of the symbols at the beginning of the text. At the foot of the page – looking to the casual observer like page numbers – were two numbers. Marcia noted down the numbers, then said briskly, "Next." It seemed to take for ever but it was only a matter of minutes before Marcia had a column of forty-nine pairs of numbers.

Marcia handed Septimus the numbers and then she opened *The Undoing of the Darkenesse*.

"Read the numbers out to me please, Septimus."

The red glow suffusing the study went out like a light. There was a collective gasp.

"SafeShield's out," Marcia said grimly.

Far below, the Barricade smashed to the ground and the first Thing walked across it, into the Wizard Tower courtyard. Twelve more followed, along with a stream of Darke Fog.

At the top of the Tower Septimus read out the first number of the first pair. "Fourteen."

With urgent fingers Marcia flipped the thick pages of *The Undoing of the Darkenesse* to page fourteen.

Septimus read out the second number of the first pair. "Ninety-eight."

As fast as she could Marcia began to count along the words on page fourteen until she reached the ninety-eighth word.

"Let."

It seemed a very small word for all the trouble finding it.

And so, agonisingly slowly, Marcia began to put together The Great UnDoing.

Outside the Wizard Tower, on the topmost marble step, a Thing reached out a long bony finger and pushed against the tall silver doors. They swung open like shed doors left unlatched in a summer breeze. The Thing walked into the Wizard Tower and the Darke Domaine tumbled in after it. The lights went out and someone screamed. In the shadows of her tiny office Hildegarde was suddenly certain that her little brother, who at the age of seven had disappeared during a Do-or-Die exercise in the Young Army, was outside the door. She ran to open it and the Darke Fog rushed in.

Things streamed in across the threshold, bringing the Darke Domaine with them. They milled around, squashing the dying floor beneath their feet, watching Wizards and Apprentices slump to the ground. As the Darke Fog began to fill the hall, the Things wandered across to the Stopped stairs and began to climb. Behind them the Darke Domaine moved slowly up through the Wizard Tower, filling every space with Darkenesse.

At the very top of the Tower, Marcia had in her hands a piece of paper with a string of forty-nine words on it, which formed, she sincerely hoped, The Great UnDoing. She and Septimus were running up the narrow stone steps to the Pyramid Library with Alther following in their wake. They flung themselves through the little door and Marcia hurried over to the window that led outside. She turned to Septimus.

"You really don't have to come," she said.

"Yes, I do," said Septimus. "You need all the Magyk you can get."

"I know," said Marcia.

"So I'm coming with you."

Marcia smiled. "Out we go then. Don't look down."

Septimus looked neither down nor up. Focusing only on the hem of Marcia's purple cloak, he followed her up the stepped side of the golden Pyramid. Alther flew slowly behind.

And so, for the second time that night, Marcia stood on the tiny platform at the top of the golden Pyramid. For some reason, she wasn't sure why, she took off her purple python pointy shoes and stood barefoot on the ancient silver hieroglyphs that were incised into the hammered gold top. She waited for Septimus to join her and then together, in voices that cut through the Darke Fog, they began the forty-nine-word incantation of *The* Great UnDoing.

"Let there be ..."

Far below, the leading Thing poked its finger lazily at the great purple door that guarded Marcia's rooms. Twelve Things stood behind it expectantly, waiting to take over their new abode. The door swung open. The Thing turned to its companions with what was possibly a smile. They stood, savouring the moment, watching the Darke Fog tumble in and swirl around Marcia's precious sofa.

At the top of the golden Pyramid, Marcia Overstrand, ExtraOrdinary Wizard, and her Apprentice, Septimus Heap, spoke the last word of The Great UnDoing.

With a great *crash* Marcia's door slammed in the Things' faces. A loud whirring ensued – the door Barred itself and, for good measure, sent out a Shock Wave. Thirteen Things screamed. A scream of thirteen Things is not one of the most harmonious sounds, but to Septimus and Marcia, teetering at the top of the golden Pyramid, it was the sweetest thing they had ever heard.

And then they saw the most beautiful sight they had ever seen – the Darke Fog rolling away. Once more they saw the Castle they loved – its higgledy-piggledy roofs, its turrets and towers, its crenulated battlements and tumbledown walls, all outlined against the pink sky of the dawn of a new day. And as they watched the sun rise, dispelling the shadows that lurked below, the first heavy snowflakes of the Big Freeze began to fall. Marcia and Septimus smiled at each other – the Darke Domaine was no more.

Some minutes later, a broadly smiling Marcia was ushering everyone into her sitting room, busily opening the windows to get rid of the dank smell of the Darke. Jim Knee was curled up in his usual place on the sofa with Jillie Djinn beside him, just as Marcia had left them. But there was something about the Chief Hermetic Scribe that made Marcia hurry over to her.

"She's dead!" Marcia gasped. And then, much more dismayed, she cried, "She's dead *on my sofa*!"

Jillie Djinn was slumped backwards, her mouth a little open, eyes closed as if asleep. Her body was there, but she herself had clearly gone – whatever it was that had been Jillie Djinn was no more. The Great UnDoing had been her undoing also.

✴ 48 ✴

RESTORATION

Marcia, Septimus and Jenna emerged from the Great Arch and paused for a moment, looking down the newly liberated Wizard Way. It was a beautiful frosty morning. The sun was creeping out from behind a bank of clouds and slanting rays of the early morning light glanced low along Wizard Way. The first serious snowflakes of the Big Freeze were beginning to fall; they drifted lazily in the fleeting sunlight and settled on to the frosty pavement.

Marcia took a deep breath of the clear, sparkling air and a wave of happiness very nearly overcame her – but she could not allow herself to be completely content until she had successfully UnSealed the Hermetic Chamber. *And found Beetle alive.*

Marcia had steeled herself to expect many things waiting for her in the front office of the Manuscriptorium but she had not expected the Port Witch Coven. They had taken a trip to see the last moments of the Wizard Tower and, becoming bored with how long it was taking, they had crowbarred the planks off the door to the Wild Book and Charm Store. They were just emerging, covered in fur, feathers and a light sprinkling of scales when, to their collective horror, they saw that not only had the lovely Darke Fog disappeared but that that ghastly ExtraOrdinary Wizard woman was waiting for them. Dorinda's piercing scream spoke for them all.

To Jenna's delight, Marcia saw the Port Witch Coven off the premises with great effectiveness. They left so fast – even the Witch Mother managed a rapid hobble in her spikes – that they forgot about Nursie, who sat unnoticed beside a collapsed pile of books. Nursie had discovered a stash of dusty liquorice snakes in the back of a drawer and was contentedly chewing them. Nursie had what she called a penchant for liquorice.

Marcia raced into the Manuscriptorium itself, closely followed by Jenna and Septimus. The place was strewn with upturned desks, ripped paper and broken lamps. Everything was covered with a sticky grey dust, which Septimus realised to his disgust was shed Thing skin. Quickly they picked their way through the debris. At the stone arched entrance to the Hermetic Chamber they stopped.

"The Seal is gone," Marcia said heavily. "I fear the worst."

The seven-cornered passage looked ominously well used – there was a slimy Thing trail on the floor. Like giant slugs, thought Septimus. He stepped into the passage and called tentatively into the dark. "Beetle . . . *Beetle*." There was no reply.

"It sounds . . . dead in there," he whispered.

"I think," said Jenna slowly, "that it sounds more like something is blocking the passageway farther up."

"It is just possible that the Seal is still holding farther in," said Marcia.

"Can it do that?" asked Septimus. "I thought it would all go at once."

"We'll just have to see, won't we?" Marcia said briskly and

she disappeared into the seven-cornered passage. Septimus and Jenna set off after her.

As he rounded the sixth corner, Septimus cannoned into Marcia. *"Oof!"*

Marcia was standing at a dead end of pitted stone. "It's still Sealed," she whispered excitedly. "It really is quite amazing. The Seal has been chipped away but I think . . . I think it's still OK."

"Does that mean that Beetle is . . ." Septimus could not finish his question. The thought that Beetle might *not* be OK made him feel sick.

"We can but hope," said Marcia grimly.

Grimacing, Marcia placed her hands on the filthy, sticky surface of the Seal. In the light of the Dragon Ring, Jenna and Septimus watched as the surface of the Seal healed itself. Soon it was smooth and shimmering with Magykal purple once more, lighting up the seven-cornered passage and showing the revolting film of slime and Thing skin in glorious detail. Septimus thought of how the Seal must have shone through the Darke when the Things had first arrived and taunted them – no wonder they had attacked it. *He* would have added a Camouflage.

Now Marcia began the UnSeal. Jenna retreated from the sudden onslaught of Magyk, which was highly concentrated in the narrow confines of the passageway and made her feel queasy. But Septimus was fascinated. He watched the shiny surface glow even brighter and slowly begin to retreat before them. Step by step Marcia and Septimus followed the Seal until it stopped at the end of the passageway. They waited anxiously, watching the diamond-hard surface slowly became translucent until they began to see the shadowy impression of the Hermetic Chamber beyond.

The Seal thinned until there was no more than a shifting swirl of Magyk dividing them from the Chamber. Through it Septimus could see Beetle slumped at the table. He could not tell whether he was alive or dead.

Once more Marcia stretched out her hands – which Septimus noticed were trembling – and laid them on the last vestige of the Seal. At her touch it melted away and a rush of air *whooshed* past them into the Chamber.

"Beetle!" Septimus ran across and shook his friend by the shoulder. Beetle felt so cold that Septimus jumped back in horror. Jenna appeared at the entrance to the Chamber. They both looked at Marcia in panic.

Marcia strode over to the siege drawer, which lay upturned on the table with a tangle of liquorice bootlaces spilling out from it. *Where was the Suspension Charm?*

"He's cold," Septimus said. "*Really* cold."

"Well, he will be cold if . . ." Marcia looked at the liquorice. It did not bode well.

"If what?" asked Septimus.

"If he's managed the Suspension." Marcia sounded worried.

And he will be if he hasn't, thought Septimus, but he said nothing. They watched Marcia gently lift Beetle so that he was sitting up, but Beetle's eyes were closed and his head flopped forward like a dead thing.

Jenna gave a gasp of dismay.

"Beetle," Marcia said, shaking him gently by his shoulders. "Beetle, you can come out now." There was no response. Marcia glanced at Jenna and Septimus. There was dread in her eyes.

Time seemed to slow down. Marcia crouched down so that she was level with Beetle's face. She placed her hands on either side of his head and gently lifted it up so that his face was level with hers. Then she took a deep breath. The buzz of Magyk filled the Hermetic Chamber once again, and from Marcia's mouth came a long stream of pink mist. It settled over Beetle's face, covering his nose and mouth.

Hardly daring to breathe themselves, Septimus and Jenna watched. Still Marcia breathed out. Still Beetle did not react, the dead white of his face shining through the pink mist above it. And then, like smoke drifting up a chimney, Septimus saw tendrils of the mist begin to disappear up Beetle's nose. *He was breathing.* Very slowly Beetle's eyes flickered opened. He looked glassily at Marcia.

Septimus rushed to Beetle's side. "Hey, Beetle, *Beetle, it's us.* Oh, *Beetle!*"

Marcia smiled with relief. "Congratulations, Beetle," she said. "The heart of the Manuscriptorium is untouched, thanks to you."

Beetle rose to the occasion with aplomb. "Gah . . ." he said.

They had gathered in the wasteland of upturned desks. Beetle looked pale and was shakily drinking a fortifying FizzFroot, which Septimus had found stashed away in Beetle's old kitchen in the Manuscriptorium backyard. Jenna, Beetle noticed, had not hung around; she had rushed off to the Palace as soon as she could. Beetle, clear-headed after his Suspension, saw what that meant. If it had been *Jenna* who had just survived two days being Sealed in an airless Chamber, *he* would not have run away at the first opportunity. *Get real, Beetle,* he told himself.

Marcia's voice broke into his thoughts.

"The Pick for the new Chief Hermetic Scribe must begin tonight," she was saying. "I must go. I intend to visit each and every scribe myself. I want to see if they are all still . . . available."

Beetle thought of Foxy and Partridge and Romilly. He thought of Larry. Of Matt, Marcus and Igor at Gothyk Grotto, even the oddly irritating people at Wizard Sandwiches. How many of them were still . . . *available*?

Marcia stopped for a quiet word with Beetle. "It's such a shame," she told him, "that you are no longer part of the Manuscriptorium. I would very much have liked your pen to have gone into the Pot."

Beetle flushed with pleasure at the compliment. "Thank you," he said. "But it would never have Picked me. I'm far too young. And I was never a proper scribe."

"That is of no consequence," said Marcia. "The Pot Picks who is right." She refrained from adding that she had no idea why it had Picked Jillie Djinn. "But perhaps you'd like to stay until the Draw and stand guard. I don't want to leave the Manuscriptorium unattended."

Once again Beetle was flattered, but he was already getting to his feet. "Sorry, but I'd better go and see Larry. Don't want to lose my job there too."

"I quite understand," said Marcia, opening the door to the front office for him. She realised that she should not have asked – Beetle clearly still found the Manuscriptorium an upsetting place to be. Marcia watched Beetle walk out into the morning sunshine and called back into the Manuscriptorium, "Septimus! You're in charge. You have my permission to use a full Restore. I shall be back soon with *all* the scribes."

From the other side of the partition Septimus then heard Marcia say loudly, "The Manuscriptorium is closed today. I suggest you come back tomorrow when it will be under new management. *What?* No, I have no idea where the witches have gone. No, I am *not* a witch, whatever gave you that idea? I am, madam, the ExtraOrdinary Wizard."

As the sounds of Nursie being rapidly escorted off the premises came through the flimsy partition, Septimus smiled. Marcia was back to her normal self again.

Outside the Manuscriptorium, Marcia found herself plagued with unwelcome intrusions. Nursie was sticking to her like Thing skin and, to top it all, she now saw the familiar figure of Marcellus Pye approaching. Marcia decided to pretend she hadn't seen him.

"Marcia! Marcia, *wait!*" Marcellus called.

"*Sorree*. Must dash!" she called out.

But Marcellus was not to be put off. He speeded up, dragging behind him an unwilling companion. As the pair drew near Marcia saw who it was.

"Merrin Meredith!" she spluttered.

Nursie's hearing was not what it had been. "Yes?" she said.

"And I thought I told *you* to go home," Marcia snapped at Nursie.

But Nursie did not hear anything. She was staring at the shambling, sniffing figure that Marcellus was dragging behind him.

A red-faced and very harassed Marcellus reached Marcia and Nursie.

"Marcia. I have something for you," said Marcellus. He

burrowed into a deep pocket, drew out a small brown box made of cheap card and handed it to Marcia.

Marcia looked at it impatiently. "Springo Spigots," she read. "Marcellus, what on earth would I want with *Springo Spigots*?"

"It's the only box that Sally had," said Marcellus. "And it's not spigots – whatever they are. I'd rather spigot a spigotty-thing any day than . . . well, you'd better take a look."

Marcia's curiosity got the better of her impatience. She opened the end of the flimsy cardboard box and drew out a small piece of bloodstained cloth. Something heavy fell into her hand. She gasped.

"Good grief, Marcellus. How did you get this?"

"How do you think?" Marcellus replied quietly. He looked pointedly at Merrin, who was staring at the ground.

Marcia took a closer look at Merrin and saw that his left hand was swathed in a bandage. An ooze of deep pink was showing on the inside of it where – Marcia now knew – his thumb no longer was. She stared at the Two-Faced Ring that lay heavy and cold in her hand and felt almost afraid.

"May I suggest that this ring be destroyed," Marcellus said quietly. "Even in the most Hidden of hiding places it will one day give some new fool – or worse – overweening powers."

"Yes, it must be destroyed," Marcia agreed. "But we no longer have the Fyres to do it."

Marcellus felt nervous as he offered his solution. "Marcia, I hope you trust me enough by now to consider my offer seriously. I would like to return to my old Alchemie Chamber. If you allow this I could start up the Fyre and within a month we could rid the Castle of the pernicious ring for ever. I give you my word I will preserve the Ice Tunnels and meddle with nothing."

"Very well, Marcellus. I accept your word. I shall place this ring in the Hidden Shelf until then."

"Um . . . I have one more request," Marcellus said tentatively.

Marcia knew what it was. "Yes," she said with a sigh. "I will second Septimus to you for the next month; I can see you will need his help. We are all in this together now. We need the Alchemie as well as the Magyk to keep the Darke in balance. Do you not agree?"

Marcellus smiled broadly as his old life opened up to him once more with all its amazing vistas. A wave of happiness spread through him. "Yes, I do agree. I most *definitely* do."

While this conversation had been going on, Nursie had taken hold of Merrin's bandaged hand and was tut-tutting over the bandage, which was, even Marcellus could see, a mess. Marcia looked at the pair and felt exasperated. What was she to do with Merrin? She blamed the evil influence of the Two-Faced Ring for much that he had done, but there was no denying that he had chosen to put it on in the first place.

Marcia knew that Nursie was the landlady of *The Doll House*, a dingy guesthouse in the Port where Jenna and Septimus had once spent an eventful night. Some time ago Aunt Zelda had told Marcia something about Nursie that she had not taken much notice of at the time – but now, as she looked at Nursie and Merrin together, and she saw the awkward way they both stood, their beaky noses and sallow skin, Marcia knew that what Aunt Zelda had told her must be true. She turned to Nursie and said, "Do you take in lodgers?"

Nursie looked surprised. "Why? You fed up with the Tower, are you? Too much cleaning, I suppose. And all those stairs must be hard on the knees. Well, it's half a crown a week, payable in advance, hot water and bedding is extra."

"I am perfectly happy in the Wizard Tower, thank you," said Marcia icily. "However, I would like to pay a year in advance for this young man here."

"A *year* in advance?" Nursie gasped, not able to believe her luck. She could get the house repainted and, best of all, she could afford to stop working for those ghastly witches.

"To include nursing services and general care and attention," said Marcia. "Also hot water, bedding *and* food. No doubt the young man would be happy to help around the house once his hand is better."

"It won't ever be better," growled Merrin. "It hasn't got a thumb any more."

"You'll get used to it," said Marcia cheerfully. "You are free of the Ring now and you have to make the best of it. I suggest you take my offer to go with the Nurse here. Otherwise all you will be seeing for the foreseeable future is the inside of the Wizard Tower Secure Chamber."

"I'll go with her. She's all right," said Merrin.

Nursie patted Merrin's good hand. "There's a good boy," she said.

"Marcellus, do you have six guineas on you?" asked Marcia.

"Six *guineas*?" Marcellus squeaked.

"Yes. You're always rattling with gold. I'll pay you back."

Marcellus delved into his pockets and very reluctantly he handed over six shining new guineas. Nursie's eyes bulged. She had never seen so much gold. Marcia added a crown from her own pocket and presented the money to the dumbstruck landlady.

"Slightly over, I think you'll find," said Marcia briskly. "But it will cover your fare back to the Port. If you hurry you will catch the evening barge."

"Come on, dearie." Nursie linked her arm through Merrin's good one. "Let's get out of this place. I never did like the Castle. Nasty memories."

"Me too," said Merrin. "It's a dump."

Marcellus and Marcia watched Merrin and Nursie head off. "Well, they seem well suited," Marcellus said.

"So they should be," said Marcia. "They're mother and son."

Foxy was the first scribe Marcia tracked down and sent off to the Manuscriptorium. On his way Foxy met Beetle coming out of Larry's Dead Languages.

"Wotcha, Beet!"

"Wotcha, Foxo!"

They surveyed each other for a moment, smiling broadly.

"You all right, Foxo?" asked Beetle.

"Yeah." Foxy grinned.

"You weren't outside when it got you then?"

"Nah. Fell asleep by the fire and woke up two days later. Mouth felt like the bottom of a parrot's cage, but apart from that all was fine. But ..." Foxy sighed. "My auntie's missing. She was out when the Domaine came over our way. Never made it back. Can't find her anywhere. And now ... well, now they're saying about a Dragon *taking* people." He shuddered.

"Oh, Foxy," said Beetle. "I am so sorry."

"Yeah." Foxy changed the subject. "But hey, you don't look so good. Was it bad in the Chamber?"

"Yeah," said Beetle. "Lots of hammering and trying to get in."

"Not nice," said Foxy.

"No. And I *never* want to see a liquorice bootlace *ever* again."

"Oh. Right." Foxy decided not to ask why. Beetle had looked strangely desperate as he'd said "liquorice bootlace."

Foxy decided to change the subject. "So, um, how's Larry?"

"Not nice either," said Beetle. "Just got fired, in fact. For coming in late."

"*Late?*"

"Two days late."

Foxy put his arm around Beetle's shoulders. He'd never seen Beetle look so down. "It's all rubbish, isn't it?" he said.

"It's not great, Foxo."

"Want a sausage sandwich?"

Beetle saw the welcome lights of Wizard Sandwiches glowing through the dimming light of the late winter afternoon and he suddenly felt ravenous. "You bet," he said.

Jenna walked slowly up to the Palace, her footprints showing trampled grass through the snow. Ahead of her the Palace was dark against the late-afternoon sky, with the winter sun already having dropped down behind the ancient battlements. It was an eerie sight, enhanced by the occasional crow call from the tops of the cedars down by the river, but Jenna did not see it that way. She had turned down offers from Silas and Sarah to come with her. This was the way she wanted to return to her Palace – on her own.

The ancient double doors were half open, left ajar by Simon

when he had fled with Sarah in his arms. And guarding them was a familiar figure.

"Welcome home, Princess-in-Waiting," said Sir Hereward.

"Thank you, Sir Hereward," replied Jenna as she stepped inside. A flurry of snow entered with her. Jenna hung up her witch's cloak in the cloakroom and closed the door on it with feelings of fondness. It had served her well and who knew? She might need it again one day.

"You'd better come in too," she said to Sir Hereward, who was still out in the snow.

"Strictly speaking, Princess, now that you have taken possession of the *whole* Palace rather than just your room, I should stay outside," Sir Hereward replied.

"I'd rather you came in," said Jenna. "I could do with some company, if you don't mind."

A smiling Sir Hereward strode in, and Jenna quickly pushed the doors to. They closed with a *bang* that echoed through the empty building. Jenna looked around the entrance hall, which was full of shadows and ghosts. She reached into her pocket for the CandleLight Charm Septimus had given her that afternoon and began lighting the first of many extinguished candles.

Later that evening Jenna was sitting in Sarah's old sitting room with a bewildered duck in her arms when she heard footsteps coming down the Long Walk. These were not the soft *tip-tap* of ghost steps but solid boot-wearing human ones. Sir Hereward, who had been standing guard beside the fire, strode off to investigate. He returned – to Jenna's surprise and delight – with Aunt Zelda and Wolf Boy.

Aunt Zelda swept her up into a huge, padded hug and Wolf Boy grinned broadly.

"We're really, *really* sorry we missed your party," he said. "But it was weird – we couldn't get out of the Queen's Room for two whole days."

Aunt Zelda settled herself beside the fire. She looked at the duck in Jenna's arms. "That creature has been in the Darke, dear," she said to Jenna a little disapprovingly. "I do hope you are not dabbling with things you shouldn't. Some Princesses of your age have done so in the past."

"Oh ..." Jenna did not know what to say. It was as if Aunt Zelda knew about her Port Witch Coven cloak hanging in the cupboard.

"Now, Jenna dear," said Aunt Zelda, "tell me *all* about it."

Jenna put some more coal on the fire. It was going to be a long evening.

❋ 49 ❋

THE CHIEF HERMETIC SCRIBE

It was Mid-Winter Feast Day. Jenna looked out of the Palace ballroom window and watched the snow falling fast, covering the lawns, festooning the bare branches of the trees and obliterating all traces of the Darke Domaine. It was beautiful.

Jenna was hosting a Mid-Winter Feast. She was determined to get rid of all traces of the Things in the Palace and she had decided that the best way to do that was to fill it with everyone she cared about. Silas, Sarah and Maxie had come over from the Ramblings. After a tearful reunion – on Sarah's part, anyway – between Ethel and Sarah, they began to help Jenna get the Ballroom ready for that evening. There was, Jenna said, a lot to do.

Silas smiled. "That's just what your mother would say," he said.

The winter morning drew on. Snow piled up outside the long windows, while the Ballroom was transformed with holly and ivy, red ribbons, huge silver candlesticks and a whole box of streamers that Silas had been keeping for a special occasion.

At the other end of Wizard Way, the Pick for the new Chief Hermetic Scribe was underway.

The previous afternoon Marcia had successfully gathered all scribes together in the Manuscriptorium. In a solemn ceremony she had placed the traditional enamel Pot on the table in the Hermetic Chamber, and then each scribe had gone in and put his or her Manuscriptorium pen into the Pot. The Pot had been left in the Hermetic Chamber overnight, and Marcia had spent an uncomfortable night in the Manuscriptorium guarding the entrance to the Chamber.

Now it was time for the Pick. All the scribes had gathered, robes freshly washed, hair combed. They filed into the dimly lit Manuscriptorium, glancing at each other, wondering who among them would be the next Chief Hermetic Scribe. Partridge had been running bets but no clear favourite had emerged.

A small, beautifully patterned square of carpet had been laid on the floor and Marcia told the scribes to gather around. The older ones looked puzzled – there had been no square of carpet at the last Pick.

Marcia began with a few carefully chosen words about Jillie Djinn, to which the scribes listened respectfully, and then she made a surprise announcement.

"Scribes. It has been a terrible time and, although most have weathered the storm, some people did not. Our thoughts go out to all who have lost anyone."

There were sympathetic glance at scribes who still had relatives and friends unaccounted for. Marcia waited a little and then continued.

"However, I do believe good has come of this. Since The Great UnDoing yesterday, we in the Wizard Tower have seen many stubborn pockets of Darke Magyk disappear and I think the same will have happened here. We have, I hope, at last got our Magyk back in balance with the Darke."

Marcia paused as a small round of applause broke out.

She continued. "During the last few days in the Wizard Tower, when I was trying to find a way to defeat the Darke Domaine, I made many important discoveries. One of them affects us all here today. Recently, in my opinion, the choice of Chief Hermetic Scribe has not been exactly . . . ideal. I believe there may be a reason for this. Over the years the Hermetic Chamber has seen much Darke Magyk, and I suspect the Pick has become corrupted. Now, with everything back as it should be, I am expecting the Pick to take a different form and give us a true result."

The scribes glanced at each other. What did Marcia mean?

Marcia allowed her comment to sink in and then she announced – loudly, to quell the murmuring – "Will the youngest scribe please step forward?"

Romilly Badger, blushing bright red, was pushed forward by Partridge and Foxy.

"Go on," whispered Partridge. "You'll be fine. Really, you will."

"Romilly Badger," said Marcia, sounding very official. "As youngest scribe I ask you to enter the Hermetic Chamber and *bring out the Pot*."

A muttering spread around the room. Normally the youngest scribe was told to bring out the *pen* that lay on the table, not the Pot.

"These are the original words as laid down in *The Undoing of the Darkenesse*," Marcia told the scribes. "And if – as I hope – the Pick has reverted to its original form, there will be *one* pen only left in the Pot, with the rest thrown out on to the table. The pen in the Pot will belong to your next Chief Hermetic Scribe. Of course, if there is only one pen on the table and all the rest are in the Pot, then we will have to accept that choice as we have done in the past – though personally I believe this method to be flawed. Does everybody agree?"

There was some general muttering and discussion, the upshot of which was agreement.

"So, Romilly," said Marcia, "if there is only one pen on the table, you will bring that out. But if there is a pile of pens, bring out the Pot. Understand?"

Romilly nodded.

Marcia carried on with the prescribed words.

"Romilly Badger, I ask you to do this so that the new Chief Hermetic Scribe may be lawfully and properly Picked. Do you accept the task? Yea or Nay?"

"Yea," whispered Romilly.

"Then enter the Chamber, scribe. Be true and tarry not."

Romilly walked self-consciously into the seven-cornered passage. After what felt like an hour – but was less than a minute – her footsteps were heard coming back along the passage. A spontaneous round of applause broke out when she appeared carrying the Pot.

Marcia broke into a broad grin. She had instantly regretted her words about the Pick, thinking that if the old method remained, then whoever was Picked would not have total authority. But now all was well. The Pick had reverted to the true method and all that remained was for Romilly to take the pen from the Pot.

"Scribe Romilly, place the Pot on the carpet," said Marcia.

Hands shaking, Romilly put the Pot down. It stood tall, its ancient dark blue enamel pitted and worn.

"Scribe Romilly, place your hand in the Pot and draw out the pen."

Romilly took a deep breath. She didn't want to put her hand in the Pot – she could not get out of her head thoughts of large, hairy spiders lurking inside – but she bravely reached into the cold, dark space.

"How many pens are there?" Marcia whispered.

"One," Romilly whispered back.

Marcia felt relieved. The Pot had worked.

"Scribe Romilly, take out the pen and show it to the scribes."

Romilly took out a beautiful black onyx pen with a swirling jade green inlay.

"Scribe Romilly, read the name scribed upon the pen."

Romilly peered at the pen. The convoluted swirls made it very difficult to tell what the name actually was.

"A candle, someone please," said Marcia.

Partridge grabbed the candle and held it up so that Romilly could read the letters. Foxy saw the pen clearly for the first time and the blood drained from his face. The next moment there was a *crash*. Foxy had fainted.

Marcia had a bad feeling. Foxy had recognised the pen – surely the new Chief Hermetic Scribe could not be Foxy? *Surely not.*

Forgetting the formal language of the Pick, Marcia said urgently, "Romilly – *whose pen is it?*"

"It says . . ." Romilly squinted hard. "Oh! I see. It says *Beetle!*"

A loud cheer broke out from all the scribes.

★   ★   ★

Foxy had a tiny room in a grubby part of the Ramblings and he'd invited Beetle, summarily evicted from his room in Larry's Dead Languages, to sleep on his floor until he found somewhere to live.

When Foxy burst in, red-faced from running all the way from the Manuscriptorium, Beetle was busy scraping some burned soup off the bottom of the pan. He hadn't known it was possible to burn soup – there was more to cooking than he had realised.

"Wotcha, Foxo," he said, a little preoccupied. "So who's the next boss, then?"

"You!" yelled Foxy.

"Barnaby Ewe? Oh well, could be worse. I think I've killed your saucepan. Really sorry."

Foxy rushed over to the tiny sink and grabbed the pan out of Beetle's hands. "No, you dingbat – it's *you*. You! Beetle, *you* are Chief Hermetic Scribe!"

"Foxy, don't kid around," Beetle said, irritated. "Give me that pan. I was cleaning it."

"Bother the stupid pan. Beetle, it *is* you. Your pen was Picked. It *was*, Beetle. I swear it."

Beetle stared at Foxy, pan scourer dripping in his hand. "But it *can't* have been. How could it get into the Pot?"

"I put it in. Remember when you got fired and you wouldn't take your pen? Well, I kept it. And that's *why* I kept it. There are no rules to say you have to be a serving scribe to go into the Pot. I looked it up specially. All that matters is your pen goes in. So that's what I did. I put it in."

Beetle was dumbfounded. "But *why*?"

"Because you deserve to be Chief Hermetic Scribe. Because, Beet, you are the *best*. And because you saved the

Manuscriptorium. You risked your life to do that. Who else could be Chief now? *No one*, Beet, that's who. No one but *you*."

Beetle shook his head. Things like this did *not* happen.

"Come on, Beet. Marcia's sent me to fetch you for your Induction. She's got the Cryptic Codex ready. *And* the Seals of Office. Everyone's waiting for you. Come *on*."

"Ah ..." Slowly Beetle was beginning to believe Foxy. He was aware that he had just crossed over one of those rare watersheds. His life a few minutes ago bore no resemblance to his life now. It was a total turnaround. He felt stunned.

"Beetle ... are you all right?" Foxy was beginning to be concerned.

Beetle nodded and a wave of happiness suddenly washed over him. "Yeah, Foxo," he said. "I am. I am *very* all right."

The Big Freeze came in fast. It was rare for it to begin on the Mid-Winter Feast Day but everyone in the Castle welcomed the blanket of white, covering all traces of the Darke Domaine, turning the Castle into a Magykal place once more. Even those who had lost family and friends — and there were more than a few — welcomed it; the silence of the snow felt right.

Walking to the Palace that evening, Septimus met Simon going the same way.

"Hi," Septimus said, a little awkwardly. "No Lucy?"

Simon smiled tentatively. "She'll be along later. Gone to collect her mum and dad. They're OK, but her mum's making a fuss."

"Ah."

They walked through the Palace Gate and headed for the Palace. Breaking the rather uncomfortable silence, Septimus said, "I wanted to say thank you."

Simon looked at his brother. "What for?" he asked, puzzled.

"For saving me. In the river."

"Oh. Oh well. I owed you."

"Yeah. Well. And I'm sorry I didn't listen about the Paired Code."

Simon shrugged. "Why should you? Stuff's happened. And I'm sorry too."

"Yeah. I know."

Simon turned to Septimus. "Quits?" he asked, smiling.

"Quits." Septimus smiled back.

Simon put his arm around his brother's shoulders – noticing that he was very nearly the same height – and together they made their way up to the Palace, leaving behind them a trail of two pairs of footprints breaking through the frosty covering that coated the blanket of snow.

That night the Palace Ballroom was ablaze with light and – for the first time for many, many years – full of people. Even Milo, Jenna's father, was there, having arrived back from a voyage a little late for her birthday, as ever. At either end of the table, at Jenna's insistence, sat Sarah and Silas. When they had first moved into the Palace, Sarah and Silas had sometimes taken those seats as a joke, with Jenna perched uncomfortably somewhere in between, but now the long table between them was full of people, laughter and conversation.

At Sarah's end of the table sat Milo, his red and gold silk robes shimmering in the candlelight while he regaled her with the details of his latest voyage. Opposite Milo was the ExtraOrdinary Wizard, who was, naturally, seated next to the Chief Hermetic Scribe. Sarah had insisted that Jenna sit next to her father, but she made a point of talking mainly to Septimus, who was placed next to her, just across the table from Beetle. Septimus looked over at his friend, resplendent in his new robes, and saw how well they suited him. Already Beetle seemed at ease in the heavy dark blue silk with the sleeves hemmed with gold, the colours echoing his admiral's jacket, which, Septimus noticed, he still wore underneath. Beetle had a glow of happiness about him that Septimus had never noticed before – it was good to see.

A burst of raucous laughter came from Silas's end of the table, where Nicko was sitting with Rupert, Maggie and Foxy. Nicko was making seagull noises. Towards the middle of the table Snorri and her mother sat quietly talking, while Ullr lay on guard beside them. Every now and then Snorri glanced disapprovingly at Nicko. Nicko did not seem to notice.

Next to Septimus was Simon. Simon's attention was mainly taken up by Lucy, Gringe and Mrs Gringe, who were talking about the wedding – or rather listening to Lucy talking about it. Occasionally Simon glanced down to a small wooden box sitting on his lap and smiled, his green eyes – unclouded for the first time in four years – gleaming in the candlelight. Written on the box was the word "Sleuth". It was a thank-you present from Marcia and it meant more to Simon than any present he had ever received.

Igor, with Matt and Marcus and his new employee, Marissa, were in deep conversation with Wolf Boy and Aunt Zelda.

Jenna, who was sitting on the other side of Septimus, nudged him. "Look at Wolf Boy. Without his long hair, don't you think he'd look just like Matt and Marcus?"

"Matt and Marcus?"

"From Gothyk Grotto. Look."

"Almost identical. That is *so* weird."

"They sound the same too, you know. Do you know anything about Wolf Boy's family, Sep? Does *Wolf Boy* know anything?"

"Never said anything to me. It was the Young Army way, Jen. I never knew I had a family until I bumped into you lot." Septimus grinned.

"Bit of a shock, that." Jenna smiled back.

"Yeah . . ." Septimus did not often think about how he might never have known who he truly was but right then, among his friends and family, a feeling akin to terror passed over him as he thought how different life might have been if Marcia had not rescued him from the snow only four years ago. He looked at Wolf Boy and realised that *he* had never found his family — surely he must have one?

"Tomorrow I shall go and ask to look at the Young Army records. There might be something in there about 409. You never know."

Jenna smiled — she'd just remembered something. She took a small present out from her pocket. "Happy birthday, Sep. It's a little late but we've been a bit busy recently."

"Hey, thanks, Jen. I got you something too. Happy birthday."

"Oh, Sep, *thank you*, that's lovely."

"You haven't seen it yet."

Jenna ripped open her present to reveal a very small and very pink crown encrusted with glass beads, sporting trailing ribbons and a pink fur trim. She burst out laughing. "That is so *silly*, Sep." She put the crown on and tied its pink ribbons under her chin. "There, that makes me Queen now. Open yours."

Septimus ripped open the red paper and extracted the set of Gragull teeth.

"Brilliant, Jen!" He put them in and the two yellowing canines slipped neatly over his lower lip. In the light of the candles Septimus looked so realistic that when Marcia finally finished her conversation with Beetle and turned to Septimus to ask him something, she screamed.

Queen and Gragull spent the rest of the evening fooling around opposite the two great dignitaries of the Castle – the ExtraOrdinary Wizard and the Chief Hermetic Scribe. Jenna felt indescribably happy. She had her old Septimus back and – as another burst of laughter and seagull noises erupted – her old Nicko too.

In the shadows two ghosts looked on contentedly.

"Thank you, Septimus," Alther had said, when asked to join the party at the table, "but I'd just like to sit quietly and be with my Alice. You Living, you're a noisy lot."

And they were. All night long.

As the sun rose the windows to the ballroom were flung open. The party climbed out into the snow and made their way down to the Palace Landing Stage. A lone ghost saw their approach and slipped away on to the trading barge that was moored at the Landing Stage, ready to leave before the Big Freeze began to ice up the river. The ghost of Olaf Snorrelssen wafted down into the cherrywood cabin that, long ago, he had made for his wife, Alfrún. He sat waiting for his wife and daughter to arrive, as he knew they surely would, and smiled. He was home at last.

But the party had not come to say goodbye to Snorri and her mother, who were not leaving until the next day. They had come to bid a final farewell to Jillie Djinn, who lay silent and snow-clad in her Leaving Boat, ready to be cast adrift to float down to the sea on the outgoing tide.

As they watched the Leaving Boat drift down the river, a rich blue silk banner fluttering from its flagstaff, Jenna turned to Beetle.

"I bet you hope she doesn't come back and haunt the Manuscriptorium," she said.

The Chief Hermetic Scribe grinned. "I've got a bit of peace and quiet first," he replied. "You know where she'll be for the next year and a day."

Jenna giggled. "Oh! *Of course* – the place where she entered Ghosthood. Marcia's *so* going to love that!"

WHAT HAPPENED IN THE DARKE DOMAINE – AND AFTERWARDS

VICTIMS OF THE DARKE DOMAINE

Marcia's Great UnDoing came just in time – three days and three nights is the longest most people can survive in a Darke Trance. Most of the Castle children woke up feeling fine, but the majority of the adults did not feel so good. They woke with a thumping headache, a raging thirst and ached from head to toe. Many assumed they had been to an extremely lively party the night before and could remember nothing about it. There were, however, some who never woke from the Castle's worst party ever.

Those who fell into the Darke Trance while in the open air fared the worst. Many succumbed to the cold and it was feared – from bloodstains found on the more exposed areas of the Castle – that the Darke dragon had taken those who were missing. Some people had been overtaken by the Darke Domaine at a dangerous moment – one died when climbing a ladder, two while trying to escape from a high window and five people fell into a fire they were tending. Three could not be woken and were taken to the Wizard Tower sick bay for DisEnchanting.

Two names on the commemorative plaques placed around the Castle will be familiar:

Bertie Bott. Ordinary Wizard. Missing, presumed eaten.

Una Brakket. Housekeeper. Found frozen in Little Creep Cut.

Maizie Smalls & Binkie

Maizie Smalls was overtaken by the Darke Domaine in her mother's house just off Wizard Way. They were sitting down to their traditional Longest Night supper prior to going out to see the lights when their front door blew open and the Darke Fog came tumbling in. They both survived, although Maizie's mother was ill for some time afterwards.

The first thing Maizie did on waking up – once she knew her mother had survived – was to rush to the Palace to try and find her cat, Binkie. Although Binkie was apparently fine, it did not take Maizie long to realise that there was something odd about the cat.

Binkie, like all the Castle cats, had been greatly affected by the Darke. The cats had acted like sponges, soaking up the stubborn pockets of Darke that lingered in dark corners and hidden places where cats liked to go. Binkie was no longer a house cat. He snarled, he spat and he scratched Maizie when she tried to stroke him. He would no longer eat the cat food that Maizie lovingly brought him – Binkie wanted blood: birds, baby rats and mice. And what Binkie wanted, Binkie got.

Five days after The Great UnDoing, Binkie left the Palace with Maizie as she set out to light the Wizard Way torches. Maizie was much encouraged by her cat's sudden desire for companionship as he followed her down the drive – but she never saw him again. Binkie stalked up Wizard Way, padded across the Castle drawbridge just before it was raised for the night and went to join the growing band of newly Darke Castle cats in the Forest. Within a few weeks there were – much to Stanley's delight – no cats at all left in the Castle.

Stanley and the Ratlets

Stanley and his ratlets spent the rest of the Darke Domaine on the Outside Path. While Stanley fretted about Jenna, Flo, Mo, Bo and Jo had a great time racing up and down the path, playing Silly Statues. When the Darke dragon roared, the one who struck the silliest pose – and kept it for the duration of the roar – won.

Once the Darke Domaine ended, Stanley and the ratlets cleaned up the Rat Office – or rather, Stanley cleaned up while the ratlets had a broom fight and then went off to hang out with their friends. Stanley did not object; he was just pleased to have everything back to normal once more and his ratlets safe.

Stanley soon found that his worries about staffing the Message Rat Service were unfounded. As word got around the Port rat community that the Castle was a cat-free zone, Stanley found he had the pick of "quality staff", as he called them. The Message Rat Service began to thrive once more – and it even acquired new drains.

Ephaniah Grebe

Ephaniah Grebe, Conservation, Preservation and Protection Scribe at the Manuscriptorium, very nearly did not survive the Darke Domaine. He locked himself in his Fume Cupboard but the Darke Fog seeped in and overpowered him. Ephaniah was weakened by his two previous encounters with the Darke: the permanent rat hex when he was fourteen and, more recently, being InHabited by a Thing.

The new Chief Hermetic Scribe found his missing Conservation Scribe squashed into the Fume Cupboard, his little rat mouth open and his tongue lolling out. Beetle thought he was dead, but a sudden twitch of Ephaniah's rat tail told him otherwise. Ephaniah joined Syrah and three other victims of the Darke Domaine in the DisEnchanting Chamber.

Marcia hopes that careful reading of *The Darke Index* may find a way of speeding up the process of DisEnchantment – the DisEnchanting Chamber is getting a little crowded.

SYRAH SYARA

Syrah survived, but only just. The DisEnchanting Chamber was a closed environment and, like a freezer when the power goes off, it would have been fine for a few hours, providing no one opened the door. But it had a narrow escape. A Thing had just pushed open the first door of the antechamber when Marcia spoke the last words of The Great UnDoing. At once the Magyk reasserted itself and the Thing was hurled across the sick bay and smashed against the wall. The sick-bay duty Wizard had to scrape it up and take it out in a wheelbarrow. Rose was excused from helping.

Septimus came to visit Syrah later that day, after he had got his Darke Week assessment from Marcia. The sick bay was busy preparing the new occupants for the DisEnchanting Chamber. Septimus squeezed in past Syrah's first new roommate – a young boy who had not yet come out of the Trance – and, remembering the last time he had visited her, suddenly felt amazingly happy and relieved that his Darke Week was over and everything was as it should be. When he told her he was safely back – with Alther – he thought he saw her eyelids flicker, just for a fraction of a second. Septimus was soon shooed out by Rose and the duty Wizards, who were bringing in another occupant. He didn't mind. Everything was all right. He walked out of the DisEnchanting Chamber with a spring in his step and went to see if anyone wanted a snowball fight.

SOPHIE BARLEY

On the opening day of the Traders' Market, Sophie Barley had just set up her stall when she found herself surrounded by five very odd customers swathed in black. One of them picked up a beautiful pendant – a winged heart with a seahorse hanging from it. She dangled it in front of Sophie's eyes and swung it back and forth ... back and forth ... back and forth. That was the last thing Sophie remembered.

Sophie awoke in the attic of Doom Dump, bound hand and foot, and there she languished while the witches took over her stall, waiting for their Princess to come along like a hunter waits beside his bait. Dorinda, who every evening fed Sophie her supper of stewed mice or coddled cockroaches, took a liking to her prisoner and began to creep away to talk to her. Sophie had just managed to get Dorinda to untie her when the Darke Domaine arrived. Unlike the witches, who revelled in the Darke, Sophie fell into a Darke Trance. She survived, and when she awoke she found Doom Dump empty. She took her chance and fled. After a reviving Springo Special Ale and a very large slab of Barley Cake at Sally Mullin's, Sophie caught the first Port barge and swore never to return to the Castle.

Jenna was worried about what had happened to Sophie. As soon as she could she went to the Port and found Sophie safe in her workshop beside the fishermen's quay. Jenna bought a beautiful pair of earrings for Sarah's birthday – and a seahorse pendant for herself.

MARISSA LANE

Marissa – along with Igor, Matt and Marcus – was trapped in Gothyk Grotto by the Darke Domaine. They retreated to Igor's own extremely secret – and embarrassingly small – SafeChamber. It was a horrible time for them all, but it did give Marissa a chance to reflect on her life. Talking to Igor made her realise what a dangerous and unpleasant path she was treading with the Port Witch Coven and she decided to Unravel her witch vows as soon as she could. After she had made her decision, Igor offered her a job as assistant in Gothyk Grotto – much to Matt and Marcus's delight. They both liked Marissa very much indeed. Igor, however, was unaware that he was storing up trouble ...

YOUNG ARMY RECORDS

Because Septimus had already been reunited with his family he was refused access to the Young Army registers. But Beetle stepped in to help. Making use of his Access-All-Areas status in the Castle, Beetle went to the Young Army Records Office, which was housed in a small building near Terry Tarsal's shoe shop. Most of the records were available for anyone to see, but those relating to families were considered private and could be seen only by those still searching for their family – or those with AAA status.

Beetle asked for the Register of Expendable Boy Soldiers.

Under the watchful eye of the records clerk (who considered him far too young to be Chief Hermetic Scribe), Beetle turned to the page headed *Numbers 400 to 499 Inclusive*. He ran his finger down the page until he came to these listings:

> *409   Mandy Marwick. Status: Forced*
> *Conscription. Traitor Family.*
> *410   Marcus Marwick. Status: Forced*
> *Conscription. Traitor Family.*
> *411   Matthew Marwick. Status: Forced*
> *Conscription. Traitor Family.*
> *412   Merrin Meredith. Status: Foundling.*
> *Mother denies child.*

The first three entries were what Beetle had suspected – Wolf Boy was one of triplets. He grinned. He hadn't suspected he'd be called *Mandy*, though.

Beetle was, however, dismayed by the entry for 412, which he knew had been Septimus's Young Army number. Surely Sep wasn't really Merrin Meredith? And then he remembered what Septimus had told him one rainy afternoon in the back kitchen of the Manuscriptorium over a mug of FizzFroot . . .

"I saw it, Beetle. Aunt Zelda was scrying in her pond and we saw moving pictures of what happened. It was weird – and really sad too. . . . The midwife snatched me away from Sarah – I mean Mum – when I was only a few hours old. She told Mum I was dead, but it was a plot. I was wanted by DomDaniel to be his Apprentice – because I am the seventh son of a seventh son. The midwife took me to the Young Army Nursery, where DomDaniel's Nurse was going to come and collect me. But when she arrived she was in a hurry and really

flustered and she just grabbed the first baby she saw – the midwife's baby. I think because the midwife was cuddling him when the Nurse arrived. The midwife went crazy – really crazy – when the guard stopped her from chasing after her own baby."

"Serves her right," Beetle remembered saying.

"Yeah. I s'pose it does. But what a horrible thing to happen – to her baby, I mean. And of course the midwife would have told everyone that I was not her child but they wouldn't have listened. They never listened to anything. As far as they were concerned I was the midwife's baby who she had suddenly abandoned. And that is how I got taken into the Young Army. I suppose I am in the Young Army register under the name of the midwife's child, which is weird. But the weirdest thing is I now know that I've met the midwife again – she was the landlady of that horrible guesthouse that Jen took us to in the Port. Aunt Zelda found that out and told me."

Beetle closed the register and handed it back to the clerk – along with the pair of white cotton gloves she had made him put on. *So it was true, Merrin Meredith was Nurse Meredith's – Nursie's – son.*

Beetle walked slowly back to the Manuscriptorium, thinking of those few moments just over fourteen years ago that had affected so many people's lives. Now he understood Marcia's reply when he had questioned her about the wisdom of letting Merrin go free. "Everyone deserves a chance to be with his mother, Beetle," she had said. At the time Beetle had actually spent so long gathering the courage to ask Marcia the question – and was so amazed when she had actually answered him civilly – that he had not liked to ask what she meant. Now he understood.

SNORRI AND ALFRUN

Snorri and her mother, Alfrún, were away for the Longest Night and missed the Darke Domaine. They returned the morning of The Great Undoing.

The previous year, Snorri had rescued her trader's barge – which actually belonged to her mother – from some boat thieves who had stolen it from Quarantine Dock. She had brought the *Alfrún* back to the Castle where Jannit Maarten's boatyard restored it.

Snorri had become unhappy living in the Palace with the Heaps. She missed her home and, she was surprised to find, she missed her mother too. It seemed to Snorri that she and Nicko had spent enough time together. Five hundred years, she said to Nicko, was long enough for anyone. It was time for them to do something new with their lives. Nicko had not answered, which had annoyed Snorri. The arrival of Alfrún Snorrelssen had made Snorri's decision for her. It was time to go home.

And so Snorri and her mother took the *Alfrún* out to sea for a test run. The barge performed perfectly and the decision was made – they would return home to the Land of the Long Nights. Snorri dreaded telling Nicko; she was sure he would not understand but to her surprise he did.

Snorri, Ullr and Alfrún left the day after the MidWinter Feast. As they waved goodbye to the little group gathered on the Palace Landing Stage, Snorri was surprised at how tearful she felt seeing Nicko waving to her as they drew away from the Palace and headed for the fast waters in the middle of the river. Snorri waved until the *Alfrún* disappeared around Raven's Rock and she could see Nicko no more, then she went below into the beautiful cherrywood cabin that her father, Olaf, had built. As Snorri sat in the cabin, looking up through the hatch at her mother on the tiller, an unexpected feeling of happiness came over her. She was going home. All would be well. It was then she saw the ghost of Olaf Snorrelssen sitting on the bench in the shadows opposite, smiling at her.

Snorri whispered, *"Papa?"*

Olaf nodded happily. "Snorri," he said. He smiled. They were a family once more.

On the Palace Landing Stage, Nicko stood gazing through the thickly falling snow at the departing *Alfrún*. And when, at last, the trading barge had disappeared from view, Nicko felt as if a weight was lifted from his shoulders. He was free.

The Room Behind the Big Red Door

Sarah and Silas set up home once more in the room behind the Big Red Door. Sarah went over to the Palace every day to see Jenna, but the Palace was now Jenna's home – not hers. The room behind the Big Red Door soon regained its previous lived-in look, and sometimes Sarah found it hard to believe they had ever left.

Thunder survived the Darke Domaine and took up residence in the stables at the back of a small house on Snake Slipway. Sarah cleaned the room from top to bottom until there was no clue that a horse had once spent a week there, although, in damp weather, Sarah still thought she could smell horse poo.

Ethel was never quite right after the Darke Domaine. The duck had had a difficult start in life and now became so nervous that she would not let Sarah out of her sight. Sarah made a duck bag – with two holes for Ethel's legs to poke through – and she carried

Ethel with her wherever she went. Silas harrumphed a lot about *that daft duck bag* but Sarah and Silas were far too happy being back home again to let a duck in a bag come between them.

THE DRAGON TRAIL

Dragon blood is indelible and the drips of blood from Spit Fyre's head wound left a track right across the Castle, from the South Gate to the Wizard Tower. While some drips fell on to roofs, most left a winding trail along tiny alleyways. The dragon blood track soon became a favourite trail for Castle children and visitors alike.

Spit Fyre recovered well from his injuries and, now that he was truly an adult dragon, he began to calm down a little – but only a *little*.

DARKE WEEK: RESULTS

Septimus passed his Darke Week.

Immediately below, for your interest, is part of a piece of paper found ripped to pieces in Marcia's wastepaper bin. Following that is Septimus's report sheet with Marcia's comments.

WIZARD TOWER SAFETY COMMITTEE

Basic Health and Safety Report for Apprentice projects. Must be completed by Wizard Tutor.

APPRENTICE PROJECT: *Darke Week*
NAME OF APPRENTICE: *Septimus Heap*
WIZARD TUTOR: *Marcia Overstrand*
AREA OF OPERATION: *the Darke Halls*

Risk-benefit analysis scaled 0 to 49 (where 49 is the greatest and 0 is the least).

RISKS: *49++ What do you expect?*
BENEFITS: *49+++*

- Do you consider that the risk–benefit ratio was acceptable? *Of course I do.*
- Would you undertake this assessment in the same manner again? *Never again, thank you.*
- What sanitary facilities were provided? *Oh, for goodness' sake . . .*

EXTRAORDINARY APPRENTICE
DARKE WEEK ASSESSMENT

TUTOR: *Marcia Overstrand. ExtraOrdinary Wizard.*
APPRENTICE: *Septimus Heap. Senior ExtraOrdinary Apprentice.*

Apprentice Assessment scaled 0 to 7 (where 7 is the greatest and 0 is the least).

RELEVANCE OF CHOSEN *DARKE* TASK: *7. Highly relevant.*
METHOD OF ENTERING THE DARKE: *6.*
Septimus, I dock one mark due to your unauthorised use of the Darke Disguise. I do realise that without it you would not have survived, but even so, I feel the rules must be given some respect here.

MAGYKAL SKILL: *7.*
Your Revoke of the Banish was word perfect first time. You used your past connection with the Flyte Charm to great effect (see me later about supervised access to this from now on). You also attained Synchronicity with a dragon. What more can I say?

DECISION-MAKING AND INITIATIVE: 7.
You used your initiative to decide where to enter the Darke and why. You used logic to reason your way through the Darke Halls. Excellent.

GENERAL CONDUCT: 7.
You were polite to the young ghost and showed great presence of mind when encountering Tertius Fume. Very good indeed.

METHOD OF EXITING THE DARKE: 7.
Very good.

SUCCESS OF DARKE TASK: 7.
Totally successful.

TUTOR'S ASSESSMENT OF SUITABILITY OF CANDIDATE TO INCORPORATE A BALANCED AND RESPONSIBLE USE OF THE DARKE IN HIS OR HER FUTURE STUDIES: 8.
I consider this candidate eminently suitable. I also reserve my right to give what mark I choose.

TOTAL SCORE OUT OF 49: *49.*

DARKE WEEK RESULT: *(strike through those that do not apply)*
~~FAIL: no retake permitted~~
~~FAIL: retake permitted~~
~~BORDERLINE PASS: retake theory only~~
~~PASS~~
~~PASS WITH MERIT~~
PASS WITH DISTINCTION

Signed: Marcia Overstrand
And on behalf of: Alther Mella. Thank you, Septimus.

Septimus Heap,
Wizard Apprentice.
Magyk is his destiny

Enjoy all of his
amazing adventures . . .

'These books open an array of dazzling worlds' *TES*

WWW.SEPTIMUSHEAP.CO.UK